Joseph Fouché

The Memoirs of Joseph Fouché

Duke of Otranto, minister of the General police of France. Vol. 2

Joseph Fouché

The Memoirs of Joseph Fouché
Duke of Otranto, minister of the General police of France. Vol. 2

ISBN/EAN: 9783337424015

Printed in Europe, USA, Canada, Australia, Japan

Cover: Foto ©Raphael Reischuk / pixelio.de

More available books at **www.hansebooks.com**

MEMOIRS

OF

JOSEPH FOUCHÉ

MEMOIRS

OF

JOSEPH FOUCHÉ

Edition strictly limited to 500 copies.

Five extra copies have been printed on Japanese vellum, but are not offered for sale.

CARNOT

THE
MEMOIRS
OF
JOSEPH FOUCHÉ

DUKE OF OTRANTO

MINISTER OF THE GENERAL POLICE OF FRANCE

TRANSLATED FROM THE FRENCH

IN TWO VOLUMES—VOLUME II

LONDON

H. S. NICHOLS

3 SOHO SQUARE AND 62 PICCADILLY W

MDCCCXCVI

Printed and Published by

H. S. NICHOLS

AT 3 SOHO SQUARE, LONDON W

CONTENTS OF VOL. II

x   CONTENTS

MEMOIRS

OF

JOSEPH FOUCHÉ

DUKE OF OTRANTO

———

I IMPOSE upon myself a great and weighty task
in again offering myself to all the severity of a public
investigation; but I impose it on myself as a duty, to
destroy the prejudices of party spirit and the impressions of hatred. I have, however, little hope that
the voice of reason will have strength enough to make
itself heard in the midst of the clamours of the two
exacerbated factions which divide the political world.
No matter; it is not for the present moment that
I write, but for the sake of a more tranquil period.
As to what concerns the present, let my destiny be
accomplished. And what a destiny, just heaven, has
that been! Of so much greatness and of so enormous
a power—a power which I never abused, except for
the purpose of avoiding still greater evils—what vestige
now remains? That which I least prize, that which
I accumulated for others, indeed remains, and remains
to an individual who, unmoved by passing events,
could have dispensed with wealth altogether—to one
who carried with him into the splendid circle of

official life the moderation of a philosopher and the sobriety of a hermit. By turns predominant, dreaded or disgraced, it is true I sought for authority, but I detested oppression. How many services have I not rendered? How many tears have I not dried up? Dare, if you can, to deny it, you whose united suffrages I concentred in my own person, notwithstanding the melancholy events which had so recently passed! Did I not become your protector, your saviour against your own resentments, and against the impetuous passions of the chief of the state? I confess that there never was a more despotic police than that whose sceptre I grasped; but will you not also admit that there never was a more protecting police under a military government, more averse to violence, more gentle in the means by which it pervaded the secret recesses of domestic life, and the operation of which was less obnoxiously obvious? Will you not, therefore, admit that the Duke of Otranto was beyond a doubt the most skilful and the most moderate of all Napoleon's ministers? I know that, at the present, you hold a different language—for this sole reason, that times have changed. You judge the past by the present; that is not my mode of judging. I have committed errors—that I grant; but the good I have done ought to be counterpoised in the other scale. Plunged in the chaos of public affairs, occupied with the unravelling of all kinds of intrigues, I took pleasure in calming hostilities, in extinguishing passions and conciliating men. It was with a degree of luxury that I sometimes tasted repose at the pure spring of my domestic affections, which, in their turn, did not escape from being poisoned at their source.

During my recent humiliations, and during my great misfortunes, can I forget that I was once the supporter and supervisor of an immense Empire; that my mere disapprobation endangered its existence, and that it ran the risk of tumbling to pieces whenever I withdrew my sustaining hand? Can I forget when, by the effect of a great reaction, and of a revolution which I foresaw, I repossessed myself of the scattered elements of so much greatness and power, and the whole vanished like a dream? Yet, nevertheless, I was considered as far superior, in consequence of my long experience—I may add, perhaps, of my sagacity—to all those who, during the catastrophe, suffered the power to escape.

At the present moment, when undeceived upon all points, I look down from a superior region upon all the miseries and fallacious splendours of greatness, when I no longer contend for any object but the justification of my political intentions, I recognise too late the extent of the gulf between the contrary parties who struggle for the government of the universe. I see and feel that a more powerful First Mover modifies and guides them, with an entire contempt of the profoundest of our calculations.

It is, nevertheless, but too true that the wounds of ambition are incurable. In spite of my reason, and in spite of myself, I am haunted by the delusive chimeras of power, by the phantoms of vanity. I feel myself dragged down towards them, as Ixion was riveted to his wheel. A deep and painful reminiscence weighs upon my mind.

And will it be said that I refrain from exhibiting all my weaknesses, all my errors, and all my repentances? A confession like this, I should think, is a sufficient pledge of the sincerity of my revelations. That pledge I owed to the importance of this second part of the Memoirs of my political life. I am thus irrevocably placed under the rigorous obligations of retracing all its peculiarities, of unfolding all its secret mysteries. This is my last labour. I shall, however, experience some compensating enjoyment in the charms of reflection, and in the fragrance of a certain number of recollections: this pleasure I have experienced in my first narrative.

In preparing these Memoirs, one consoling idea has never abandoned me: I shall not entirely descend into the grave—perhaps, I said to myself, into that grave which already yawns to receive me at the termination of my exile. I cannot dissemble it from myself. However I may elude the decay of my spirit, I have but too strong conviction of the decay of my bodily strength. Urged as I am to haste by the pursuing footsteps of destiny, let me proceed with a perfect feeling of sincerity to recapitulate the events which passed between my disgrace in 1810 and my fall in 1815. This division of the subject is the most serious and the most thorny of all my political confessions. How many incidents, how many mighty interests, how many conspicuous characters, how many acts of turpitude are associated with the last act of a transitory power! But fear nothing, enemies or friends; it is not the police which here denounces; it is history which reveals.

Pretending as I do to raise myself above the influence of every description of frivolous compromise, I am not less resolved to place myself beyond the atmosphere of satire and libel, as well as of hypocrisy and falsehood. That which is disgraceful I will disgrace; that which is respectable I will respect. In a word, I will grasp my pen with an unshaking hand; and, in order that it may not deviate, I will never lose sight of the synchronism of public events.

From these preliminaries, intended to awaken attention and stimulate reflection, I am about to pass to the recital of facts which confirm, of details which reveal, of traits which characterise. The result will, I persuade myself, be a picture which may be named, as the reader pleases, either history or materials for history.

At the end of the first portion of these Memoirs will be found the discursive point of my history. It is distinguished by the event of my disgrace, which transferred the portfolio of the superior state police into the hands of Savary. It must be borne in mind that the Empire was then in the zenith of its power, and that its military limits had no longer any bounds. Possessor of Germany, master of Italy, absolute disposer of France, invader of Spain, Napoleon was, moreover, the ally of the Cæsars and of the autocrat of the North. So dazzling was the halo of his power that the ulcer of the Spanish war, which was gnawing the vitals of the Empire in the South, attracted little notice. Everywhere else Napoleon had only to desire in order to obtain. All moral counterpoise had disappeared from his government. Everything gave way; his agents, his functionaries, his dignitaries, exhibited nothing but a group of flatterers and mutes, anxious to catch the least sign of his decisions. In short, he had just dismissed in me the only individual of his council who would have dared to restrain his successive encroachments. In me he kept aloof a zealous and watchful minister, who never spared him useful admonition nor courageous reproof.

An imperial decree constituted me governor-general of Rome.[1] But I never, for a single moment, thought that it was the Emperor's wish that I should exercise so important a trust. This nomination was nothing but an honourable veil, woven by his policy, in order to conceal and tone down to the public eye the too glaring intensity of my disgrace, in the secret of which

---

[1] *Letter of the Emperor to M. the Duke of Otranto.*

MONSIEUR, THE DUKE OF OTRANTO,

    The services which you have rendered us in the difficult circumstances which have occurred, induce us to confide to you the government of Rome, until we have provided for the execution of Article 8 of the Act of the Constitution of the 17th of last February. We have determined, by a special decree, the extraordinary powers with which the particular circumstances in which that department is at present placed require that you should be invested. We expect that you will continue in your new post to give us proofs of your zeal for our service and attachment for our person.

    This letter having no other object, we pray God, M. the Duke of Otranto, to take you into his holy keeping.

                    (Signed)   NAPOLEON.

St. Cloud, the 3rd of June, 1810.

    Letter of the Minister of General Police to S.M., I. and R.

SIRE,

    I accept the government of Rome to which your Majesty has had the goodness to raise me, as a recompense for the humble services which I have been so fortunate as to perform.

    I must not, however, dissemble that I experienced a very poignant regret in quitting your Majesty; I lose at once the

his intimates alone were. I could not be mistaken; the mere choice of my successor was in itself a frightful indication. In each saloon, in every family, in short, throughout Paris, there was a general horror manifested at seeing the general police of the Empire thenceforth confounded with the military police of the chief magistrate; and, moreover, given up to the fanatical subserviency of a man who made it his chief honour to execute the secret orders of his master. His name alone created a universal mistrust, a kind of stupor, the impression of which, perhaps, may have been magnified out of due proportion.

I no longer communicated, except under extreme precaution, with my intimate friends and private agents. I soon obtained confirmation of all I had foreseen. During several days my wife's apartments were never free from distinguished visits, carefully masked under the appearance of congratulation on the subject of the imperial decree which raised me to the government-general of Rome. I received the confidential testimonies of crowds of exalted personages, who, while signifying their regrets, assured me that my retreat would carry with it the disapprobation of

happiness and the information which I daily derived from your communications.

If anything can mitigate that regret, it is the reflection that I furnish under the circumstances, by my absolute resignation to the will of your Majesty, the strongest testimony of my boundless devotion to your person.

I am, with the most profound respect, Sire,
Your Majesty's very humble and most obedient
servant and faithful subject.
(Signed)   DUKE D'OTRANTO.

Paris, June 3rd, 1810.

all such men as were most esteemed for their influence or rank in society.

"We are not indeed satisfied," they said, "whether
the regret of the Faubourg St. Germain be not at least
as deep as that displayed by the multitude of conspicuous characters who feel an interest in the fortunes
of the Revolution." Testimonials of this kind offered
to a fallen minister are neither suspicious nor doubtful.

It was necessary for me, in consequence of my
position and the claims of decorum, to put up with
the annoyance of acting in the character of Savary's
mentor during the *début* of his ministerial noviciate.
It will be readily understood that I did not push my
politeness so far as to initiate him in the upper
mysteries of the political police. I took care not to
give him a key which might one day contribute to
our common safety. Neither did I initiate him in the
tolerably difficult art of arranging the secret bulletin,
the conception and often the digest of which was
properly reserved for the minister alone. The wretched
amount of Savary's experience in this walk was already
known to me. I had previously obtained, without his
being aware of it, copies of the bulletins of his counter-
police. What villainies did they not contain? To
confess the truth, I was so perplexed by his perpetual
questions and stupid self-sufficiency that I amused
myself with telling him old women's tales.[1]

---

[1] It was, doubtless, this circumstance which since occasioned
the Duke de Rovigo, in referring to Fouché, to say, "That
personage made us believe a great deal." It must be, however,
understood that this phrase, as we have heard it quoted in
society, comprises all the members of the imperial government.—
Note by the French Editor.

By way of amends, I assumed the air of instructing him in the forms, the customs, and the traditions of the office. I particularly magnified the profound views of the three councillors of state who, under his direction, were about to search all the recesses of the administrative police, by quartering France among them. He was quite dazzled with the measure. I introduced and frankly recommended to him the chief agents and missionaries whom I had previously had under my orders; the only one whom he accepted was the treasurer, a little round personage, and the little inquisitor, Desmarets, on whom I never placed any reliance. This latter individual, endowed with a certain degree of tact, had instinctively bowed his body towards the rising sun. To Savary he made a complete stalking-horse.

Nothing in the world was ever more ludicrous than to see this military minister giving his audiences, *spelling* the list of the solicitors, got up by his *huissiers* of the ante-chamber, with notes by Desmarets under his eye; the latter constituted *guide-âne* for promises and refusals, which were almost always accompanied by oaths or invectives. I had not failed to tell him that I had disobliged the Emperor by being *trop bon;* and that he, in order with more efficiency to watch over his master's valuable days, ought to show himself as replete with indocility as possible.[1] Puffed up by an insolent self-conceit, he affected, from the first moment of his

[1] This would be going much too far for any other individual but Fouché; by nature revengeful, and indulging towards the Duke de Rovigo a hatred, the evidences of which he suffers too conspicuously to transpire. *Note by the French Editor.*

accession to office, to imitate his master in his frequent fits of passion and his broken and incoherent phrases. He considered that there was nothing of any utility in the entire police, but secret reports, espionage, and the money chest. I had the happiness of beholding him in the midst of his bouncing fits, as well as of his mood, on the day when I put in his hands the agreeable computation of all the budgets which were merged in the private chest; *it appeared* to him like a new wonderful lamp.

I was in positive torture till I got rid of this ministerial pedagogueship; but on the other hand I resorted to pretexts, in order to prolong my stay in Paris. Ostensibly I carried on my preparations for my departure for Rome, as if I had never for a moment doubted that I was about to be installed there. The whole of my household was arranged upon the scale of a governor-generalship, and even my equipages were superinscribed in large characters, "*Equipages of the Governor-general of Rome.*" Being duly apprised that all my proceedings for the journey were being watched, I employed more care in the arrangement of trifles such as these.

At length, receiving neither decision nor instructions from court, I requested Berthier to obtain my audience of leave from the Emperor. The only reply I could get was that the Emperor had not appointed a day for my audience, and that it would be prudent, in consequence of the popular gossip, for me to go to my country-seat, and there await the orders that would be immediately sent to me. I accordingly went to my château de Ferrières,[1] but not without indulging in the venial malice of causing it to be inserted in the Paris journals, by a circuitous means, that I was departed for my new government.[2]

In my last interview with Berthier I had not found much difficulty in detecting the Emperor's inclinations towards me. I perceived how impatient he was at finding public opinion decidedly pronounced against my dismissal, and as strongly declared against my successor. Nothing was now recognised in the functions of police but a pro-consulship and a gendarmerie. All these indications confirmed me in the opinion that I should with great difficulty escape the consequences of an actual fall.

In fact, I had scarcely reached Ferrières when a relation of my wife, who had secretly quitted Paris, hastened to me at midnight to convey the important intelligence that I should be arrested on the following

[1] The château de Ferrières is distant about three quarters of a league from the estate of Pont Carré, emigrant landed property, about six leagues from Paris, which Fouché had acquired from the state, but for which it is asserted that he had paid the full value to the proprietor. The château of Pont Carré being then in a dilapidated state, it would seem that Fouché caused it to be demolished, and devoted its site to pasture land. Ferrières and Pont Carré, united with immense wooded estates, which are now attached to them, constitute, according to report, one of the most magnificent domains in the kingdom: it comprises an extent of four leagues. It was to the château de Ferrières that Fouché retired immediately after his disgrace, and subsequently after his return from his senatorship at Aix, as will be seen in the progress of these Memoirs.—*Note by the French Editor.*

[2] The author almost always neglects dates. We believe that it was on the 26th of June, 1810.—*Note by the French Editor.*

day, and that my papers would be seized. Although the particulars were magnified, the information was positive ; it came from an individual attached to the Emperor's private cabinet, and long engaged in my interest. I immediately went to work and stored away all my most important papers. As soon as the operation was completed, I resigned myself with stoical fortitude to whatever might occur; and at eight o'clock my confidential emissary J—— arrived full post with a letter from Madame de V—— in a feigned hand, informing me that Savary had just told the Emperor that I had carried off his secret correspondence and confidential orders to Ferrières. I saw in the twinkling of an eye from whom Madame de V. obtained her information. It confirmed the first intelligence, but the papers now appeared to be the only matters of interest. Although thus reassured as to the subject of actual violence to my person, I was picturing to myself the arrival of the chief *Sbire* and his archers, when my people informed me that a carriage, preceded by outriders, was entering the court of the château. But Napoleon, restrained I presume by some remains of decency, had spared me the mortification of coming in contact with his police minister. It was Berthier who entered my apartment, followed by the councillors of state Réal and Dubois.

From their embarrassment I gathered that I had not entirely lost my influence, and that their mission was conditional. In fact, Berthier, commencing the business, told me, with a constrained air, that he came by the Emperor's orders to demand his correspondence; that he imperiously insisted upon it; and that if I refused, the police prefect, Dubois, who was present, had orders to arrest me and place a seal on my papers. Réal, assuming a tone of persuasion, and addressing me with more unction as an old friend, begged of me, nearly with tears in his eyes, to submit to the Emperor's wishes. "I," said I calmly, "I resist the Emperor's wishes? Can such a thing enter your heads? I who have always served the Emperor with so great a degree of zeal, although wounded by his unjust suspicions, even at those times when I served him most effectually. Come into my closet; search everywhere, gentlemen. I will give my keys into your hands; I will myself put you in possession of all my papers. It is lucky for me that the Emperor has put me to this unexpected test, from which it is impossible but that I shall go forth with advantage. The rigorous examination of all my papers and my correspondence will give the Emperor means of convincing himself of the injustice of the suspicions with which the malice of my enemies alone could have inspired him against the most devoted of his servants and the most faithful of his ministers." The calmness and firmness which I had assumed while making this harangue produced its effect, and I proceeded in these words: "As to the private correspondence with me during the exercise of my functions, as it was of a nature which required its being buried in eternal secrecy, I partly burned it when I resigned my office, not wishing to expose papers of so great an importance to the chances of an indiscreet investigation. As to the rest, gentlemen, you will still find, with this exception, the papers which the Emperor requires. They are, I believe, in two locked and ticketed *cartons*. You will have no difficulty in recognising them, nor will you be likely to confound them with my private papers, which I give up with the same frankness to your research. Once more, I fear nothing, and have nothing to fear from my subjection to this proof."

The commissioners grew perfectly confused with protestations and excuses. On recovering they proceeded to examine my papers, or rather I examined them myself, in the presence of Dubois. I must do this justice to Dubois, that although he was my personal enemy, and more especially charged with the execution of the Emperor's orders, he conducted himself with as much reserve as decorum. Whether it was that he already had a presentiment of his own disgrace shortly following mine,[1] or whether he judged it prudent not to disgust too much a minister who after two falls could reascend the pinnacle of power.

Influenced probably by my *openness*,[2] the imperial commission contented itself with some insignificant papers, which I wished to consign to it; and, in conclusion, after the customary forms of politeness, Berthier, Réal, and Dubois re-entered their carriage and returned to Paris. At the close of night I made my exit by the little gate in my park, got into the cabriolet of my *homme d'affaires*, and, accompanied by a friend, hurried to Paris, where I was set down *incognito* at my hotel

---

[1] M. the Count Dubois was succeeded by M. Pasquier, in his functions of prefect of police, on the 14th of October, 1810. Fouché has intimated one of the motives of his disgrace in the first part of his Memoirs.—*Note by the French Editor.*

[2] The word *openness* (*candeur*) was underlined in the original notes.—*Note by the French Editor.*

in the Rue du Bac. There I learnt two hours afterwards (for all my strings were in motion) that the Emperor, on the report of what had passed at Ferrières, had fallen into a violent passion ; that after having broken out in threats against me, he had exclaimed that I had played off a trick upon the commissioners ; that they were *imbéciles*; and that Berthier was in regard to state affairs no better than an old woman, who had suffered himself to be mystified by the craftiest man in the Empire.

The next day at nine o'clock in the morning, having concerted my plan, I hastened to St. Cloud, and there presented myself to the grand marshal of the palace. " Here I am," said I to Duroc ; " I am prompted by the most urgent interest to see the Emperor without delay, and to prove to him that I am very far from deserving his cruel mistrust and unjust suspicion. Tell him, I entreat you, that I am waiting in your closet till he deigns to grant me a few minutes' audience." " I will go instantly," replied Duroc, " and I am very glad to see that *you have mixed a little water with your wine.*" Such was the exact phrase he used, and it squared with the idea which I wished to give him of my deportment. Duroc, returning, took me by the hand, led me forward, and left me in the Emperor's closet. From the first aspect and deportment of Napoleon, I guessed what was passing in his mind. Without giving me time to say a single word, he embraced me, flattered me, and went even so far as to testify a kind of repentance for the dissatisfaction he had expressed with regard to me ; then, with an accent which seemed to say that he himself offered me a pledge of reconciliation, he concluding by requiring, and, in short, demanding his correspondence. "Sire," I replied with a determined tone, "I have burnt it." "That is not true; I must have it," replied he, with compressed vehemence and anger. "It is reduced to ashes." "Withdraw!" These words were pronounced with a scowling motion of the head and a withering look. "But, Sire——" "Withdraw, I say!" This was repeated with such emphasis as to dissuade me from staying. I held ready in my hand a brief memorial, which I laid on the table as I retired; an action which I accompanied with a respectful bow. The Emperor, bursting with anger, seized the paper and tore it to pieces.

Duroc, who saw me so soon returning, perceiving neither trouble nor emotion depicted in my appearance, imagined that I was restored to favour. "You have come off well," said he; "I prevented the Emperor yesterday from causing you to be arrested." "You spared him," I returned, "the commission of a very foolish act—an act which would at all events have been impolitic, and which would have supplied malignity with matter to work on. The Emperor by that means would have scattered alarm among those individuals who are most devoted to the interests of his government." I perceived from Duroc's manner that this was also his opinion, and taking him by the hand I said, "Do not suffer yourself to be alienated, Duroc; the Emperor stands in need of your prudent counsel."

I quitted St. Cloud, somewhat reassured by this half-confidence of the grand marshal, for which I was indebted to a mistake; and returned, pondering on the position of the affair, to my hotel.

I was about to return to Ferrières, after having dispatched some urgent business, when the Prince de Neufchâtel was announced. "The Emperor," said he, "is very angry. I never saw him in so violent a passion; he has taken it into his head that you have deceived him, and carried audacity so far as falsely to maintain to his face that you had burnt his letters, in order to avoid giving them up. He pretends that it is a punishable misdemeanour to persist in retaining them." "This suspicion," said I to Berthier, "is the most unjust part of the whole affair. The correspondence of the Emperor would, on the contrary, be my only guarantee, and if I possessed it I would not give it up." Berthier urgently implored me to yield; but, finding me silent, he concluded by threats in the Emperor's name. "Go to him," I replied, "and tell him that I have been accustomed for these five and twenty years to sleep with my head on the scaffold; that I know the extent of his power, but that I do not fear it; and add, that if he wishes to make a Strafford of me he is at full liberty to do so." We then separated; I more than ever resolved to stand firm, and scrupulously to retain the undeniable proofs that all which was most violent and iniquitous in the exercise of my ministerial functions had been imperiously prescribed, by orders emanating from the cabinet, and stamped with the seal of the Emperor.

Neither was it the effect of public disgrace which I so much feared as ambuscades prepared against me in darkness. Determined by my own reflections, as well as the entreaties of my friend and of all I held most dear, I threw myself into a post-chaise, taking with me only my eldest son and his tutor. I then took the road to Lyons; there I found my old secretary Maillocheau, general commissary of police, who was indebted to me for his place. I obtained from him all the papers I thought I might want, and rapidly traversed a great part of France. Thence passing with the same celerity into Italy, I arrived at Florence with a boldly conceived design, which I thought was calculated to secure me from the Emperor's resentment. But such was the state of my physical irritability, and the excess of the fatigue with which so rapid and so long a journey had overwhelmed me, that it was necessary to give up two entire days to repose, before I could find myself in a proper condition to provide for my own safety.

It was not unintentionally, and this I will explain presently, that I had sought refuge in that classic land, beloved from time immemorial by gods and men. Beautiful and free Tuscany, which had at first fallen under the dominion of the Medicis, subsequently under the sceptre of the house of Austria, princes who had always governed it rather in the character of fathers than of kings, was at that time plunged in the gulf of the French Empire.

I pass over the delusive cession made by Napoleon to the Infant of Parma, under the title of King of Etruria, a cession revoked almost as soon as it was concluded. Tuscany was reserved for other destinies. Ever since 1807 Eliza, Napoleon's sister, ruled over it under the title of grand duchess. And it was I, by inconsistent and extraordinary vicissitudes! it was I who now came to place myself under the protection of a woman I disliked; who formerly giving strength to the Fontanes and Molé coterie, had contributed to my first disgrace; of that woman of whom I shall have to say in this place more in her favour than against her, in order to be just; for I have a habit of speaking and writing according to the associations of the epoch, but without passion or resentment. Such ought, in fact, to be the standing maxim of the statesman; the past ought in his eyes to appear in no other light than history; everything is comprised in the present.

When, besides, the question concerns women subjected to the influence of strong passions, it admits of an easy explanation. At my resumption of office I had found it expedient to conciliate Eliza. I had successively protected two individuals, Hin—— and Les——, to whom she was much attached, and who, within a short interval, had rendered themselves in the strongest degree necessary to her inclinations. The one, in the character of a broker, had been bitterly persecuted by the Emperor; the other, more obscure, had plunged himself into a disgraceful transaction. It was not without trouble that I succeeded in hushing the matter up.

I had, moreover, persuaded Napoleon in 1805 to confer on his sister the sovereignty of Lucca and Piombino. I was, therefore, almost certain of still finding the heart of Eliza disposed to feelings of gratitude; and I did not hesitate to assure myself of the fact on the very day when my disgrace was aggravated by my last interview with the Emperor. Having presented myself to the grand duchess, who was then at Paris to assist in the marriage ceremony, I had solicited from her, without entirely confiding to her all the thorny points of my position, letters for her dominions, through which, as I told her, I was about to pass, in order to proceed to Rome. Eliza assented with infinite affability, giving me warm recommendations, and designating me in her letters by the amiable epithet of the "common friend." This it is necessary to explain. I had in Tuscany some friends, whom I had stationed there, to their pecuniary advantage, and the grand duchess gave them all the latitude I required to serve me. Such was the steadiness of their character that I could, without risk, reveal to them all the difficulties of my situation.

The intelligence received nearly at the same time from Paris, and from my family, who had stopped at Aix, brought nothing of a reassuring description. On the contrary, it portrayed the Emperor, goaded by Savary and inclined to break out into violence against my alleged obstinacy, which was termed indiscreet and even mad. No one at that time could entertain the idea of a single individual daring to resist the will of him to whom all things, whether potentates or nations, bowed the knee. "Is it your intention," wrote one of my friends to me, "to make yourself more powerful than the Emperor?" My head became giddy with the supposition, and I was in my turn intimidated. In my sleepless nights, and in my dreams, I imagined myself surrounded by executioners, and seemed as if I beheld in the native country of Dante the inexorable vision of his infernal gates. The spectre of tyranny depicted itself on my imagination with more frightful features than during the most sanguinary despotism of Robespierre, who had condemned me to the scaffold. Here I was less in dread of the scaffold than of a dungeon. I knew, alas! but too well the man with whom I had to deal.

My head becoming by degrees more and more heated, I returned to the first idea which had presented itself to my mind; and I took the desperate resolution of embarking for the United States, that common refuge of the unfortunate friends of liberty. Secure of Dubois,[1] director of police in the grand duchy, who was indebted to me for his place, I obtained blank passports, and proceeded to Leghorn, where I freighted a vessel, giving out that I was going by sea to Naples, whence I intended to proceed to Rome. I went on board; I even set sail, fully determined to pass the straits and cross the Atlantic. But, just heavens! to what a terrible affliction was my frail, irritable habit of body subjected! A dreadful sea-sickness loaded my bosom and tore my entrails. Vanquished by my sufferings, I began to regret that I had not attended to the remonstrances of my friends and family, whose future existence I was about to compromise. I nevertheless struggled on, and resisted as much as possible the idea of

---

[1] This individual must not be confounded with Count Dubois, prefect of police. We have been informed that the Dubois, director of police in Tuscany, and M. Maillocheau, commissary-general of police at Lyons, were severely reprimanded by the Duke of Rovigo for having favoured the furtive journey of Fouché. The commissary-general of Lyons was even cashiered. —*Note by the French Editor.*

yielding to the influence which oppressed me. But I had already lost my senses, and was about to expire, when I reached land. Overwhelmed by this rough trial, I subsequently declined the offer of a generous English captain, who wished to convey me to his native island, on board of a commodious vessel and a good sailer, promising me at the same time such attention and antidotes as would secure me against the return of sea-sickness. I had no longer the means of complying. I was resolved to endure everything sooner than again trust myself to an element incompatible with my habits of life. This cruel proof had, besides, changed my ideas; I no longer saw objects under the same point of view. By degrees I perceived that there was a possibility of coming to some kind of compromise with the Emperor, whose rage pursued me even to the shores of the Tuscan Sea. I still wandered there for a short time, in order to mature my plan, and obtain opportunities for its realisation. At length, my resolution being taken and my batteries prepared, I returned to Florence. There I wrote to Eliza, already well disposed to do me service. I conveyed a letter to the Emperor, under cover to her, in which, without flattery or humiliation, I confessed that I was sorry for having displeased him; but that, being in dread of falling a defenceless victim to the malignity of my enemies, I had considered myself entitled, perhaps wrongfully, to retain possession of papers which composed my only guarantee. That on reflection, and in deep sorrow for having incurred his displeasure, I had placed myself under the protection of a princess who, by the ties of blood as well as by the goodness of her heart, was worthy of being his representative in Tuscany; that to her I consigned my vindication, and that I entreated his Majesty to grant me, under the auspices of the grand duchess, in exchange for the papers which I had determined to give up in compliance with his wish, some kind of indemnity for all the measures and acts which I might have executed by his orders during the period of my two ministerial functions; that a pledge of this description, which was necessary to my security and repose, would constitute a sacred ægis, capable of defending me against the attacks of envy and the shafts of malice; that I had already more than one reason to believe that his Majesty, out of regard to my zeal and services, would deign to reopen the only access which remained to his goodness and justice by permitting me to retire to Aix, the chief place of my senatorship, and to reside there in the bosom of my family till further orders.

This letter, sent by *estafette* to the grand duchess, had a full and entire effect. Eliza interested herself zealously. The courier's return announced to me that the Prince de Neufchâtel, vice-constable, was commissioned by an express order from the Emperor to deliver to me a receipt in exchange for the correspondence and orders which the Emperor had addressed to me during the exercise of my ministerial office, and that I might, with full security, retire to the chief place of my senatorship.

In this way, through the intervention of the grand duchess, was effected, not certainly a reconciliation between me and the Emperor, but a kind of compromise,

which I should have regarded as impracticable three
weeks before. I was less indebted for it to inclination
on my part, or sincere submission, than to the results
of a sea-sickness, the tortures of which I was, from
habit of body, incapable of supporting.

Restored to my family, I was at length enabled at
Aix to enjoy the tranquillity so necessary to the decay
of my strength and the condition of my mind, which
was irritated without being humiliated. It was not
without a very painful internal contest that I had consented to bend my spirit before the violence of the
despot. If at length I decided upon yielding, it was
by capitulation; but sacrifices such as these are not
made without effort by anyone who feels the native
dignity of man, and who has no other wish than to
live under a reasonable government. There were for
me many other motives of bitterness and alarm in contemplating the secret and hurried march of a power
which was proceeding to devour itself, and the springs
of which were so familiar to me that their results could
no longer escape the foresight of my calculations.

Although I had reason to believe myself condemned
for a tolerably long term to perfect obscurity and
nullity, this mode of life, which might have conducted
me to apathy and indifference, was very ill accordant
with a mind broken in to the habits and exercise of
great affairs. What others were blind to I perceived:
flashes of light escaped from the insipid and lying
columns of the *Moniteur* which attracted my notice.
The cause of the diurnal event was revealed to me by
the very announcement of its result; truth was in my
respect almost always supplied by the affectation of

reserve; and the lucubrations of the chief magistrate revealed to me alternately the joy and torments of his ambition. I penetrated the most secret actions, even to the servile eagerness of his intimate partisans and most tried agents.

Nevertheless details were wanting; I was too far from the scene of action. How, for example, could I divine the sudden incidents and the unforeseen accidents which occurred out of the ordinary circle of things? There was always some commotion or some storm in the interior of the palace. If some scattered and broken rumours of these transpired, they seldom reached the extreme limits of the provinces without being altered or mutilated through ignorance or passion.

The inveterate custom of desiring to know everything pursued me; and I yielded the more easily to it, in the midst of the *ennui* of a tranquil and monotonous state of exile. By the assistance of steady friends and faithful emissaries I arranged my secret correspondence, corroborated by regular bulletins, which, as they reached me from various quarters, might be reciprocally checked; in a word, I established my counter-police at Aix. This amusement, which was at first weekly, was repeated subsequently more than once a week, and I was informed of all that occurred in a more *piquante* manner.

Such were the occupations of my retreat. There, surrounded by the calm atmosphere of reflection, my Parisian bulletins arrived in such a manner as to stimulate my political meditations. Oh! ever courageous, witty, and faithful V——; you who grasped almost all the threads of the network of information and of truth; you who, endowed with superior sagacity and reason, and who, always active and calm, remained faithful under all circumstances to gratitude and friendship — accept the tribute of respect and tenderness which my heart longs to renew, even to the moment of my last sigh. You were not, however, the only agent employed for the common interest, in weaving the patriotic web which had been preparing for more than a twelvemonth, to meet the probable chance of a catastrophe.[1] The amiable and profound D——, the beautiful and alluring R——, seconded your noble zeal. You also had your knights of secret mystery enrolled under the banners of the hidden graces and virtues. It must be confessed: in the midst of social decomposition, whether under the Reign of Terror or during the two directorial and imperial tyrannies, whom did we find so capable of a rare disinterestedness as to devote themselves for the common good? Some half-dozen ladies. What do I say?—a large number of ladies, who retained the generosity of their ideas uninfected by that contagion of venality and baseness which degrades human nature and bastardises nations.

Alas! we were at that time approaching, after many misfortunes, the boundaries of that fatal cycle in which we had everything to deplore or fear as a nation; we were approaching that frightful future, and more frightful because it was near, in which everything was likely to be compromised and subjected to question: our fortune, our honour, our repose. We

---

[1] Fouché in this place only lifts a corner of the veil; what follows will apprise the reader of all which the ex-minister at present conceals.—*Note by the French Editor.*

had been indebted for them, it is true, to the great man himself; but that extraordinary personage persevered, in spite of the lessons of all ages, in attempting to exercise a power without counterpoise and without control. Devoured by the fever of domination and conquest, raised to the pinnacle of human authority, it was no longer in his power to stop in his career.

Thanks to my correspondence and secret information, I followed him step by step in his public proceedings as well as in his private actions. If I did not lose sight of him, the reason was that the whole Empire was himself; the reason was that all our power, all our fortune, resided in his fortune and his power: an alarming incorporation, beyond a doubt, because it placed at the mercy of a single man, not only one nation, but a hundred different nations.

Arrived at the zenith of his power, Napoleon did not even make a single halt. It was during the two years which I passed in absence from affairs that the germ of his decline, which was at first imperceptible, began to develop itself. On that account I thought, therefore, to advert in this place to the rapid effects of it, less for the sake of gratifying a vain curiosity than of contributing to the utility of history. It will, moreover, be by means of this highly natural transition that I shall be conducted without any gap to the subject of my reappearance[1] on the stage of the world, and my direction once more of state affairs.

---

[1] This word [*ré-apparition*], which well expresses what the author means, is not French: it is borrowed from the English, and can only be supplied by a paraphrase.—*Note by the French Editor.*

The year 1810, at first distinguished by the marriage of Napoleon and Maria Louisa, and afterwards by my disgrace, was also rendered remarkable by the disgrace of Pauline Borghese, the Emperor's sister, and by the abdication of his brother Louis, king of Holland. Let us investigate these two events, in order to be better enabled to explain what followed.

Of the three sisters of Napoleon, Eliza, Caroline, and Pauline, the latter, who was celebrated for her beauty, was the individual whom he most loved, without, however, suffering himself to be subjected by her influence. Full of levity, inconsistency, and laxity of morals, without talent, but not without some smartness and some information, she delighted in splendour, in dissipation, and all kind of flattery. Never had she conceived so great a hatred for any man as for Leclerc, her first husband, and still greater for one of the most amiable of men, Prince Camille Borghese, to whom Napoleon had united her by her second marriage. Her first marriage was what is called a garrison marriage. Being taken ill, and refusing to follow Leclerc in his expedition to San Domingo, she was carried by Napoleon's orders in a litter on board the admiral's ship.
- Consumed by the burning heat of that tropical climate, and banished by the unfortunate result of that expedition to the island De la Tortue, she, in order to divert her mind, plunged into every species of sensuality. On the death of Leclerc, she hastened to take ship, not like an Artemisia, nor like the wife of Britannicus, dissolved in tears, and embracing the funeral urn of her husband, but free, triumphant, and eager again to revel in all the luxuries of the capital.

There, for a long while eaten up by a complaint, the seat of which is an accusing witness against incontinence, Pauline had recourse to all the treasures of Esculapius, and recovered. Strange effect of her miraculous cure! far from impairing her beauty, it derived from it a greater degree of lustre and bloom, like some curious flowers which are brought to blossom by manure, and rendered more beautiful by the rottenness out of which they spring.

Desiring nothing but unrestrained and unlimited enjoyment, but dreading her brother and his rough severity, Pauline formed a project, in conjunction with one of her women, of subjecting Napoleon to the full dominion of her charms. She employed so much art, and so much refinement for the purpose, that her triumph was complete. Such was the intoxication of the despot that more than once his familiars heard him exclaim, on emerging from one of his fits of transport, that his sister was the most beautiful of the beautiful, and, in short, the Venus of the age. Her beauty, however, was only of a masculine description. But let us lay aside these portraits, which are more worthy of the pencil of Suetonius and Aretin than of the graving-tool of history. Voluptuous château de Neuilly! magnificent palace of the Faubourg St. Honoré! if your walls, like those of the palaces of the kings of Babylon, could reveal the truth, what licentious scenes would you not depict in characters of exaggerated size!

For more than a year the infatuation of the brother for the sister maintained its dominion, although unaccompanied by passion; in fact, no other passion but that of dominion and conquest could master that

haughty and warlike spirit. When, after the battle of
Wagram and the peace of Vienna, Napoleon returned
in triumph to Paris, preceded by the report of his
approaching divorce with Josephine, he went that very
day to his sister, who was in a state of agitation and
the most anxious anticipation of his return. Never
had she displayed so much love and adoration for her
brother. I heard her say on that very day—for she
was not aware that there was any mystery to be preserved towards me—"Why do we not rule in Egypt?
We might then act like the Ptolemies. I might
divorce my husband and marry my brother." I knew
her to be too uninstructed to have conceived such an
idea herself, and immediately detected in it an ejacu-
lation of Napoleon.

The bitter and concentrated disappointment which
Pauline felt may be conceived when some months after
that time she saw Maria Louisa, adorned with all her
native frankness, make her appearance at the nuptial
ceremony and take her seat on the throne by the side
of Napoleon. The imperial court then underwent a
thorough reform in its habits, its morals, and its
etiquette. The reform was complete and rigorous.
From that moment the licentious court of Pauline was
deserted; and that woman, who united all the weaknesses to all the graces of her sex, considering Maria
Louisa in the light of a fortunate rival, conceived a
mortal jealousy against her, and nourished the most
intense resentment in the recesses of her heart. Her
health was impaired by it. By the advice of her
physician she had recourse to the waters of Aix-la-
Chapelle, as well for the purpose of recovery as for

that of escaping the *ennui* to which she was a prey. Having undertaken her journey, she passed the line of direction in which Napoleon and Maria Louisa were travelling towards the frontier of Holland. There compelled to appear at the court of the new Empress, and eagerly seizing an opportunity of insulting her as much as possible, she went so far as to make, behind her back, while she was passing through the *salon*, a sign with her two fingers, and that accompanied by an indecent tittering, which the common people apply, in their gross style of derision, to credulous and deluded husbands. Napoleon, who witnessed and was shocked by the impertinence, which the reflection of the mirrors had even revealed to Maria Louisa, never forgave his sister: she that day received an order to withdraw from court. From that time, disdaining submission, she preferred to live in exile and disgrace, till the period of the events of 1814, a period which restored her past affection, and proved her fidelity to the misfortunes of her brother.

The disgrace of Louis, king of Holland, was of a more dignified description.

Up to this time the Emperor had only persecuted and despoiled legitimate sovereigns, as if by that means he had really intended, according to his own imprudent disclosure, to make his own family the most ancient in Europe. But now, preserving no more terms, he went so far as to depose a king of his own race, whose brow he himself had bound with the royal diadem. The question was asked whether he had proclaimed his brother King of Holland in order to reduce him to the condition of his prefect. Louis, who was of a mild

character and a friend of justice, beheld with deep
sorrow the ruin of his kingdom, occasioned by the effect
of that continental system which destroyed all industry
and commerce. He secretly favoured a maritime trade,
notwithstanding the threats of his brother, who applied
to his conduct the epithet of *fraudeur*, exasperated by
seeing himself thus disobeyed, and forgetting that he had
told his brother, when investing him with the royal
office, and in order to vanquish his repugnancy, that
it was much better to die a king than live a prince.
Louis, finding himself incapable of preventing the occupation of his states by the soldiers and custom-house
officers of his brother, abdicated the crown in favour
of his son, announcing his resolution by a message to
the legislative body of Holland in these terms: "My
brother, although much exasperated against me, is not
so against my children; he will certainly never destroy
what he has erected for their sakes; he will not take
away their inheritance, since he will never have occasion
to complain of a child who cannot govern for himself.
The Queen, appointed to the regency, will do her utmost
to conciliate the Emperor, my brother. She will be
more fortunate than I, whose exertions have never been
crowned with success; and, who can tell? perhaps I
may be the only impediment to a reconciliation between
France and Holland. If that be the case, I shall readily
seek consolation in passing the remainder of my life
in wandering and suffering far from the chief objects
of my profoundest affection."

An abdication like this was not undignified. The
message was hardly delivered, when Louis secretly
quitted Holland, and retired to Gratz, in Styria, in the

Austrian states, having nothing more to live upon than a trifling pension. His wife Hortense, more greedily disposed, appropriated to herself the two millions of revenue which Napoleon decreed in favour of his disinherited brother.

This first example of Bonapartean abdication struck me, and induced me to reflect. Shall I confess the truth? It gave me the idea of the possibility which existed of one day saving the Empire, by means of an abdication imposed upon him who might by his extravagance compromise its prosperity. It will be seen in what manner this idea, which was at first confined to myself, germinated afterwards in other political heads.

It may be thought that the abdication of Louis would have disconcerted Napoleon. But was he not surrounded by men, incessantly occupied with the task of varnishing over his invasions and encroachments? Does anyone want to know what was the rhetoric employed upon this subject by Champagny, Duke de Cadore, his minister for foreign affairs, successively promoted to the highest offices, and of whom Talleyrand had formed so accurate a judgment when saying that he was a man fit for every kind of place on the evening preceding the day of his appointment? This minister, so well instructed, commenced by proving, in a jumble called a report, that the abdication of the King of Holland, he being incapable of such an act without the consent of Napoleon, was null by virtue of that circumstance, and of no effect. From this he deduced the marvellous inference (and this grand effort of logic was anticipated) that Holland ought to be considered as a conquest, and reunited to the French Empire; an inference which an imperial decree decided without appeal.

This event had a characteristic scene for its last act. Napoleon caused the son of Louis, still a child, and whom he had created Grand Duke de Berg, to be brought into his presence; and addressed him in the following short harangue: " Come hither, my son ! the conduct of your father afflicts my heart: his disorder alone can explain it.[1] Come to my arms! I will be your father; you shall lose nothing by the event; but never forget, in whatever situation my policy may place you, that your paramount duty is owing to me; and that all your duties towards the people committed to your care are subordinate." In this manner it was that Napoleon rent asunder the veil of so measureless an ambition, that he placed himself above the King of kings and the sovereignty of all nations.

For the present, let us say a word on the true cause of the usurpation of Holland: I can speak of it with so much the more certainty, since it is in some degree connected with my fall. When the marriage with an archduchess was resolved on, Napoleon had a glimpse of a general pacification, which I exerted myself to mature into a firm and reasonable determination. I knew by my emissaries that the cabinet of London was attached to two decisive points: the independence of Holland and of the Peninsula. With

---

[1] This insinuation of Napoleon against his brother was calumnious. Louis was melancholy and valetudinarian ; but his sound and right-minded judgment was not affected by that circumstance.—*Note by the French Editor.*

Louis at its head, the maintenance of the separation of Holland might be counted on. As to the Peninsula, Napoleon would only consent to withdraw his pretensions to Portugal, and for this sole reason, that he found nothing but impediments in the way of his consummation of the conquest.

I did not, however, despair of filling him with disgust at the occupation of Spain, which had already cost him so great an effusion of blood, and which was everything but secure. By his authority, I concerted with his brother Louis, during his residence in Paris, in 1810, a plan of secret and special negotiation with London. Louis wrote to his minister of foreign affairs that Napoleon was so enraged against him and the English, in consequence of their clandestine trade with his dominions, that it would be impossible to prevent the forcible reunion of Holland with France, unless a maritime peace instantly took place, or, at least, unless changes in the British system of blockade and orders of council were effected. He authorised his minister to come to an understanding with his colleagues on this head—but always as if acting of their own accord—and to dispatch to London an agent, who, being invested with a certain degree of consideration, might make overtures of negotiation in their especial names. This agent was instructed in the first instance to press on the notice of the cabinet of St. James the immense disadvantage which would result to the commerce, and even the future safety of England, should Holland, by means of its union with the Empire of Napoleon, become an instrument of aggression in the hands of the latter ; that he would, doubtless, take measures to preclude it from all commercial connection.

The ministers of Louis chose for their agent M. Labouchere, a banker of Amsterdam, who repaired to London, with instructions to set on foot, in conjunction with the Marquis of Wellesley, a secret negotiation. He was more especially to insist on the necessity of making changes in the execution of the orders of council of the month of November, 1807. But the Marquis of Wellesley refused to enter into a detached negotiation on the subject of Holland, in the full persuasion that its independence could only be ensured as long as it was Napoleon's pleasure, and he till then had shown himself little disposed to recognise the rights of any of the nations placed under his influence. However, with a view to sound the sincere intentions of Napoleon, he authorised, about the same epoch (April, 1810), the English commissioner Mackenzie, then charged with the function of continuing the negotiation at Morlaix relative to the exchange of prisoners, to open a negotiation for a maritime peace, which was to be concealed by the ostensible negotiation going on with the French commissioner employed to superintend the treaty of exchange.[1] The cabinet of St. James, through the agency of the commissioner Mackenzie, left to Napoleon his choice between three modes of treating; viz., 1st. The state of possession before hostilities; 2nd. The state of present possession; 3rd. Reciprocal compensation. But Napoleon, intoxicated by his pros-

---

[1] M. the Marquis du Moutier, at this time ambassador from Charles X., in Switzerland.—*Note by the French Editor.*

perity, refused to listen to any of these bases of negotiation, rejecting every description of peace but that of which he should prescribe the conditions.

From that moment the Marquis of Wellesley refused to receive any overture from the banker Labouchere, and even from M. Fagan, whom I had commissioned to address him with the same view. The English ministry was too well persuaded of the efficacy of its system of blockade to accede to any modification in that respect. The negotiation, therefore, was irredeemably broken off; and Napoleon, perceiving that he could not compel England to yield to his will, resolved, in the spirit of vengeance, to invade the kingdom of his brother, hoping by that means to withdraw Holland for ever from the influence of English commerce. At the same time he conceived that he could no longer defer the disgrace of his minister of police, who incessantly laboured to bring him back to a reasonable system of administration and policy. He was the more induced to make a sacrifice of me in consequence of his private correspondents repeating, in reference to myself, and in accordance with certain London pamphleteers, "that he trembled before his own work, without having the courage to destroy it." He was waiting for the opportunity for several months past. It has been seen[1] how uneasy he was respecting my connection with Bernadotte. In this case there appeared to him a more plausible motive for my disgrace. He pretended that, under pretext of negotiating on the subject of Holland,

---

[1] In the first part of these Memoirs.— *Note by the French Editor.*

my agents in London had done nothing but abandon themselves to intrigues and fraudulent speculations: by that means seeking to make me responsible for the rupture of a negotiation which had only failed through his bad faith and domineering spirit. Such is an elucidation of the true motives of the invasion of Holland, and of my disgrace, the accuracy of which I can guarantee.

This system of irreconciliation and violence was perpetuated by an imperial decree,[1] the purport of which was that all English merchandise which existed in places subjected to the Emperor's dominions, or conquered by his arms, should be publicly burnt. This was an appendix to the Berlin and Milan decrees; that is to say, that the same steps were to be taken at Amsterdam and Leghorn as had already been taken at Berlin, Frankfort, Mayence, and Paris. If the observation could not here be made, that "to burn was not to answer," it could at least be said that "to burn was not to govern."

Such were the consequences of the continental system, which, according to silly and dastardly counsellors, was ultimately to put England *hors de combat* and deliver the whole world to Napoleon. And this incendiary idea, which became with him in particular a fixed belief, was nothing but a political tradition, inherited by him from the directorial government, which the jurists of clubs and gazettes had persuaded that the only way to reduce England was to exclude her from the ports of the continent.

But in order to do this it was first necessary to

---

[1] From the 19th of October, 1810.

subjugate continental Europe, of which Napoleon did not yet possess more than one-third; the rest languished under the dead weight of the kings, his allies, his friends, or his tributaries. What a spirit reigned in the notes which the minister Champagny successively addressed to them, in order to persuade them to close their ports against all English vessels! "That there was no longer any neutrals for the European states; that they should not carry on any commerce, active or passive, on their own account, and that France alone, by means of licenses negotiated at London, would provide them with such goods as it was indispensable for them to receive." Such was the famous continental system, which tended to abolish the commerce of the world, and which on that very account was impracticable. Besides, it would have been soon found necessary to modify it, or rather to merge it in the system of licenses invented by England.

Bonaparte was, therefore, himself impelled from the end of 1810 to impart a latitude to this system by granting permission, for a given sum, to introduce into France a certain quantity of colonial produce; but on condition of exchanging it for goods of French manufacture, which were most frequently thrown into the sea on account of the difficulties raised by the English custom-house officers.

And who obtained the greatest profit by this unprecedented monopoly? Undoubtedly not the minor speculators, nor the commissioners *tarifés* by the great speculator in chief, who were reduced to little more than a trivial profit of commission. But the Emperor's profit was clear and net. Every day he observed, with an access of joy which he did not disguise, the accumulation of treasure stored in the cellars of the Pavillon Marsan; they were completely encumbered with them. These treasures already amounted to near five hundred millions in specie;[1] it was a residue of the two milliards of circulating medium introduced into France by the effect of conquest. The desire of gold might thus have superseded eventually the desire of conquest in the mind of Napoleon, if the inexorable Nemesis had suffered him to grow old.

To form an idea of the accumulation of wealth identified with the development of this individual's power, forty millions of movables and four or five millions of plate, preserved in the imperial mansions, must be added to the treasures concealed in the cellars of the Tuileries; five hundred millions distributed under the name of *dotations* to the army; and, finally, the *domaine extraordinaire*, amounting to more than seven hundred millions, and which was unlimited, since it was composed of property "which the Emperor, exercising the right of peace and war, acquired by conquests and treaties." With such an indefinite text as the above, it was impossible for anything to escape him. Already the funds of this *domaine extraordinaire* were composed of whole provinces, of states whose fate had not been decided, and of the produce of confiscations throughout the Empire. It would have, doubtless, concluded by absorbing all the public revenues and

---

[1] The voluntary companions of the captive of St. Helena have since confirmed this disclosure; but they only compute the especial treasure of their idol in the best times at four hundred millions.—*Note by the French Editor.*

property which might chance to escape from the two other institutions of *imperial domains* and *private domains*. To subject the whole of France to a new form of vassalage, and attach it to his domain, by annual fiefs, was also one of the favourite ideas of Napoleon.

What a magnificent *régime* of military spoliation on the one hand and of gifts and prodigality on the other! Whither was it likely to conduct us? To shed our blood in order to subject the whole world to a state of vassalage. And, besides, there was but little hope of satiating the voracity of the favourites and votaries of an insatiable conqueror.

Such animadversions proceeding from my pen, and the reflections which accompany them, will occasion some readers, I doubt not, to smile or sneer. How, it will be said, was it that this minister, so mortified because he was disgraced, remained a stranger to the abuses of lucrative gratuities which he now, perhaps, exclaims against because their source is dried up? Was he not himself loaded with honours and riches? And who denies it? What, because a man has shared in the individual advantages of an outrageous, pernicious, and insupportable system, should he abstain from telling the truth when he has pledged himself to reveal everything? The time for reservation is past. It is, besides, necessary in this place to state the causes of the fall of the greatest Empire which ever adorned or desolated the universe.

It will be seen how Napoleon, with very little interval of delay, voluntarily precipitated himself beyond all the bounds of moderation and prudence.

As one consequence of the usurpation of Holland, he declared in a message addressed to the senate,[1] that new guarantees were indispensable to him, and those which had appeared to him most urgent, was the reunion of the mouth of the Scheldt, of the Meuse, of the Rhine, the Ems, the Weser, and the Elbe; and the establishment of an interior navigation in the Baltic. Thence resulted a Senatus Consultum,[2] decreeing that Holland, a considerable portion of the north of Germany, and the free towns of Hamburg, Bremen, and Lübeck, should thenceforth form an integral part of the French Empire, and comprise ten new departments. It was thus that Napoleon, without thinking of consolidating what he had acquired, incessantly tormented himself with the thirst for new acquisitions.

This violent incorporation was effected without any motive of right, even ostensible; without any preparatory negotiation with any cabinet whatsoever ; and under the futile pretext that it was rendered indispensable by the war against England. Napoleon by this act destroyed even his own creations; neither the states of the Confederation of the Rhine, nor the kingdom of Westphalia, nor any other territory were exempted from furnishing their quota towards this new spoil of the lion.

But he thus obtained for himself a new frontier line, which deprived the southern and central provinces of Germany of all communication with the northern sea, which passed the Elbe, separated

---

[1] The 10th of December, 1810.
[2] Of the 13th of December, 1810.

Denmark from Germany, established itself on the Baltic, and exhibited a tendency to unite with that line of Prussian fortresses on the Oder, which we occupied in spite of treaties.

It will be readily perceived that this of itself was an act sufficient to disturb the neighbouring powers by thus establishing on the flanks of Germany a new French dominion; and that by a simple decree, by a Senatus Consultum, imposed upon a servile senate. I immediately concluded that the treaty of Tilsit, the principal object of which was to establish a line of demarcation between the two empires, was by that means annulled; and that France and Russia, thus brought into contact, would not be long before they would fall to blows.

When I learnt, by means of my correspondents at Paris, the uneasiness which the junction of the Hanse towns caused to Russia, Prussia, and even Austria, I was confirmed in the opinion that there was not only comprised in that circumstance the germ of a new universal war, but of a conflict which would finally decide whether we were to have a universal monarchy in the hands of Napoleon Bonaparte, or the restoration of all which the Revolution had dispersed or destroyed.

Alas! with this great question was incorporated another; namely, the identical question of the interest of the Revolution, and of the safety of the individuals who had founded and established it. What was to become of them? Could I remain cold, alien, and insensible to so disturbing a future prospect?

Among the princes recently despoiled was the Duke of Oldenburg, of the house of Holstein-Gottorp; that

is to say, of the same house as the Emperor of Russia ;
and Napoleon thus took away the patrimony of a prince
whom policy urged him to ingratiate. A negotiation
was opened on this subject between the court of St.
Petersburg and the cabinet of the Tuileries. Napoleon,
by way of indemnity, offered the Duke of Oldenburg
the city and territory of Erfurt. When I learnt that
this offer had just been haughtily rejected, that the
Emperor Alexander had, by a formal protest, reserved
the rights of his family from encroachment, and that
his ministers had received orders to present that protest
at the various courts, I no longer entertained a doubt
that war was on the point of breaking out. But, reflecting on the circumspect and measured character of
the Emperor Alexander, I concluded that the approach
of the crisis would neither be abrupt nor precipitate.

Let us now pass to the year 1811, during which
all the elements of a frightful tempest were maturing
in the midst of a deceitful calm, the illusions and de-
ceptions of which I detected. From day to day my
Parisian bulletins and my private correspondence became more animated and more unremitting. I will
give a sketch in this place in order to connect the
chain of facts and the most striking details and features,
scarcely allowing myself to combine with them some
short reflections, or some necessary elucidations. I
have, moreover, already said that, anxious as I am to
arrive at the period of my re-entrance into office, an
abridged historical transition, which will conduct us to
the catastrophes of 1813, 1814, and 1815, will be most
accordant with the spirit of my design.

The first event which offers itself to notice is that

of the birth of the child, proclaimed King of Rome on
the 20th of March, 1811, at the first moment of its
existence.   As if a son of Bonaparte could not be
born anything else than a king!   This sudden revival
of the kingdom of Tarquin the Proud appeared to
some persons in the light of a bad omen.   It recalled
too glaringly the spoliation recently operated upon the
Holy See and the oppression exercised upon the person
of the Sovereign Pontiff.   Ridiculous reports respecting
the birth of this infant king were propagated, I believe,
in Paris.   If these reports—derived at once from the
upper and lower classes—did not prove a hostile state
of public opinion at that epoch against the perpetuity
of the new dynasty, I might dismiss all allusion to
them as unworthy of the dignity of history.   Malice
exhibited itself in an ingeniously credulous point of
view.   A pretended pregnancy was at first supposed.
As if an archduchess, when becoming barren, could
ever belie the well-known Latin distich.   The consequence of this supposition led to another fable,
according to which the King of Rome was identified
with a child lately born from a connection between
Napoleon and the Duchess de M——.   Some news-
mongers pretended that he was substituted in the place
of a still-born child; others in the room of a female
infant.   At all events, the arch-chancellor, Cambacérès,
could not have been mistaken.   The calumnies of the
malignant were inexhaustible.   It is, however, true that
the labour of Maria Louisa was horribly protracted;
that the *accoucheur* got bewildered; that the child was
concluded to be dead; and that he was only recovered
from his lethargy by the effect of the repeated report

of a hundred pieces of artillery. As to the Emperor's transport, it was very natural. Some flatterers inferred from it, in the first instance, that Napoleon, more fortunate than Cæsar, would have nothing further to dread from the Ides of March, since the 20th of March was distinguished as a day of good fortune both for himself and the Empire. Napoleon believed in horoscopes and predictions. What a mistake was his calculation in March, 1814 and 1815!

He departed from Rambouillet with Maria Louisa towards the end of May in order to visit Cherbourg. On their return to St. Cloud on the 4th of June, 1811, they presided at the baptism of their son, whom Napoleon, lifting in his arms, himself exhibited to the numerous assistants. All things seemed to conspire in announcing the most brilliant destinies for this child. Three years sufficed to overthrow the colossal power of his father—and yet the court, the great officers, the ministers, and the entire Empire went on at that time in the most unprophetic security. There was scarcely to be discovered, even by the most sagacious among us, the least sign of apprehension and vague disquietude.

- Some few days afterwards (the 16th of June, 1811), Napoleon, opening the session of the legislative body, announced that the birth of the King of Rome had accomplished his wishes and fulfilled the prayers of his people. He spoke of the incorporation of the Roman states, of Holland, of the Hanse towns, and of Valois, and concluded by saying that he flattered himself that the peace of the continent would not be broken. France easily understood the purport of these last words, which were not dropped without a design of preparing the public mind for war.

The ukase intended by the Emperor Alexander to extricate his Empire out of the embarrassment in which the continental system retained it was made known to me. Russia could not renounce her maritime commerce for a longer period. I, moreover, knew that the faction of the old Russians began to predominate in the councils of Alexander. The ukase confined the importation of merchandise to certain specified ports; and among those which were subjected to tariff no article of French manufacture was found. I saw in that a retort to the arbitrary seizure of the Hanse towns.

As to our commerce, compressed from day to day within our immediate limits, it only existed in land carriage; we had no other vessels of burden than waggons and drays. The great reputation of our industry was, at that time, based upon the manufacture of sugar from beetroot. It was a lucky experiment for certain adventurers in the line of national industry, who thereby obtained from the government advance money, premiums, and grants of land. The administration exhausted its funds in these juggleries, the actors of which promised us beetroot sugar at the same price as colonial. According to my Parisian correspondents, the Emperor had already under a glass on his mantelpiece at St. Cloud a loaf of refined beetroot sugar, which would bear comparison with the best colonial sugar that ever issued from the warehouses of Orleans. It was so perfect a specimen that his minister of the interior had presented it to him with all the pomp which might correspond with a rarity worthy of figuring in a museum. Specimens of it were sent to the prince primate and to all the little potentates of the Confederation of the Rhine. If it was beyond the reach of the masses in consequence of its high price, they had, by way of compensation, under this policy, syrup of raisins and indigenous coffee of chicory at a reasonable price. In the midst of this parsimony of colonial produce, some new manufactures flourished in the interior, and some hundred manufacturers, who shared in the distribution of prizes and premiums, loudly cried up the activity of our internal commerce.

All other commerce languished ; and, what was still more deplorable, the people began to suffer from dearth occasioned by a bad harvest, and aggravated by the extent of those exportations on which the government obtained a profit. To say the truth, indeed, in order to render misery less importunate, mendicity depôts were established in different parts of the Empire, where one portion of the population was successively penned up and provided for by means of economical soups. But the people who persevered in their *panivorous* propensities accused the Emperor of selling our corn to the English. It is certain that the corn monopoly exercised by Napoleon partly contributed to produce the famine. The spirit which reigned in the *salons* was not more favourable to the Emperor ; it was even becoming hostile. Such was the manner in which public opinion was moulded since Savary directed it.

That individual, who was dazzled by the pomp of

rank and the illusion of outward circumstances, imagined that he should arrive at a state of influence and power, if he possessed creatures, parasites, and literary men, marshalled at his table and dragooned to his orders. He conceived that, in order to profit by my legacy, all that was necessary was to ingratiate the Faubourg St. Germain without divesting his police of its odious and irritating qualifications. In a word, he thought it possible to form the public spirit of the Empire as Madame de Genlis formed the manners of the new court. It was then that the famous *déjeûners à la fourchette* were established, at which Savary presided, and at which all the hired jurists, who corresponded with the Emperor, and all the journalists who aspired to receive orders and gratifications, were to be found. It was there that Savary, animated by his camp habits of dictation and by the incense of a plentiful breakfast, imparted commands to each of his guests as to the colour they should give to the literature of the week.

The direction of this moral portion of the police was confided to the poet Esmenard, a writer of real talent, but in so much discredit that I thought it necessary to keep the bridle constantly in his mouth whenever I set him to work. Perverting in a short time the superiority of his position to a bad account, he completely led the new minister by the nose, through the application of flattery to his passions and his absurdities. I had paid due respect to learning and to letters. My successor, in the very act of pretending to make himself a protector of the Academies, treated them in a military manner, imposing his own creatures upon them as candidates; and appearing to have nothing more at heart than the desire of humiliating and scandalising the organs of knowledge and of public opinion. I paid respect to the proprietorship of the journals; Savary invaded its rights with audacity, and divided its shares among his familiars and agents. But in this manner he deprived himself, in consequence of the degradation of the journals, of one of the principal levers of public opinion. It was in the same way that Napoleon took a dislike to Madame de Staël, and, in concert with the poet Esmenard, did all he could to injure her; an impolitic persecution, because he thus made of the numerous coteries of that celebrated woman a hotbed of opposition to the imperial *régime* and of animosity to the Emperor.

In the upper police there was the same system and the same violence; and there little Desmarets was to be found acting the part of effective minister. What was to be expected from a man of such slender talents, and from the combinations of a minister of his description? Awkward inventions, repulsive acts, and a vexatious practice. Some idea may be formed of it by the following example: a certain Baron de Kolly, a Piedmontese, who was commissioned by the British government to attempt the liberation of Ferdinand of Spain from his captivity, disembarked about the beginning of March, 1810, in Quiberon Bay; thence he proceeded to Paris, where I ordered him to be arrested and conveyed to the château de Vincennes. What, forsooth, does my successor do? He imagines a plan of trying Ferdinand's inclinations, by means of a false Baron de Kolly, supplied with the papers and the letter of credit belonging to the real emissary. Ferdinand VII. was, however, upon his guard; he saw the snare, avoided it, and left Savary to put the best face he could on his defeat.

The Queen of Etruria, deprived of her states, lived at Nice, in exile, where she was shamefully treated: emissaries were sent to induce her to throw herself into the arms of the English. This unhappy queen, driven to despair, embraced what appeared to her the only means of safety; she was arrested and threatened to be carried before a military commission, and two of her officers were shot. When there is no conspiracy, a sham one is easily imagined, or a real one excited. It was in this manner that some unfortunate inhabitants of Toulon, said to be implicated in an obscure plot against our arsenals, were dragged to punishment in a city already bleeding with the memory of its past afflictions.

In the meanwhile opinion remained mute. There was no more communication; no more confession; no more confidence among the citizens. It was only in the interior of the domestic circle, or in the bosom of friendship, that the public grief dared to express itself in stifled accents of affliction. In default of public opinion, the Emperor wished to be supplied with that which emanated from the *salons* of Paris. A factitious opinion was manufactured expressly for his service by the three hundred police spies, hired at large salaries. There were, in this manner, several statistical surveys of public feeling; the five or six polices supplied theirs. The least insignificant was, beyond dispute, that of the director-general of posts, Lavalette. Already a correspondent and confidential emissary of Napoleon, when he was only a general, he was *au fait* to all that was agreeable to him in this line. The Emperor, who was soon enabled to appreciate what was wanting in these secret researches, the true spirit of which no one but myself had seized, demanded facts. These were furnished; but miserable facts they were; and he concluded either by rejecting or not reading them, so tiresome and incoherent did he find them. In my retreat some of these bulletins, got up by the pupils of the police system, were brought to me. At a later period Savary transcribed from one end to the other all that immediately issued from his own cabinet, believing that he should by that means impart more importance to his vague discoveries.

If from the moment of my disgrace the police had degenerated in its most essential functions, it was the same with another public office, which was also the asylum of mystery. I allude to the office of foreign relations, where, since the resignation of M. de Talleyrand, the spirit of conquest, of violence, and oppression were no longer repressed by moderation or restraint. Napoleon had fallen into the impolicy—and the consequences will be seen by and by—to disgust that personage, so independent in mind, so brilliant in talent, and so practised and refined in his taste; who, moreover, had, by his diplomacy, done him at least as much service as I myself had been able to render him in the higher affairs of state, which concerned the security of his person. But Napoleon could never forgive Talleyrand for having always spoken of the war in Spain with a disapproving freedom of speech.

In a short time the *salons* and the boudoirs of Paris became the theatre of a secret warfare between the adherents of Napoleon on the one side and of Talleyrand and his friends on the other—a war in which epigrams and *bons-mots* constituted the artillery, and in which the victor of Europe was almost always beaten. This species of satirical encounter contracted a more serious character, in proportion as the Spanish war grew more envenomed in its progress. On their side, M. and Madame de Talleyrand only exhibited greater kindness to the princes of the house of Spain, banished to their château de Valency by a petty refinement of malice on the part of Napoleon. His pique at Talleyrand's conduct continually augmenting, he one day perceived him at his levee in the midst of his courtiers, and hoping, in order to humiliate him, to take advantage of an affair of gallantry alleged to have passed at Valency, he put a question to him which, to a husband, is considered as one of the greatest of insults. Without exhibiting any emotion in his countenance, Talleyrand replied in a dignified manner, " It would be well both for the glory of your Majesty and myself if the princes of the house of Spain were never mentioned." Never did Napoleon display so much confusion as after receiving this severe lesson, which was couched in the most refined terms of politeness. All things shortly announced a complete disgrace, and the position of Talleyrand was gradually becoming more difficult. His hotel, his friends, and his servants were given up to a perpetual espionage, which Savary himself did not even affect to disguise. He boasted to his familiar partisans that he kept Talleyrand and Fouché in perpetual alarm. The public drew the inference that the chief magistrate, by means of his suspicious character, had deprived himself of the services of two men whose advice would always have been beneficial; and that there was not, either in the police department or that of foreign affairs, sufficient moderation or ability from the moment of their quitting office. The police was nothing more than a fruitless and irritating inquisition. As to foreign affairs, people became accustomed to look upon treaties as hollow truces or expedients calculated to lead to new wars. To such a pitch was this habit brought that no one at last blushed at making the most scandalous avowals. "We do not want principles," said Champagny-Cadore, who succeeded Talleyrand, and the same individual who had presided over the violence exercised on the person of the Pope and the princes of the house of Spain. Yet, nevertheless, this same minister, when out of the diplomatic sphere, or rather beyond the influence of Napoleon, was one of the mildest men in France in deportment, and one of the most moderate in opinion. As it was no longer possible to maintain place except by flattering the passions of the individual who had the source of all power and favour, the monopolisers of imperial policy set themselves briskly to work in order to accelerate the fall of England and the humiliation of Russia. Memorials and projects followed each other under cover of the secret police of Desmarets and Savary, whose function it was to make themselves responsible for the daily muster-roll of projectors. The Emperor no longer received any reports but those in which the truth of facts and their consequences were either distorted or disguised; he no longer imbibed any information but such as was derived from impassioned correspondence, replete with proposals and projects of intrigues, adventures, and acts of violence.

The idea was at length entertained of manœuvring England at the same time as Russia. I had endeavoured without effect, while I held the reins of the superior police, to calm the Emperor down to more sober ideas respecting England. The Emperor esteemed the English, and had no especial dislike to England; but he feared the oligarchy of its government. It was his belief that England, under a system of this description, would never suffer him to enjoy a substantial peace, but only a truce of three years at the utmost, after which it would be necessary to begin again. I could never succeed in destroying the prejudices and misapprehensions of the Emperor on this head. Other persons, by the coarsest sophistries, inflamed his ruling passion against the nature of the British constitution, a passion which plunged him once more into a universal war. It was a revolution in earnest which Bonaparte wished to effect in England; he thirsted with a desire to strangle the liberty of the press and the liberty of parliamentary discussion. Induced to wish for the moment when he could behold that island in her turn delivered up to the horrors of a political revolution, he sent envoys there, who deceived him as to its actual condition. I told him a hundred times that England was as powerful by the effect of her institutions as of her naval force: but he preferred believing the representations of interested spies. It was in the hope of causing internal dissensions to explode that, during the year 1811, he chiefly occupied himself with the project of entirely excluding English commerce from the continent. His emissaries did not fail to attribute the distress of the manufactures in that kingdom to the continental blockade, as well as the numerous bankruptcies, which, during the course of that same year, struck deadly blows at the stability of English credit. They announced the approximation of serious tumults; and maintained that England could not much longer support a state of war, which cost her more than fifty millions sterling.

In fact, tumultuous meetings of work-people without work broke out in Nottinghamshire. The mutineers assembled in organised bodies, burnt or destroyed the looms, and committed all kinds of excesses. They described themselves to be under the orders of a Captain Ludd, an imaginary personage, whence they derived the name of Luddites. The Emperor considered this in the light of a national wound, which it was his policy to enlarge like that of Ireland. In a short time, indeed, the system of insurrection extended its sphere of action, and involved the neighbouring counties of Derby and Leicester. It was affirmed in the cabinet of Napoleon that persons of note were not strangers to the commotion, and were even its instigators.

In case of serious insurrection, supported by corresponding movements matured in London, the co-operation, more or less efficacious, of our prisoners, who amounted to fifty thousand, was calculated upon. Such was one of the motives which influenced Napoleon in not consenting to their proposed exchange. As we had no more than 10,000 English prisoners in France, but near 53,000 Spanish and Portuguese, the Emperor feigned to consent to a *cartel*, but only in the proportion of one Englishman and four Spaniards or Portuguese against five Frenchmen or Italians. He was sure beforehand that England would reject an exchange founded upon this principle. In fact, the mere proposal was scouted by the English ministry.

Napoleon, who increased the rigour of his continental system, in proportion as he saw the distress of England increasing, exacted a more complete closing of the ports of Sweden, to which power he only left the choice between war with England or with France. This impolitic rigour exhibited towards an independent power proceeded in some degree from his discontent with Bernadotte, who had been proclaimed the year preceding (the 21st of August, 1810), by the unanimous vote of the Swedish states, prince royal and hereditary successor of King Charles XIII. This sudden elevation had not pleased Napoleon at the bottom of his heart, and his resentment against his old companion in arms had continually augmented from the period of the commission, which I had consigned to him in 1809, for the defence of Antwerp. Napoleon was persuaded that there was a secret intelligence between Bernadotte and myself at that time, and that if he had then experienced any striking reverse, I should have caused Bernadotte to be proclaimed either First Consul or Emperor, in order to close the gates of France against him for ever. It was on this account, on the other hand, that he saw him depart for the North, in the first instance, without regret, considering himself too happy to be delivered from the presence of a man whom Savary and his familiars represented to him in the light of an adversary, and who might one day become formidable. Considering, moreover, for some months that he should be able to retain him compulsively within the orbit of his own politics, he addressed note upon note, and injunction upon injunction, to the government of Charles XIII., to induce it to keep its ports rigorously closed against English commerce. Exasperated that sufficient promptitude was not exhibited in accomplishing his views, he caused his privateers to seize such Swedish vessels as were loaded with colonial produce, and persevered in the occupation of Pomerania. Mutual complaints being thus engendered, Napoleon gave new disquietude to the government of which Bernadotte had become the hope and the arbiter. The whole of the year 1811 was spent in altercations between the two states.

The knowledge which I had of the character of Bernadotte gave me sufficient reason to foresee that he would conclude by throwing himself into the arms of Russia and England, either to guarantee the independence of Sweden, or to secure the rights of inheritance to a crown of which Napoleon plainly revealed that he was envious.

My old ties of connection with the Prince of Sweden, imparted to the Emperor (as misinterpreted by Savary) the idea that I secretly excited Bernadotte to maintain himself in an attitude of opposition to the cabinet of St. Cloud. I soon learnt, beyond the possibility of doubt, that I was spied upon, and that my letters were opened. And here I beg to ask, what would be thought of me if I had not put myself in a condition to counter-work the ridiculous investigations of a police, all the windings of which I was acquainted with? I was not, however, ignorant of what was passing at Stockholm, nor even in the North; I had Colonel V. C—— near the person of Bernadotte, who supplied me with all that was necessary to know.

Let us conclude, by some reflections on the Peninsular War, our sketch of the political events of 1811, which will conduct us to the fatal expedition into Russia. The resistance of the Spanish people had already assumed the character of a national war; and it was Napoleon himself who had opened this field of battle on the continent to England's advantage.

Ever since the beginning of 1810, the war had become so complicated in Spain, it already offered so many chances to the ambition and the rivalries of the various generals, that when King Joseph came to Paris to attend the nuptials of the Emperor, he made an express demand that all the troops should be withdrawn, or that they should be placed under his immediate orders, or rather under the direction of his major-general. The Emperor took good care not to grant him the recall of the troops, but he invested him with their command. Joseph accordingly took with him from Paris Marshal Jourdan, who bore the title of major-general to the King of Spain. The generals-in-chief were subjected to his orders, and were to hold themselves accountable to King Joseph and to the Emperor at the same time. But these measures remedied nothing; there were always several armies, and the generals depending at once on Paris and

Madrid, took precautions to depend upon neither; their first and principal object was to remain masters of the provinces which they occupied, or for which they were contending with the enemy.

In the meanwhile we had been twice driven from Portugal, where the English army found infinite resources and a secure place of refuge. All things ought to have convinced Napoleon that in order to subject the Peninsula, it was, in the first place, indispensable to effect the conquest of Lisbon, and compel the English to re-embark. To this he had, in some sort, pledged himself in the face of Europe. But his genius was in fault in this instance, as in many other decisive circumstances where the irritability and impetuosity of his character ought to have given way to a greater breadth of view, or at least to the most ordinary foresight. How could it have escaped his notice that he was risking not only his Spanish conquest, but even his own fortune, in suffering a military and hostile reputation to establish itself in the Peninsula? Europe had a sufficient number of soldiers; all that she wanted was a general capable of guiding them, and of making a stand against the French army, no matter how. It is incredible how this view of the subject could have escaped the observation of Napoleon. It was only through an access of confidence in himself and his good fortune. With the same fatuity, instead of marching in person at the head of a formidable army, to drive Wellington out of Portugal (and this the state of the continent at that time permitted), he sent Masséna there, the most skilful, doubtless, of his lieutenants, an individual endowed with unusual courage and remarkable perseverance, whose talent grew with the increase of danger, and who, when vanquished, always appeared ready to recommence the struggle as if he were the victor. But Masséna, who was a daring depredator, was also the secret enemy of the Emperor, who had compelled him to disgorge three millions of money. Like Soult, he indulged himself in the belief that he also might be enabled to win a crown at the point of the sword: the examples of Napoleon, of Murat, and of Bernadotte were, besides, so alluring that Masséna's mind easily gave way to ambitious visions of reigning in his turn. Replete with hope, he began his march at the head of sixty thousand soldiers; but at the very outset of the first difficulties of the expedition, he received certain intelligence that the Emperor was disposed to restore Portugal to the house of Braganza, provided that England consented to his appropriation of Spain, and that a secret negotiation was opened for that purpose. Masséna, piqued and discouraged, suffered the fire of his military genius to evaporate. Moreover, in an operation so decisive as that he had undertaken, no one could supply Napoleon's place; he alone could dare to sacrifice from thirty to forty thousand men in order to carry the formidable lines of Torres Vedras, which encompassed Lisbon like an actual girdle of steel. Everything was about to depend, nevertheless, on the issue of this campaign of 1810, both with reference to Napoleon and to Europe. It showed a real deficiency of tact and genius to have failed in perceiving this intimate co-relation.

What was the consequence? The campaign failed

Lord Wellington triumphed. Masséna, falling into disrepute, returned to dance attendance in the saloons of the Tuileries, only obtaining, after a month's solicitation, a private audience, in which he detailed the reverses of the campaign; and, in short, the Peninsular War, notwithstanding many great exploits, exhibited upon the whole an alarming aspect. Suchet alone, in the eastern provinces, transmitted titles of incontestable glory to the French name. He effected the conquest of the kingdom of Valencia, and was always equal to himself. While he thus rendered himself in other words independent, Soult, who was not able to make himself King of Portugal, enacted the part of king in Andalusia; and Marmont, rallying the wrecks of the army of Portugal, acted for himself on the Douro and the Tormes; in a word, the lieutenants of Bonaparte established distinct military governments, and Joseph was no more than a fictitious king. He could no longer quit Madrid without having an army for his escort; more than once he narrowly escaped being taken by the *guerrillas;* his kingdom was not his own; the provinces which we occupied were, in reality, no more than French provinces ruined by our armies, or devastated by the *guerrillas,* who harassed us without intermission. I lay it down as a position, that all the reverses subsequent to those of the Peninsula are attributable to the errors of the campaign of 1810, so falsely conceived and so lightly undertaken. Towards the end of 1811, Joseph dispatched the Marquis of Almenara, invested with full powers, to sign his formal abdication at Paris, or to obtain a recognition of the independence of Spain.

But Napoleon, diverting his whole attention towards Russia, postponed his decision regarding Spain till after the issue of the great and distant enterprise in which he was about to engulf himself beyond redemption.

The Russian war was not a war undertaken for the sake of sugar and coffee, as the vulgar at first believed, but a war purely political. If the causes of it have never yet been accurately understood, it is because they are shrouded by the mysterious veil of diplomacy; they could only be grasped by enlightened observers and practical statesmen. The seeds of the Russian war were inclosed even in the treaty of Tilsit. In order to prove this position, it will be sufficient for me to exhibit in this place a sketch of its immediate results. The foundation of the kingdom of Westphalia for the Napoleonic dynasty; the accession of the larger number of the princes of the north of Germany to the Confederation of the Rhine; the erection of the duchy of Warsaw, which was meant to be a nucleus for the entire re-establishment of Poland, a constantly variable bugbear in the hands of its inventor, and which he might direct as it best pleased him, either against Russia or against Austria; the re-establishment of the republic of Dantzic, of which the independence was guaranteed, but whose permanent subjection gave to Napoleon a port and a depôt of arms on the Baltic; finally, military roads secured to the French army across the Russian states, and which broke down every barrier interposed between France and the Russian frontiers—such were the conditions to which the Russian cabinet subscribed in exchange for eventual acquisitions in Turkey, which soon turned out to be illusory. It is true this was not the same with Finland. How, nevertheless, was it possible to avoid confessing that if the Russian autocrat acknowledged an equal in Napoleon, he also recognised in him a conqueror, who, sooner or later, would reap the benefit of his advantages?

But, in the first instance, directing his ambitious views towards the South, Spain, Portugal, and Spanish America became the immediate objects of his cupidity. Thence, the respite which a captious treaty offered to the Russian Empire. Besides, Napoleon found little difficulty in fascinating the eyes of those whom he caressed while he was concerting their ruin. At one time I looked with a favourable eye at his views upon Russia : and I confess that, seduced by the grandeur of his plans, I had once indulged in the hope of seeing the re-establishment of Poland founded upon the base of liberty; but Napoleon, repelling Kosciusko, or, at least, endeavouring to draw him into a maze, I perceived that his only object was to extend his dominion beyond the Vistula, and the example of his ravages in Spain soon restored a greater degree of sobriety to my judgment.

In fine, it was well understood that the Emperor Alexander, in order to preserve peace, found it necessary to temporise in all respects with Napoleon, his cabinet, his ministers, and his ambassadors ; and that it was incumbent upon him not to deviate, in any respect, from the obligation of acknowledging his supremacy and of obeying his will.

While proceeding to the conquest of Spain, Napoleon had put the finishing hand to his federal system, and thus prepared the way to universal monarchy. The last defeat of Austria followed; next the forced marriage of an archduchess, and the change brought about in the policy of the latter power. All hope then vanished for the capacity of the European continent to shake off the yoke as long as the Emperor Alexander remained faithful to his alliance with the chief of the federal Empire, already named, by way of eminence, the Great Empire. But how was it possible to breathe in the neighbourhood of so oppressive an atmosphere of ambition? Russia already began to recognise that the infallible results of the continental system for every nation which submitted to it was the ruin of commerce and of industry, the establishment of excessive imposts, the burden of immense armies nearly foreign to their princes, and of princes incapable of protecting their trembling subjects from the grip of the usurper of Europe.

The Emperor Alexander, after three years of an ambiguous and burdensome alliance, at length opened his eyes. It was found necessary to summon all the strength of his empire, in order to secure his independence. Instructed by his emissaries that the anti-French party, or that of the old Russians, began to prevail in the cabinet of St. Petersburg, Napoleon returned, with regard to Russia, to his plan of 1805 and 1806, which he had only at that time postponed with the view to the better maturing its eventual execution.

This was his plan: to divide or abolish the Russian Empire, or compel the Emperor Alexander to make a humiliating peace, followed by an alliance between Russia, France, and Austria, the basis and the price of which were to be the restoration of Poland and the dissolution of the Empire of the Crescent. This was to be followed by the accession of all Europe to the continental system, which, in the case of Bonaparte, was only another name for universal domination.

But, in the first instance, it was indispensable to gain Russia by intimidation, or otherwise to make a deadly war upon her, for the purpose of abrogating her power, or expelling her into Asia. Exertions were made at a distance to shake the fidelity of the Poles, by preparing their minds through the effects of mysterious negotiation.

When Napoleon had determined that all the springs of his diplomacy should be put in motion towards the North, he changed his minister of foreign affairs, the complication of so many intrigues and manœuvres becoming too much, not indeed for the zeal, but for the energy of Champagny-Cadore. Napoleon did not think himself secure in confiding the weight of affairs so important to any other person than Maret, the chief of his secretariate—that is to say, all external affairs were from that moment concentrated in the single focus of his cabinet, and received no other impulse than from him. Under this point of view, Maret, who was a true official machine, was the very man whom the Emperor wanted. Without being a bad man, he really admired his master, all whose thoughts, secrets, and inclinations he was acquainted with. He was, moreover, his confidential secretary, and the individual best acquainted with the art of connecting or transfusing into grammatical phraseology his effusions and political imaginations. It was also he who kept the secret register in which the Emperor made his notes of such individuals of all countries and parties who might be useful to him, as well as of men who were pointed out to his notice, and whose intentions he suspected. He also kept the *tarif* of all the pensioned courts and personages from one end of Europe to the other: in short, it was Maret who, for a long time past, had directed the emissaries of the cabinet. Constantly devoted to the caprices of Napoleon, and opposing nothing but the calmness of unconquerable resignation to the violence of the Emperor, it was in perfect good faith, and under the impression that he was following the line of his duty, that Maret unscrupulously lent himself to proceedings which attacked the security of the state. Never did it enter his mind to dispute the will of Napoleon; he therefore enjoyed a constantly augmenting state of favour.

These mysteries of the cabinet, the unusual tone of some of the notes in 1811, the indication of great preparations secretly set on foot, and manœuvres and external intrigues, awakened the attention of Russia. The Czar had already found that the time was come to penetrate Napoleon's projects, and desiring to obtain some better guarantee than that of his ambassador, Kourakin, who was perfectly cajoled at St. Cloud, and himself a partisan of the continental system, he had dispatched Count Czernitscheff to Paris, ever since the month of January, on a confidential mission. This young nobleman, who was colonel in a regiment of Cossacks in the Russian imperial guard, attracted the notice of the court of Napoleon, on his first appearance, by his politeness and chivalrous deportment. He appeared in all circles and at all festivals; and he obtained there, as well as among the highest ranks, so great a success that he soon became the rage among all such ladies as contended for the empire of elegance and beauty.

They all aspired to the homage of the amiable and brilliant envoy of the Russian Emperor. For some time he appeared to be doubtful about his choice, but at length it was to the Duchess of R—— that the Paris of the Neva gave the apple. This intrigue produced more stir, inasmuch as it was the Emperor, and not his minister of police, who first suspected that, under the mask of gallantry, under the exterior of amiable and showy accomplishments, the Russian envoy concealed a mission of political survey. Suspicions multiplied when he was found to return upon a new mission in a month after his departure. Confounded at the circumstance of having been anticipated and forewarned by Napoleon, Savary, in order to please him, commissioned his factotum, Esmenard, to let fly some pungent satires at the Czar's emissary. The very evening previous to his arrival (the 11th of April, 1811), the semi-official scribe inserted in the *Journal de l'Empire* an article which recorded the career of an officer named Bower, in the employ of Russia, whom Prince Potemkin commissioned at one time to hire a dancer at Paris, at another time to purchase *boulargue* in Albania, water-melons in Astracan, and grapes in the Crimea. The allusion was obvious. Czernitscheff felt himself insulted, and complained in common with his ambassador. The intention of Napoleon not being to hazard a rupture, he pretended to be exasperated at a satire of which he had himself supplied the idea; and, by way of reparation, pronounced the ostensible disgrace of Esmenard, who was temporarily banished to Naples, though loaded at the same time with money and secret favours. These gifts were fatal to him. He was two months after (the 25th of June, 1811) run away with by some over-spirited horses, which dashed him down a precipice on the road to Fondi, and the unfortunate man was killed by the fracture of his skull against a rock.

Meantime Napoleon and his ministers never ceased complaining at St. Petersburg of the effect produced by the ukase of the 31st of December, which favoured the interest of England by permitting the introduction of colonial goods. The Paris journals went so far as frequently to announce that English vessels were admitted into Russian ports. From that time all clear-sighted men felt convinced that a new rupture was inevitable. It was well understood that the apparent causes of irritation merely served as disguises for political complaints, which had become the subject of animated debates between the two empires. In the autumn of 1811 the war was considered even in England to be imminent, and the cabinet of London was persuaded that Napoleon could no longer send to his armies in Spain the reinforcements which his brother Joseph solicited.

It was also from this epoch—an epoch vividly depicted on my memory—that by the sole medium of rumours and conjectures scattered through society, and repeated in all classes, public prepossession was created, accompanied by so eager a curiosity, which, during six or eight months, absorbing all the attention of the popular mind, concentrated it upon the immense enterprise which Napoleon was about to undertake. I was so deeply interested in its contemplation that I became possessed with the most vehement desire of drawing nearer to the capital. I hoped to be enabled to change my relative position there, and by that means find myself in a condition to present to the Emperor, while time remained, some observations calculated to make him abandon his resolution, or induce him to modify his projects; for a secret presentiment seemed to warn me that he was in this case rushing on to his destruction.

Great difficulties, however, obstructed this design. In the first instance, I could not disguise from myself that I had become an object of suspicion and disquietude to the Emperor. I knew that an order to supervise my conduct had been repeatedly given, but that the superior police had found itself so much at fault as to be obliged to allege that my great distance and mode of life rendered all supervision abortive; that, in a word, I evaded all kind of search with infinite adroitness. Upon this datum I founded my chance of success for the direct demand, which I addressed to the Emperor, through the intervention of Duroc; and I caused it very adroitly to be supported by the Count de Narbonne, who was at that time rising rapidly in favour.

I alleged that the climate of the South was particularly prejudicial to my health; that such was the opinion of my physicians; that, moreover, a residence of some months at my estate of Pont Carré was rendered indispensably necessary by the interests of my family; that I should experience great pleasure from being enabled to retire into seclusion, for which I had always entertained a decided predilection. I immediately received permission; but Duroc at the same time confidentially advised me to live at Ferrières, in the greatest possible privacy, in order to give no cause of umbrage, especially as I had the police, as well as a great body of prejudice, arrayed against me. I consequently changed my residence, but without display and, if I may so express myself, *incognito.* As soon as I arrived at Ferrières I began to live in seclusion, receiving nobody, and ostensibly occupying myself with no other care than that of benefiting my health, educating my children, and improving my estate. It was necessary to employ infinite caution, in order to receive from Paris, in the vicinity of which I now was, that secret information, a thirst for which I had now nursed into an invincible habit. Looking to the importance of the conjuncture, I soon perceived that nothing could be a sufficient substitute for those confidential conversations which I possessed the art of drawing out, without ever having an occasion to reproach myself with breach of confidence. But, situated as I was, it was only by stealth, and at long intervals, that I was enabled to obtain a few clandestine interviews with trusty and devoted persons. When this happened, they always gained access to me, without the knowledge of my people, by means of a small door, of which I myself possessed the key, and under cover of the shades of night. It was in a secret corner of my château that I received them, and where we ran no risk of being heard or surprised.

Of all the individuals connected with the government, or composing a part of it, the estimable and worthy Malouet was the only one who possessed the courage to visit me openly and without disguise. It was this which enabled me to appreciate all the merit of that worthy man. I was profoundly affected by thus seeing him defy authority, in order to extend a friendly hand to an ancient fellow-pupil and companion of his youth;[1] and that notwithstanding we had held opposite opinions in politics, and were even now distinguished by strong shades of difference. He had always been a prudent and moderate royalist, I had been an enthusiastic republican. Alas! what am I saying? However, Malouet had on this account entertained prejudices of too well-founded a description against me on his return to France. Those prejudices were only dissipated when he was enabled to judge for himself that I was a different man from what he had supposed, employing the vast power with which I was invested for no other purpose than to disarm hostile passions and heal the wounds of the Revolution. He then did me justice, and concluded by the profession of an inviolable friendship. This flattering feeling, which he carried with him to the tomb, is beyond a doubt the most honourable pledge that I can offer either to my enemies or my friends.

How deep and exquisite were our mutual moments

[1] Fouché and M. Malouet had been fellow-students at the Oratoire.—*Note by the French Editor.*

of confidence! Although divided by shades of opinion, we soon found ourselves united on the same ground, surveying the encroachments of power with the same eyes, impressed with the same anxieties, and convinced that Europe was upon the eve of one of the most terrible social crises which had ever shaken the nations of the earth. The Russian war, now considered inevitable, and the extravagant ambition of the chief magistrate, composed the text of our commentaries and reflections. I learnt from Malouet that Napoleon had proposed to the Emperor of Russia that the latter should invest his ambassador, Kourakin, with powers to enter into negotiations on the subject of the three points in dispute; namely, first, the ukase of the 31st of December, which, according to our cabinet, had annulled the treaty of Tilsit, and the conventions consequent upon it; secondly, the protest of the Emperor Alexander against the occupation of the duchy of Oldenburg, Russia having no right, according to our cabinet, to meddle with anything that concerned a prince of the Confederation of the Rhine; thirdly, the order which Alexander had given his Moldavian army, to direct its march towards the frontiers of the duchy of Warsaw. But Alexander, whose eyes were already open to the consequences of his alliance with Napoleon, eluded the proposition, at the same time promising to send to Paris Count Nesselrode, who had superseded Count Romanzoff in his favour.

On a full examination of the matter, we considered the point in dispute to be nothing but pleas, mutually put forward, in order to conceal the real question of state; that question consisted in the power and rivalry

of two empires which had latterly become too proxi-
mate not to be induced to contend for the continental
supremacy. While he regarded as useless and abortive the representations which I proposed to make to
Napoleon on the subject of the danger of this new
war, Malouet did not endeavour to dissuade me from
the attempt; on the contrary, he told me that it was
a kind of protest which I owed to my country, to
myself, and to the importance of the office I had
filled, and which it was proper to make for the exoneration of my conscience. I showed him my sketch,
which he approved, remarking to me, however, that I
ought not to exhibit too much anxiety, since, as
nothing official nor ostensible could be shown to occasion my solicitude, I should have the air of having
intermeddled with a state secret; that it depended on
myself alone to seize the opportune occasion, for
which, according to all probability, I should not have
long to wait. We took leave of each other, and I
resumed my task.

The Emperor, with a view to ingratiate himself
with his new subjects in Holland, departed in September on a journey along the coast. On his return
he immediately commenced occupying himself with
his immense preparations for the Russian war. For
form's sake, some privy councils were held, at which
none but the most servile instruments of power
attended. Never had Napoleon exerted that power,
materially or morally, in a more despotic manner—
retaining his ministers and council of state in a condition of dependence upon him, by means of Senatus
Consulta which emanated from his cabinet, dispensing

with the legislative body by means of the senate, and with both by means of the council of state, which was entirely under his thumb. Besides, he never took the least heed of the advice of his ministers, and governed less by means of decrees submitted on their part to his approbation than of acts secretly suggested to him by his correspondents, his private agents, and more frequently by his own impulses or impatience. It has been seen to what a degree flattery had obtained possession of his court, of his officers, of his ministers, and council. Panegyric had become so outrageous that adoration was a matter of command, and from that moment it became a matter of disgrace.

The rumours of the Russian war daily increasing in consistency, became, in consequence of the general fever of the public mind, the subject of all conversation and all remark. At length the very acts of the government began to lift a corner of the veil. A Senatus Consultum of the 20th of December placed 120,000 men, of the conscription of 1812, at its disposal. The harangue of the government orator and the report of the committee of the senate were not made public, and this furnished additional motives for ascribing everything to the approaching rupture.

I had settled my ideas as to the amount of the danger likely to result from a distant war, which would admit of no comparison with any other ; I had nothing more to do, therefore, than to make a fair copy of my memorial, which it was now time to present. It was divided into three sections. In the first I treated of the unseasonable period selected for the Russian war, and I drew my principal inferences from the dangers which would result from undertaking it, at the very moment when the flames of war in Spain, instead of being extinguished, were daily augmenting in the violence of their conflagration. I proved by examples that it was a combination entirely adverse to the rules of policy established by conquering nations. In the second section I treated of the difficulties inherent, if I may use the phrase, in the war itself; and I deduced my arguments from the nature of the country and from the character of the inhabitants, considered under the double point of view of nobility and people. I did not omit to notice the character of the Emperor himself, which I considered myself warranted in concluding to be falsely judged, or ill comprehended. Finally, in the third and last section, I treated of the probable consequences of the war, looking at them under the two hypotheses of a complete success or an entire reverse.

In the first case, I affirmed that the pretence of arriving at a universal monarchy, through the conquest of an empire bordering upon China, was nothing but a magnificent chimera; that from Moscow the conqueror would inevitably be drawn on to fall at first upon Constantinople, and thence to proceed to the Ganges, by the effect of the same irresistible impulse which had formerly impelled, beyond the bounds of true state policy, Alexander the Macedonian; and subsequently another still more profound and reflecting genius, namely, Julius Cæsar, who, on the eve of undertaking his war against the Parthians (the Russians of that period), indulged the frantic hope of making the tour of the world with his victorious legions. It may be easily perceived that, with this matter for my text, I could not sink beneath my subject with respect to general considerations. "Sire," said I to Napoleon, "you are now in possession of the finest monarchy upon earth; is it your wish incessantly to enlarge its boundaries, in order to leave the inheritance of an interminable war to a weaker arm than your own? The lessons of history repel the idea of a universal monarchy. Take care that too much confidence in your military genius does not induce you to overleap all the bounds of nature and shock all the precepts of wisdom.

"It is full time to pause. You have, Sire, reached that point of your career in which what you have acquired is more valuable than all which additional efforts can add to your acquisitions. All new increase of your dominion, which already passes reasonable bounds, not only for France—overwhelmed, perhaps, as she may be said to be, under the weight of your conquests—but also for the well-understood interest of your own glory and security; all that your power can gain in superficial extent, will be lost in substantial value. Pause while you have the time: enjoy, in short, the advantages of a destiny which is, beyond a doubt, the most brilliant of all which in modern times the spirit of social order has permitted a bold imagination either to desire or possess.

"And what empire is it which you seek to subject? The Russian Empire, which is enthroned upon the Pole and supported by eternal snows; which is only assailable during one quarter of the year; which offers to its assailants nothing but hardships, sufferings, and the privations of a barren soil, and of a region uni-

versally benumbed and dead?   It constitutes the true
Antæus of fable, over whom it was impossible to
triumph, except by strangling him in the uplifted
arms.   What, Sire! is it your intention to plunge
into the depths of the modern Scythia, without heed-
ing either the rigour and inclemency of the climate,
or the impoverishment of the country which it will
be necessary to pass; nor the roads, lakes, and forests
which are sufficient to arrest your march; nor the
enormous fatigue and unmeasured dangers which
will exhaust your army, let it be as formidable as it
will?   True, no force in the world, beyond a doubt,
can prevent you passing the Niemen and plunging
into the deserts and forests of Lithuania; but you
will find the Dwina a much more difficult obstacle to
surmount than the Niemen, and you will still be a
hundred leagues distant from St. Petersburg.   There it
will be requisite for you to choose between St. Petersburg and Moscow.   What a balance of chances, just
heaven! will that be, which will decide the fate of
your march to one or the other of those two capitals!
In one or the other will be found the destiny of the
universe.

- "Whatever may be your success, the Russians will
dispute with you inch by inch these desert countries,
in which you will find none of the necessaries of war.
You must draw everything from a distance of two
hundred leagues.   Whilst you will have to fight, perhaps, thirty battles, the half of your army will be
employed in defending your lines of communication,
weakened by extension, and menaced and broken by
clouds of Cossacks.   Take care lest all your genius be

unable to save your army, a prey to fatigue, hunger, want of clothing, and the severity of the climate; take care lest you be afterwards compelled to fight between the Elbe and the Rhine. Sire, I conjure you in the name of France, for the sake of your own glory and of ours, replace your sword in its scabbard. Think of Charles XII. It is true that prince could not, like you, command two-thirds of continental Europe, together with an army of six hundred thousand men; but on the other hand, the Czar had not four hundred thousand men and fifty thousand Cossacks. Perhaps you will say, his heart was of iron, while nature has bestowed the mildest character upon the Emperor Alexander; but do not deceive yourself, mildness is not incompatible with firmness, especially when such vital interests are at stake. Besides, will you not have as opponents his senate, the majority of the nobles, the imperial family, a fanatical people, hardy and warlike troops, and the intrigues of the cabinet of St. James? Even now, if Sweden escape you, it will be by the sole influence of British gold. Take care lest that irreconcilable island should shake the fidelity of your allies; take care, Sire, that your people do not reproach you with a mad ambition, and do not anticipate too much the possibility of some great misfortune. Your power and glory have laid asleep many hostile passions; one unexpected reverse may shake all the foundations of your Empire."

This memorial being finished, I sought an audience of the Emperor, and was introduced into his cabinet at the Tuileries. He had scarcely perceived me when, assuming an easy manner: "Here you are, Duke;

I know what brings you." "What, Sire?" "Yes, I know you have a memorial to lay before me." "It is not possible." "Never mind; I know it; give me the paper, I will read it. I am not, however, ignorant that the Russian war is no more to your taste than the Spanish." "Sire, I do not think that the present war will be successful enough for us to fight without risk, and at the same time, beyond the Pyrenees and the Niemen. The desire and the necessity of seeing your Majesty's power secured upon a lasting basis have emboldened me to submit to your Majesty some observations upon the present crisis." "There is no crisis; the present is a war purely political; you cannot judge of my position nor of the general aspect of Europe. Since my marriage the lion has been thought to sleep; we shall see whether he does or not. Spain will fall as soon as I have annihilated the English influence at St. Petersburg. I wanted eight hundred thousand men, and I have them. All Europe follows in my train, and Europe is no longer anything but an old rotten strumpet, with whom I may do what I please, with my eight hundred thousand men. Did you not formerly tell me that you made genius to consist in finding nothing impossible? Well, in six or eight months you shall see what plans upon a vast scale can effect, when united to a power that can execute them. I am guided by the opinion of the army and the people rather than by that of gentlemen who are too rich and who only tremble for me because they fear any sudden shock. Make yourselves easy; regard the Russian war as dictated by good sense and by a just view of the interests and the tranquillity of all Europe. Besides, how can I help it, if an excess of power leads me to assume the dictatorship of the world? Have not you contributed to it, you and so many others who blame me now, and who are anxious to make me a good sort of a king (*roi débonnaire*). My destiny is not accomplished: I must finish that which is but as yet sketched. We must have a European code, a European Court of Cassation, the same coins, the same weights and measures, the same laws. I must amalgamate all the people of Europe into one, and Paris must be the capital of the world. Such, my lord duke, is the only termination which suits my ideas. At present you will not serve me well, because you imagine that all is again to be placed in doubt; but, before twelve months are over, you will serve me with the same zeal and ardour as after the victories of Marengo and Austerlitz. You will see something superior to all that: and it is I who tell you so. Farewell, my lord duke: do not let it appear that you are either disgraced or discontented, and place a little more confidence in your sovereign."

I withdrew quite thunderstruck, after having made a profound bow to the Emperor, who turned his back upon me. Having recovered from the astonishment I felt at this singular conversation, I began to conjecture by what means the Emperor could have been so exactly informed of the object of my proceedings. Not being able to arrive at any satisfactory conclusion, I hastened to Malouet, supposing that, perhaps, some involuntary indiscretion on his part had put the high police, or one of the Emperor's confidants, upon the scent. I explained myself; but soon convinced by the protestations of

the most upright man in the Empire that nothing had
escaped him, I found the circumstance still more extraordinary, as I could not fix my suspicions upon a
third person. How then could the Emperor have learnt
that it was my intention to present a memorial to him ?
I was then subject to espionage at Rome. Suddenly
a thought struck me ; I recollected that one day a man
had suddenly entered my room without giving my *valet
de chambre* time to announce him, and had availed
himself of some specious pretext to keep me in conversation. After having weighed all the circumstances,
I inferred that he was an emissary ; and upon a review
of all that had taken place, my suspicions became still
stronger. I ordered inquiries to be made, and learnt
that this man, whose name was B——, was a returned
emigrant, who had purchased, near my château, a small
estate, for which he had not yet paid : that he was
mayor of his commune : but was, to all appearance,
an intriguer and an impostor. I procured some of his
writing, and recognised it as that of a former agent,
commissioned at London to be a spy upon the Bourbons,
the emigrants of rank, and the Chouans. I had his
number of correspondence ; and this datum enabled
me to set the *bureaux* at work respecting this worthy
gentleman. One of my former confidential agents undertook to come at the fact ; and succeeded. The affair
was as follows.

Savary, having been ordered by the Emperor to
inform him how the ex-minister Fouché was engaged
in his château of Ferrières, presented a first report,
announcing that he was under the surveillance of an
agent sufficiently qualified to fulfil the intentions of

his Majesty. He, however, remarked to the Emperor that the investigation was of a very delicate nature, the ex-minister being invisible to all strangers in person, not even the country people having access to the château. After some research, Savary cast his eyes upon the Sieur B——. Having sent for this man, who is tall, well-made, of pleasing manners, and an insinuating character, cunning, adroit, possessing great volubility, and an imperturbable assurance, he said to him, " Sir, you are mayor of your commune; you know the Duke of Otranto, or, at least, you have been in correspondence with him, and you must be able to form some idea of his character and habits; you must give me an account of what he is doing at Ferrières; this information is absolutely indispensable, for the Emperor requires it." " My lord," answered B——, " you have given me a commission extremely difficult to execute; I consider it as almost impossible. You know the man; he is distrustful, suspicious, and constantly on his guard; besides, he is inaccessible; by what means, or under what pretext, can I gain an entrance into his house ? Indeed, I cannot." " It does not signify," answered the minister; "this commission, to which the Emperor attaches great importance, must be executed: I expect you will procure me this intelligence, as a proof of your devotion to the person of the Emperor. Go, and do not return without having accomplished your object; I allow you a fortnight."

B——, in the greatest embarrassment, ran about, making inquiries, and found, through an indirect channel, that one of my farmers was prosecuted by my steward for large arrears of rent. He went to see him, and pretending to be extremely interested for him, obtained from him the documents relative to the affair. Furnished with these papers, he took a cabriolet, and with a face of great concern, presented himself at the gate of my château, announcing himself as the mayor of a neighbouring commune, who had taken a great interest in an unfortunate family unjustly prosecuted. Being first stopped at the gate, he easily talked over my porter, who allowed him to reach the grand steps. There my *valet de chambre* refused to let him enter my apartment. Without, however, being disheartened, B—— begged, solicited, and entreated so earnestly that at last he prevailed upon the *valet de chambre* to announce him; but, at the moment when the valet was entering my room, he pushed him on one side and entered; I was at my writing-desk with my pen in my hand.

The sudden entrance of a stranger surprised me. I asked him what was his pleasure: " My lord," said B——, " I am come to solicit from you a favour, an act of justice and humanity the most urgent; I am come to entreat you to save an unhappy father of a family from total ruin "; and here he employed all his rhetoric to interest me in favour of his client, and explained the whole affair to me in the clearest manner possible. After a moment's hesitation, I rose and proceeded to search in a portfolio for the papers relative to my farms. Whilst, my back being turned, I was searching for the documents, B——, still speaking, succeeded in deciphering a few lines of my writing; and what particularly struck him were the initials,

V. M. I. et R.; he immediately inferred that I was preparing a memorial to be presented to his Majesty. Upon returning to my desk, after two or three minutes' search, and persuaded by the fine speeches of the man, I settled the affair with him in favour of his client, with the utmost simplicity, and wished him adieu, expressing my thanks to him for having given me an opportunity of performing a praiseworthy action. B—— left me, and immediately proceeded to Savary, to whom he related the success of his undertaking, and Savary immediately hastened to make his report to the Emperor. I confess that when made acquainted with the details of this piece of mystification I was extremely chagrined. I could scarcely forgive myself at having been thus duped by a scoundrel, who for a long time had sent me secret intelligence from London, and in whose favour I advanced annually a sum of twenty thousand francs. It will be seen later (1815) that I did not allow myself to be actuated by too great a resentment.

Although this was a wretched intrigue, I yet derived from it an advantageous position, which gave me more security and confidence, by making me persevere in my system of circumspection and reserve. It was evident that a great part of Napoleon's suspicions respecting me was dissipated, and that I had no longer any reason to apprehend, at the moment that he was about to penetrate into Russia, being made the object of any inquisitorial and vexatious measure. I knew that in a cabinet council, to which the Emperor had only summoned Berthier, Cambacérès, and Duroc, the question had been discussed whether it would be advantageous to make sure, either by arrest or severe banishment, of M. de Talleyrand and me; and that, upon mature consideration, the idea of this *coup d'état* had been rejected as impolitic and useless; impolitic, inasmuch as it would have shaken public confidence too much, and aroused apprehensions for the future in the minds of the high officers and dignitaries of the state; useless, because no act or deed could be laid to our charge as a motive for such a measure. Engaged, moreover, in the preparations for the expedition into Russia, the government experienced uneasiness more real and disappointments more distressing. France was daily suffering more and more from a scarcity of corn. Risings had taken place in several places; these had been repressed by force, and military commissions had condemned to be shot many unfortunate wretches who had been urged on by despair. It was not without feelings of horror the public ascertained that, among the victims of these bloody executions, a woman in the town of Caen had been included.

It became, however, necessary to withdraw a part of the veil which concealed the mystery of the vast hostile preparations of which all the north of Germany was already the theatre. An extraordinary meeting of the senate was ordered, for the purpose of receiving the communication of the two reports which it was determined should be presented to the Emperor; the one by the minister for foreign affairs, the other by the minister for war. The sole object of this farce, at once warlike and diplomatic, was to obtain a levy of such men as had escaped the conscription, and the formation of cohorts of the first ban, according to a new organisation of the national guard, which divided into three bans or classes the immense majority of our male population.

There was no exaggeration this time in considering France as one vast camp, whence our phalanxes marched from all parts upon Europe as upon a prey. In order to colour this levy of those classes which had been free from the conscription, fresh motives and new pretexts were necessary, since it was not desirable at present to reveal the true motives of such extraordinary measures. Maret spoke to the senate of the necessity of compelling England to acknowledge the maritime rights established by the stipulations of the treaty of Utrecht—stipulations which France abandoned at Amiens. But the levy of the first ban of the national guards was granted by a Senatus Consultum, and a hundred cohorts were placed at the disposal of the government; we members of the senate evincing admirable docility and subserviency. At the same time two treaties of alliance and reciprocal assistance were signed with Prussia and Austria. All doubt was now removed. Napoleon was about to attack Russia, not only with his own forces, but also with those of Germany and of all the petty sovereigns who could no longer move out of the orbit of his power.

War was fully decided upon, when the Emperor caused his confidential minister to open fresh negotiations with London; but these proposals not only came late, but were made without any ability. Some persons who were in the secret of nearly every intrigue assured me at this time that the cabinet employed this clumsy expedient in concert with the principal Russians of the French party. Seeing themselves on the eve of being expelled from the councils of St. Petersburg, they imagined that the Emperor Alexander, alarmed at the possibility of an arrangement between France and England, would re-enter the continental system to prevent his being isolated, and that he would once more submit to Napoleon's will. But however this may be, Maret wrote to Lord Castlereagh a letter containing the following propositions: To renounce all extension of territory on the side of the Pyrenees; to declare the *actual dynasty* of Spain independent, and to guarantee the independence of that monarchy; to guarantee to the house of Braganza the independence and integrity of Portugal, as well as the kingdom of Naples to Joachim and the kingdom of Sicily to Ferdinand IV. As to the other objects of discussion, our cabinet proposed to negotiate them upon this basis—that each power should keep what the other could not wrest from it by the war. Lord Castlereagh replied that if, by the *actual dynasty* of Spain, the brother of the chief of the French government was meant, he was commanded by his sovereign to declare candidly that he could not receive any proposals of peace founded upon that basis.

Here the matter dropped. Ashamed of its overtures, our cabinet, whose only object was to have drawn Russia into some act of weakness, perceived too late that it had impressed upon our diplomacy a character of fickleness, bad faith, and ignorance. As all was transacted in the utmost secrecy, what most puzzled the politicians was that in France, and even in Russia, the exterior forms of amity were kept up amid the immense preparations. The Emperor Alexander's ambassador was still at Paris, while Napoleon had his at St. Petersburg. Nor was this all; Alexander had his confidential diplomatist, Count Czernitscheff, resident in the French capital. This amiable Russian, in the midst of the dissipations of a brilliant court and the mysteries of more than one amorous intrigue purposely ill managed, did not neglect a secret commission of the highest importance to his master. Seconded by women, some of whom were stimulated by love, and others by a spirit of intrigue, he managed his plans so as to discover Napoleon's real intentions of invading Russia. Suspicion having been raised as to the secret object of his mission, he was watched and placed under surveillance, but all to no purpose. At length Savary sent to him a person attached to the police, who gave him some false information, and drew from him in return some fresh indications which increased the suspicion already indulged. But, favoured by his gallant connections, Czernitscheff was warned in time. He avoided the snare, insulted the spy, and went to Maret to complain of having been subjected to such revolting proceedings.

That very day the Emperor, having been informed of the subject of his complaint, determined upon communicating to him the secret accounts which inculpated him. Czernitscheff came out triumphant from this ordeal, by giving an explanation of his conduct and of the cause of his complaints. The police at once received formal orders to take off the surveillance. Being thus at liberty to continue his investigations, he succeeded in executing the object of his mission. He was particularly anxious to procure the lists of the intended movements of the French army. These he obtained through the medium of a clerk named Michel, belonging to the *bureau des mouvements.* An oversight of this person, who thus betrayed the secret of the Emperor's operations, having awakened some suspicions, he was arrested. Czernitscheff was immediately informed of it, and left Paris with the greatest precipitation, carrying off with him some most important documents. In vain was a telegraph order given to seize his person. He had got the start by five or six hours, and this advantage was sufficient to enable him to cross the Rhine. He had just passed the bridge of Kehl when the telegraphic order for his arrest reached Strasburg.

His precipitate flight from Paris prevented him from burning his secret correspondence, which it was his custom to conceal under the carpet of his room; and as the latter was necessarily the object of minute search, the police agents discovered the papers of Czernitscheff. The first thing found in them was the proof that a great intimacy had been kept up between this Russian nobleman and several ladies of Napoleon's court, amongst others the Duchess of R——. She, however, it is said, exculpated herself by alleging that she had acted in concert with her husband, to endeavour to ascertain the secret object of Czernitscheff's mission. Among the papers discovered was also a letter in Michel's handwriting; so convincing a proof of his guilt sealed his fate—he expiated his treason with his life. This affair brought to light a very singular fact; namely, that the Russian cabinet had foreseen, even from the epoch of the interview at Erfurt, the possibility of a rupture with France. It was then that Romanzoff said, in order to justify his complaisant policy, and with reference to Napoleon, " We must wear him out " (*Il faut l'user*).

The circumstances of Czernitscheff's flight, which was soon known in the *salons*, made considerable noise, and accelerated the rupture. The Emperor, whose departure was determined upon, anxious to obtain some popularity, visited the different quarters of Paris, examining the public works, and acting little preconcerted scenes, either with the prefect of Paris or the prefect of police, Pasquier. He also went frequently to the chase, affecting to appear more occupied with his pleasures than with the vast enterprise he had engaged in. I saw him at St. Cloud, whither I went to pay my respects to him, without any intention of soliciting or obtaining an audience. The mournful aspect of that court, and the anxious looks of the courtiers, appeared to me to form a strong contrast to the confidence of the Emperor. He had never enjoyed such perfect health ; never had I seen his features, formed after the antique, lighted up with a greater glow of mental vigour, of greater confidence in himself, founded on a deep conviction of his prodigious power. I experienced a feeling of involuntary melancholy, which I should have been unable to define had not the most gloomy presentiments taken possession of my mind.

In the meantime the cabinet of St. Petersburg,

whether its real intention was to employ every possible means of reconciliation, compatible with the independence of the Russian Empire, or whether it had only the view of obtaining some certain information respecting the true intentions of Napoleon, ordered Prince Kourakin to make known to the French government the bases of an arrangement, which his sovereign was willing to accede to. These were the deliverance of Prussia, a reduction of the garrison of Dantzic, and the evacuation of Swedish Pomerania: upon these conditions the Czar engaged to make no change whatever in the measures prohibiting a direct trade with England, and to concert with France a system of licenses to be granted in Russia.

Kourakin's note remained unanswered for a fortnight. At length, on the 9th of May, the day of the Emperor's departure for Germany, Maret asked Kourakin if he had full powers for treating; Kourakin replied that the character of ambassador with which he was invested should be considered as sufficient. Being only able to obtain evasive and dilatory answers, he demanded his passports, which were refused him under various pretences. It was not till the 20th of June they were sent him from Thorn, an artifice, the object of which was to allow Napoleon time to cross the Niemen with all his forces, in order to surprise his august adversary at Wilna, before he could receive the least intelligence from his ambassador.

The die was cast; the Niemen was crossed by six hundred thousand men, by the finest and most formidable army ever assembled by any conqueror of the earth. We will now leave Napoleon—we will leave this illustrious madman to rush on to his ruin: it is not his military history I am relating.

Let us ascertain the state of public opinion at the moment when, traversing Germany and stopping at Dresden, he riveted upon himself the anxious regards of twenty nations. Let us first see what was thought of him in the saloons of Paris, those very saloons for whose good opinion he was so anxious; prayers were there put up for his humiliation, and even for his fall, so much did his aggression appear the effect of a mad ambition. In the middle and lower classes the disposition was not more favourable to him. The discontent, however, had nothing of hostility in it. The general wish was only to save Napoleon from his own follies, and to restrain him within the bounds of moderation and justice.

Some persons have imagined that an organised resistance on the part of his marshals and the army would have succeeded in ruling his will, and eventually in obtaining the mastery over him. But such persons could understand but little the fascinations of a military life and the manners of a camp. I have had the means of being convinced that not the least political idea calculated to guarantee us from the abuses of victory, or from the dangers of a reverse, ever proceeded from the brains of any discontented general.

There was, moreover, at the bottom of all this spirit of disapprobation, a feeling superior to it: that of anxious expectation and intense curiosity respecting the issue of the vast expedition of the extraordinary man whose ambition devoured whole ages. It was generally admitted that he would remain conqueror and master of the field.

As to politicians, by taking into consideration the destruction of Poland on the one hand, and the encroachments of the Revolution on the other, they saw Germany destroyed by two vast irruptions ; that of the French from the west and the Russians from the east. It was these latter that Napoleon wished to drive back upon the polar ice, or into the steppes of Asia. This man, who drew after him one-half of the military population of Europe, and whose orders were implicitly executed in the space comprehended within nineteen degrees of latitude and thirty degrees of longitude—this man, who had now set foot on Russian ground, was about to risk his own fate and the existence of France.

Upon advancing beyond the Niemen and proclaiming war, he exclaimed, with an affectation of prophetic inspiration : " The Russians are urged on by fate—let the destinies be accomplished!" His adversary, who cared not to await him at Wilna, more calm, recommends to his people to defend their *country and their liberty*. What a contrast between the two nations, between these two adversaries and their language!

At first, the forced retreat of the Russians—who, being the weakest and least inured to war, endeavoured to avoid the *rencontre*—and the devastation of the country which they systematically effected, were considered as two grand measures, the result of a plan preconcerted for the purpose of drawing Napoleon into the heart of the Empire.

But the imagination soon took the alarm when,

after a furious combat, Napoleon, against the advice of the majority of his marshals, and in contempt of a kind of engagement he had entered into at Paris with his council, left in his rear Smolensk, the only bulwark of Russia on the frontiers of Poland. The public anxiety was still further increased when he was seen advancing, without the least hesitation, on the line of Moscow, braving all the chances of war, and equally regardless of the character of his enemies, the disposition of Europe impatient of her yoke, the season, the distance, and the severity of the climate.

Inflated with gaining the most sanguinary battle of modern times, a battle in which a hundred thousand soldiers were victims to the ambition of one man,[1] and not in the least affected by the miserable and wretched appearance of his bivouacs, Napoleon imagined that he could at length effect the destruction of a vast and powerful empire, as he formerly accomplished the instantaneous fall of the republics of Geneva, Venice, and Lucca.

The Russians had retreated; armed with torches, they had burnt Smolensk, Dorogobouj, Viazma, Gjatsk, and Mojaisk, and yet he imagined they would spare him Moscow. The conflagration of this fine capital, while it undeceived Napoleon too late, enlightened France with its ill-omed flames; the sensation was deep. It was now, alas! that I saw all my presentiments realised; I perceived its object—that of depriving the victor of a pledge and the vanquished of a motive for concluding peace.

[1] The battle of the Moskowa, or Borodino, fought on the 7th of September, at twenty-five leagues in advance of Moscow. - *Note by the Editor.*

How did Napoleon act upon witnessing this grand national sacrifice? He encamped for forty days on the ashes of Moscow, contemplating his vain conquest, not doubting his ability to conclude the campaign by negotiations, and never even suspecting that two Russian armies, the one from the Livonian Gulf, the other from Moldavia, had been ordered to effect a junction at Borisow, a place one hundred leagues in his rear. He was ignorant, perhaps, that Russia, without a single ally at the commencement of the campaign, had just signed, one after the other, three defensive treaties— with Sweden, England, and the Regency of Cadiz.

In the interval, the interview at Abo between the Emperor Alexander and Bernadotte, in presence of Lord Cathcart, took place—an interview at which the first appeal was made to Moreau, whom it was desired to oppose to his persecutor, to him who was now designated the oppressor of Europe. The ruins of Moscow had been abandoned to Napoleon, who could not at all comprehend a system of warfare completely in opposition to his principles of strategy. For twenty-two days he awaited a suppliant message from the Russian Emperor, whose cabinet kept in play his prolocutors and negotiators. Napoleon was as blind at Moscow as in Spain. Prudent measures smacked too much of methodical arrangement, which he utterly detested.

At length he commenced his retreat, but not till the death-knell of his power had been tolled; he commenced his retreat, and on the very day of his tardy evacuation of Moscow, the 13th of October, the Malet conspiracy, so humiliating for the Emperor, for his adherents, and for his police, burst out; a conspiracy which had nearly cost him his Empire, from the wish of gratifying his vanity in dating a few decrees from Moscow. The Malet conspiracy has never well been understood—Malet was not a mad but a bold man.

Little known as a general, he was at first compromised in 1802, in the Senate conspiracy, as it was called, of which Bernadotte was the mover, Madame de Staël the centre, and himself the principal agent; a conspiracy in which I was myself denounced as an accomplice by Dubois, the prefect of police. It being expected that Malet should be the scapegoat, he was thrown into prison. Upon being restored to liberty by the amnesty granted on the occasion of the coronation, he was employed in 1805 in the army of Italy: and upon his return was engaged in fresh plots against the Emperor, involving at one time Brune, at another Masséna; at length, in 1808, he was imprisoned in the castle of Vincennes. It was in the gloom of this prison that he hatched his double conspiracy, which was to rally the disaffected of every party against the Emperor's government. The whole of this plot, however, was not the offspring of Malet's brain.[1] Its conception belonged to the royalists, its execution to the republicans. In fact, success was impossible without the agreement of two opposite opinions, which were cemented by a hatred common to both, and a mutual necessity of overthrowing the oppressor in order to restore public liberty. All was favourable to the conspirators engaged in the boldest of enterprises. From the instant that the mode of execution depended only upon one man, and that man

[1] This deserves attention.—*Note by the Editor.*

was decided, full of courage, there was every reason to calculate upon the probability of success. The rest was left to chance. Let us see what this was; and, first, let us consider into what hands the power was delegated in the Emperor's absence. It is certain that the arch-chancellor, Cambacérès, was the depositary of it; a weak and vicious man and a true sycophant. Among the ministers, one alone prided himself upon being at the head of the police, which for him remained mute as to any discoveries; but this man, a headstrong officer of gendarmerie, was a mere cipher in politics and state affairs. Next on the list was Pasquier, prefect of police, an excellent magistrate in all that regarded mud and lanterns, in regulating the police of the markets, gambling-houses, and prostitutes, but without intelligence, extremely verbose, and entirely devoid of tact and investigation. So much for the civil power.

We will now proceed to the military. The strength of the sword was intrusted to Hullin, commander of Paris, a dull, heavy soldier, but firm, although equally stupid and awkward in politics as the others. Let it also be observed that the exercise of authority having become for the principal functionaries a kind of mechanism, they perceived beyond that nothing but passive obedience: that the Empress Maria Louisa resided at St. Cloud; that at this time, in the garrison of Paris, there were none of those old fanatical troops who, in the name of the Emperor, would have carried fire and sword everywhere; that they had been replaced by cohorts recently organised, the greater part of which were commanded by old patriotic officers; and, lastly, that the anxiety respecting the

event of the Muscovite expedition began to make the
high functionaries apprehensive for their security. It
is evident, therefore, that Paris in this state of things
would, by an ably directed and vigorous *coup de main*,
remain in possession of the first that seized it. The
immense distance of the Emperor, the irregularity and
frequent interruption of the couriers, by increasing the
anxiety and preparing the public mind, threw all the
chances in favour of the person who should be daring
enough to take advantage of a momentary stupor and
alarm. The *Emperor is dead;* the abolition of the imperial government by a senatorial decree and the establishment of a provisional one, were the pivot of the
conspiracy, of which the mover and the head was
Malet. He had himself drawn up the Senatus Consultum decreeing the abolition of the imperial *régime.*

But, it may be said, you see there was no decree
of the senate, there was no provisional government,
the Emperor was full of life and vigour, and the
conspiracy was only founded on a fiction. Besides,
how could Malet have accomplished it, supposing even
that he had remained master of Paris?

It is true there was no decree of the senate, but
is it equally certain that there was not in the senate
a nucleus of opposition which might have been made
to act *according to circumstances!* I will suppose the
fact that, out of one hundred and thirty senators,
nearly sixty,[1] who were generally guided by M. de

---

[1] The same, no doubt, who, eighteen months after, on the
2nd of April, 1814, had the *courage,* protected by two hundred
thousand bayonets, to declare Napoleon *fallen from the throne.*—
Note by the Editor.

Talleyrand, M. de Semonville, and me, would have seconded any resolution which should have a salutary object, upon the mere manifestation of the junction of this triple influence. Now such a coalition was neither improbable nor impracticable.

This possibility explains the creation of an eventual provisional government composed of MM. Matthieu de Montmorency, Alexis de Noailles, General Moreau, Count Frochot, prefect of the Seine, and a fifth not named. This fifth person was M. de Talleyrand, and I myself was to fill the place of Moreau during his absence, whose name had been introduced either to satisfy or divide the army.

As to Malet, a mere instrument, he would voluntarily have resigned the command of Paris to Masséna, who, as well as myself, lived at that time in retirement and disgrace.

" But answer," it may be said, " this last and strongest objection—the Emperor was living." True, but it should be recollected how the imperial revolution which overthrew Nero was effected—although there be no wish to compare the two characters. It was operated with the assistance of false rumours and alarms, by a servile but suddenly unshackled senate. Where was Napoleon at the moment when Malet executed his enterprise? He was evacuating Moscow; he was commencing his disastrous retreat, which had only been foreseen, but which once ascertained for fact, would have decided the general defection, if fifteen or twenty people of influence had replaced, in the name of *the safety of France*, the first movers of the conspiracy. Let it be recollected that the couriers and bulletins were already intercepted ; that the twenty-sixth and twenty - seventh bulletins, announcing the evacuation and the retreat, and dated the 23rd of October, were only followed by the twenty - eighth, dated the 11th of November ; being an interval of twenty days, which would have amply sufficed to ensure the success of a plot, the ramifications of which will, for a long time, remain unknown. For a month nothing was heard of but a continual succession of disasters, the knowledge of which alone might have closed the gates of France against the Emperor for ever. At first believed to be dead, he would only have been resuscitated, to be again struck down by the decree of his forfeiture. Never did a more favourable opportunity present itself for the overthrow of his military dictatorship ; never would it have been more easy to have established the basis of a government which would have reconciled us with ourselves and with Europe. This supposition being admitted, how many fresh calamities would our country have been spared ?

Now let us examine what were the causes of Malet's failure, in the midst even of his triumph. Shall I avow it ? It was for having regulated his means of execution upon a basis too widely extensive in philanthropy. We will explain. Malet, a republican, belonging as well as Guidal and Lahorie his accomplices, to the secret society of the Philadelphians, was justly apprehensive lest he should revive the alarm of the return of those sanguinary and mournful days which France remembered with horror. This moral conviction overcame every more decisive consideration, and instead of immediately putting to death Savary, Hullin, and the two adjutants, Doucet and Laborde, the chief of the staff, Malet thought it would be sufficient to arrest them without effusion of blood. He at first succeeded with respect to the police, which was disorganised the moment that Savary and Pasquier permitted themselves to be surprised and ignominiously dragged to prison. But when Hullin's resistance had forced Malet to discharge his pistols, his hesitation lost everything, not being able to fire at the same time upon Hullin and Laborde. The latter, being at liberty, had time to rally a few men round him, and, rushing upon Malet, disarmed and arrested him. The conspiracy failed. Malet died with great *sang-froid*, carrying with him the secret of one of the boldest *coups de main* which the grand epoch of our Revolution bequeaths to history.

The facility with which this surprise of power was effected seemed to indicate that it was not unexpected. All was prepared at the Hôtel de Ville for the installation of the provisional government. Pale and trembling, the arch-chancellor remained, till ten o'clock in the morning, a prey to the most dreadful alarms, at one moment imagining he was about to be killed, at another that he should at least share the dungeon with Savary. As to the people, it is true, they did nothing for the success of an enterprise at first enveloped in complete obscurity; but they indirectly seconded it by that *vis inertiæ* which is always opposed to bad governments. In short, although it had failed, this conspiracy was a home-thrust to Napoleon's dynasty, by revealing a secret, fatal for its founder, his family, and his adherents, viz., that his political establishment would end with his life.

It was at Smolensk, on the 14th or 16th of November, that the Emperor, amid the horrors of his retreat, received the first information of the conspiracy, and the prompt punishment of its authors. He was much troubled at it. " What an impression," said he, " will that make in France ! " Savary and Cambacérès urged him to keep a strict eye upon the army, in which plots were formed against his life. Extraordinary precautions were immediately taken ; a sacred band of officers most devoted to him was formed, the command of which was intrusted to Grouchy, but this chosen body was soon involved in the general wreck. Jealous in the extreme of all that could menace his throne, Napoleon felt far more anxiety to preserve that than to save the wrecks of his army, the retreat of which he hurried on at any cost. Thanks to the unskilful pursuit of Kutusow, he gained three days' march upon the Russians, arrived at the Beresina, eluded the generals of the Moldavian army, and, under protection of a most horrible disaster, gained the opposite bank. The whole army in the meantime was completely disbanded. The only remains which could here and there be perceived of it were wandering spectres sinking under the severity of cold, fatigue, and wretchedness. Napoleon, having made up his mind to end an expedition which would deprive him of his laurels as a general and tear from him his reputation as a statesman, like a deserter, betook himself to flight in a sledge, and intrusted himself solely to Caulaincourt's devotedness. Disguised, and with the utmost haste, he made for Paris, where everything conspired to make him tremble for the loss of his crown. At Warsaw he himself revealed to his ambassador his situation and the state of his mind by those well-known words, " From the sublime to the ridiculous there is but a step." Still alive to the fear of never reaching France, he strove to surmount danger by the rapidity of his flight, travelling in an impenetrable *incognito*. In Silesia he was very nearly taken by the Prussians, and at Dresden he only escaped a plot for his seizure because Lord Walpole, who was at Vienna, dared not give the signal.

And as if fortune had wished to pursue him to extremities, he re-entered the palace of the Tuileries on the 18th of December, the day after the publication of his twenty-ninth bulletin, which carried mourning into so many families. But this was on his part a new snare, held out to the devotedness and credulity of a generous nation, who, struck with consternation, thought that their chief, chastened by misfortune, was ready to seize the first favourable opportunity of bringing back peace, and of at length consolidating the foundation of general happiness.

This was the reason why France willingly made the greatest sacrifices to sustain a man whose only success had been that of spurning the ashes of Moscow, of carrying desolation into a vast extent of country which he had left covered with the corpses of a hundred and fifty thousand of his own subjects and those of his allies, after abandoning a still greater number of prisoners and the whole of his artillery and magazines.

Of four hundred thousand men in arms who had crossed the Niemen, scarcely thirty thousand repassed that river five months afterwards, and of those two-thirds had not seen the Kremlin.

Napoleon, however, appeared at first far less concerned on account of the loss of his army than about the conspiracy which had revealed so fatal a secret as the fragility of the foundation of his Empire. Tormented by his death having been anticipated, his care-worn brow appeared bending beneath clouds of gloom. The conspiracy was the object of his first words, his first inquiries. He closeted himself with Cambacérès, and sifted him narrowly in a long and secret conversation. Savary was next sent for, whom he overwhelmed with questions and reproaches; he afterwards gave audience to several members of his council, and appeared still wholly occupied with the conspiracy, while his ministers and agents were in the utmost alarm. But his police, being interested in representing the plot as an isolated one, affirmed that the whole of it originated in Malet; such was also the opinion of Cambacérès, of the minister at war, and of the confidential advisers, who confirmed Napoleon in the idea that the greatest danger he had to fear, and against which he should be on his guard, was in the reminiscences of the republic. Enraged against the prefect of the Seine, a pupil of Mirabeau, who, as we have seen, truckled to the conspirators, he issued a philippic against *pusillanimous magistrates*, who, said he, "are the destruction of the Empire, of the laws and of the throne. Our fathers had for their rallying cry, 'The king is dead: long live the king!'

A few words," added Napoleon, "containing the principal advantages of monarchy." All the bodies of the state immediately came to assure him of their present and future fidelity. Lacépède, the speaker of the senate, designating the body to which he belonged as "the first council of the Emperor," added with great rapidity, "whose authority exists only when the monarch requires it, and gives it movement." This allusion to the spring of which Malet had availed himself struck the senators very forcibly. In his answer to the council of state, Napoleon, attributing all the misfortunes which "beautiful France had undergone" to ideology (gloomy metaphysics), took occasion to cast reflections upon philosophy and liberty. He did not perceive that by ceasing to keep up the Revolution and its principles, he ceased to command its aid and support, and that by preaching up the maxims of monarchical legitimacy, he was opening to the Bourbons the ways which the Revolution had closed against them. And yet, in great crises, the Bourbons were ever uppermost in his thoughts. Besides what I have myself seen and heard of him in this respect, I was at this time made acquainted with the following fact. Ney, when relating to me the disasters of the retreat, and putting the firmness of his own military conduct in opposition to the want of foresight and the stupor of Napoleon, added that he observed in him a kind of mental aberration. "I thought him mad," said Ney to me, "when, struck with the greatness of his misfortune, at the moment of his departure he said to us, like a man who saw himself utterly deprived of all resource:

' The Bourbons will take advantage of this ' "—an observation the sense of which escaped Ney, who was incapable of combining two political ideas.

Napoleon's object, therefore, now was to establish the superiority of the *fourth dynasty* over the *third*, and to surmount the crisis. All the different bodies of the state were now seen occupied in resolving a new question of public right, in consequence of the impulse of the cabinet, and the first words which fell from their master's lips : " I will," said he to them, " reflect upon the different epochs of *our* history." Everyone immediately began thinking of the means to secure the hereditary succession ; the different speakers hastened to develop and explain the new doctrine ; nothing was now heard of but succession, legitimate rights ; these were the theme of all the preconcerted speeches. The King of Rome, said they, must be crowned upon the express demand of the senate, and a solemn oath must in anticipation unite the Empire to the succession to the throne.

Such was the measure upon which the man intended to rely who, indebted to the Revolution for a vast power, the magic of which he had just destroyed, renounced that very Revolution, and separated himself from it. He, however, felt all the instability of a throne the sole support of which is the sword.

Whilst he was thus exclaiming against the men and the principles of the Revolution, he recollected me—me against whom he had indulged so much suspicious jealousy. Besides, could he ever pardon me my hints of disapprobation and my importunate and officious foresight ? I was informed that he had instituted a secret inquiry respecting my conduct in connection with the Malet affair; but that all the reports had agreed as to my circumspection and non-participation in it. Unable to reach me, he wounded me in the person of my friend, M. Malouet, whom he never pardoned for having openly visited me during my disgrace, being rendered more uneasy by this undisguised friendship between a revolutionary and a royalist patriot; besides which he was irritated against him on account of the spirit of opposition which Malouet evinced in the discussion at the council board, against so many extravagant and vexatious measures. Being removed from the council of state, Malouet was exiled to Tours, where he led the life of a philosopher, less affected by his own disgrace than by the ills which afflicted his country. His disgrace was for me an additional motive to persist in the same reserve towards a government which in its despair, in its vengeance, could be restrained by no consideration. Its power already began to totter, and experienced eyes could perceive the elements of its destruction. But, seconded by his intimate counsellors, Napoleon employed every artifice calculated to palliate our disasters and conceal from us their inevitable consequences. He assembled the whole phalanx of his flatterers, now become the organs of his will; he gave them their lesson, and all with one voice attributed the loss of our army and the fatal issue of the campaign solely to the rigour of the elements. By the aid of deception of every kind, they succeeded in making it believed that all might be repaired if the nation did but show itself great and generous; that fresh sacrifices should be considered as nothing when weighed against the preservation of its independence and glory. The public spirit was stimulated by addresses begged from the chiefs of cohorts of the first bans of the national guards, who desired to march against the enemy out of France, and also by offers from the departments and communes to furnish cavalry, offers commanded by the government itself. Napoleon endeavoured at the same time to gain over new creatures to his interest and to secure vacillating affections. He distributed secret bribes drawn from his own treasures, which he had already diminished by nearly a hundred millions for his expenses in the Russian war. This time he was about to make unlimited demands upon them, for the double purpose of creating a new army and of keeping in pay the ministers of certain cabinets, in order to maintain them in his interests. It was in his treasures that he found an army of reserve.

In the meantime he held privy councils, which were attended by Cambacérès, Lebrun, Talleyrand, Champagny, Maret, and Caulaincourt. Maret, who had arrived from Berlin, affirmed that he had received from the Prussian ministers, and from the King himself, the strongest protestations that they would persevere in our alliance; he added that every circumstance ought to set the Emperor's mind at ease respecting the affairs of the North. Whether Maret really spoke sincerely, or whether all was concerted for the purpose of spurring on the council, which leaned towards negotiations, Napoleon, affecting greater confidence, said that he could rely upon Austria, and, according to all appearance, upon Prussia: that, consequently, there was nothing alarming in his situation; that, besides, he found his brother Joseph again at Madrid, and the English driven into Portugal; in addition to which he had already under arms one hundred cohorts and the anticipated levy of the conscripts of 1813. He decided that the Spanish war and that of the North should be prosecuted with the utmost vigour.

On the other hand, the contents of Otto's[1] correspondence got wind. It was known that Lord Walpole had made Austria the most brilliant offers; that he had represented all Germany as ready to rise, and France on the eve of a revolution. Otto added that the defection of Austria might be expected. But this cabinet, being soon informed that Napoleon had again seized the reins of power, that he was making fresh levies, and that in the interior there was no appearance of a crisis, hastened to dispatch to Paris Count Bubna. Otto also changed his tone, and his letters were in perfect unison with the assertions of Austria, whom he represented as only desirous of interfering as a mediator for a general pacification.

Full of confidence, Napoleon gave the word to his official organ, the *Moniteur*. According to its representations, "Austria and France are inseparable; no continental power will detach itself from him; besides, forty million of Frenchmen have nothing to fear. . . . If it be desired to know," adds he, "the conditions to which I would subscribe for a general peace, reference must be made to the letter written by the Duke of Bassano to Lord Castlereagh previous to the campaign of Russia," which was equivalent to saying that he

[1] Napoleon's ambassador at Vienna.

consented—as if he had experienced no reverse at Moscow—to leave Sicily to Ferdinand IV., and Portugal to the house of Braganza, but that no other sacrifice was to be required of him.

The news of the defection of a Prussian corps commanded by Yorck having arrived, " What sufficed yesterday," cried Napoleon, " is not sufficient to-day ; " and all his councillors perceived that very instant what use was going to be made of such an event. Maret drew up a report, stuffed according to custom with invectives against the British Government, and concluding by proposing a levy of three hundred and fifty thousand men. Regnault hastened to the senate, and in the name of the Emperor required the service of the young Frenchmen forming the hundred cohorts, and who had been assured that they would only be occupied with military games and martial exercises in the interior : a Senatus Consultum placed them at the disposal of the Emperor. The legislative body was assembled in order to vote the supplies. " Peace," said Napoleon, in his opening speech, " is necessary to the world ; but I will never make but one which is honourable and consonant with the greatness of my Empire." Nothing could be more pompous than the *exposé* of his situation presented by Montalivet, the minister of the interior ; everything—population, agriculture, manufactures, commerce, public instruction, and even the navy—was in the most flourishing and prosperous condition. Then came the presentation of the budget by Count Molé, councillor of state ; and here the worthy pupil of Fontanes, astonished at so much prosperity, exclaimed in concluding his speech,

" To produce so many wonders only twelve years of war and one single man sufficed." And immediately eleven hundred and fifty millions were, without discussion, placed at the disposal of this one man.

He had placed as the first thing on his list of urgent affairs, the accommodation of his differences with the Pope, who, since the month of June, had been confined to the palace of Fontainebleau. Under pretence of a hunting party, Napoleon hastened to extort from him a new concordat despoiling him of his temporalities, but which the Holy Father retracted almost immediately afterwards. Religious matters became in consequence more and more embroiled. The open defection of Prussia no longer left any doubts upon the progress of the coalition. Frederick William, suddenly quitting Berlin, had fled to Breslau, protected by the kindness of our ambassador, Saint-Marsan, and in some degree under the ægis of Augereau, who had become humanised. Nothing could be more kind and amiable than our generals and our ambassadors since our reverses. Upon receiving the news that the King of Prussia had escaped him, Napoleon regretted he had not treated him as he had done Ferdinand VII. and the Pope. " This is not the first instance," said he, " that in politics generosity is a bad counsellor." He, indeed, generous towards Prussia !

In the meantime the reflux of the war, setting in from the ruins of Moscow, proceeded rapidly towards the Oder and the Elbe. Eugène, who had rallied a few thousand men, had successively retired upon the Walthe, the Oder, the Spree, the Elbe, and the Saale. The German insurrection, excited by the secret societies, spread itself from town to town and from village to village, and the number of Napoleon's enemies daily increased. How could we depend upon our allies? From the defection of Prussia we had reason to anticipate that of many others. Determined to brave everything, Napoleon, like a spendthrift, anticipating his revenue of men, ordered the conscription of 1814 to be rendered available. He and his favourites flattered themselves with an army of a thousand battalions, presenting an effective force of eight hundred thousand men and four hundred squadrons, or one hundred thousand horse; in all a million of soldiers to feed and pay. He soothed himself with this flattering chimera, and his ministers already demanded an additional sum of three hundred millions.

On the other hand one hundred and sixty thousand conscripts were wandering about the country, deserting from their standards, and protected by the disaffected spirit of the provinces. Napoleon dreaded this silent rebellion to military law, which would soon only need chiefs when an opportunity presented itself. What did he do? By the most artful of plans he collected together in a guard of honour ten thousand young men, selected from the richest and most illustrious families; these were so many hostages of their parents' loyalty.

The mediation of Austria being unsuccessful, Napoleon again endeavoured to open a direct communication with the English minister. For this purpose he dispatched the banker Labouchere, who, however, did not meet with a more favourable reception than he did in my time. On her side Prussia, who had just entered into alliance with Russia, proposed an armistice, upon condition that Napoleon would content himself with the line of the Elbe, and would cede all the places on the Oder and the Vistula. In our cabinet a party still persisted in affirming that peace was still possible. M. de Talleyrand said that one had always the power of not fighting. Lebrun and Caulaincourt were likewise of opinion that the offer of Prussia should be accepted, and that negotiations should be entered upon. But how could Napoleon be persuaded to give up the fortresses? He could not make up his mind to cede anything by negotiation. "Let them take them from me," said he, "but I will not give them up."

He made his journals say, "Spain belongs to the French dynasty. No human effort can hinder it." Being informed on the 31st of March that the Russians had begun to cross the Elbe, he himself declared, through the medium of these same journals, "that hostile batteries placed upon the heights of Montmartre should never make him yield an inch of territory."

And yet he received from every quarter pacific counsels and useful advice.

It hurt me to see M. de Talleyrand, if not restored to favour, at least recalled to the council board, whilst I remained forgotten and in disgrace. I perceived the reason of it to be the impression left by the Malet plot, to which a republican and liberal colour had affectedly been given. It might also be imputed to my remonstrances against the war with Russia. Certain, however, that sooner or later my services would be required, I thought it expedient to hasten the period. I was not ignorant that an address from Louis XVIII. to the French people, dated Hartwell, 1st of February, was

being clandestinely circulated, in which the senate was
invited to be the *instrument of a great service*. I knew
that the Emperor was aware of this document, the
authenticity of which, however, might be questioned,
as it had not given rise in England to any public
observation or discussion. I procured a copy of it,
which I addressed to him, assuring him at the same
time of its genuineness. I showed him in my letter
that his triumphs had lulled the Faubourg St. Germain,
but that his reverses had again roused them; that these
reverses had produced a vast change in the opinion of
Europe; that even in France the public mind had
undergone a change; that the partisans of the Bourbon family were on the alert; that they would secretly
reorganise themselves the instant that the power of
the head of the state should lose its fascination : that
an indisposition to war was the most general and the
deepest feeling; that nothing short of the national
honour was necessary to enforce the necessity of
conquering peace by a new campaign, in which the
whole population were to be in arms, in order to support negotiations so anxiously expected ; that, for our
safety and his own, he must either make peace or
convert the war into a national one; that too implicit
a confidence on the alliance of Austria would inevitably be his destruction ; that great sacrifices must be
made to Austria, and that what could not be withheld from her should be ceded with the utmost
promptitude; that I did not consider M. Otto as a
person adequate to the discussion of such complicated
political interests, especially when opposed to M. de
Metternich ; and I pointed out M. de Narbonne as

alone able to penetrate the real intentions of Austria, whose conduct was so very equivocal.

It was not till after the lapse of a fortnight or three weeks that I had a proof that my letter (though unanswered) had produced its effect, by the mission of M. de Narbonne to Vienna. I neither wished for nor expected more; the rest must follow sooner or later. I could rely upon the influence and credit of M. de Narbonne, whose mission was of the highest importance.

It must not excite astonishment if, at the moment when Prussia obtained the levy *en masse* of the people of Germany, in the rear of the armies of the northern confederacy—if, at the moment when she held out to the nation its deliverance as the object of the war, that Napoleon voluntarily rejected his best defence, that of a national war. He was well aware he could only obtain a burst of patriotic enthusiasm by recovering public opinion—by making to us concessions easy to another, but which would have cost him his heart's blood, as they would have inflicted a wound upon his pride, and have been a curb upon his power. I was therefore convinced that he would no more acquiesce in such a measure than in ceding to Prussia the places upon the Vistula and the Oder, and to Austria the Tyrol and Illyria. Napoleon thought he could meet all difficulties by the formation of a new army of three hundred thousand men, and by appointing a regency in case even of his death.

By conferring it upon Maria Louisa, with the right of assisting at the different councils of state, his object was twofold: to flatter Austria and at the same time to prevent any plot of a provisional government. But as the regent could not authorise by her signature the presentation of any Senatus Consultum, nor the promulgation of any law, the part she had to act was limited to her appearance at the council board. Besides, she was herself under the guidance of Cambacérès, who was himself directed by Savary. The ex-minister, Champagny, made also part of the regency, under the name of secretary, whose duty it was to enter into a new register, ridiculously called the State-book, the *definitive* intention of the absent Emperor. In fact, after the regency was set in motion, the *soul* of the government did not the less travel post with Napoleon, who made no difficulty of issuing forth his decrees from all his movable headquarters.

The allies, after several battles, were preparing to cross the Elbe, when the Emperor, after having displayed extraordinary activity during three months in his preparations, quitted Paris on the 15th of April, and proceeded to place himself at the head of his troops.

He first astonished Europe by the creation and sudden appearance, in the heart of Germany, of a new army of two hundred thousand men, which enabled him to act on the offensive. By gaining two battles successively, the one at Bautzen, in Saxony, the other at Wurschen, beyond the Spree, he recovered the reputation of his military talents. The first consequence of these victories was to bring back to us the King of Saxony, who entered into our alliance with the utmost precipitation.

The Prusso-Russians, whom Napoleon had defeated —that is to say, the troops of Frederick William and the Emperor Alexander—continued their retreat towards the Oder, and he permitted himself to be drawn on in pursuit. But, in proportion as he advanced, he separated himself from his reinforcements, whilst the allies, on the contrary, fell back upon theirs.

Suddenly the news of an armistice was noised about Paris. Napoleon acceded to it, as he stood in need of reinforcements of every kind, and because he feared, under the cloak of mediation, the armed interference of Austria.

The question was now as to the line of demarcation between the two armies. The two points which occasioned the most animated discussion were Hamburg and Breslau. The Prussians insisted, with the greatest obstinacy, upon being left in possession of Silesia, and Napoleon, although he was apprehensive that the enemy's object in the armistice was rather to strengthen themselves for war than to use it as a preliminary to peace, determined to acquiesce, the general wish around him being for a suspension of arms. He therefore gave up Breslau, abandoned the line of the Oder, and consented to withdraw his army upon Lignitz. The armistice was concluded on the 4th of June at Plessevig; and Napoleon again fixed his headquarters at Dresden.

Such were the events that occupied the two first months of a campaign which was about to decide the fate of Europe. They had, both on this and the other side of the Rhine, wound up public attention to the highest possible pitch of excitement and anxiety.

The armistice was as a respite ; the nation now flattered itself with the hope of an approaching peace, the object universally desired. Was it not thus, besides, that Napoleon, after all his victories, had succeeded in pacifying Europe ? But to the observer how much times were changed ! Up to this moment, for want of information that could be depended upon, there was in Paris nothing but crude ideas upon events of the secret and spring of which we were equally ignorant. I was expecting news from headquarters by an indirect channel, when I received from the arch-chancellor an invitation to confer with him upon a subject of importance. He informed me that he was commanded by the Emperor to make a communication to me. The Emperor, who had determined upon again accepting my services, desired that, at the same time he wrote to the King of Naples, requesting him to repair to Dresden, I should avail myself of the intimacy I enjoyed with that prince to determine him not to defer acquiescing in the Emperor's wish. I was to represent to him that it became absolutely necessary that we should make in Saxony the greatest display possible of our forces, and of our resources, both military and political, in order to induce the enemy to conclude a peace which should be honourable for us. The arch-chancellor gave me the Emperor's letter to read, to which he added his own entreaties, adding that he had not the least doubt that I should be immediately called to fill a mission which would not be inferior either to my talents or rank. I replied that I was ready to fulfil the Emperor's wishes ; that I would that moment write to the King of Naples, and would communicate its contents to him, in order that he might report them to his Majesty.

Although, from preceding circumstances, I had expected that I should soon be recalled into political activity, I was rather in doubt as to what I should direct my views. I was mistrustful of Italy, which, in case of the resumption of hostilities, would only be for me an honourable exile dictated by suspicion. However, I wrote to Murat, who was himself in no ordinary position.

Joachim Murat, a brave and noble-minded general, but a king without any firmness or decision in his resolves, had created for himself at Naples a species of popularity and military power; with this he was so blinded as to wish to shake off the yoke of Napoleon, who only considered him as an obedient vassal. It was not without difficulty that he had obeyed Napoleon's orders in forming part of the Russian expedition with his contingent, formed of twelve thousand Neapolitans and a part of his guard. It was to him that Napoleon, when he fled, confided the command of the wretched remains of his army. Joachim, foreseeing the changes which were about to take place in the political system of Europe, resolved to return to his kingdom, and endeavour to preserve himself from the consequences of such a disaster. He quitted the army at Posen, and ten days after (the 27th of January, 1813) the *Moniteur* announced his departure in these terms: "The King of Naples, being indisposed, has been obliged to retire from the command of the army, which he has resigned into the hands of the prince viceroy. The latter is more accustomed to the direction of large masses, and possesses the entire confidence of the Emperor."

This sally of official anger was the more galling to
Murat, from the Emperor having, during the two preceding years, made him feel that he was but a vassal
of the Grand Empire. Murat, perceiving that he must
expect the fate of his brother-in-law, Louis, if the
Emperor, surmounting his disasters, should recover
his ascendency, sought the alliance of Austria, which
was not as yet detached from Napoleon. His first
communications with the court of Vienna were managed by Count Mier, the Austrian minister at Naples.
Some negotiations also took place with Lord Bentinck,
commander of the English forces in Sicily. Joachim
and Lord Bentinck had even a secret interview in the
island of Ponza; but Murat was watched by Bonaparte.

When it was known at Naples that the Emperor,
after gaining the battles of Lützen and Bautzen, was
assembling a numerous army in Saxony, Queen Caroline wrote to her brother requesting he would be more
considerate towards her husband, and used all her
influence with the king to induce him to break off
his rash connections with Austria and England.
Napoleon wrote to Murat, who at first refused to
proceed to Saxony. He then caused a very affectionate letter to be written to him, in which Berthier,
in the name of the Emperor, entreated him to repair
to headquarters, assuring him that in all probability
the campaign would not be opened; that negotiations
for peace were about to be commenced, and that his
own interests imperatively demanded his presence.
My letter was nearly in the same terms; and I
flattered him by adding that glory was to be won
there, and that his honour required that he should

make one among his brothers in arms. Murat no
longer hesitated. Before even he could have received
my dispatch, a courier from Dresden brought me an
order from the Emperor, requiring my presence at
headquarters. I immediately concluded that, being as
much apprehensive of my presence at Paris as of that
of Murat at Naples, we might consider ourselves as
two hostages whom he was anxious to have in his
power. I made some hasty preparations, and set off
for Dresden *viâ* Mayence.

The defence of Mayence, our principal key to the
Rhine, was confided to Augereau, with whom I was
anxious to have an interview, and who was ordered
to form a corps of observation on the Maine. I found
him very incredulous as to the peace, finding much
fault with Napoleon, and expressing much pity for
the poor inhabitants of Mayence, who were in the
utmost alarm at the idea of a siege and the ruin of
the beautiful environs of their city. Finding that he
was completely master of all that had occurred, I set
him a-babbling. " Adieu, now," said he, " to our days
of glory! Alas! how little do these two victories,
with which Napoleon makes all Paris re-echo, re-
semble those of our famous campaign in Italy, where
Bonaparte was my pupil in a science which he now
only abuses. How great is the difficulty now to
make even a few marches in advance! At Lützen
our centre had given way; several battalions even
had disbanded themselves. In vain did our two wings,
by extending themselves, threaten to surround the
forces accumulated by the enemy in the centre; we
should have been lost but for sixteen battalions of the

young guard and forty-eight pieces of cannon. I tell you," continued he, "we can only calculate upon the superiority of our artillery; we have taught them to beat us. After Bautzen, he forced the passage of the Elbe, and made himself an opening into the north; but he was obliged to stop before Wurschen, on the other side of the Spree, and there we only carried the position and the entrenched camp by immense loss of blood. I have letters from headquarters, and from these I learn that all this horrible butchery has been productive neither of result, cannon, nor prisoners. In a cross country like this, the enemy are everywhere found intrenched, and dispute the ground with invariable success. The battle of Reichenbach was disadvantageous to us. Observe also that in this short opening of the campaign a cannon-ball carried off Bessières on this side the Elbe, while another killed Duroc at Reichenbach—Duroc, the only friend he had left! The same day Bruyères and Kirgener fell also under random bullets. What a war!" cried Augereau, continuing his disheartening reflections, "what a war is this! It will be the end of us all! What is he now about at Dresden? He will not make peace; he will get himself surrounded by five hundred thousand men—for, rely upon it, Austria will be as little faithful to him as Prussia. Yes, if he persist, and be not killed, which he will not be, good-bye to us all."

These observations sufficiently convinced me of the truth of what I had already heard, that an impatience for peace and for returning to Paris formed the anxious desire of almost every general whose fortune was made. Dresden presented to me at the same time the idea of a vast intrenched camp and a capital city. The forests in the vicinity were being felled by the axes of the pioneers. Upon my arrival I everywhere found the earth dug up, trees felled, ditches, and palisadoes. The Emperor was continually on horseback, overlooking the works and studying the surrounding country, accompanied by Berthier, Soult, and the chief geographical engineer, Bacler d'Alby; he was almost continually with the map in his hand examining the openings which led into the plain of Dresden. The construction of bridges, the tracing of roads, the erection of redoubts, and the formation of camps, formed also principal objects in his excursions and rides.

All these fortifications and lines might be considered as the advanced works of Dresden, the central point of a strong position on the higher bank of the Elbe; the works on the right bank round the city were nearly finished; peasants, put in requisition from all parts of Saxony, were labouring at their completion. The Emperor had completely surrounded the city by ditches and palisadoes, supplying the intervals left by the walls; the approaches were also defended by a line of advanced redoubts, the cross fires of which commanded the country to a considerable distance. Not confining himself to fortifying the environs of Dresden, he had established along the whole line of the Elbe, upon the banks of that river, his cavalry, the van of which was at Dresden, while its rear reached to Hamburg. The towns of Königstein, Dresden, Torgau, Wittenberg, and Magdeburg were his principal fortified points upon the Elbe, and secured to him the possession of that large and beautiful valley. All these works, begun and prosecuted with the utmost ardour, sufficiently revealed that Napoleon's plan was to concentrate a great part of his forces in the environs of Dresden, there to await the course of events. Thus I found him much occupied with negotiations, after having chosen the suburbs of Dresden for his field of battle, and the line of the Elbe for his rallying point. The majority of his generals considered Dresden as possessing all the advantages of a central position proper to serve as a pivot for the Emperor's intended operations. There were, however, some who owned to me that if Austria declared itself, we should find ourselves in an awkward predicament, being exposed to an attack between the Elbe and the Rhine. They considered the division of the enemies' forces, though separate, as forming three grand masses. Towards the north, on the Berlin road, the army of Bernadotte, Prince of Sweden; towards the east, on the road to Silesia, the army of Blucher; and behind the mountains of Bohemia, the Austrian army of observation, under Schwartzenberg; for at headquarters the Austrians were already looked upon as on the point of declaring against us.

Being informed that the Emperor had returned to the palace of Marcolini, in Frederichstadt, I hastened to present myself at his levee. He made me enter his cabinet; I found him there very serious. "You have come late, my lord duke," said he to me. "Sire, I have used the utmost diligence in obeying your Majesty's commands." "Why were you not here before my grand discussion with Metternich; you would have fathomed him." "Sire, it was not my fault." "These people wish to dictate laws to me without a sword being drawn; and do you know who most annoy me at this moment? Your two friends, Bernadotte and Metternich; the one makes an open, the other an underhand, war against me." " But, Sire!——" " Call upon Berthier; he will communicate to you everything respecting our present situation, and will put you *au fait* of all; you must then give me your ideas upon this infernal Austrian negotiation, which is slipping through my fingers; all your ability is required to preserve it. However, I will in no way compromise my power or my glory! Those scoundrels are so hard! They want, without fighting, the money and the provinces which I only obtained at the sword's point. I have arranged matters well, as to the chief point. Narbonne has undeceived us; you will see what his opinion is. Speak with Berthier as soon as possible, give the matter mature consideration, and let me see you in two days."

Upon withdrawing I found it was impossible for me that day to converse with Berthier, who having become, since Duroc's death, the favourite both in politics and military affairs, was continually with the Emperor, and was a constant guest at his table. He put off the interview till the day following. In the meantime a member of the cabinet made me acquainted with two circumstances which had just overshadowed our political horizon, and which rendered the hopes of peace still more uncertain. I mean the political dispute of Count Metternich with the Emperor (of which I shall soon speak) and the intelligence which arrived that very day of the complete defeat of our army in Spain, at Vittoria; a defeat which left the Peninsula at the mercy of Wellington, and carried the war to the foot of the Pyrenees. Such an event, known at Prague, could not fail of producing a baleful influence upon the pending negotiations. The Emperor, confounded at this first reverse, which he imputed to the inability of Joseph and Jourdan, looked around for a general adequate to the reparation of so many errors. His choice fell upon Marshal Soult, at that time near his person. He enjoined him to go and rally his forces, and to defend, inch by inch, the passage of the Pyrenees. Soult would not have hesitated had not his wife, recently arrived at Dresden with a splendid equipage, shown some repugnance, refusing to return to Spain, " where," said she, " nothing was to be got but blows." As she possessed considerable influence over her husband, Soult, being much annoyed, had recourse to the Emperor, who immediately sent for the duchess. She made her appearance with an air of vast importance : and, assuming an imperious tone, declared that her husband should not return to Spain ; that he had served too long, and stood in need of repose. " Madam," cried Napoleon, enraged, " I did not send for you to hear this insolence. I am not your husband ; and if I were, you would conduct yourself differently. Recollect that woman's province is to obey ; return to your husband and let him be quiet." She was obliged to submit ; to sell horses, carriages, &c., and in dudgeon take the road to the western Pyrenees. This scene with a haughty duchess furnished much amusement at headquarters, and acted as a diversion to the malicious chit-chat, of which one of our most beautiful actresses, Mademoiselle de Bourgoin, had recently been the object. Having been sent for to Dresden, with the *élite* of the Comédie Française, and being invited one day to breakfast with the Emperor, in company with Berthier and Caulaincourt, she had, it is said, after laying aside the character of Melpomene, successively assumed that of Hebe, Terpsichore, and Thaïs.

But let us pass on to more serious circumstances. I at length obtained an interview with Berthier, who had a small lodging in the Bruhl[1] palace. It would be tiresome to relate *verbatim* our long conversation upon the military and political position of the Emperor at this time. I shall only give here the portion really historical, introducing some ideas drawn from my own recollections. We will commence by the Austrian negotiation. Narbonne, writing from Vienna towards the end of April, was the first to inform us that Austria could be but little depended upon, he having forced from M. de Metternich the avowal that the treaty of alliance of the 14th of March, 1812, no longer appeared suitable to existing circumstances ; he called for a serious attention to the demands and armaments of Austria. The Emperor immediately conceived the idea of at least neutralising the cabinet of Vienna by means of two negotiations : the one official, the other secret. He flattered himself with destroying the influence of the northern coalition, both with the Emperor, his father-in-law, and M. de Metternich.

The Emperor had formed an erroneous opinion of

---

[1] It is supposed to be the palace of Marcolini, which was occupied by Napoleon, and formerly belonged to the Count de Bruhl, a minister of Augustus III., the Elector of Saxony, and King of Poland.—*Note by the French Editor.*

this statesman, who had resided for three years at
Paris as ambassador, and who had negotiated, in quality
of prime minister, the treaty of Vienna and of alliance.
Of all European statesmen he was indisputably the
one who best understood the government and court of
Napoleon. In this he had succeeded, through his high
connections, by successively paying his interested de-
voirs to Hortense and Pauline, and those which were
the result of predilection to Murat's wife, afterwards
the Queen of Naples.

The Emperor formed a superficial judgment of a
diplomatist who, under the exterior of a man of the
world, agreeable, gallant, and devoted to pleasure,
masked one of the strongest thinkers of Germany, and
concealed a mind essentially European and monarchical.
Still deceiving himself, even after his reverses, the
Emperor imagined that intrigue at Vienna would be
superior to considerations of state ; such was the source
of his errors. Imagining that he had cut the Gordian
knot of policy in the fields of Lützen and Wurschen,
he thought he had fully succeeded in regaining Austria
to his interests. M. de Bubna was dispatched to him.
This minister did not dissemble, in the midst of his
flatteries, that his court would demand in Italy the
Illyrian provinces, on the side of Bavaria and Poland
an increase of frontiers, and lastly in Germany the
dissolution of the confederation of the Rhine. Napoleon,
considering it weakness to purchase a mere neutrality
with such sacrifices, in answer to the autograph letter
of his father-in-law, replied that he would die fighting
rather than submit himself to such conditions. The uncertainty respecting the alliance being prolonged, after the

armistice. Bubna was seen going to and fro between Vienna and Dresden, Dresden and Prague, and at length he announced that Russia and Prussia would adhere to the mediation of his court.

A congress at Prague now became the topic of conversation. Narbonne followed the court of Austria thither; and scarcely was he in the neighbourhood of Dresden than he repaired thither to receive fresh instructions. "Well," said the Emperor to him, "what do they say of Lützen?" "Ah! Sire," replied the witty courtier, "some say you are a god, others that you are a devil; but every one allows you are more than a man." Narbonne, a deep observer of mankind, was not, however, mistaken respecting the supernatural power of him whose head he compared to a volcano.

The secret negotiation turned upon two conditions, the withdrawing from the Illyrian provinces and the payment of a provisional subsidy of fifteen millions, as a small compensation for what Austria affirmed she had refused, namely, ten millions stirling, offered her by the cabinet of London, in order to induce her to declare against us. She had already received ten millions in equal payments.

After having conferred with Narbonne, Napoleon decided that the negotiations should be opened direct with M. de Metternich, and that I should repair to Dresden, as I had for a long time been in possession of a clue to the labyrinth of diplomacy.

Whilst a courier was dispatched for me M. de Metternich arrived, bringing with him the answer of his cabinet to the pressing notes of the minister of foreign affairs. The alliance, being considered as incompatible with the mediation, was first to be broken off. The Austrian minister, also, no longer dissembled the intentions of his court to place itself between the belligerent powers, to prevent their communicating with each other, but through the chancery of Vienna. Here fresh difficulties arose, as Napoleon would not understand this unusual mode of negotiation. Prince Metternich, being the bearer of a private letter from his master, came to deliver it to the Emperor, who granted him a private audience. Here the altercation began by Napoleon complaining that a month had already been lost, that the mediation of Austria had the character of hostility, and that she would no longer guarantee the integrity of the French Empire. He complained that she had interfered to arrest his victorious progress, by the mention of armistice and mediation. "You talk of peace and alliance," said he to M. de Metternich, "and the political horizon becomes still more clouded. The ties of the coalition are drawn still closer by the treaties cemented with English gold. Now that your two hundred thousand men are ready, you come to dictate laws to me: your cabinet is eager to take advantage of my embarrassment to recover all or part of what it has lost, and to propose our ransom before we have fought. Well! I will consent to treat; but let us have a candid explanation. What are your demands?" "Austria," replied Metternich, "is only desirous of establishing an order of things which, by a wise distribution of the European power, may place the guarantee of peace under the ægis of a confederacy of independent states." "Be more explicit. I have offered you Illyria; I have consented to a subsidy to induce you to remain neutral; my army is quite sufficient to make the Russians and Prussians listen to reason." M. de Metternich then made the avowal that things were at such a pass that Austria could not remain neutral; that she was forced to declare for or against France. Thus pressed, Napoleon, without flinching, seized a map of Europe, and desired Metternich to explain himself. Finding that Austria insisted not only upon Illyria but the half of Italy, the return of the Pope to Rome, the re-establishment of Prussia, the ceding of Warsaw, of Spain, Holland, and the confederation of the Rhine, he could no longer contain himself. "Your object, then," cried he, "in going from camp to camp is partition; you want the dismemberment of the French Empire! With a single dash of the pen you pretend to throw down the ramparts of the fortresses of Europe, the keys of which I could only obtain by dint of victory! And it is without striking a blow that Austria thinks to make me subscribe to such conditions! And it is my father-in-law who makes an offer in itself an insult! He deceives himself, if he thinks that a mutilated throne can be an asylum for his daughter or his grandson. Ah! Metternich, how much has England paid you to induce you to act this part against me?"

At these words the statesman, offended, replied only with a haughty silence. Napoleon, confused, became more calm, and declared that he did not yet despair of peace; he insisted that the congress might be opened. Upon dismissing M. de Metternich, he told him that the cession of Illyria was not his *ne plus ultra*. The Austrian minister did not quit Dresden (June 30th) till after he had caused the mediation of his court to be accepted, and prolonged the armistice till the 10th of August. When Napoleon was asked if the five last millions of the subsidy must be paid: "No," said he, "these people would soon demand all France of us." Such was the state of affairs on my arrival at Dresden.

I did not conceal from Berthier, whose judgment was sound and whose opinions were just, that I had not the least doubt that Austria would join the coalition, unless the Emperor abandoned, at least, Germany and Illyria. I added that, if hostilities were resumed, I foresaw the greatest disasters, as there had never existed since the Revolution so firm a principle of coalition against our power.

Berthier coincided with me in opinion. "But," said he, "you cannot imagine how much circumspection is necessary with the Emperor; an open contradiction would irritate beyond my power to pacify him. I am obliged to use the most indirect means, unless he demands my opinion. For example, ever since Austria has appeared desirous of dictating to us, we are often discussing plans of campaign upon the supposition of a rupture; there I am at home. Well, would you believe it? I did not dare persuade him to abandon the line of the Elbe for the purpose of approaching that of the Rhine, which would cover the whole of our disposable forces. How did I act? In an indirect manner I seconded the plan of a very intelligent officer,[1] a plan which consisted in calling in all the troops we

---

[1] We have reason to believe that the person here alluded to is Lieutenant-General Rogniat, commander of the engineer department in the campaign of Saxony.—*Note by the Editor.*

had on the other side of the Elbe, in reuniting all the
detached corps, and in retiring *en masse* upon the Saale,
and from thence upon the Rhine. One very serious
consideration pleaded in favour of this plan. Allowing
that Austria declared herself, she would immediately
open the gates of Bohemia, permit the allies to turn
our position, and, in a word, cut us off from France.
Nothing could make an impression upon the Emperor.
'Good God!' cried he, 'why ten defeats could scarcely
reduce me to the position in which you place me all
at once. You are apprehensive of my situation in the
heart of Germany being a very precarious one. Was
I not in a much more hazardous situation at Marengo,
Austerlitz, and Wagram? Well! I conquered at Wagram, Austerlitz, and Marengo. What! do you think me
in a precarious situation who am protected by all the
fortresses of the Elbe and by Erfurt? Dresden is the
pivot upon which I shall manœuvre to make head
against every attack. From Berlin to Prague the
enemy develop themselves upon a circumference of
which I occupy the centre. Do you imagine that so
many different nations will long keep up a connected
system of operations for such an extent of line? I
shall sooner or later surprise them in false movements.
The fate of Germany must be decided in the plains of
Saxony. I repeat it : the position I have chosen gives
me such chances that the enemy, if they even gained
ten battles, could scarcely drive me back upon the
Rhine ; while I, if once victorious, would take possession of the hostile capitals, disengage my garrisons
upon the Oder and the Vistula, and force the allies to
make a peace which would leave my glory untouched.

At any rate, I have calculated upon everything; fate must do the rest. As to your plan of retrograde defence, it cannot suit me: besides, I do not ask you to furnish plans of campaign; do not make them; be satisfied with entering into my ideas, in order to execute the commands I may give you.'" "But," said I to Berthier, "if every general and staff-officer of the army thought as you, which I have no doubt is really the case, do you not conceive that this combination of a moral opposition would force the Emperor not to compromise everything by his obstinacy?" "Do not deceive yourself," replied Berthier; "opinions are much divided at headquarters. Because we have been a long time victorious, it is imagined we shall be so still, no allowance being made for the vast changes in the times. Besides, see how the Emperor is surrounded: Maret is completely drawn into his system; nothing, therefore, can be expected from him. If Caulaincourt, who enjoys his confidence in a still greater degree, sometimes speaks his mind and forces the truth upon him, he is not less obsequious. The Emperor now rarely consults his two bravest generals, Murat and Ney, except on the field of battle; and he is in the right. Those usually about his person encourage his mania for war—all but Narbonne, Flahault, Drouet, Durosnel, and Bernard, who are distinguished exceptions, and who might easily be brought over to more reasonable views. As to his other favourites, especially Backer d'Alby, who, with his maps, is constantly at his side, they, like their master, indulge the hope that the allies will commit faults which may be turned to their destruction. They speak of them with contempt, as acting without any plan. They will not see that all has undergone a change since our unfortunate Russian campaign ; that we have taught them how to beat us ; and that, if they cannot attain the velocity and the precision of our manœuvres and the superiority of our artillery, other advantages, especially that of numbers, will ensure their eventual triumph ; for, as in the days of Marshal Saxe, it is still *gros bataillons* who gain the victory. Do not forget, also, the co-operation of the people, who are now stirred up in insurrection against us, not only by secret societies, but even by their governments, no doubt ; add to which we are also in want of spies and a good cavalry." "Enough," said I, taking leave of him ; "I will commit to writing your ideas, to which I will add my own ; and, thus provided, I will see the Emperor and tell him the truth, as I have done upon every opportune occasion."

My intention was not to enter into a military discussion, nor even into a profound political disquisition, for I was perfectly aware that either the abruptness of his dialogue, of his questions, or of his dogmatic tone would not allow me the time. My first audience gave me to understand that two men were uppermost in his thoughts, Bernadotte and Metternich. As to the latter, I knew well my cue. The former was a more difficult subject to deal with ; it was, however, necessary. I had been assured that, at the Abo interview (September, 1812), the Emperor of Russia had said to him, "If Bonaparte be unsuccessful in his invasion of my empire, and if in consequence of that the throne of France should become vacant, I know no one better qualified to ascend it than yourself." Were not these words, which are a sufficient explanation of Bernadotte's conduct, rather employed as a stimulus than as an index of the real sentiments of the august personage who uttered them? France was at this time in no way prepared for such an event : how many chances were against it even being probable ? After the disasters of Moscow the European cabinets could not make a question about replacing the military chief of France by another soldier of fortune. They began to recollect that there was a dynasty of the Bourbons. Many doubts were removed by the expected arrival of Moreau on the continent, in the suite of Bernadotte. The first operations of Charles John, who, previous to the armistice, had landed at Stralsund with the Swedish corps, was to retake Pomerania from us. His future line of policy might easily be conjectured by his being always accompanied and almost watched by the English General Stewart, the Austrian Baron de Vincent, the Russian General Pozzo di Borgo, and the Prussian General Krusemarck.

Amid such distrust, some glimmerings of hope shone over Napoleon's fortunes ; for almost all parties had their representatives at his headquarters, even the faction of the malcontents, of which Madame de Staël was the life and soul. Napoleon had just learnt that, availing himself of the armistice, Charles John had recently visited the Emperor Alexander and the King of Prussia at their headquarters of Reichenbach, in order to confirm them in their resolution not to sign peace so long as a single French soldier should be left on the right bank of the Rhine. The temper in which I was about to find him may easily be conjectured. I prepared myself for the interview, and presented myself at the gardens of Marcolini. Being almost immediately introduced, I found the Emperor surrounded with maps and plans. He had scarcely perceived me, when, rising, he addressed me thus : " Well, my lord duke, are you now acquainted with our situation ? " " Yes, Sire." " Shall we be between two fires—between the howitzers of your dear Bernadotte and the bombs of my most excellent friend Schwartzenberg ? " " In my opinion, there cannot be the least hesitation, at least, to conciliate Austria." " I will not do so ; I will not tamely submit to be stripped without fighting. I know full well that the ambition of all, and the bad passions of many, have been set in action against me. Your Bernadotte, for example, may do us much harm by giving up the key to our policy and the tactics of our army to the enemy." " But, Sire, has not your cabinet endeavoured to induce him back into a less hostile system ? " " By what means ? He is subsidised by England. I have, however, written to him, and have about him a man I can depend upon ; but his head has been turned with seeing himself courted and flattered by these legitimates." "Sire, all this has appeared to me in so serious a light that I also have taken up the pen to endeavour to open the Prince of Sweden's eyes, who is at perfect liberty to come and parade up and down in Germany ; but who ought not, in any case whatever, to make war upon France." " But, France ! France ! I am France." " Will your Majesty condescend to inform me if you approve of my letter. I prove in it to the Prince of Sweden that he is making himself the instrument of Russia and England for the overthrow of your power, and for the resuscitation of the cause of the Bourbons." (I then delivered my letter to the Emperor, who read it attentively.) "Very well; but how will you get it conveyed to him?" "I think your Majesty might avail yourself of the medium of Marshal Ney, so long the friend and companion-in-arms of the Prince of Sweden, and who might add his own personal solicitations, your Majesty authorising him to choose for his emissary Colonel T——." "No, that officer was formerly a Jacobin." "Sire, Lieutenant T——, of the gendarmerie, might be employed: his devotion and intelligence is well known to your Majesty." "Well, let it be so; instructions shall be given him, and he shall wait upon Ney." After two minutes' silence, the Emperor suddenly resumed: "Have you considered the means of prosecuting the secret negotiation with Austria?" "Yes, Sire." "Have you drawn me up a note?" "Yes, Sire, here it is." The Emperor, after having read it: "What! does all appear to you unavailing? Do you see in my plans nothing but palliatives and half-measures? Do you range yourself in the lists with those who would wish to see me disarmed and reduced to an equality with a village mayor? Rely upon it, my lord duke, you will never find a more secure ægis than mine." "Sire, of this I am so well persuaded that it is precisely one of the motives which make me so ardently desire to see your Majesty's throne no longer exposed to the chances of war. But it is my duty not to conceal from your Majesty that the reaction of Europe, for a long time arrested by your glorious victories, can no longer be so but by other triumphs more difficult to obtain. The same ministers who were always ready to negotiate with your cabinet, and whom it was formerly so easy for you to divide and intimidate, now boast that their voices shall no longer be stifled in the councils of kings by a narrow and short-sighted policy; they pretend that they have at stake the salvation of Europe!" "Well, I have at stake the salvation of the Empire, and certainly I shall not undertake a part which they have rejected." "But a disjunction must be effected; if you do not disarm Austria, or if she do not embrace your cause, you will have all Europe against you, for this once firmly united. The best thing to be secured would be peace; it is practicable by abandoning Germany to preserve Italy, or by ceding Italy in order to keep a footing in Germany. I am beset, Sire, with melancholy presentiments; in the name of Heaven, for the glory and consolidation of that magnificent Empire I have assisted you in organising, avoid, I entreat, the rupture, and avert while there is yet time a general crusade against your power. Think that this time, upon the least reverse of fortune, the face of everything will be changed, and that you will lose the rest of your allies, who are even now wavering; that by rejecting a national defence, the only safeguard against disaster, your enemies will turn to their advantage the *vis inertiæ*, so fatal to the power which isolates itself; it is then that old dormant hopes will be revived, and that England, ever on the watch, will pour into Bordeaux, La Vendée, Normandy, and Morbihan, its agents, commissioned on the first favourable opportunity to revive the cause of the Bourbons. I conjure you, Sire, for the sake of our safety and your own glory, not to stake your crown and power on the chances of a throw. What will be the event? That five hundred thousand soldiers, backed by a second line consisting of a population in arms, will compel you to abandon Germany, without giving you time to enter into fresh negotiations." At these words the Emperor, raising his head, and assuming a warlike attitude, " I can yet," said he, " fight ten battles with them, and one is sufficient to disorganise and crush them. It is a pity, my lord duke, that a fatal tendency to discouragement and despair should have thus pervaded the best inclined minds. The question is no longer the ceding this or that province; our political supremacy is at stake: and, as to myself, upon that depends my existence. If my physical power be great, my moral power is in- finitely more so; it is magic; do not let us break the enchantment. What occasion for all this alarm? Let events develop themselves. As to Austria, she should deceive no one; she wishes to profit by my situation in order to wrest great concessions from me. I have made up my mind to it to a great extent; but I can never be persuaded that she consents to ruin me utterly, and thus place herself at the mercy of Russia. This is my line of policy, and I expect you will serve me to the utmost of your ability. I have appointed you Governor-general of Illyria: and, to all appear- ance, you will have to cede it to Austria. Go, set off for Prague, there make your dispositions for the secret negotiations; and from thence proceed to Gratz and Laybach; after which you will act according to circumstances; use all dispatch, for poor Junot, whom you replace, is certainly stark mad; and Illyria has need of an able and firm hand." "I am quite ready, Sire, to answer the confidence with which you honour me; but, if I dared, I would beg you to observe that one of the principal springs in the secret negotiation would doubtless be, independently of the withdrawing from the provinces, the perspective of the regency, such as it has been organised by your Majesty in its greatest latitude." "I understand you well! say all you please upon the subject; I give you *carte blanche*."

My sole object was now, supposing that a rupture should take place, to turn my new situation to the advantage of the state. Besides, the secret negotiation with Austria appeared to be without an object the moment the Emperor refused to make to that power the concessions by which alone he could retain it in his interests. My mission was therefore, with respect to Austria, nothing but a blind; and towards myself nought else but a pretext to remove me during the crisis from the centre of affairs. The Emperor had also two other objects. First, to keep as long as possible the court of Austria still in suspense, and to keep up a party there quite disposed to second him if in case of a rupture he should succeed, by some grand defeat, in disuniting the northern coalition. Secondly, he earnestly wished to make me traverse the Austrian monarchy from one end to the other, on my way to my government, being persuaded that I should not make my observations upon it in vain. Berthier owned to me that such was the Emperor's intentions; that he even desired I would stop at

Prague as long as possible, in order to concert matters with Narbonne, and to penetrate the ulterior views of Austria. He did not fail to expatiate much upon the high powers with which I was invested in the Illyrian provinces, powers which, being at the same time both civil and military, conferred upon me a kind of dictatorship; but I knew perfectly well what I had to expect from this Illyria, whether war broke out again, or whether this province was ceded to Austria. As to my sojourn and my observations at Prague, I was convinced that it became me less than any other person to prolong the one or extend the others beyond the limits of propriety.

I was, however, desirous of prescribing to myself some plan, founded equally upon reason and utility; for I knew that nothing could be worse than to act at random. The actual state of existing politics affording me no data, I arranged my ideas upon the probabilities of the future. The Emperor, said I, must succumb under a general confederacy; he may perish in the field, or may be attainted by a decree of forfeiture, after a series of fresh reverses which would entirely dissipate the fascination of his power. In spite of the egotism, the blindness, and even the baseness which predominate among the chief functionaries of the state, it is impossible but that ideas of self-preservation must take root in some of the strongest thinkers of Paris; this may bring about one of those revolutions, determined by the weight of circumstances and the exigencies of public opinion. Such a revolution may have important consequences, for if England, the soul of this new coalition, should take upon herself the political direction of it, the chances would be found to be on the side of the Bourbons.

I have no need to say that my former proceedings did not permit me to turn my thoughts to that quarter, even supposing the overthrow of the Empire; and perhaps I shall be considered as being too candid in confessing that, during the last six months of 1813, the Bourbons would have found, in the high offices of state, but few men of credit upon whom they could rely with any degree of safety. In fact, all the revolutionary interests which were falling off from the Emperor, those even of the royalists which had become incorporated with the imperial government, must first necessarily endeavour to rally under the power of the regency, of which Napoleon himself had laid the basis, if a few men of ability were to be enabled to effect the change in case of a reverse. But it was clear that one ought not to calculate that all was lost. Austria was much interested in seeing a regency established under the aegis of an archduchess, and in maintaining a system which, by allying her to France, reconciled to Europe and reduced within its natural limits the Alps and the Rhine, would enable her immediately to counterbalance the too great preponderance about to be acquired by Russia. It was upon this basis that I arranged my ideas, and explained them in a memoir, in which I established the hypothesis of an effective regency, the eventual direction of which might be left to statesmen. According to my plan, all interests and parties were to be represented in the council of regency. I naturally was to be a member of it, as well as MM. Talleyrand, Narbonne,

Macdonald, Montmorency, and two other persons, whose names I shall not mention. As to the ambition of the marshals, it would have been provided for by the erection of large military governments, which were to be shared amongst them, and which would have increased their influence in the state; in a word, according to my ideas, the regency would have conciliated all minds and all opinions. The government, instead of being the oppressor, would have become the protector of its subjects; while its form would have been that of a limited monarchy, with a mixture of a moderate aristocracy (*aristocratie raisonnable*) and of a representative democracy.

This was undoubtedly the plan best suited to the serious character of the circumstances, as it would preserve France from the twofold danger of invasion and dismemberment. I had the greatest reason for believing that it would be favourably received by the statesman at that time at the head of the Austrian policy, whose solidity of character and depth of views were well known to me—I mean M. de Metternich. His kindness for me took its rise from the Austrian declaration of war in 1809. At that time I received orders from the Emperor to have him seized, in defiance of the laws of nations, by a brigade of gendarmerie, to be conducted under this escort to the confines of Austria, subjecting him at the same time to every severity which could increase the insult offered to him. Much hurt at such unheard-of treatment, I undertook, at least, to soften down the execution of it. I immediately ordered my carriage, and repaired to the ambassador's. I explained to him the object of my visit, and expressed the deep regret it caused me. A mutual explanation followed, sufficient, at least, for us to understand each other. Having requested Marshal Moncey to appoint a captain of gendarmerie whose amiable and polite manners might qualify, in some degree, the insulting nature of his commission, I ordered him to take his seat in the travelling-carriage of the ambassador, to whom I allowed the requisite time for preparation. Upon taking leave, he expressed to me his deep sense of obligation for the attentions and delicacy I had observed upon this occasion.

My ideas, therefore, being thus settled, and being urged by the Emperor and Berthier, I began my journey, in company with M. de Chassenon, inspector-general of the grand army, and took the road to Prague—not, however, without having, previous to my departure from Dresden, paid my respects to the venerable monarch of Saxony, who had devoted himself with so much perseverance to the French cause. I had an opportunity of remarking how much the Saxons regretted seeing their King thus identified with the interests of Napoleon, and how clearly they foresaw the misfortunes which might accrue from it.

- I arrived at Prague at the moment of the expected opening of the congress, upon which, however, I founded not the slightest hopes, as in my eyes it was nothing more than one of those diplomatic farces played off to justify the employment of force. M. de Metternich and the plenipotentiaries of Russia and Prussia had just arrived, and the whole Austrian chancery had already taken up its quarters. Of the two French plenipotentiaries I only found Narbonne; he was expecting

Caulaincourt, and was ordered not to act without his colleague. Some difficulties had already preceded the meeting of the congress; Napoleon had just protested against the nomination of M. d'Anstett, the Russian plenipotentiary, a Frenchman by birth, born in Alsace, and whom he designated in his *Moniteur* as a most active agent of war. Besides these altercations, it was expected that questions relating to form and ceremony would arrest the progress of affairs at their very outset. Napoleon had entered into the same explanation with Narbonne as with me. "The peace that I will not make," he had said to him, "is that which my enemies wish to impose upon me. Be assured, he who has always dictated peace cannot, in his turn, tamely submit to it. If I abandon Germany, Austria will fight with still more ardour till she obtains Italy; if I cede Italy, she will, in order to secure her possession of it, hasten to expel me from Germany." The only positive instruction Narbonne had yet received was to endeavour not to place Austria in a hostile position. I communicated to him the Emperor's intention relative to a secret negotiation, and he augured as unfavourably from it as I did myself.

I found myself at Prague in a sphere entirely new to me, and on a ground with which I was equally unacquainted. It was known that I had arrived there merely on my way forward. Much delicacy was required in getting an interview with the head of the Austrian chancery. I everywhere found the same distrust with respect to Napoleon, and complaints, more or less well founded. I was assured, for example, that since the month of December, 1812, he had offered to abandon to Austria Italy, the Illyrian provinces, the supremacy of Germany, and, in short, to re-establish the ancient splendour of the court of Vienna; but that he no sooner saw himself enabled to open a new campaign than he had eluded all his promises, confining himself to cede nothing but a few trifling advantages, which could bear no proportion whatever to what Austria naturally expected, in order to resume her rank and preponderance in Europe.

The cabinet of Vienna evidently wished to profit by the diminution of our power, to recover what it had lost by the peace of Presburg and that of Schönbrunn. It attached but little value to the regaining of Illyria, which could not fail, on the first shot, returning under its vast dominion.

I learnt at Prague that the northern coalition had just declared against the Confederation of the Rhine, at the opening even of the campaign; and that on the 25th of March, Marshal Kutusow had announced, by a proclamation published at Kalisch, that the Confederation of the Rhine was dissolved. This was a species of sanction offered beforehand to the defection of the German troops employed in our armies. I likewise learnt that the conference at Reichenbach had been just resumed at Trachenberg; that the Emperor of Russia, the King of Prussia, and the Prince Royal of Sweden were present at them, as well as M. de Stadion on the part of Austria, and the Earl of Aberdeen for England, as well as the generals-in-chief of the combined army. There the forces which the coalesced powers were about to devote to the most determined war ever undertaken against Napoleon were decided upon ; there their movements of attack and their offensive operations were planned; in short, the rendezvous of the three grand armies was appointed to be *in the very camp* of the enemy. It was impossible not to perceive that the understanding with all the contracting parties was about to be cemented by treaties of partition and subsidy.

It was, however, decided to open the congress, but to inclose Napoleon in it in the circle of Popilius. Although not openly admitted to the conferences, England was undoubtedly the soul of them. It was she who was about to direct the negotiations. Thus there was no longer any doubt that Austria was on the eve of joining the northern confederation and strengthening it by two hundred thousand troops of the line. To all that we could confidentially urge in order to dissuade her, she replied that it was scarcely possible to find in Napoleon any guarantee that she should not be exposed to fresh spoliations while the state of affairs allowed him the means of oppression.

All my efforts to renew the secret negotiation were unavailing. As to my private views, as their object was the future guarantee of our political establishment, I was informed that the plan of a regency in the interests of Austria might influence the determinations of its policy, but not till suppositions should be converted into realities. I could not succeed in getting any provisional engagement entered into on the basis of contingent events. I merely obtained the assurance that they would only commence by the destruction of the external power of Napoleon, and that Austria would refuse to be a party to any plan for a violent change in the interior. I ought not to forget to mention that, among the complaints made to me by the Austrian chancery, I remarked its reproaches against Napoleon on account of the diatribes of his *Moniteur*, as well as of certain articles inserted in other journals. I quitted Prague certainly with more information, but without having found there the least shadow of a guarantee for the future; on the contrary, I carried with me the melancholy conviction that a million of soldiers were about to decide the fate of Europe; and that in this vast conflict it would be difficult to stipulate in time for the interests which I had combined, and of which no diplomacy would make an object of primary importance.

In traversing the Austrian monarchy on my way to Illyria, my journey, although a very rapid one, afforded me much instruction. I first was convinced that this compact monarchy, although composed of so many different states, was better governed and administered than is generally supposed; that it was also inhabited and defended by a loyal and patient people; that its policy possessed a kind of long-suffering well calculated to rise superior to reverses, for which it had always palliatives in reserve. By its perseverance in its maxims of state it triumphed, sooner or later, over the shifting policy of circumstance and contingency; in short, it was evident that Austria, by the entire development of its power, was about to throw a decisive weight into the balance of Europe.

I proceeded by the way of Gratz, the capital of Styria, and by the Styrian Alps towards Laybach, the ancient capital of the duchy of Carniola, at that time considered the chief place of our Illyrian provinces. I arrived there towards the end of July, and immediately installed myself in quality of governor-general. These provinces, ceded by the treaty of peace of Schönbrunn in 1809, were composed of Austrian Frioul, of the government of the port and town of Trieste, of Carniola, which includes the rich mines of Istria, of the circle of Willach, and of a part of Croatia and Dalmatia; that is to say, all the country situated to the right of the Save, reckoning from the point where that river quits Carniola, and takes its course as far as the frontier of Bosnia. This last country includes Provincial Croatia, the six districts of Military Croatia, Fiume, and the Hungarian shore, Austrian Istria, and all the districts on the right bank of the Save, to which the Thalweg served as a boundary between the kingdom of Italy and the Austrian territory. From this description it will be perceived that they were an assemblage of heterogeneous parts, each repelling the other; but which, had they been longer united to the French Empire, might have formed one whole, and acquired from their position considerable importance— the more so as Dalmatia and a part of Albania were comprised in them.

The sensation caused by my arrival in these provinces was the greater because my name, as former minister of the general police, was known there, and I replaced in the civil and military government an aide-de-camp of the Emperor, one of his favourites, Junot, Duke of Abrantes, who had just given an evident proof of madness. The circumstances relative to poor Junot are these: the corrosive effect of the severe climate of

Russia upon the wound which had disfigured him in Portugal, domestic cares, and resentment at not having obtained a marshal's staff, had so affected his senses that six weeks before my arrival the aberration of his mind had been evinced in public. One day, making his aide-de-camp get into his *calèche*, to which six horses were harnessed, and which was preceded by a picket of cavalry, he himself, covered with his decorations, and having a whip in his hand, mounted the coach-box. Thus exposed, he rode for several hours, from one end of the town of Goritz to the other, in the midst of the crowd of astonished inhabitants. The next day he dictated the most absurd orders and letters, which he ended with this formula: " I therefore, sir, pray that *Saint Cunegunda* will take you into her gracious favour and protection." Actions still more deplorable followed this, and the unfortunate Junot was sent back to France, where he died a fortnight after in consequence of a paroxysm, in which he threw himself out of a window in his father's château. Such was the man whom I had come to replace in the government of the provinces, which, though least harmonising with what was called the French Empire, were still governed upon the principles of conquest. It is true I was to be seconded by Lieutenant-general Baron Fresia, appointed commander-in-chief, subject to my immediate orders. This general officer, one among the Piedmontese who had most distinguished himself in the French armies, possessed much penetration and ability, and commanded a division of cavalry in the grand army at Dresden, when the Emperor sent him into the Illyrian provinces.

We were here under a pure and mild climate; the country around us offered the greatest variety, and, though sometimes wild, was always picturesque; while among its inhabitants might at times be perceived the traces of advanced civilisation, at others the manners of the primæval ages. Upon quitting Dresden, when taking leave of the Emperor, he told me that in his hands Illyria was an advanced guard upon Austria, and adequate to be a check upon her; a sentinel at the gates of Vienna to force obedience; that, notwithstanding, it had never been his intention to retain it; that he had only taken it as a pledge, it having been at first his intention to exchange it for Gallicia, and now of offering it to his father-in-law to retain his alliance. I, however, had perceived from his vacillation that he formed various projects upon this said Illyria. He told me, besides, that at all events he intended sending to the prince viceroy, Eugene Beauharnais, orders to be in readiness upon the Italian frontier, to make a vital attack upon the hereditary states should the court of Vienna declare against us. He added that at the same time he would give directions to the Bavarian army, to Augereau's corps of observation, and the corps and cavalry under General Milhaud, to second the enterprise of the viceroy, whom he had ordered to penetrate even as far as Vienna. But might not Napoleon deceive himself in these his gigantic views, and might he not propose them merely with the view of intimidating Austria?

I had scarcely arrived at my government when I was convinced that the season for bold projects was passed, and that all idea of carrying out any powerful diversions in the very heart of the hereditary states must be abandoned. In Illyria we had nothing but feeble detachments, and since the disasters of the campaign of Moscow the military power of Italy was almost annihilated. Three corps of observation having been successively drawn from it since 1812 had completely exhausted all the French and Italian battalions; the garrisons were completely drained of troops, and the different depôts had nothing but the numbers of the regiments; the viceroy, however, had just received a positive order to raise a new army with the utmost expedition. For this purpose the conscriptions of the departments bordering upon the kingdom of Italy were assigned over to him. The recruiting was rapid, but the skeleton regiments were with difficulty being completed, and this army, which was to consist of fifty thousand men, was still unorganised and without *matériel*, when Narbonne informed me, by a letter from Prague, of the rupture of the congress. It was there that the fiat of Austria had at length been pronounced on the 7th of August. She had demanded the dissolution of the duchy of Warsaw, and the partition of it between herself, Russia, and Prussia; the re-establishment of the Hanseatic towns in their independence; the re-integration of Prussia with a frontier on the Elbe; and the cession to Austria of all the Illyrian provinces, including Trieste. The question of the independence of Holland and Spain was referred to a general peace. Napoleon employed the whole of the 9th in deliberating. He at length decided upon giving a first answer, in which, accepting one part of the conditions, he rejected the others. The 11th was passed in awaiting the effect; but he soon learnt that in the morning the congress was broken up. The same day Austria abandoned our alliance for that of our enemies, and the Russian troops penetrated into Bohemia. Napoleon accepted too late, in their full extent, the conditions prescribed by M. de Metternich: but these concessions, which would have insured a peace on the 10th, were of no avail on the 12th. Austria declared war, and adjourned *sine die* the question of the reassembly of the congress. Upon receiving this letter I had not the least doubt that the attack would commence by Illyria.

When travelling through the hereditary states, the continual movement of the Austrian troops did not escape my notice. I learnt that Field-marshal Hiller was expected at Agram; that he had been preceded there by Generals Frimont, Fenner, and Morshal; that the strength of the army of which he was about to take the command would amount to forty thousand men; and that the troops in Austrian Croatia had been already placed upon a war footing. Upon my arrival I had immediately dispatched intelligence of this to the prince viceroy. Every report I received announced that among the inhabitants of French Croatia there were secret practices and silent machinations being carried on by Austrian agents sent for that purpose on the other side of the Save. They were organising an insurrectionary movement which might assist the invasion. In fact, on the 17th of August, the day after the expiration of the German armistice, two Austrian columns, without any previous declaration of war, crossed the Save at Sissek and at Agram, directing their march upon Carlstadt and Fiume. General Jeanin, in command at Carlstadt, the chief town of French Croatia, made at first some show of defence, but, abandoned by the Croatian soldiers under his orders, and attacked by the insurgent inhabitants, he effected his retreat almost alone to Fiume. Less fortunate, the governor of Croatia, M. de Contades, being arrested during his flight, was in danger of losing his life. Having almost by a miracle escaped the rage of the inhabitants, who were infuriated against all persons employed in the French administration, he was detained a prisoner by General Nugent, who would not consent to restore him his liberty, without being authorised so to do by the court of Vienna.

The behaviour of the Croatians upon this occasion occasioned me no surprise. I was aware of their attachment to the Austrian government. Almost all the other parts of the Illyrian provinces followed the example of Croatia. The towns even of Zara, Ragusa, and Cattaro, defended by Generals Roise, Montrichard, and Gauthier, with weak garrisons of Italians and a few French officers, were soon besieged by the Austrian troops, seconded by the free companies of Dalmatia. Upon the first intelligence of these movements, I had caused the fortresses of Laybach and Trieste to be put into a state of defence. Having gained intelligence that the Austrian general, Hiller, commander-in-chief of the enemies' forces, was uniting at Clagenfurt the greatest part of his forces, with the view of forcing Willach and Tarvis, and of afterwards penetrating into the Tyrol by the valley of the Drave, I immediately sent information of it to the prince viceroy. He had already set his army in march upon Illyria. The arrival of the Italian division of General Pino at Laybach enabled me to make head against hostilities.

I however did not deceive myself; Hiller was manœuvring with forty thousand men, besides which all the population was in his favour. The viceroy, reduced either by the numerical weakness of his army or the inexperience of his troops to a defensive war, with the mere hope of gaining time, could not think of re-occupying the line of the Save, which the enemy had already left behind. As the greatest part of the Austrian forces were in march upon Clagenfurt, it was really to be feared that the enemy might succeed in forcing the positions of Tarvis and Willach. This movement would have exposed the left of the viceroy's army, and opened to the Austrians an entrance into the Tyrol, through the valley of the Drave. The prince took up the position of Adelberg, his left being at the sources of the Save, and his right inclined towards Trieste. Upon his extreme left he had ordered the passes of the Tyrol to be guarded by a detached corps.

The enemy, however, continued offensive operations. Fiume and Trieste, which they had taken without much effort, were retaken by General Pino with like facility. Willach, which was successively lost and recovered, suffered more from the battle than the combatants themselves. The only operation of vigour was the carrying the camp of Felnitz, by Lieutenant-general Grenier.

Thus passed all the month of September. As the Emperor had observed, the fate of Italy was to be decided in Germany. At Dresden the rupture had been followed by military events of far greater importance.

But the battle of Dresden, while it diffused joy among the Emperor's adherents, proved but a transient gleam of hope for them; they found themselves again plunged in doubt and alarm. The intelligence of the reverses of Katsbach, Grossbeeren, and Culm began to transpire at Paris and Milan. I learnt from my correspondents that eighteen days had elapsed without the arrival of any couriers at Paris. Rumours ·began to spread a gloom over France; the Emperor was losing the confidence of his people. I was informed that royalist intrigues were again afloat in La Vendée and at Bordeaux; and that it was whispered in the parties and the saloons of the metropolis, "This is the beginning of the end."

The same might be said of Italy. Since the last news from Germany, the Austrian generals opposed to us showed themselves more and more confident; while on our side the Italian troops no longer manifested the same ardour.

One of their chiefs, General Pino, who had at first manœuvred under my direction, for the defence of Illyria, revealing the secret dismay which pervaded the ranks, suddenly quitted the army, and retired to Milan, where he awaited the result of the campaign.

I went to confer upon the state of affairs with the prince viceroy, whom I found extremely uneasy, but firmly devoted to the Emperor. He was much hurt at the rupture, and had no longer any confidence in the fortune of Napoleon. "It had been better," said he to me, " if he had lost without too great a sacrifice the two first battles in the commencement of the campaign; he would have retreated in time behind the Rhine." I did not conceal from him that I had given him that advice at Dresden, but that nothing could make an impression upon him. "It is," I said to him, "the more unfortunate, because at the first battle he loses in person, the political reorganisation will be settled without him." Eugene was struck with this reflection, and for the first time, perhaps, he was awake to the instability of his political establishment. I did not open myself further upon this occasion, having but little confidence in those about him. He at length owned to me, what I had foreseen, that he had strong reasons for believing that Bavaria was at this moment about to detach itself from our alliance; that the Bavarian army upon the frontiers of Austria had made no movement to arrest those of the Austrians, who were advancing in great force, although slowly, through the valley of the Drave towards the Tyrol; that himself being no longer able to govern Italy, he was about to retreat behind the Isonzo, in order to interpose the defiles between him and the enemy. "If, contrary to all expectation," said I to him, "you cannot make a stand there, endeavour—for I have more confidence in your talents than in your troops—at least to dispute for some time the country between the Piave and the Adige, in order to allow time for events to develop themselves. It will be doing a great deal, if, during the approaching winter, you can cover Mantua, Verona, Milan, and the mouths of the Po."

He immediately made his arrangements for retreating, and I on my side evacuated Laybach, after having

left in the castle the shadow of a garrison, chiefly
composed of convalescents, whom I placed under the
command of Colonel Léger. I followed the army,
which had just occupied the line of the Isonzo. The
same day the Austrians having appeared in force upon
Trieste, Lieutenant-general Fresia finally evacuated that
place by my orders, leaving in the castle a very small
garrison only, commanded by Colonel Rabić, who, after
a very gallant defence, capitulated about a month afterwards. From the headquarters of Gradisca, I addressed
my report to the Emperor. I represented to him that
the viceroy, thinking it his duty only to listen to pru-
dential motives, had just ordered the retreat upon
Isonzo; that in consequence of this movement the
Illyrian provinces were henceforth lost; but that the
objects to which the arms of Italy would direct its
efforts possessed also their advantages; that they left
nothing to chance, and might for some time yet in-
sure the tranquillity of Italy. I added that, as my
mission was now nearly at an end, I begged him to
give me another appointment, and that I awaited his
orders.

In expectation either of events or of Napoleon's
decision with respect to me, I was induced to take a
view of Lombardy, of that magnificent country to the
liberty of which I had devoted myself when entering
the career of high official duties. Alas! that also was
a sufferer under imperial oppression, and its political
destiny depended but too much upon that of Napoleon.

By conquering Italy we had introduced into it our
activity, industry, and a taste for the arts and for
luxury. Milan was the city which derived the greatest

advantages from the French Revolution, which we had transplanted there. Milan received a still greater lustre when it became the capital of a kingdom. A court, a council of state, a senate, a diplomatic corps, ministers, civil and military appointments, and tribunals of justice, added nearly twenty thousand inhabitants to its population, which exceeded one hundred thousand souls. Milan was considerably improved and embellished; but its brilliant period was of short duration, like that of all the kingdoms which the ambition of the conqueror soon exhausted both of men and money in his vain determination of subjecting the world. The Viceroy Eugene was soon nothing more in the eyes of the Lombards than the obedient executor of all his wishes. After the affair of Moscow, all the springs of government in Italy, as in France, had lost their elasticity. The conviction of Napoleon's power was destroyed the moment the illusion of his military fortune became eclipsed. Latterly, Eugene seemed to fear making himself popular, lest he should give him offence. Eugene, although a brave soldier and of approved loyalty, was parsimonious, rather light, too docile to the advice of those who flattered his taste, but little acquainted with the character of the people whom he governed, and placing too much confidence in a few ambitious Frenchmen: he needed a degree of political knowledge equal to that which he possessed of military affairs. During these latter days of difficulty this prince completed the people's discontent by conscriptions and forced requisitions; in short, the viceroy yielded too much both to the example and the impulse of the sovereign ruler. Eugene's position became the more difficult, as he had soon opposed to him both the partisans of Italian independence and those of the ancient order of things. The first becoming daily more irritated, looked round for assistance. Like his adoptive father, Eugene found no other hope for the maintenance of authority but in his army, which he lost no time in organising and disciplining.

All was suspense in Italy. It was known that three large armies in Germany surrounded, so to speak, the Emperor's, with the intention of manœuvring upon the basis of his line of operations at Dresden; and if the events of war should prove favourable to them, of uniting in the rear of this line between the Elbe and the Saal. It was likewise known that to oppose these three grand allied armies, Napoleon had scarcely two hundred thousand men, divided into eleven bodies of infantry, four of cavalry, and his guard, which presented a formidable reserve. Lastly, we had just learnt that he had resolved, in order to avoid being completely surrounded, to abandon his central position at Dresden and manœuvre at Magdeburg and on the Saal. Suddenly, towards the end of October, I received from the viceroy's headquarters a note conceived in these terms: " For refusing to give up anything, he has lost all." My anxiety and impatience to know the extent of what had taken place may easily be imagined. The next day gloomy reports were propagated respecting the fatal battle of Leipsic, which would have the effect of forcing Napoleon back upon the Rhine, followed by all Europe in arms. Now were realised all my presentiments, all my foresight. But what would become of us? What fate was reserved for the tottering Empire?

It was easy to foresee that the Emperor's enormous power, if not entirely destroyed, would at least be diminished. On the one hand I did not shut my eyes to the species of opposition he might meet with in the interior of the Empire; all the constituent elements of public power were known to me; I could appreciate the persons possessing more or less influence, and form an opinion of their courage and energy. A bold man was now necessary, and there were none but cowards. The only man who, by his talents and ability, could direct events and save the Revolution, had no political nerve, and was fearful of losing his head. As to myself, who certainly would not have been wanting in resolution, I was far removed from the centre, whether by fortuitous chances or by pre-concerted arrangements. I was burning with impatience; and, having resolved to brave everything in order to re-enter the capital, there to resume the secret clues of a plot which would have conducted us to a happy issue, was already on my way, when a letter from the Emperor, dated Mayence, ordered me, in answer to my last dispatch, to proceed to assume the government of Rome, which till then I had only nominally enjoyed. I perceived the blow, but there were no means of parrying it: the man who was thus being the destruction of the Empire found himself still secure amid the wrecks of his military power. I lingered on my journey, in order to observe the course of events, and in expectation of receiving from my confidential friends in Paris positive information as to the sensation which would be produced by the sudden return of the Emperor, after these fresh disasters.

But how well I knew the ground, and how correctly had I judged of the men who occupied it! There were not twenty senators who did not consider the Empire out of danger because the Emperor was safe!—not a grand functionary who suspected that the arms of Europe were able to cross the Rhine. In spite of the stupor which universally prevailed, a wilful blindness still created illusions in favour of power. I must, however, except that able man, whom I have sufficiently designated with a profound and hidden irony; he seemed to anticipate the moment of a fall, which appeared to him not to have yet arrived at its lowest point.

Italy in the meantime was undergoing great changes. Abandoning successively the Isonzo, the Tagliamento, the Piave, and the Brenta, the viceroy had recently repassed the Adige, and fixed his headquarters at Verona. The Austrian army, continually advancing and receiving reinforcements, established itself at Vicenza, at Bassano, and Montebello, already forming the blockades of Venice, Palma Nuova, and Osopo. In the secret negotiations with which I had been intrusted, the cession of the Venetian states as far as the Adige had been consented to, as one of the preliminaries of peace with Austria. But where would the pretensions of that power now stop? The two armies remained thus in presence of each other, as in winter quarters. It was upon the south of Italy that all eyes were fixed, and whence were expected the military and political events which would impart activity to the two armies in observation of each other, on the Brenta and the Adige. Murat, conceiving the fortunes of Napoleon entirely lost after the affair of Leipsic, returned in all haste to Naples to resume the plan which he supposed would maintain him on the throne, even after the ruin of him who had placed him on it. In an interview with Count de Mier, at the headquarters of Ohlendorf in Thuringia, on the 23rd of October, he sketched out, so to speak, his accession to the coalition and his treaty with the Austrian court. I had not at that time any certain data respecting Murat's intentions, but I foresaw his change of policy. I have learnt that upon arriving at Lodi, on his way from Leipsic and Milan, whilst he was changing horses, several Italians of distinction were surrounding his coach, and upon one of them asking if he would soon come and assist the viceroy, " Certainly," he replied, with his Gascon manner; " before a month is over I shall come to assist you with fifty thousand good ——," using a most indelicate expression, and he set off with the rapidity of lightning. I inferred from this that he said just the contrary to what he intended. In fact, it thus formed part of Murat's plans to enter into alliance with Austria at the same time that he represented himself to the Italians as the support of their independence. I also learnt that, while traversing Northern Italy, he received very graciously several Italian noblemen and general officers, who were labouring for the liberation of their country, promising them to embrace their cause and lead an army on the Po.

Upon my arrival at Rome I found General Miollis and Governor Janet full of mistrust and suspicions respecting Murat's conduct, who, they told me, was openly making his court to the coalition, and was organising a new army, partly composed of Neapolitans, Italian deserters, Corsicans, and Frenchmen. Every information from Naples announced that he had just abolished the "continental system" in his dominions, granting at the same time the entry of his ports to vessels of every nation : it was asserted that he was not only negotiating with the court of Vienna, but also with Lord William Bentinck, hoping to conclude a separate peace with Great Britain. The fears of the military commandant of Rome were shared by the viceroy, who dispatched his aide-de-camp, Gifflenga, to Naples in order to ascertain the King's intentions. This young officer, but little accustomed to the arts of that court, was cajoled by a few fair promises of peace and friendship.

Murat, declaring himself for the independence of Italy, found a party within the Roman states among the Carbonari and the Crivellari, a species of political *illuminati*, who were raised among the chief grandees, the jurisconsults, and the Roman prelates. A priest of the name of Battaglia had just roused to insurrection the country about Viterbo; he had placed himself at the head of a band of insurgents, seizing the public treasuries and levying contributions upon persons attached to the French interest. At the same time incendiary writings and proclamations were profusely spread throughout the pontifical domains. Miollis, setting in motion the armed force, soon dispersed the bands of insurgents. Battaglia having been arrested and conducted to Rome, his depositions sufficiently proved that he was the agent of the Neapolitan consul, Ruccari, who was employed by his court to excite insurrection against the French dominion. It appeared to me that great circumspection and prudence were requisite in opposing the practices of the Neapolitans, and that nothing should be undertaken unadvisedly.

Murat, however, had set his troops in motion in the north of Italy. Early in December a division of Neapolitan infantry and a brigade of cavalry, with sixteen pieces of artillery, entered Rome; these troops were commanded by General Carascosa. Although the Emperor had given orders that the King of Naples should be treated as an ally, *who was ready to show good intentions*, and notwithstanding the movement of this body had been concerted with the viceroy, General Miollis received the Neapolitans with much mistrust, ordering Civitá Vecchia and the castle of St. Angelo to be put into a position of defence: the money chests and other precious articles being all removed to the latter fortress. Three or four Neapolitan divisions succeeded each other, taking the road through the Abruzzo upon Ancona, and through Rome either upon Tuscany, Pesaro, Rimini, or Bologna. It was to this last city that Murat had just sent Prince Pignatelli Strongoli, less to trace the route of his army, the object of whose appearance on the Po seemed to be that of checking the Austrians, than to dispose all the friends of the independent cause to assist him in his enterprises. Pignatelli was commissioned to gain him partisans.

In the meantime I received from the Emperor an order to repair to Naples, to endeavour to dissuade Murat from declaring against him. I was instructed to conciliate him, and to employ the utmost address in this negotiation, and even to flatter him with the prospect that the Marches of Pesaro and Ancona, the spoils of the Roman state, and the objects of his ambition, should be ceded to him. My arrival at Naples was preceded by three letters from the Emperor addressed to Joachim, one of them announcing my mission. I made my entry at the court of Naples about the middle of December. Joachim's court was certainly a singular one, and his Vesuvian royalty (*royauté du Vésuve*) most precarious. Murat possessed great courage but little mind ; no great personage of his time carried further than himself whatever was ridiculous in ornament and the affectation of pomp; it was he whom the soldiers called *King Franconi*. Napoleon, however, who did not mistake his brother-in-law's character, erroneously supposed that Queen Caroline, his sister, an ambitious and haughty woman, would govern her husband, and that without her Murat could not be a king. But from the commencement of his reign, suspecting the authority to which they wished to subject him as a husband, he endeavoured to free himself from it ; and the political circumstances in which he then found himself the more effectually opposed the queen's ascendency, as he was wholly surrounded by advisers who urged him to declare against Napoleon, representing that this system of veering about was a political necessity.

In a court where policy was nothing but cunning, gallantry but dissoluteness, and external magnificence but theatrical pomp, I found myself nearly—if the comparison be not considered too flattering to myself—as

Plato did at the court of Dionysius. Upon my arrival I was beset by the intriguers of both nations, among whom, under the mask of a kind of ingenuousness, I recognised some emissaries from Paris. There were also some of these in the King's council; and I was particularly on my guard against a certain Marquis de G——— who, of the two meanings attached to his name in Latin, had all the vigilance of the one and none of the candour of the other. In my first conferences, in the presence of Murat, I was obliged to maintain a great reserve. I affected to be without instructions, and begged the King would explain his political situation to me. He confessed that it was critical and embarrassing; that on the one hand he was placed between his people and his army, who detested all idea of persevering in an alliance with France; on the other, between the Emperor Napoleon—who had left him without the least guide, and was continually giving him fresh cause for disgust— and the allied sovereigns, who insisted upon his immediately declaring his complete co-operation with the coalition. Again, that the Italian chiefs required him to concur in declaring the independence of their country, while the viceroy was decidedly opposed to all measures favourable to the independents, whether by the Emperor's orders or to forward his own views. "Lastly," added the King, "I have to contend against the manœuvres of Lord Bentinck, who, from his headquarters in Sicily, is endeavouring to effect an insurrection in Calabria, and who assists with money and promises the Carbonari throughout the whole extent of my kingdom." I told the King that it was not for me to offer him any advice; that as to himself a decided resolution was all that was necessary; that to induce him to take one, and when taken firmly to adhere to it, was the utmost my duty required of me.

The King, upon the breaking-up of the conference, owned to me that having, a month ago, communicated to the Emperor his fears that an Austrian detachment would march towards the mouths of the Po, he had entreated him upon that occasion freely to renounce the direct possession of Italy, and, by declaring its independence, thus complete the benefits he had already bestowed upon that country. I replied to the King that it was difficult to imagine the Emperor would make a virtue of necessity; but that, supposing he did, I should claim the priority for France—I who had so often and so vainly entreated Napoleon to render the war a national one.

My other conferences were all equally useless. Murat had committed himself; his council impelled him more and more into the interests of the coalition—a political situation incompatible with his project of calling Italy to independence. I pointed this out to him, but in vain; I then confined myself to advise him in a secret conference to increase his army, to have good troops, and, at any cost, to attach to his cause the sect of the Carbonari, whom he had, with much impolicy, persecuted, and who seemed to me to acquire greater consistence in proportion as events became more serious. I concluded by counselling the King not to rely too much upon his princely crowd of Neapolitan nobles, but rather to surround himself by people whose *excellence* did not alone consist in their title, and to whose firmness and devotion he could intrust himself.

My mission to Naples was not without its charms. I respired, in the midst of winter, the air of the finest climate in Europe. I found myself courted and respected by a brilliant court; but all my thoughts were turned towards France, and towards her my eyes were continually directed. She was threatened with invasion; foreigners were at her gates. What would the Emperor do? what would become of him? I was convinced that he would not have greatness of soul sufficient to induce him to identify himself with the nation. Isolated, his ruin was certain; but the effects of his gradual fall might for a long time prove disastrous to the country.

Receiving no certain information, and having but uncertain notions upon the state of affairs in Paris, I hastened to retake the road to Rome, to which city my private correspondence was addressed. I considered it the more imperative upon me to quit Murat's court, as I had certain intelligence that the arrival of Count Neyperg, the Austrian plenipotentiary, empowered to conclude the King of Naples' accession to the coalition, was hourly expected, and I should then have found myself compromised at Naples. Having once more entered the ancient capital of the world, I flew to open my dispatches from Paris. They contained the intelligence I had every moment expected, of the violation of the neutrality of Switzerland by the allies, and the invasion of our territory on the eastern frontier. By them I also learnt that the Emperor could scarcely assemble between Strasburg and Mayence some sixty thousand men in the space of a month, so great had been the ravages inflicted upon his armies by epidemic disorders and disorganisation ; but that he still obstinately rejected the fundamental bases (*bases sommaires*) which the allies had just sent him from Frankfort, notwithstanding that Talleyrand in the council strongly urged him to make peace, assuring him in the most positive terms that he deceived himself as to the energies of the nation, and that it would not second his efforts, and that he would ultimately find himself abandoned. Deaf to these prudent counsels, what did Napoleon meditate at this important crisis? A *coup d'état :* that of proclaiming himself dictator. Indebted for his rise to the factions and storms of a Revolution in which *words* did much, he persuaded himself (from a confusion of ideas respecting ancient history) that the title of dictator alone would produce a great effect. He, however, gave this up, upon the representations of Talleyrand and Cambacérès. They observed to him that he must exercise the power without assuming the name ; that he could even lock up the senate-house without arrogating any fresh title. He acted upon their suggestions ; the senate - house was from this moment placed under a guard.

Such was the sum total of my correspondence ; and, yielding to the impressions such intelligence produced, I wrote to the Emperor the following letter :

"I have bid adieu to the King of Naples; I ought not to conceal from your Majesty any of the causes which have paralysed the natural activity of that prince.

"1st. It is the uncertainty in which you have left

him with respect to the command of the armies of Italy. The King, in these two last campaigns, has given you so many proofs of his devotion and his military abilities that he expected from you this proof of confidence. He feels himself subject to a twofold humiliation, that of being the object of your suspicions and of being reduced to an equality with your generals.

" 2nd. It is continually suggested to the King that if, in order to preserve Italy to the Emperor, you exhaust your kingdom of troops, the English will effect a landing there, and will excite insurrections the more dangerous because the Neapolitans loudly complain of French influence. Besides, it is added, what is the situation of this Empire? That of being without an army, and of being discouraged by the events of a campaign which the enemy do not consider the termination of its misfortunes, since the Rhine is no longer a barrier, and since the Emperor, far from being able to preserve Italy, can scarcely prevent the invasion of his German, Swiss, and Spanish frontiers. Take care of yourself, rely only upon your own resources, is the advice he is continually receiving from Paris. The Emperor can no longer do anything for France; how then can he secure your dominions? If, at the period of his greatest power, it had been his intention to have incorporated Naples in the Empire, what sacrifice can you expect him to make for you now? He would, at this moment, abandon you for a fortress.

" 3rd. On the other hand, your enemies opposed to this picture of the situation of France that of the immense advantages which are likely to accrue to the King by joining the coalition: this prince, by so doing, consolidates his throne and aggrandises his power; instead of making the Emperor a useless sacrifice of his glory and his crown, he will diffuse over both the most brilliant lustre by proclaiming himself the defender of Italy and the guarantee of her independence. If he declare himself for your Majesty, his army abandons him, and his people rise in insurrection. If he abandon your cause, all Italy crowds beneath his banners. Such is the language addressed to the King by men who are closely attached to your government. Perhaps, by doing so, they only deceive themselves as to the means of being serviceable to your Majesty. Peace is necessary to the world; and to persuade the King to place himself at the head of Italy is in their opinion the surest method of forcing you to make peace.

"I arrived at Rome on the 18th; there, as throughout all Italy, the word *independence* has acquired a magical virtue. It cannot be denied that under this banner are ranged opposing interests: but each country demands a local government; and each complains of being obliged to make their appeal to Paris, upon subjects even of the least importance. The French government, at so great a distance from the capital, only causes them heavy charges without any equivalent.

"'All,' say the Romans, 'that we know of the government of France is conscriptions, taxes, vexations, privations, and sacrifices. Add to which, we have neither interior nor exterior commerce: we have no means of disposing of our produce, and for the trifling articles we obtain from foreign countries, we pay most extravagantly.' Sire, when your Majesty was at the acme of glory and power, I had the courage to tell you the truth, for it was the only thing of which you then stood in need. I ought now to declare it to you with the same fidelity, but with greater delicacy, since you are unfortunate. Your speech to the legislative body would have made a deep impression upon Europe, and would have touched all hearts, if your Majesty had added to the wish you expressed for peace a magnanimous renunciation of your former plan of universal monarchy. So long as you are not explicit upon this point, the allied powers will believe, or will say, that this system is only deferred, and that you will avail yourself of events to recommence it. The French nation itself will be subjected to the same apprehensions. It appears to me that if under these circumstances you were to concentrate all your forces between the Alps, the Pyrenees, and the Rhine, and make a candid declaration that you would not overstep those natural frontiers, you might then command both the wishes and the arms of the nation in defence of your Empire; and truly, this Empire would still be the finest and most powerful in the world; it would still be sufficient for your glory and the prosperity of France. I am convinced that you can never procure a real peace but at this price. I tremble at being the only one to hold this language to you! Mistrust the lying lips of your sycophants; experience should have taught you to appreciate them. These are they who induced you to march into Spain, Poland, and Russia; who persuaded you to remove your real friends; and who still more recently dissuaded you from signing peace at Dresden. These are they who now deceive you, and who exaggerate your resources. You have still enough left to be happy, and to make France peaceful and prosperous; but that is all, and of this truth all Europe is persuaded: it is even useless any longer to employ delusion—to deceive her is no longer possible.

"I conjure your Majesty not to reject my counsels; they are the effusions of a heart which has never ceased to be attached to you. I have not the egotism of affecting to see more or better than others; were all equally candid they would hold the same language to you. They would have spoken as I did after the peace of Tilsit, after the peace of Vienna, before the war against Russia, and, lastly, at Dresden.

"It is mortifying for the dignity of human nature that I am the only one who dares to tell you what I think. Should your Majesty have to undergo new misfortunes, I shall not have to reproach myself with having suppressed the truth. In Heaven's name put an end to the war; let mankind enjoy at least a momentary repose."

My letter was scarcely sent off, when Napoleon struck his last *coup d'état*, the dissolution of the legislative body. From the palace of the Tuileries, which ought only to have resounded with protestations of homage and fidelity, but which was suddenly transformed into an arena for pride, rage, and malice, legislators, magistrates, generals, and public functionaries were seen departing, struck with fear and apprehension. All were penetrated with profound grief at seeing a separation between the chief of the state and the nation, at the moment when there was the greatest necessity of mutual confidence and assistance. Under what auspices then was the third lustrum of the Empire about to be opened? Was this year to be the last of its duration? What gloomy prospects for the defence of the country, invaded by five foreign armies, marching under the banners of all the potentates of Europe! In order to continue to impose upon Austria, the Emperor, who still thought he had it in his power to detach that kingdom from the coalition whenever he pleased, at the commencement of the decisive campaign, intrusted the regency to Maria Louisa; so that the Empire in its last struggles had actually two governments—the one at Napoleon's camp, the other at Paris. He soon even increased the absurdity both in theory and practice of this regency, by nominating his brother Joseph to the lieutenancy-general of the Empire, almost at the very moment he had invested the Empress with the executive power. This was only infusing one more ingredient of division into his government.

Such had not been the idea I had formed of a regency of which, but for the evil destiny which detained me on the other side of the Alps, I could have insured the success.

I ask, who in this jumble of power was the person or authority that could really be considered as the depositary of Napoleon's will? Joseph was but a counterpoise to the arch-chancellor Cambacérès, who himself counterbalanced the Empress and Joseph, and the Empress was only introduced for form's sake. Cambacérès was therefore the grand pivot of the regency of Paris; but he was subjected to the surveillance of the minister of police, a real domestic inquisitor. In itself the police is nothing but a hidden power, the strength of which consists in the opinion it can impart of its force; then indeed it can become one of the greatest state weapons; but in the hands of a Savary the talisman of the police was broken for ever.

From what has been observed it may be seen that no government was ever ready to fall under so many precautions, perhaps even from excess of precaution. It is, however, a fact that all the authorities were unanimously of opinion on one point, namely, the impossibility of preserving the government in the hands of Napoleon. But no one had the courage to declare this openly, and to act in consequence. What a disgrace that so many able and experienced men should have tamely permitted the destruction of the state, and have effected, under foreign protection, a revolution which the country in tears entreated to be permitted to commence! O you who have said to me since, after the blow was struck, "Why were you not there?" how does this reveal your baseness! I was not there precisely because I ought to have been there, and because it was foreseen that, by the force of things alone, all the interests of the Revolution of which I was the representative would have prevailed and averted the catastrophe. I was so little mistaken as to our real situation that, anxious to hasten my return and terminate my mission, I wrote the Emperor a second letter, in which I represented to him how contrary it was to his dignity that I should remain in the quality of his governor-general at Rome when invaded by the Neapolitans; besides that, it became impossible that Rome,

Tuscany, and the Genoese states could be preserved if the King of Naples acceded to the coalition; and that, in my opinion, policy required that he should enter into arrangements with that prince to abandon to him the provisional military occupation of the countries that it would be impossible for us to guard or defend; that by this we should obtain the double advantage of saving our garrison and indirectly re-attaching the King of Naples to the French cause; that, as to myself, finding my dignity wounded at Rome, where my authority could no longer possess any weight, I had taken the road to Florence, where I should await his final instructions.

I found Florence, like the rest of Italy, unquiet, in suspense, and divided as to the opinion that might be formed of the movements of Murat towards Upper Italy. The adherents of Napoleon asserted that the Neapolitans, still faithful and devoted to his cause, only marched on the Po to second our efforts against the common enemy, and that Murat would come to command them in person. The partisans of independence saw nothing in the approach of the Neapolitans but the near arrival of auxiliaries who would assist them in throwing off the French yoke. Others, lastly, could not see without uneasiness, upon the theatre of Upper Italy, a new army, which in their eyes was nothing but a collection of vagabonds and thieves, forced into the service and completely undisciplined. What, said they to me, is to be expected from a Carascosa, a man who supplies a want of ability by boasting; from a Macdonaldo, the former aide-de-camp of the old Cisalpine general, Trivulzi, whose mistress he married, and who, not being able to obtain employment either in France or the kingdom of Italy, has entered the service of Murat in despair; what from the ex-general Lecchi, a Lombardian, one unfortunately notorious for his cruelties, his exactions, and his plunderings in Spain, and who, brought before a council of war in France, was dismissed without employment? Perhaps young Lavauguyon will be panegyrised, recently restored to Murat's favour, who in a jealous fit had disgraced him in 1811; a time when at the head of the chosen body-guard he was, according to some, too much remarked by Queen Caroline; and to others, a still more happy rival to Murat. The other generals possessed neither consistency nor respect. Thus I soon knew to what extent I could rely upon this Neapolitan army. It was composed of forty battalions, twenty squadrons: in all twenty thousand men and fifty pieces of artillery; in other respects it was tolerably provided, but its discipline was very bad.

The government of Tuscany was the more uneasy respecting its arrival, as on the 10th of December the English had effected a landing at Via Reggio, and had afterwards appeared before Leghorn; but the firmness of the French garrison had compelled them to reembark. This attempt of theirs, however, appeared to me only to be a first essay of their strength.

It was in the midst of these circumstances that I presented myself at the court of the grand duchess, where I met with a most gracious reception. In the duchess I found a very singular woman; and this time I had leisure to study her character. Ungifted with beauty and personal charms, Eliza was not void of wit, and the first movements of her heart were good; but an incurable defect in judgment, added to very amorous propensities, continually betrayed her into errors and even excesses. Her mania consisted in imitating the habits of her brother, affecting his *brusquerie*, his predilection for pomp and military parade, and neglecting the arts of peace, and even literature, of which formerly she had from taste professed herself the protectress. In a country where agriculture and commerce had flourished to so great a degree she was solely occupied in forming a splendid and servile court, in organising whole battalions of conscripts, appointing and cashiering generals. There, where formerly the universities of Pisa and Florence, and the academies della Crusca, del Cimento, and del Disegno, had shed so great a lustre, she permitted learning to languish and decay, granting her protection solely to actors, rope-dancers, and musicians. In short, Eliza was feared, but not beloved.

As to myself, far from having reason to complain of her, I found her discreet, affectionate, resigned even to the crosses with which she was threatened, and willingly yielding her own opinions to my experience and advice. From that moment I directed her policy. She allowed me to perceive how much she was hurt that Napoleon was about to lose not only the Empire through his obstinacy, but even to sacrifice without hesitation the establishment of which his family was in possession. I then guessed all her fears, and well understood that she was alarmed at the precarious situation of Tuscany, which it grieved her to think she was about to be deprived of. I did not conceal from her that at Dresden I had given Napoleon the most sincere and wholesome advice ; that I warned him he was about to stake, single-handed, his crown against the whole of Europe ; that he ought to give up Germany, and then intrench himself upon the Rhine, calling the nation to his assistance ; that he would be compelled against his own inclination to have recourse to this ; but that then he would adopt too late a measure exacted by necessity.

In the meantime, the different *corps d'armée* of Murat successively arrived at their destination, either at Rome or in the Marches. General Lavauguyon, his aide-de-camp, who was at Rome at the head of five thousand Neapolitans, suddenly announcing himself as commander-in-chief of the Roman states, took possession of the country. General Miollis, who had only eighteen hundred Frenchmen under his command, shut himself up in the castle of St. Angelo. Lavauguyon immediately summoned him to surrender, and invested the castle ; he demanded an interview with Miollis, which the latter decidedly refused.

But shortly afterwards Murat himself, who had left Naples on the 23rd of January, made his entry into Rome with all that pomp to which he was so fondly attached, and was received by the independents with great demonstrations of joy.

Murat caused it to be proposed to General Miollis, as well as to General Lasalcette, who defended Civitá Vecchia with two thousand men, to return to France with their garrisons. Both generals rejected his offer, and the king left a corps of observation to blockade both these places. At the same time he had caused the siege of Ancona to be commenced, a citadel into which General Barbou had retired. However, as yet there had been no open hostilities; but the King of Naples, at the head of nine thousand infantry and four thousand cavalry, having entered Bologna, occupied Modena, Ferrara, and Cento. His equivocal conduct, and the movements of his troops, which were advancing upon Parma and Tuscany, no longer left any doubt upon his intended defection. Joachim entered Bologna on the 1st of February. That very day he detached from his army General Minutolo, with eight hundred men, to take possession of Tuscany, to the government of which he nominated General Joseph Lecchi. Intelligence of this had no sooner arrived than the utmost consternation reigned in the court of the grand duchess, who complained bitterly of being thus despoiled by her brother-in-law. Being summoned to the council, and having been previously informed that the people everywhere met the Neapolitans with open arms, I advised the grand duchess to yield to the storm, and to retire either to Leghorn or Lucca. This resolution being taken, she enjoined her husband, Prince Felix Baciocchi, to evacuate Tuscany.

I was a witness to this convulsion, which, upon a smaller scale, was but the type of what was soon to take place at Paris. But in Tuscany there was no effusion of blood: on one side it was nothing but a flight, and on the other but a sarcastic war of words, with which the Florentines pursued the leaders and inferior officers of the government. Thus Baciocchi, upon the change in his fortune, had thought proper to change his name, and to adopt that of Felix (the happy) instead of Pascal, a name as ridiculous in Italy as that of Jocrisse in France. The Florentines, therefore, in allusion to this, upon his forced retreat, indulged this *jeu de mot*, " Quando eri Felice, eravamo Pasquali ; adesso che sei ritornato Pasquale, saremo Felici."

The prefect of Florence, my intimate friend, was not exempted from persecutions of this kind. He was very strict with respect to the conscription, and whenever a person underwent his examination generally sent him off to the army with the expression, *bon à marcher;* when the authorities therefore were obliged to leave the city, he found written on his door, in large characters, *bon à marcher.* Whilst the grand duchess and I had retired to Lucca, Baciocchi was still in possession of the citadel and fortifications of the cities of Florence and Volterra. I expected from day to day the powers I had requested for the military evacuation of Tuscany and the Roman states. The grand duchess was equally desirous of seeing Tuscany delivered from the French troops, in the hope of coming to some arrangement with Murat, whose fortune appeared to her to offer more fortunate chances than that of Napoleon. She was especially mistrustful of little Legarde, whom the Emperor had set over her in quality of commissary-general of police, and who was indebted to me for his fortune. She even went so far as to suspect that he sent Napoleon accounts injurious to her as well as to me. Eliza spoke very freely on the subject, and one day expressed her anxious wish to get the portfolio of this emissary in her possession, in order to see if her suspicions were well founded. Being myself persuaded that Legarde's correspondence would be more unfavourable to me than to the grand duchess, I did not attempt to dissuade her from it when she told me that she intended employing him on a mission to Pisa, and that she would afterwards have him stopped upon the road by men hired and masked for that purpose. I was much gratified in seeing a commissary-general of police thus robbed on the highway—one, too, who while affecting bluntness and extreme good-nature, boasted of possessing more cunning than the most wily Italian. It was necessary to undeceive him as to his ability. In fact, upon his return from Pisa, the persons hired for the purpose stopped him, made him alight from his coach, and, whilst two of them held him on the edge of a ditch, the others carried off his money, jewels, and even his papers, which were in a trunk in the front of the carriage. When we saw people in the greatest alarm come to inform us of the misfortune of the commissary-general, the grand duchess and myself had great difficulty to preserve our gravity, and we were obliged to withdraw aside to give vent to our inclination for laughter. This *opera seria*, however, disappointed us; the pretended papers of the commissary-general which were brought us consisted of a set of numbers of the *Moniteur*, which Legarde, having a coach with a false bottom where he concealed his secret papers, had placed in the box in front. He escaped with the loss of his money and his jewels; and, according to every probability, with fear alone, for he could not fail to indemnify himself either at Florence or Paris.

In the meantime, Murat, who now kept the diplomatists in full play, endeavoured to fill all Italy with his name. He wrote me letter after letter, repeating that his alliance with the coalition appeared to him the only means of preserving the throne, and requiring me to tell the Emperor the whole truth upon the actual state of Italy. I answered that I had anticipated him in that point, and that he had no need to encourage me to tell the Emperor the truth; that I had always thought that to conceal it was to betray princes; I insisted upon the necessity of the King of Naples keeping up a good army as a means of influence with the coalition; above all I recommended him to away with all irresolution; it was extremely essential to his interests, I told him, to create for himself a great respect, and to make his character an object of esteem; and since his resolution appeared wavering, I owed it to the friendship he had testified for me to own to him that the least hesitation would be fatal; that it would draw upon him general want of confidence; that he could, besides, promote the interests of his country by contributing to the general pacification, and by supporting the dignity of thrones and the independence of nations. I added that I witnessed with regret the risings in the country; that those passions which could not be gratified ought not to be raised. Being also requested by this prince to send him in writing the reflections which I had made to him at Naples upon the constitutions required of him by the partisans of liberty, I warned him against letting himself be induced to throw into the midst of Neapolitan people ideas for which they were not all prepared; in short, said I to him, I fear that the word constitution, which I hear everywhere upon my road, is nothing with the majority but a pretext for throwing off all obedience.

The troops of Murat had arrived on the southern banks of the Po. By taking possession of Tuscany and the Roman states, he had declared against the Emperor his brother-in-law in favour of Austria. He had bound himself, without binding the opposite party; for the treaty he had signed at Naples on the 11th of January, with the Count de Neyperg, was not ratified. In consequence of the seriousness of events, I judged it expedient again to confer with Murat in person, and I had a secret interview with him at Modena. There I convinced him, since he had taken a decisive part, that he ought to announce it. "If you had," said I to him, "as much firmness of character as excellence of heart, you would be superior in Italy to the coalition. You can only conquer it here by much decision and frankness." He still hesitated. I communicated to him the latest news I had received from Paris. Determined by this, he confided to me his idea of a proclamation, or rather declaration of war, in which I suggested some alterations, which he made. This proclamation, dated from Bologna, was conceived in the following terms:

"Soldiers! so long as I thought the Emperor Napoleon fought for the peace and the happiness of France, I fought at his side; but now illusion is impossible: the Emperor's whole wish is for war. I should betray the interests of my former country, those of my dominions, and yours, did I not immediately separate my arms from his, to unite them with those of the allied powers, whose magnanimous intentions are to re-establish the dignity of thrones and the independence of nations.

" I know that attempts are made to warp the patriotism of the Frenchmen who compose a part of my army, by false sentiments of honour and fidelity; as if any honour and fidelity were shown in subjecting the world to the mad ambition of the Emperor Napoleon.

" Soldiers! there are no longer but two banners in Europe; upon one you read: ' Religion, Morality, Justice, Moderation, Laws, Peace and Happiness; ' upon the other, ' Persecution, Deceit, Violence, Tyranny, War, and Grief in every family '—choose."

I had also to treat with Murat upon a particular business which involved my own interests; I had to claim, as governor-general of the Roman states and afterwards of Illyria, the arrears of salary, amounting to the sum of one hundred and seventy thousand francs. The King of Naples, having seized the Roman states and the public revenues, became responsible to me for my debt. He gave an order for it, the execution of which was attended with some delay; however, before leaving Italy, I was enabled to say that I had not lost my time there for nothing.

At Lucca I again found the grand duchess still in much trouble, and extremely uneasy respecting the aspect of affairs. I announced to her that Murat was at length determined upon raising troops, but that I, nevertheless, doubted whether his operations would be directed by sufficient vigour and rectitude to engage the confidence of his new allies; that the Austrian ministers reproached him with being a Frenchman, and, above all, of being too much attached to the Emperor; that the revolutionists, who at this moment governed Florence, affirmed openly that the King of Naples was in intelligence with France, and that he was deceiving the Italians; that they even went so far as to impute to my counsels the inaction of the Neapolitan troops, whom the Austrians were impatient to see marched against the viceroy, who was about to be immediately attacked by General Count Bellegarde. I lastly informed her that I had left Murat ill with vexation; that he was aware of the critical situation in which he was placed; but that henceforth it would be difficult for my counsels to reach him.

A few days after I received from the minister of war a dispatch, containing the Emperor's instructions relative to the evacuation of the Roman and Tuscan states. To these was added a letter for the King of Naples, which I was ordered to remit to him in person: I was also instructed to make him at the same time certain confidential communications, to be modified according to the position in which I found that prince. I immediately set off for Bologna, where Murat then was. As far as Florence I experienced no difficulty; but, on my arrival in that town, the new authorities notified to me that I could neither continue my journey nor stop at Florence, and that I must retire to Prato, there to await the King's answer. I immediately dispatched a courier to him, and returned to Lucca, preferring a residence in that town, Prato being already in insurrection. I soon received Murat's answer, who informed me that he had already ordered his generals to treat with me respecting the evacuation of Tuscany and the Roman states.

The powers with which the Emperor had invested me came very *à propos*. The greater part of the French troops which were in Tuscany were concentrated at Leghorn; those who were at Pisa seemed disposed to make resistance. The Neapolitan general, Minutolo, had already marched with a column of Murat's army from Florence to Leghorn; at Pisa there had been some hostilities between this troop and a French detachment; they were now about to become more serious. Informed of this event, I left Lucca with the utmost expedition, and presented myself at the advanced posts. Having made known my powers, I immediately stipulated a convention by which the French troops were to give up the posts and fortresses they occupied, and return to France; I immediately gave orders to the garrisons of Leghorn and Tuscany to fall back upon Genoa.

A few days afterwards, in virtue of the same powers, I treated with Lieutenant-general Lecchi, the King of Naples' governor in Tuscany, for the evacuation of the Roman states. This new convention stipulated the giving up of the castle of St. Angelo and of Cività Vecchia to the Neapolitans. The French garrisons were to be conveyed by sea to Marseilles at the expense of the King of Naples.

Thus ended my mission in Italy, the termination of which I so impatiently desired, in order to re-enter my country, at that time in so wretched a condition: inundated by foreign troops, who were advancing nearer and nearer towards the capital, the approaches even to which Napoleon was reduced to defend. At such a distance I had some difficulty in accounting for the progress of certain events; thus, why the two allied armies again separated after having beaten Napoleon at La Rothière, instead of marching direct and without delay to Paris. Such a movement would have anticipated by two months the events which occurred at the close of March, and consequently avoided many disasters, and prevented the useless effusion of much blood and many tears. But the allies had nothing ready at that time in Paris; and the cabinets, who were not inclined for the regency, prolonged, doubtless with much regret, the calamities of war, in order to form other plans and produce different results. As to the congress of Châtillon, I imagined it would terminate as that of Prague had done. Everything announced that the catastrophe of this grand drama would soon arrive.

Before setting off for France I proceeded to Volta, the headquarters of the prince viceroy. He had effected his retreat upon the Mincio, and, upon the King of Naples' declaration of war against France, had fought with the Austrians one of those battles which, having no real decisive effect on politics, is only productive of military glory. I had two private conferences with the viceroy, in which I represented to him that fighting battles was now the more useless, as everything would be decided within the environs of Paris. I dissuaded him from obeying the Emperor's orders to march the army of Italy upon the Vosges; first, because it was now too late for a junction to be effected; and, secondly, because by crossing the Alps he would for ever lose his Lombardian possessions. Eugene owned to me that

Murat had made him a secret proposal to unite their forces, for the purpose of sharing Italy, after having sent away the French troops, and that he had rejected this absurd offer; that his declaration of war had placed him, Eugene, in the greatest embarrassment; and that he feared he could hold out no longer, if Murat should serve the Austrians with any degree of zeal. I made him easy upon this point, being well acquainted with the uncertain character of Murat, and knowing, besides, that his wishes for the independence of Italy had already been counteracted by the allies.

I was at Eugene's headquarters when Faypoult, formerly prefect, a man in whom Murat placed some confidence, arrived. He had been sent by Napoleon to Murat, as well as to Eugene, with the intelligence of the recent successes he had obtained at Briey and at Montereau. These advantages were purposely exaggerated for the double object of keeping up Eugene's hopes and damping Murat's zeal in the cause of his new allies. Count Tacher, one of Eugene's aides-de-camp, whom he had dispatched to Napoleon, had returned also with the utmost expedition, and reported to him the very words which the Emperor, intoxicated with some brilliant but transient success, had addressed to him: "Return to Eugene," said Napoleon; "tell him how I have trimmed these scoundrels; they are a set of rabble whom I will whip out of my dominions." The most general joy prevailed at headquarters. I took Eugene aside, and told him that such boastings ought to inspire with confidence only such as were mad enthusiasts, but that they could have no effect upon reasonable people; that these latter saw in its full extent the imminent danger which threatened the imperial throne; that arms were not wanting to defend the government, but rather the sentiment to set them in action; and that by separating himself from the nation, the Emperor by his despotism, had destroyed all public spirit. I gave Eugene some advice, and began my route for Lyons, leaving Italy a prey, so to speak, to four different armies, the French, Austrian, Neapolitan, and English—for this time Lord Bentinck had really landed at Leghorn, from that place having signified to Eliza that he acknowledged neither the authority of Napoleon nor hers as grand duchess, and in this manner dictating the law to Tuscany, he formed a junction with the Neapolitans, who occupied Bologna, Modena, and Reggio. Thus I left Italy in a most uncertain and embarrassed situation; nothing could be then more precarious than our possessions beyond the Alps. Neither the viceroy nor Murat—and certainly neither of them was deficient in valour—had sufficient political talents, nor even consistency enough in the eyes of the Italians, to arrest the wreck of our power in Italy, especially as both rulers proceeded in opposite directions.

To own the truth, I was much more troubled about the alarming condition of France than the tottering situation of the viceroy, or even of Murat; in fact, the fate of Italy was about to depend on the result of the contest then proceeding in so vigorous a manner between Napoleon and the allied monarchs, who endeavoured to establish themselves between the Seine and the Marne.

It was in the midst of these circumstances that I

entered Lyons towards the beginning of March. Everything there was in a state of confusion and uncertainty as to the result of the campaign. The prefect, the commissary-general of police, and some subordinate generals were disposed to defend Lyons, as a consequence of the universal persuasion that Paris would also be defended; and it was by throwing up earthworks that a pretence was made to arrest the enemy's progress before the second city of the Empire, which was threatened by the arrival of a reinforcement of 45,000 Germans. Augereau was invited; a general who depreciated Napoleon, but possessed little skill as a politician, and who in this crisis, yielding to evil counsels, could discover no benefit for France, except by identifying her with his destiny. A line of fortifications was hastily traced, and all kinds of means employed to impart a national character to this popular resistance. But the same inclinations, then discovered at Paris, the seat of government, prevailed also at Lyons. The prefect Bondy did his utmost to animate the patriotism of the lethargic Lyonnese, which was extinguished by the same causes which made it languish in other parts of France.

The very night of my arrival I was admitted to a conference with the chief public functionaries, which took place every evening at the house of Marshal Augereau. I perceived from the first moment that all which bore any character of factious desperation obtained no favour from any party but the prefect, a few of the general officers who had arrived with a corps from the army of Aragon, and Saulnier, commissary-general of police. I made a frank confession of the defection of the King of Naples, and of the probability that a million of men were about to penetrate France, which it was no longer possible to save, except by some master-stroke of policy. I saw that my opinions as well as my disclosures were in opposition to the functionaries, who, urged by their zeal for the Emperor, were disposed to undergo the horrors of a siege. They did not disguise the mortification which my presence gave them, and I soon perceived that they had received secret instructions in regard to me. Augereau having refused to listen to the only prospect of deliverance which was concentred in the interests of the Revolution, of which, nevertheless, he was a zealous partisan, concluded by concurring with the measure proposed by the prefect and commissary-general of police, the object of which was to compel me to quit Lyons, and to reside provisionally at Valence. I gave way, though with reluctance, and took the road to Dauphiné, casting at the same time an impatient glance towards that of Paris, which was the only one whereon I could have wished to have travelled post.

It was at Valence that I learnt the arrival of Count d'Artois at Vesoul, and the terrors of Napoleon at the first daybreak of royalism which had just burst forth at Troyes, in Champagne. I learnt a few days after, and in succession, the arrival of the Duke d'Angoulême at the headquarters of Lord Wellington; the loss of the battle of Orthez by Soult; the loss of the battle of Laon by Napoleon; the entry of the Duke d'Angoulême into Bordeaux. How much deeper my regret then became, to behold myself more than a hundred leagues from the capital, where a political revolution

was of necessity to be expected as a consequence of
so many disasters! The occupation of Lyons by the
Austrians almost immediately followed; and Marshal
Augereau withdrawing his headquarters to Valence, I
departed for Avignon, in order to wait the issue of
events, and in full readiness to hurry to Paris at the
first signal. But surrounded by different *corps d'armée*,
reduced to the uncertainty of conjectures, and to depend upon vague rumours by the interruption of the
couriers and by the difficulty of communication, I
doubtless hesitated too long in taking the decisive step.
How much I subsequently repented of not having
clandestinely proceeded to Paris through the centre of
France, which was at that time free from foreign invasion! A single consideration was calculated to dissuade me. I had reason to fear that secret instructions referring to me were transmitted to each prefect
individually.

I was residing at Avignon, uninvested with any
political character, and I inhabited the same apartment
in which the unfortunate Brune was assassinated a year
afterwards. There I found the public mind so greatly
opposed to Napoleon that I was enabled to publish
notice that I would receive all the public bodies and
constituted authorities, to whom I announced the
approaching downfall of the imperial government, and
added that Murat, in Upper Italy, was labouring for
the good cause. To a greater extent than at Lyons
and Valence, an inclination to see the fall of Napoleon,
followed by some kind of settled authority, was manifested at Avignon. At length the news of the events
of the 31st of March reached me. Compelled to make

a long circuit, in order to follow the road of Toulouse and Limoges, I did not arrive at Paris till towards the beginning of April; but it was already too late. The establishment of a provisional government, of which I ought to have constituted a part; the deposition of Napoleon, which I had myself aspired to pronounce, but which was effected without my aid; in short, the restoration of the Bourbons, which I had opposed in order to substitute my plan of a regency—annihilated all my projects and replunged me into a state of political nullity in the presence of princes to whom I had given matter of offence. I was aware that clemency might be in harmony with the goodness of their hearts; but I was also aware that it was not less incompatible with the principle of legitimacy.

I subsequently heard this double question mooted : If the Duke of Otranto had been at Paris, would he have formed a part of the provisional government ? and, if he had done so, what would have been the result of the revolution of the 31st of March ?

I owe in this place some elucidations to my contemporaries, relative to secret circumstances which I have not judged fitting to parcel out in my narrative, in order to exhibit them to the light in a better form ; for there are some confessions which are only to be justified by conjunctures, and which ought not to be hazarded except at favourable opportunities.

I will admit, in the first instance, that, impressed with the necessity of preventing a European reaction, and of saving France by the assistance of France, the events of 1809—that is to say, the war with Austria and the attack of the English on Antwerp—supplied only the first steps towards the execution of a plan of revolution, the object of which was the dethronement of the Emperor. I confess, moreover, that I was the moving soul of this plan, which was alone capable of reconciling us with Europe, and of bringing us back to a reasonable state of government. It required the concurrence of two statesmen, one directing the cabinet of Vienna, and the other that of St. James; I mean Prince Metternich and the Marquis of Wellesley, to whom I had sent for that purpose M. de Fagan, an old officer in the Irish regiment of Dillon, and whose insinuating character was adapted for so delicate a mission.

Before proceeding to overtures of this description, I had not neglected, in the interior of France, to obtain the co-operation of the only man who was indispensable to me. It will be easily guessed that I refer to Prince Talleyrand. Our reconciliation had taken place in a conference at Surêne, at the house of the Princess of Vaudémont. From the first moment of interview, our political ideas sympathised; and a kind of coalition was established between our reciprocal future plans. I had not, however, been able to escape from the epigrammatic causticity of my noble and new ally, who, being questioned by his intimate friends after our interview as to what his opinion was with regard to me, replied, " True ! I have seen Fouché ; he is *papier doré sur tranche*."

The observation was of course brought to me. I did not show that I was offended at it ; political considerations in my case have always superseded the irritability of self-love.

I had been equally aware of the necessity of placing myself in direct communication with one of the most influential of the senators, M. de S——, who was himself in close connection with the secretaryship of state, by means of Maret, an old fellow-prisoner.

An acquisition of this description was so much the more valuable to me, inasmuch as since the disgrace of Bourrienne I did not possess in the secretary's office any other persons than mere subalterns in my interest, who often suffered the thread of the higher class of intrigues to escape from their grasp. But how was I to obtain the friendship of a person whom I had reckoned for a considerable time among the number of my declared antagonists? The senatorship of Bourges had just become vacant; that I resolved should be the price of our reconciliation; I manœuvred in consequence; S—— obtained it; and from that moment I gained a friend in the senate, and, as it were, an additional eye for ever on the watch in the cabinet of Napoleon.

Another individual was requisite to my plans—Marshal M——, chief of the gendarmerie. Up to that time he had been opposed to me. Appointed to the command of a *corps d'armée* in Catalonia, he was unprovided, although in high employment, with the necessary funds for his outfit. I knew his embarrassment, and sent him, by the advice of a friend, a little hoard of eighty thousand francs, which it was in my power to employ, and for the transfer of which I had the Emperor's authority. In this manner, in the space of a very few months, I made friends of all enemies. I had two offices on my hands: the home department

and that of the police. I had the gendarmerie at my
disposal, and a multitude of spies at my command; as
a lever of public opinion, I had also the immense
patronage of the old republicans, as well as of the determined royalists, who found a shield of protection in
the maintenance of my credit. Such were the elements
of my power, when Napoleon, engaged in the double
war of Spain and Austria, and thenceforth considered
as an incorrigible disturber, appeared to me to be involved in so inextricable a position that I concerted
the plan which I have disclosed in a preceding passage.
Whether it was that Napoleon's sagacity divined what
I was about, or that indiscretion inherent in the native
character of Frenchmen had awakened his suspicions
(for as to being betrayed, I certainly was not), my
disgrace, which was almost sudden, as I have related
at the end of the events of 1809, postponed for five
years the subversion of the imperial throne. And it
was under the protection of feelings such as these, and
under the support of a body of public opinion, which
had never abandoned me either at the time of my
disgrace or of my exile; it was, moreover, while fortified by the reputation of a statesman, who, with the
precision of cool and calculating foresight, had prophe-
sied the fall of Napoleon, that I found myself overtaken
by the events of the 31st of March. If I had been at
Paris at that time, the weight of my influence, and
my perfect knowledge of the secret bearings of parties,
would have enabled me to impart an entirely contrary
direction to the bias of those extraordinary events. My
preponderance and prompt decision would have prevailed
over the more mysterious and tardy influence of M. de

Talleyrand. That distinguished individual was incapable
of making any progress, unless when yoked with me
to the same car. I should have revealed to him all
the ramifications of my political plan; and in spite of
the odious policy of Savary, the ridiculous administration of Cambacérès, the lieutenant-generalship of the
puppet Joseph, and the total prostration of the senate,
we should have rekindled fresh life in the *caput mortuum*
of the Revolution; and degraded patriots would have
no longer thought, as they have done when it was too
late, of preserving nothing but themselves. Impelled
by me, they would, before the intervention of foreign
powers, have pronounced the downfall of Napoleon, and
proclaimed a regency, according to the forms which
I had laid down. This *dénouement* was the only one
capable of imparting security to the Revolution and its
principles. But the fates had otherwise decreed.[1]
Napoleon himself conspired against his own blood.
What shifts, what pretexts, did he not employ to keep
me at a distance from the capital, where he even
feared the presence of his son and of his wife; for
the order, which he left to Cambacérès, to cause the
immediate departure of the Empress and the King of
Rome at the earliest appearance of the allies, cannot,
without great misrepresentation, be imputed to any

[1] Rather say, that in spite of so many intrigues, of all the
military power of Bonaparte, and of the protracted aberrations
of European policy, Providence at length determined that our
native princes should resume the sceptre of France. We are
now at length consoled for so many wars and calamities by the
reign of Charles X., which the wise foresight of Louis XVIII.
enabled him to prepare for our advantage.—*Note by the French
Editor.*

other motive than that of averting such a revolution as might be effected by the establishment of a national regency. After having suffered himself to be juggled out of his capital by the Emperor Alexander, he wished to have recourse to the regency as a last shift. But it was then too late. The combinations of M. de Talleyrand had prevailed, and it was when a provisional government was already framed that I arrived to make my appearance, before the Restoration.

What a position, just Heaven, was mine! Impelled by the consciousness of the many claims which I possessed to power, and withheld by a sentiment of remorse; impressed at the same time with the grandeur of a spectacle perfectly new to the generation which surveyed it—the public entrance of a son of France, who, after being the sport of Fortune for twenty-five years, again saw, in the midst of acclamations and universal rejoicing, the capital of his ancestors adorned with the standards and emblems of royalty. Moved, I confess, by the affecting picture of royal affability, intermingling with royalist intoxication, I was subjugated by the feeling.[1] I neither dissembled my regret nor my repentance: I revealed them in full senate, while I urged the senators to send a deputation to his Royal Highness; at the same time declaring myself

[1] Another effect of the same Providence. What a sublime and affecting spectacle was that return of a son of France on the immortal day of the 12th of April, 1814! That spectacle affected the soul of a regicide; the feeling of remorse overcomes him; he recognises in the great catastrophe the hand of Divine Providence, which prepared, ten years before, the way for the mild and paternal rule of Charles X., of that chivalrous king who was saluted by the acclamations of the Parisians on the very threshold of our restoration.—*Note by the French Editor.*

unworthy to form a part of it, and of appearing in my own person before the representative of monarchy, and withstanding to the utmost of my influence such of my colleagues as wished to impose restraints upon the Bourbons.

A month had not yet elapsed when, tormented by the secret disquietude with which the residence of Napoleon at the isle of Elba inspired me, a residence which I foresaw might prove fatal to France, I took up my pen and addressed him in the following letter, which I surrender to the impartial judgment of history.

"SIRE,—When France and a portion of Europe were at your feet, I never flinched from telling you the truth. Now that you are in misfortune I entertain more fear of wounding your sensibility while I address you in the language of sincerity; but it is a duty which I owe to you, because it is useful, and even necessary, to your own welfare.

"You have accepted the isle of Elba and its sovereignty for your retreat. I lend an attentive ear to all which is dropped on the subject of that sovereignty and of that isle. I think it is my duty to assure you that the situation of that isle in Europe is not adapted for you, and that the title of sovereign over some acres of land is still less fitted for an individual who has been the master of a mighty Empire.

"I entreat you to weigh well these two considerations, and you will perceive that they are well founded. The isle of Elba is at a very short distance from Africa, Greece, and Spain; it nearly touches the shores of Italy and France. From that island, tides, winds, and a little felucca may suddenly bring you in conjunction with countries most exposed to agitation, to chances, and revolutions. There is stability nowhere; and in this general condition of national ductility a genius like yours may always excite disquietude and suspicion among European powers. Without being criminal you may be accused, and without being criminal you may also do mischief, since a state of alarm is a great evil for governments as well as for nations.

" A king who ascends the throne of France must desire to reign exclusively by justice; but you know well what numerous passions besiege a throne, and with what ingenuity malice gives the colour of truth to defamation.

" The titles which you preserve by constantly re-calling what you have lost to your mind, can only serve to aggravate the bitterness of your regret; they will not so much assume the shape of power in ruins, as of a stimulant mockery of grandeur passed away. I will go farther : without doing you honour, they will expose you to the greatest danger. It will be said that you only preserve your titles with a view to the preservation of your pretensions ; it will be said that the rocky island of Elba is the *point d'appui* on which you will fix your lever in order a second time to shake the system of the social frame.

" Permit me, Sire, to express with frankness all that passes in my mind. It will be more glorious and more consolatory for you to live in the character of a private individual ; and the more secure an asylum for an individual like yourself is the United States of America. There you will recommence your existence in the midst of a nation still in its youth, and which can admire your genius without standing in dread of its effects. You will be under the protection of law, equally impartial and inviolable, like everything else in the country of Franklin, Washington, and Jefferson. You will prove to the Americans that, if you were born among them, you would have thought and voted as they have done, and that you would have preferred their virtues and their liberty to all the sovereignties on earth."

This letter, which I am disposed to consider as creditable to my character, was subsequently submitted, by the royalists, to the Count d'Artois, in conjunction with the following letter, which I addressed to his Royal Highness:

"MONSEIGNEUR,—It has been my wish to offer a last service to the Emperor Napoleon, whose minister I was for ten years. I think it my duty to communicate to your Royal Highness the letter which I have just written. His welfare cannot be a matter of indifference to me, since it has excited the generous pity of the powers which have conquered him. But the greatest of all interests for France and Europe, that to which all others ought to give way, is the tranquillity of nations and governments after so many storms and misfortunes; and that repose, even though established upon solid bases, will never be sufficiently guaranteed, will never, in short, be permanently enjoyed, as long as Napoleon remains in the isle of Elba. Napoleon, residing on that rock, may be regarded, with respect to Italy, France, and the whole of Europe, with the same feelings as Vesuvius by the side of Naples. I see no place but the New World and the United States, in which he can be precluded from imparting renovated shocks of disturbance."

The prince, whose sagacity is certainly unquestionable, was enabled by this letter to judge, what he but imperfectly surmised before, that I was not to be reckoned among the adherents of Napoleon.

On being consulted by ministers and courtiers, I frequently repeated to them, " Be silent about the evils which have been done ; place yourselves at the head of the benefits which the last twenty-five years have created ; attribute all that is injurious to preceding governments, or still more justly to the force of events ; employ alternately the virtue which oppression has engendered, the energy which our discords have developed, and the talents which popular ferment has brought out. If the King do not make the nation his *point d'appui*, his authority will diminish, his courtiers will be reduced to the necessity of extorting barren tributes of homage on his behalf, which will be his ruin. Take care," I added, " not to touch upon the colour of the national cockade and flag ; that question is not yet entirely understood ; it is frivolous only in appearance, but it determines much ; it is under the question of its standards that the nation will rally ; the colour of a ribbon may also decide the colour of a future reign. A sacrifice like this, on the part of the King, resembles that made by Henry IV. to the ritual of the mass." It will be seen that in my advice I did not hesitate to constitute the King into a head of the Revolution, to which, by this measure, a guarantee much stronger than that of the charter itself would

be presented : my opinions, and the interests of my
country, as well as my own, prescribed this course.
But if, on the one hand, I possessed numerous partisans,
either among the royalists or among the men of the
Revolution, I had, on the other hand, against me the
Bonapartists and the relics of Savary's police.   The
latter represented me as devoured by chagrin at not
having been able to assist in the overthrow of an
edifice which I had indulged in erecting ; and as
hurrying to the legitimate throne, making a parade of
my remorse, and offering my services to the august
family which I had outraged, at any price which they
chose to fix.   The former, on the contrary, depicted
me as the only man calculated to maintain the security
of the Bourbons ; as a most sagacious minister, capable
of disposing of a portion of the elements of the political
body.   I do not think that I deceive myself when
I affirm that such was the prevailing opinion in the
Faubourg St. Germain.

I commenced a correspondence with several important personages of the court ; among others, with
my friend Malouet, who, since his exile at Tours, had
been appointed by the King to the office of marine.
All the letters which I wrote to him were placed
under the King's eye.   I recommended to him, as
well as all those who came on his Majesty's behalf,
to ask my advice, not to establish a warfare between
old and new opinions, between the nation and the
emigrants ; but there was not energy enough to follow
any part of my recommendation ; and the torrent of
opposite opinions was suffered to prevail.

Towards the end of June, the King had ordered

M. de Blacas to have a conference with me; accordingly I had a visit from that minister, whom I coldly received. I knew him to be surrounded by persons who were my enemies, and who enjoyed no credit with the public; such as Savary, Bourrienne, Dubois (the old prefect of police), and a certain Madame P——, a woman in bad repute and very notorious; I knew that the whole of them, united, exerted themselves to delude and circumvent M. de Blacas. His unconciliatory manner and his inexperience in business, joined to the aversion with which his cabal inspired me, prevented him from fully comprehending me, while it precluded me from yielding him my entire confidence. However, as Louis XVIII. would be informed that I had shown reserve and distrust in my communications with his minister, I took up my pen, and the next day wrote a detailed letter to M. de Blacas, under the conviction that the King would be shortly made acquainted with it. I told him that the agitation of France was caused among the people by a dread of the re-establishment of feudal rights; by disquietude respecting their acquisitions, on the part of the possessors of emigrant property; by a doubt as to their personal security on the part of those who had taken a high tone in declaring either for the Republic or for Bonaparte; by the loss of, and regret for, so many prospects of glory and fortune on the part of the army; and, finally, by the astonishment produced on the publication of the charter (which the King had chosen to characterise as an emanation from his hereditary power) on the minds of the constitutionalists. Among these causes, the most dangerous of all was precisely that which all

the wisdom of the King and his ministers could not
entirely foresee nor exclude from operation. I refer
to the discontent of the army, and I explained its
motives. Among others, I stated that an army, and
more especially an army raised by conscription, always
imbibes the general feeling of the nation in which it
lives, and that it always ends with being either
contented or discontented, like the nation, and in
conjunction with the nation. With this cause of discontent, I added, the genius of Bonaparte still interfered. "A nation," I observed, "in which, for five and
twenty years, opinions and feelings have been thrown
into so strong an action as to impart disturbance to the
universe, cannot, without long gradations of interval,
return to a tranquil and peaceable condition : to attempt to stop the force of that activity would be
impolitic ; new fuel must be found for its rapacity ;
the boundless careers of industry in all the branches
of commerce, of the arts, of the sciences, and of the
discoveries which they have effected, must be thrown
open and enlarged as much as possible ; in short,
everything which extends the faculties and the power
of man. The nineteenth century has scarcely begun ;
it ought to bear the name of Louis XVIII., as the
seventeenth bore the name of Louis XIV." I made
corresponding efforts to plead the cause of the liberty
of the press and individual liberty ; and I concluded
in the following terms : " Great numbers of Frenchmen,
who devoted themselves to participate in the misfortunes of the Bourbons, as they had in their prosperity,
have returned with the dynasty of their kings; they
can no longer pretend to the re-acquisition of their

estates without exciting violent troubles and a civil war. Be it so; let one of the king's ministers, inspired by the logic of a reflecting mind, and imbued with the eloquence of a soul alive to what is due to great misfortunes and great virtues, ask of the two chambers the allotment of an annual sum for the purpose of indemnifying calamities and privations, so deserving of succour, at the hands of a feeling and heroic nation. I will take upon myself to predict that such a project mooted in the chambers would be passed into a law by acclamation."

But such counsels could only be expected to be fruitless, as they resulted from an individual placed beyond the sphere of power. Supported and urged by a numerous party of royalists, the ramifications of which extended as far as the court, I confess that I was suffered to have glimpses of office, for the purpose of exerting an influence over events; but I had opposed to me M. de Blacas, who had subjected himself to the crafty influence of Savary; and the latter, being sold to Bonaparte, trembled at the idea of a door of access to the King's councils being opened to me. I had, moreover, too many momentous interests, and especially rival pretensions, opposed to me. I did not disguise from myself that the main argument which was constantly reiterated against me was undeniable. I felt my real position, and departed with my family for my château of Ferrières, whence I proposed to cast an observing eye upon events. It was necessary to oppose the wishes of my friend in order to station myself in this manner at a distance from the capital.

I was convinced beforehand that the feeble and incompetent individuals who grasped the helm of government would continue to follow erroneous maxims of policy and to impart a false direction to affairs.

What serious reflections, therefore, assailed my mind with regard to the equivocal and incoherent position of the new government! As a statesman, it could not escape my notice that a restoration had been effected without a revolution, since all the wheel-marks of the imperial government still subsisted, and there was nothing changed, if I may so express it, but the individuality of power. And, in fact, what could be found after the lapse of twenty years in an immovable condition? Clergy, nobility, institutions, municipalities, hereditary proprietorships, nothing had escaped the general overthrow. The Bourbons, in reascending the throne, found support in public inclination, but not in national interest. Such was the origin of the commotion, the first indications of which already began to exhibit themselves to my eyes. France was prostrated between the votaries and adversaries of the Restoration. Louis XVIII. reigned over a suffering and divided nation. All the favourers of imperial despotism, all the individuals who had distinguished themselves in our revolutionary crisis, feared to be obliged to share their dignities with the ancient nobility. They had required securities, and they had obtained them, or imagined they had obtained them, by that declaration which was solicited from the King, and promulgated by that prince before his entrance into his capital.

But, on the other hand, the reverses of Napoleon had succeeded each other with so much rapidity that the possessors of superior employments and great incomes had not sufficient time to retrench the luxury of their establishments. When the Bourbons were recalled, some calculation was necessary on their part, and it was indispensable to put a sudden stop to the unlimited course of their expenses. Here was a plentiful source of discontent and irritation among the upper ranks of the social order. Another still more alarming cause of instability for the new government was to be found in the as yet unmodified scale of the army. It had not received its *congé* (an enormous error), for all the old soldiers and all the prisoners who were restored to France were imbued with a spirit at variance with the Restoration, and devoted to the interests of the ex-Emperor.

The King, instead of accepting the charter, had granted it—another subject of discontent to that great body of Frenchmen whose political era dated from the Revolution. The charter, it is true, confirmed titles, honours, and in some respects places. It legalised the acquisition of national property; but that was not entirely satisfactory for so many restless and prejudiced individuals. The charter, moreover, had a multitude of objectors. According to one party, it was not sufficiently liberal; according to the partisans of the ancient *régime*, the old constitution of the kingdom was preferable. To this state of things must be added the laxity and uncertainty of the ministers, who, without being either royalists or patriots, took it into their heads that they could render France ministerial. The general apprehension must also be borne in mind which was entertained of the congress of Vienna, which, while employed in the reconstruction of Europe, menaced such states as had become the seat of revolution with subjection to an anti-revolutionary *régime ;* in this manner the interests produced by twenty-five years of troubles were thrown into alarm. The royalists enfeebled and divided their party in the same proportion as their adversaries, shuddering at the very name of Bourbon, exhibited more pertinacity in disputing their rights. The possibility of Napoleon's return, considered at first as a chimera, became the favourite idea of the army; plots were formed and the royal police countermined. It is easy to conceive that, having occupied so many elevated posts in the state, and still preserving such numerous links of connection with public affairs, and with so devoted a body of clients in the capital, my observations extended over all the intrigues which were concocting.

I was in this disposition of mind when an individual, who had possessed much influence, and who was then on the point of losing it, wrote to induce me to make one of a secret committee, the object of which was a counter-revolutionary result. I wrote this answer upon the letter, which did not remain concealed. " I never work *en serres chaudes ;* I decline doing anything which is incapable of assuming a dignified air."

In the meantime affiliations were forming; and influential men were contracting political engagements to each other. It was soon obvious to me that the state was proceeding towards a crisis, and that the adherents of Napoleon had coalesced in order to accelerate its advent. But no success was possible without my co-operation; I was anything but decided to concede it to a party against whom I entertained a grudge of long standing. Repeated applications were made to me, and many plans suggested ; all tended to the dethronement of the King, and subsequent proclamation either of another dynasty or of a provisional republic. A military party made me a proposal of offering the dictatorship to Eugene Beauharnais. I wrote to Eugene, under the impression that the matter had already assumed a substantial form ; but I only received a vague answer. In the interim all the interests of the Revolution congregated round myself and Carnot, whose letter to the King produced a general sensation which testified still more efficaciously against the unskilfulness of the ministry. The affair of Excelmans gave additional strength to the persuasion that a considerable party, the focus of which was in Paris, desired the re-establishment of Napoleon and the imperial government.

When, as winter approached, I returned to the capital, the royal government appeared to me undermined by two parties, hostile to legitimacy, and itself thenceforward without resource. The King, by his good pleasure, had commissioned the Duke d'Havre to supersede M. de Blacas in his confidential communications with me. The true nobility of this nobleman's character, as well as his frank deportment, procured him my entire confidence. I opened my whole heart to him ; and found myself disposed to a freedom of communication which I had never before known. Never had I in any moment of my life felt so little inclination to reserve ; never before did I find myself endowed with an eloquence so true and a sensibility so intense as those which accompanied the recital of the circumstances by which I had been fatally induced to vote for the death of Louis XVI. I can say it with truth that this confession extorted from my feelings was imbued at once with remorse and inspiration. I cannot, indeed, at this time recall to mind without profound emotion the tears which I observed in the eyes of my virtuous interlocutor—of that illustrious duke, who was a personification of true and loyal French chivalry.

Our political conversations were minuted, for the purpose of being subsequently communicated to the King. But the wounds of the state were beyond remedy, and a great crisis was inevitable. Placed, on the one hand, between the Bourbons, who only conceded to me a semi-confidence, whose system closed all the avenues of power and honour against me, and with regard to whom I was in a false position, while at the same time I had no kind of engagement towards them; and on the other hand, between the party to which I was indebted for my fortune, and to which a community of opinions and interests attracted me, at the moment when a prolonged state of doubt on my part might have isolated me from both, I threw myself entirely into the arms of the latter. It was not against the Bourbons that I resolved within myself to wage war, but against the dogma of legitimacy. I was, however, thwarted in my combinations by the existence of a Bonapartist party, which, exerting all its influence over the army, kept us all in a state of dependence. It was my former colleague Thibaudeau who first disclosed to me the progress of the faction in the isle of Elba, whose principal agent he certainly was. I saw that there was no time to lose; I moreover considered that Napoleon would at all events serve as a rallying point for the army, reserving in my own mind the intention of putting him down afterwards, which appeared to me so much the more easy, as the Emperor, to my view, was nothing but a worn-out actor, whose first performance could not be re-enacted. I then consented that Thibaudeau should make overtures to some intimates of Napoleon, and I allowed Regnault, Cambacérès, Davoust, S——, B——, L——, C——, B—— de la M——, M. de D—— to be admitted to our conference. But I exacted concessions and securities, refusing to unite with that party, if their chief, abjuring despotism, did not adopt a system of liberal government. Our coalition was cemented by the reciprocal promise of an equal participation of power, either in the ministry or in the provisional government at the moment of the explosion. According to the plan arranged with Thibaudeau, I hastened to dispatch my emissary, J——, to Murat, to induce him to declare himself the arbiter of Italy; at the same time, the grand committee dispatched Dr. R——, to the isle of Elba. Lyons and Grenoble became the two pivots of the enterprise in the South; in the North a military movement, directed by D'Erlon and Lefèvre - Desnouettes was to determine the flight or capture of the royal family, which in their turn would occasion the formation of a provisional government, of which I was to form a part, with Carnot, Caulaincourt, Lafayette, and N——. To resume the supreme power in the midst of the general confusion, such was the drift of our combinations. Solicited to reconcile himself with

Napoleon, and hoping to remain master of Italy, Murat, although the ally of Austria, was the first to take up arms on treacherous pretences. This show of hostilities apparently directed against Louis XVIII., caused great sensation in the King's council. Thirty thousand men were immediately marched towards Grenoble and the Alps, or rather thrown in Napoleon's way. The adroitness of this manœuvre was not duly appreciated. In the meanwhile the disembarkation of the Emperor took place at Cannes; and it may be alleged in proof that we are not a nation of conspirators that for the preceding fortnight the overthrow of the Bourbons had been publicly avowed by all parties, and had been a subject of universal conversation. The court alone persevered in refusing to see what was as clear as the sun to everybody else.

Before touching on the events of the 20th of March, let us throw a retrospective glance over the past. It will have been seen that I had at first no intention of joining the party of revolt; I had only desired to induce the cabinet of the Tuileries to grasp the reins of the Revolution, and guide them with a vigorous hand through the midst of surrounding obstacles. I think I may avow, without arrogating too much to myself, that I alone was capable of heading and superintending such a system. At the court, in Paris, and in the provinces, I was selected by all parties as fittest for this bold attempt. I had to contend against rivalries, which my predecessors appeared to furnish with invincible arms; but up to the latest moment I never ceased seeking for some *mezzo-termine*, some mode of conciliation, which might have excused me from recurring to the desperate expedient of the Emperor's return. It has been seen how in yielding to it I yielded to the necessity of the case. It was only at the moment of Napoleon's landing that I was thoroughly informed of the fatal combination which brought him back to our shores. Its object embraced three distinct subdivisions: the return of Napoleon to Paris; the captivity of the King and the royal family; and the smuggling of Maria Louisa and her son from Vienna. The first subdivision of the plan was the execution of that which was least liable to obstruction, considering the disposition to defection manifested by almost all the troops. The same could not be said of the seizure of the King and the royal family; for that purpose it would have been necessary for an army to have suddenly marched on the capital, an expedient which precluded the possibility of a secret; and it was on that account that the attempt of Lefèvre-Desnouettes failed. As to the smuggling of Maria Louisa and her son, that also was attempted and had nearly succeeded. Shrinking with a kind of horror from the idea of sacrificing to a military *coup de main* the family of a monarch who had shown so much generosity in my case as to take my advice, I requested an audience of the King as soon as I learnt that Napoleon was marching upon Lyons. This interview was not granted me; but two gentlemen came, on his Majesty's behalf, to receive my communications. I apprised them of the danger which Louis XVIII. incurred, and I engaged to stop the progress of the fugitive from the isle of Elba, if the court would consent to the terms which I required. My proposals resulted from the actual nature

of the events which were in the act of being unfolded.
A patriotic party not less inimical than myself to imperial despotism had just completed its organisation;
it had for its chiefs MM. de Broglie, Lafayette,
d'Argenson, Flaugergues, Benjamin Constant, &c.
They had agreed to require of the King the dismissal
of his ministers; the nomination of forty new members
selected from men of the Revolution to the chamber
of peers; and that of M. de Lafayette to the command
of the national guard. It was, moreover, proposed
to send into the provinces patriotic missionaries, in
order to stop the defection of the troops, and kindle
a national energy in their hearts. I was no stranger
to the motions of this party, by means of which I
subsequently became minister. I was, however, aware
that it was indispensable to rally all the elements of
the Revolution in order to oppose them in one body
to the power of the sword; that it was necessary to
oppose one name against another, and the charm of
those recollections, which the heir of the first mover
of the Revolution would excite in the hearts of free-
men, against that of a glory which, by its sudden
resurrection, dazzled the genius of the camp. When
the King's ministers desired to know what were the
means which I proposed to employ in order to prevent
Napoleon from reaching Paris, I refused to communicate them, being disinclined to disclose them to any
person but the King himself; but I protested that I
was sure of success. The two chief conditions which
I exacted was the appointment of the first prince of
the blood to the lieutenant-generalship of the kingdom and the consignment of power and the direction

of affairs into my hands and those of my party. This experiment of my political measures was declined, and we therefore found ourselves necessitated in some sort to second the impulse of the party which I had wished to paralyse; conceiving myself, besides, in a condition to substitute a more popular government in the room of that which Napoleon threatened to revive.

The alarm in the palace of the Tuileries hourly increasing in proportion as the march became more rapid and more secure, the court again turned its attention to my assistance. Some royalists interfered to obtain at least for me an interview with Monsieur, the King's brother, at the house of Count d'Escars. I only required permission to go clandestinely to the château by night, the publicity of such a proceeding being otherwise calculated to compromise my influence with my party. Everything was regulated accordingly. Monsieur did not allow me to wait long; he was only accompanied by the Count d'Escars. The affability of this prince, his condescending deportment, his eager address, in which solicitude for the destinies of France and of his family was depicted; to sum up all, his generous and affecting language touched my heart and doubled my regret that an interview of so vital an importance was decided upon too late. I declared with grief to this frank and loyal prince that there was no longer time, and that it was now impossible to serve the King's cause. It was at the conclusion of an interview which will never be erased from my mind that, subjugated by the charm of so august a confidence, and finding in the painful conviction of my own powerlessness a sudden inspiration of hope, I exclaimed, as

I took leave of the prince, "Take measures to save the King, and I will take steps to save the monarchy."

Who could have imagined that, after communications of so lofty an importance, there should almost immediately be set on foot against me and against my liberty, a kind of plot—for plot it was, and a plot totally at variance with the genuine sentiments of the magnanimous sovereign and his noble brother. Its authors I will reveal. But, whatever may be its cause, I was sitting, without any distrust, in my hotel, when some agents of the Parisian police, at the head of which Bourrienne had just been placed, suddenly made their appearance, accompanied by gendarmes to arrest me. Having timely intelligence, I hastily took measures for my escape. The agents of police had already proceeded to active search in my apartments, when the gendarmes, commissioned to execute the order of the new prefect, presented themselves before me. These men, who had so long obeyed my orders, not daring to lay their hands on my person, contented themselves with giving me their written authority. I took the paper, opened it, and confidently said, "This order is not regular; stay where you are while I go and protest it." I entered my closet, seated myself at my desk, and began to write. I then rose with a paper in my hand, and making a sudden turn I precipitately descended into my garden by a secret door; there I found a ladder attached to a wall contiguous to the hotel of Queen Hortense. I lightly climbed it; one of my people raised the ladder, which I took and let fall on its feet on the other side of the wall; this I quickly scaled, and descended with still more promptitude. I arrived, in the character of a fugitive, at the house of Hortense, who extended her arms to me; and, as if by some sudden transition of an Eastern tale, I suddenly found myself in the midst of the *élite* of the Bonapartists, in the headquarters of the party, where I found mirth and where my presence caused intoxication.

This impromptu circumstance completed the dissipation of that distrust which the party entertained towards me; and the same individuals who till then had considered me in the light of an almost acquired partisan of the Bourbons, now beheld in me nothing more than an enemy proscribed by the Bourbons.

Let it be here understood that political considerations had nothing to do with the attempt to arrest me. His Royal Highness Monsieur went so far as to say to some influential members of the second chamber that it was against his knowledge that the attempt had been made to arrest me, and that he would answer for the safety of my person.

This attempt was nothing but the result of an interested contrivance between Savary, Bourrienne, and B——; whatever might be the issue of the 20th of March, this triumvirate, or rather the three members of this *tripot*, had determined to secure to themselves the working of the machine, and they had convinced themselves that it was necessary to sacrifice me, in order that their ambitious cupidity might acquire a kind of guarantee and consideration.

If I had once fallen into their hands, what would they have done with me? It has been said that their object was to transfer me to Lille; but no! it was not

Lille. This I have learnt since; but it was to the castle of Saumur; and I repeat my question, what was the lot they intended for me there? If I may rely on discoveries that my return to power elicited, one of my enemies—for all the three were not capable of crime—would have caused my assassination, and subsequently imputed my death to the royalists, who would have borne the odium.

Such was my singular position that the departure of Louis XVIII. and the arrival of Napoleon were requisite to give me entire liberty. Being one of the first to obtain intelligence that the Tuileries was vacant, I learnt at the same time that Lavalette had sent an express to Fontainebleau, where Napoleon had just arrived, to apprise him of the King's departure. Madame Ham——, who had intrigued so much in producing this situation, was mortified that others should get the start of her, and, dispatching an express with orders to overtake the preceding one, obtained by that means the honour of conveying the first intelligence.

Carried onward by his soldiers and some portions of the populace, Napoleon resumed possession of the Tuileries in the midst of his partisans, who exhibited the most clamorous triumph. I was not present at first among the other dignitaries of the state, with whom he conversed on the present aspect of his affairs. But Napoleon sent for me. "So they wanted to carry you off," he said, as I approached him, " in order to prevent you from being useful to your country. Well! I now offer you an opportunity of doing her fresh service. The period is difficult, but your courage, as well as mine, is superior to the crisis. Accept once more the office of minister of police." I represented to him that the office of foreign affairs was more an object of my ambition than any other, persuaded as I was that I could in that quarter more than elsewhere do my country effectual service. "No," rejoined he, "take the duty of police. You have learnt to judge soundly of the state of the public mind; to divine, prepare, and direct the progress of events. You understand the tactics, the resources, and the pretensions of the various parties. The police is your *forte*." There was no way of receding. I gave him to understand in all its extent the dangerous position of affairs; and, as if he wished to engage me more deeply in his interest, he assured me that Austria and England, in order to balance the preponderance of Russia, secretly favoured his escape and return to France. Without giving credit to this assurance, I accepted the office.

The next day I learnt, through Regnault, who was devoted to me, that Bonaparte, always suspicious and distrustful in my case, would have wished to keep me out of the circle of government; but that he had yielded to the solicitations of Bassano, Caulaincourt, and of Regnault himself, and his chief partisans, who in disclosing their engagements with me, impressed upon his mind the importance of strengthening himself by my popularity and the adherence of the party which I directed.

Cambacérès, who foresaw the fatal issue of this new interlude, did not accept till after much hesitation the office of minister of justice; the portfolio of war was given to Davoust, who was much more attached to his fortune than to Napoleon.

Caulaincourt, in the conviction that no relationship could be established with foreign powers, at first refused the office for foreign affairs. Napoleon offered it to Molé, who declined having anything to do with it, and refused the home department at the same time. Too much devoted to the Emperor to leave him without a minister, Caulaincourt at length acceded. From hand to hand the home department at length passed into the possession of Carnot, a nomination which was considered as a national guarantee. The marine was given to the cynical and brutal Decrès, and the secretaryship of state to Bassano, notorious for the reputation of thinking with Napoleon's thoughts and seeing with his eyes. Out of deference to public opinion Savary was omitted; however, Moncey having refused the gendarmerie, it was given to him: he was at least so far in his proper place. Champagny and Montalivet, who had appeared invested with the highest employments when Napoleon, almost master of the world, did not stand in so vacillating a position, modestly contented themselves, the one with the superintendence of public buildings, and the other with that of the civil list. Bertrand, equally amiable, insinuating, and zealous, superseded Duroc in the function of grand marshal of the palace. Napoleon restored to their duty about his person almost all the chamberlains, grooms, and masters of the ceremonies who surrounded him before his abdication; but ill cured of his old unhappy passion for great lords, he must have them at any price: he would have thought himself in the midst of a republic if he had not contrived to be environed by the ancient *noblesse.*

Yet, nevertheless, those who had assisted him in crossing the Mediterranean pretended that he had thought as much of re-establishing the Republic or the Consulate as the Empire. But I knew in what to trust on that head; I knew what trouble I had among his adherents in getting them to abandon his oppressive system, and to engage him to give pledges to the liberties of the nation. His decrees from Lyons had not been voluntary; he had there pledged himself to give a national constitution to France. "I return," he then said, "in order to protect and defend the interests which our Revolution has engendered. It is my wish to give you an inviolable constitution, which shall be the joint work of the people and myself." By his decrees at Lyons he had abolished the chamber of peers by a single stroke of his pen, and annihilated the feudal nobility. It was also at Lyons that, in the hope of averting the resentment of foreign powers, he had commissioned his brother Joseph, then in Switzerland, to make known to them, through the intervention of their ministers to the Helvetic Confederation, that he was positively determined on no longer troubling the repose of Europe, and on faithfully maintaining the treaty of Paris.

This compulsory disposition on his part, the distrust which he perceived was felt in the interior of France as to the sincerity of his secret thoughts, and I may add my own repellant attitude, prescribed bounds to the impulses of a man who was prompted to rekindle the flames of war throughout Europe. In fact, on the very night of his arrival at the Tuileries, he commenced a deliberation as to the expediency of renewing the scourge of war by an invasion of Belgium. But a feeling of dislike having exhibited itself among those who surrounded him, he found it necessary to abandon this project; he succumbed beneath the hand of necessity, although once more armed with his ancient military power. That power, however, since the Lyons decrees, had changed its nature.

By a decree of the 24th of March, suppressing the censorship and the regulation of publications, he consummated what it was agreed to call the imperial restoration. The liberty of the press, so tumultuous a liberty in France, and which is, nevertheless, the mother of all other immunities, had been reconquered; nor had I in a slight degree contributed to that reconquest, even in the presence of its greatest enemy. Napoleon objected to me that the royalists, on one side, would employ it to aid the cause of the Bourbons, and the Jacobins, on the other, to render his sentiments and projects suspected. "Sire," I rejoined, "the French require victory or the nourishment of liberty." I insisted also that his decrees should contain no other epithets than that of Emperor of the French, inducing him to suppress the *et cætera*, which I remarked with uneasiness in his proclamations and decrees from Lyons.

But he rejected the idea of being indebted to the patriots for his re-installation at the Tuileries. "Some intriguers," said he to me with bitterness, "wanted to appropriate the credit to themselves, and turn it to their own advantage. They now lay claim to having prepared my progress to Paris; but I know to whom

I am indebted—the people, the soldiers, and the sub-lieutenants have effected everything; it is to them and them only that I owe the whole." I felt what was meant by these words, and that they were intended as a reproof for my party and myself.

It will be obvious that, with such feelings, it was indispensable for him to obtain a different police from mine. He sent for Réal, whom he had just invested with the office of prefect of police; and, after having allured him with fine promises and more substantial gifts, sent him to Savary, in order to devise means of tracing and counteracting my designs; but I was aware of them.

In the meanwhile he learnt with anxiety that Louis XVIII. proposed remaining in observation on the frontiers of Belgium. He had, besides, another cause of vexation: Ney, Lecourbe, and other generals wished him on extortionate terms to purchase their services: he grew indignant at this. The result of the royalist enterprise rather contributed to tranquillise him. He was astonished at the courage which the Duke d'Angoulême exhibited in La Drôme, and at that of Madame at Bordeaux. He admired the intrepidity of this heroic princess, whom the desertion of an entire army had not been able to dispirit. I ought here to do justice to Murat. On being informed that Grouchy had just made the Duke d'Angoulême prisoner, in contempt of the capitulation of Palud, to which the ratification of Napoleon was alone wanting, and which was in fact obtained but not sent off, Murat concealed the arrest of the prince from Napoleon, transmitted his original orders, and only apprised him of the nullification of the convention when the obscurity of night rendered all telegraphic communication impossible.

The next day it was proposed in council to obtain the crown diamonds, which were worth forty millions, in exchange for the Duke d'Angoulême. I recommended the Emperor to throw M. de Vitrolles into the bargain, if the restitution could be obtained. "No," said Napoleon angrily; "he is an intriguer and an agent of Talleyrand. It was he who was dispatched to the Emperor Alexander, and who opened the gates of Paris to the allies. This man has been arrested at Toulouse, in the act of conspiring against me. If he had been shot Lamarque would have done no more than his duty." I, however, represented to him that, if military executions had been resorted to on both sides, France would soon have been covered with blood; that political reasons prescribed a more temporising system; and that in restoring the Duke d'Angoulême to liberty, some stipulation could be made for M. de Vitrolles, who was only the avowed agent of the Bourbons. To this he at length acceded, and I instantly set on foot a negotiation on the subject.

We had many other causes of inquietude. Caulaincourt had just had an interview, at the house of Madame de Souza, with Baron de Vincent, the Austrian minister, whose passport was designedly delayed. This minister did not disguise that it was the resolution of the allied powers to oppose Napoleon's retention of the throne; but he suffered it to be perceived that Napoleon's son did not inspire the same repugnance. It has been seen that it was upon this basis that I previously modelled the plan of an edifice, which I considered myself at that time in better condition to erect.

Napoleon caused the Emperor Alexander and Prince Metternich to be written to by Hortense, and also the latter by his sister the Queen of Naples, hoping in this way to deaden the force of the blows which he was not yet prepared to encounter. He at the same time commissioned Eugene and the Princess Stephanie of Baden to neglect nothing in order to detach them from the coalition. Meanwhile he caused overtures to be made to the cabinet of London by an agent whom I pointed out to him. And in conclusion he hoped to ingratiate himself with the English parliament and nation by a decree abolishing the negro slave trade.

Notwithstanding this, all our external communications were intercepted by order of the various cabinets. The proceedings of the congress of Vienna furnished a subject of deep attention and the most painful anxiety at the Tuileries. We at length learnt, in a specific manner, what the public already knew—the declaration of the congress of Vienna, dated the 13th of March, which pronounced the outlawry of Napoleon. France was from that time terrified at the evils which the future prepared for her; she groaned at the thoughts of being exposed to the horrors of a new invasion for the sake of a single man. Napoleon affected not to be moved; and told us in full council: "This time they will find that they have not to deal with the France of 1814; and their success, if they obtain it, will only serve to render the war more sanguinary and obstinate; while, on the other hand, if victory favour me, I may become as formidable as ever. Have I not on my side Belgium and the provinces on this side the Rhine. With the aid of a proclamation and a tricolour flag I will revolutionise them in twenty-four hours."

I was far from allowing myself to be lulled into security by such gasconades as these. The moment I obtained knowledge of the declaration, I did not hesitate to request the King, by means of an agent on whom I could rely, to permit me to devote myself, when opportunity occurred, to his service. I demanded no other condition in return but the right of preserving my repose and fortune in my seclusion at Pont-Carré. The overture was fully accepted and sanctioned by Lord Wellington, who arrived just then at Ghent from the congress at Vienna. The same kind of convention had already been concluded, as far as I was concerned, between Prince Metternich, Prince de Talleyrand, and the generalissimo of the allies.

It will not be irrelevant to explain in this place the occasion of that good feeling which I met with from the Wellesley family, not only on the part of the marquis, but also on that of Lord Wellington. It had its origin in the zeal which I manifested at the period of my second ministry, in putting an end to the captivity of a member of that illustrious family, who was detained in France in consequence of the rigorous measures enforced by Napoleon's orders.

The treaty of the 25th of March, by which the great powers engaged on their side not to lay down their arms while Napoleon was on the throne, was only the natural consequence of the decision of the 13th. All indirect overtures had completely failed. "No peace, no truce, with that individual," replied the Emperor Alexander to Queen Hortense; "with any but him." Flahaut, who was sent to Vienna, was not allowed to pass Stuttgart; and Talleyrand refused to enter the service of Napoleon. Notwithstanding, however, the manner in which his first overtures were discountenanced, he decided on making new applications to the Emperor of Austria. At the same time that he sent the Baron de Strassart to him, he dispatched to M. de Talleyrand MM. de S. L—— and de Monteron, well known by their connection with that statesman, and the last being his most intimate and devoted friend. But these attempts of the second order could scarcely produce much effect upon the general course of things.

I daily became an object of greater umbrage to Napoleon, especially as I never let slip any occasion of repressing his despotic inclination and the revolutionary measures which he promulgated. I was known by no other name among his partisans than that of the minister of Ghent. The following were his new sources of disquietude: M. de Blacas, who, deaf to all advice, suffered the affair of the 20th of March to ripen, without believing it, and without troubling his head about it, forgot, in the hurry and anxiety of his departure, a mass of papers, which might have compromised a great number of respectable individuals. On being informed of this fact, I had been prompted by an instinctive foresight, from the 21st of March, to authorise the notary Lainé, colonel of the national guard, to occupy M. de Blacas' cabinet, arrange all the papers, and burn all such whose signatures might have contributed to disturb the peace of individuals.

Savary and Réal having tracked me in this operation, the Emperor made a demand upon me for the papers, which I presented to him in a bundle. Finding nothing among them but unimportant matters, he did not fail to suspect me of having withdrawn those which he had an interest in seeing.

On the 25th of March he exiled by decree to the distance of thirty leagues from Paris the royalists, the Vendean chiefs, and the royal volunteers and *gardes du corps*. As I was opposed to this general measure, I had the chief of them summoned into my presence, and after having testified the sympathy I felt for their situation, and explained the attempts I had made to prevent their exile, I authorised them generally to remain at Paris.

The vexation which the royalist intrigues gave Napoleon, and my desire to mitigate measures, induced him to promulgate his famous decree, which is thought to have been concocted at Lyons, though it did not see the light till it reached Paris, by which he ordained the trial and sequestration of the property of MM. de Talleyrand, Raguse, d'Alberg, Montesquiou, Jaucourt, Beurnonville, Lynch, Vitrolles, Alexis de Noailles, Bourrienne, Bellard, Larochejacquelein, and Sosthène de Larochefoucauld. Among this list was also found the name of Augereau; but it was erased at the entreaty of his wife and in consideration of his proclamation on the 23rd of March. I expressed myself very openly in the council on the subject of this new proscription list; in getting up which all private deliberation had been eluded. I maintained it was an act of vengeance and despotism, an early infraction of the promises made to the nation, and which would not fail to be followed by public disapprobation. In fact, some echoes of it had already been heard within the palace of the Tuileries.

Meanwhile England and Austria were on the point of successively adopting a decisive policy, the object of which was to aggravate the isolated position of Napoleon. In her memorandum of the 25th of April, England declared that by the treaty of the 29th of March she had not engaged to replace Louis XVIII. on the throne, and that her intention was not to prosecute the war with a view of imposing any government whatever upon France. A similar declaration on the part of Austria appeared on the 9th of May following. In the interim I was very near committing myself in a serious manner with respect to Austria. A secret agent of Prince Metternich having been dispatched to me, that individual, in consequence of his imprudence, was suspected, and the Emperor ordered Réal to have him arrested. Terror was of course employed to extort confessions from him. He declared that he had remitted me a letter from the prince, and a sign of mutual recognition, which was to be employed by the agent whom I was about to dispatch to Bâle, in order to confer with M. Werner, his confidential delegate. The Emperor instantly sent for me, as if he wanted an interview on public business. His first thought was to have my papers seized, but that he quickly abandoned, in the persuasion that I was not a man to leave traces of what might compromise me. Not having the slightest intimation that Prince Metternich's envoy had been arrested, I neither exhibited embarrassment nor anxiety.

The Emperor inferring from my silence on the subject of this secret correspondence that I was betraying him, convoked his partisans, told them I was a traitor, that he had proofs of it, and that he was about to have me shot. A thousand protestations were immediately heard against it: it was suggested to him that proofs clearer than daylight were indispensable, in order to warrant an act which would produce the most violent sensation in the public mind. Carnot, seeing that he persevered, told him, "It is in your power to have Fouché shot, but to morrow at the same hour your power will have departed." "How?" said the Emperor. "Yes, Sire," returned Carnot, "there is no longer any time to dissemble; the men of the Revolution will only suffer you to reign as long as they have security that you will respect their liberties. If you cause Fouché to be put to death by martial law, Fouché whom they consider as their strongest guarantee, you may be assured of it that to-morrow you will no longer possess any influence over public opinion. If Fouché be really guilty you must obtain convincing proofs of it, expose him subsequently to the nation, and put him on trial according to form." In this opinion all the rest coincided. It was decided that efforts should be made to detect the intrigue, and that an agent should be sent to Bâle in order to obtain the necessary proofs for my conviction. The Emperor confided this mission to his secretary, Fleury.[1] Supplied with all the necessary signs of recognition, he immediately departed for Bâle, and subsequently opened communications with M. Werner, as if he had been sent by myself.

[1] Baron Fleury de Chaboulon.—*Note by the French Editor.*

It may be easily guessed that the first question he put to him was to inform himself of the means on which the allies calculated for the destruction of Napoleon. M. Werner said that nothing was decided on the subject; that the allies were not inclined to resort to force but at the last extremity; that they had hoped that I might be able to find some means for delivering France from Bonaparte without new effusion of blood. Fleury, continuing to act his part, said, "There only remains then two methods to pursue—to dethrone him or assassinate him." "To assassinate him!" exclaimed M. Werner, with indignation; "never did such an idea present itself to the mind of M. de Metternich and the allies." Fleury, notwithstanding all his artifices and his captious queries, could obtain no other attestation against me, except the conviction of M. de Metternich that I hated the Emperor, and the circumstance that such conviction had prompted him to open communications with me.

I had taken so little pains to disguise my opinion in that respect from Prince Metternich that the preceding year (1814), at a similar epoch, on seeing him at Paris, I reproached him warmly with not having caused Bonaparte to be confined in a fortress, predicting that he would return from Elba to renew his ravages in Europe. Fleury and M. Werner separated, one to return to Vienna and the other to Paris, in order to provide themselves with fresh instructions, and with a promise of meeting at Bâle again in eight days.

But Fleury had scarcely resumed his journey to Bâle when a second direct emissary having given me intimation and enabled me to make a discovery of what was passing, I put the letter of Prince Metternich in my portfolio; and after my business with the Emperor was done, feigning a sudden recollection: "Ah, Sire," I said to him, with the tone of a man awaking from a long forgetfulness, "how overwhelmed I must be with the state of public affairs. I am positively besieged in my cabinet, and so it is that for several days I have forgotten to lay a letter of Prince Metternich under your eye. It is for your Majesty to decide whether I shall send him the agent which he requires. What can be his object? I can scarcely doubt that the allies, in order to avert the calamities of a general war, wish to induce you to abdicate in favour of your son. I am satisfied that such is the especial desire of M. de Metternich; indeed, I must reiterate that such is mine. I have never concealed it from you; and I am still persuaded that it will be impossible for you to resist the arms of united Europe." I instantly perceived by the play of his physiognomy that he was suffering an internal struggle between the dissatisfaction which my frankness occasioned him and the satisfaction he derived from the explanation of my conduct.

When Fleury returned, the Emperor sent him to me to make a confession of the whole proceeding, as if his intention had been to subjugate my confidence. I had no great difficulty in cajoling a young man replete with animation and impetuosity, and who employed a serious and studied *finesse* in order to prevent my divining the second rendezvous which he had at Bâle. I suffered him to depart; he arrived there post haste, and had the fatigues of his journey and the heat of his vehement zeal for his pains. Meanwhile Monteron and Bresson, who came from Vienna, commissioned to bring me confidential communications on behalf of M. de Metternich and M. de Talleyrand, renewed the feeling of distrust which Napoleon entertained towards me. He sent for them both : questioned them for a considerable time ; and could extract nothing of a positive nature from either. Urged by his uneasy feelings, he wanted to place them under surveillance ; but he learnt, with much dissatisfaction, that Bresson had suddenly departed for England, with an ostensible commission from Davoust, for the purchase of forty thousand muskets contracted for by a gunsmith. He did not fail to suspect a secret intelligence between Davoust and me, and that Bresson was an instrument.

Situated as I was, it was incumbent on me to neglect nothing to preserve the favourable opinion of the public : I also possessed my vehicles of popularity, in my circulars and anti-royalist reports. I had just established throughout France lieutenants of police who were devoted to me ; the choice of secret agents was centred in me alone; I got possession of the journals, and thus became master of public opinion. But I had soon upon my hands an affair of quite different importance—the unseasonable insurrection of La Vendée, which disconcerted all my plans. It was incumbent on me to have the royalists on my side, but not to suffer them to meddle with our affairs. In this particular my views corresponded with the interests of Napoleon. He was apparently much chagrined at this new fermentation of the old leaven.

I hastened to make him easy by assuring him that I would soon extinguish it; that he had only to give me *carte blanche*, and to place twelve thousand of the old troops at my disposal.

In the conviction that I should not sacrifice them to the Bourbons, he left me at full liberty to take my own measures. I easily persuaded some idiots of the royalist party, whose opinions I modelled after my own fashion, that this war of some few fanatics was unseasonable; that the measures which it would suggest would reproduce the Reign of Terror and occasion the revolutionary party to be let loose; that it was absolutely necessary to obtain an order from the King to cause this rabble to lay down their arms; that the grand question could not be decided in the interior, but on the frontiers. I immediately dispatched three negotiators, Malartic, Flavigny, and Laberaudière, furnished with instructions and orders to confer with such of the chiefs as the public effervescence had not yet involved in this party, and who would be glad to be supplied with a plea for waiting the course of events. All was soon arranged; the affair was brought to a conclusion at the expense of a few skirmishes, and at the decisive moment La Vendée was all at once repressed and composed.

The commencement of war by Murat caused me another description of uneasiness, and so much the more serious as neither the Emperor nor myself was possessed of efficacious means of supporting or directing him. Unfortunately the impulse came from us, for it was necessary that some one should *bell the cat*. But that individual, who always overstepped the bounds of moderation, was not able to stop in proper time ; I wrote to him in vain at a later period, as well as to the queen, begging him to be moderate, and not to urge events too violently, which we should, probably, too soon be obliged to obey. When I learnt that his troops were already engaged with the troops of Austria, I said to myself, " That man is lost ; the contest is not equal." The issue was that he engulfed himself in the billows which he had set afloat.

Towards the end of May he disembarked as a fugitive in the Gulf of Juan. This news had all the sinister effect of a fatal omen, and involved the partisans of the Emperor in consternation.

On the other hand, Napoleon found himself involved in a labyrinth of affairs, each more serious than its predecessor, and in the midst of which all his feelings were absorbed by one supreme idea, that of confronting the armaments of Europe. He would have wished to transform France into a camp, and its towns into arsenals. The soldiers appertained to him, but the citizens were in the hands of others. It was, moreover, not without fear that he set the instruments of the revolution in motion, by authorising the re-establishment of popular clubs and the formation of civic confederations : circumstances which gave him occasion to fear that he had regenerated anarchy—he who had boasted so much of having disenthroned it. What solicitudes, what anxieties, and what constraint was he compelled to infuse into his measures, in order to mitigate the violence of associations so dangerous to be controlled !

This affectation of popularity had upheld him in

public opinion until the moment of his "acte additionnel aux constitutions de l'empire." Napoleon considered the latter as his title deeds to the crown, and in annulling them he would have considered himself in the light of commencing a new reign. He who could only date from possession *de facto* preferred to model his system in a ridiculous manner, after the fashion of Louis XVIII., who computed time according to the data of legitimacy. Instead of a national constitution, which he had promised, he contented himself with modifying the political laws and the Senatus Consulta which governed the Empire. He re-established the confiscation of property, against which almost all his councillors protested. In fine, he determined, in a council held upon this subject, not to submit his constitution to public query, but to present it to the nation as an *acte additionnel*. I strongly contended against his resolution, as also did Decrès, Caulaincourt, and almost all the members present. He persisted, in spite of our exertion, to comprise all his concessions within the compass of this irregular design.

The word *additionnel* disenchanted the friends of liberty. They recognised in it the ill-disguised continuation of the chief institutions, created in favour of absolute power. From that moment Napoleon, to their view, became an incurable despot; and I, for my part, regarded him in the light of a madman delivered bound hand and foot to the mercy of Europe. Confined to that description of popular suffrage which Savary and Réal directed, he caused some of the lowest classes to be assembled, and the latter, under the name of

Fédérés, marched in procession under the windows of the Tuileries, uttering repeatedly exclamations of " Vive l'Empereur!" There he himself announced to this mobocracy that if the kings dared to attack him he would proceed to encounter them at the frontiers. This disgusting scene humiliated even the soldiers. Never had the extraordinary individual in question, who had worn the purple with so much lustre, contributed so greatly to degrade it. He was no longer, in patriotic opinion, considered in any other light than as an actor subjected to the applauses of the vilest of the populace. Scenes of this humiliating description made a strong impression on my mind; well assured, moreover, that all the allied powers, unanimous in their resolution, were preparing to march against us, or, rather, against him, I proceeded early the next day to the Tuileries; and a second time I represented to Napoleon, in still stronger colours, that it was an absolute impossibility for France, in her divided condition, to sustain the assault of universal and united Europe; that it was incumbent upon him to explain himself frankly to the nation; to assure himself of the ultimate intentions of the allied sovereigns, and that if they persisted, as everything gave reason to infer, then there would be no possibility of hesitation; that his interests, and those of his country, imposed upon him the obligation of withdrawing to the United States.

But from the reply which he stammered, in which he mingled plans of campaigns, punishments, battles, insurrections, colossal projects, decrees of destiny, I perceived that he was resolved to trust the fate of

France to the issue of war, and that the military faction carried the day in spite of my admonitions.

The assembly of the Champ-de-Mars was nothing but a vain pageantry, in which Napoleon, in the garb of a citizen, hoped to mislead the populace by the charm of a public ceremony. The different parties were not more satisfied with it than they had been with the *acte additionnel;* one faction wished that he had re-established a republic; and the other that in divesting himself of the crown he had left the sovereign people in possession of the right of offering it to the most worthy; and finally, the coalition of statesmen, of whom I constituted the soul, reproached him with not having availed himself of that solemnity to proclaim Napoleon II.; an event which would have given us a *point d'appui* in certain cabinets, and, probably, would have preserved us from a second invasion. It will not be denied that, in the critical position of France, the last expedient would have been most reasonable.

As soon as we had acquired the conviction that all attempts to produce this result in the interior of France would be unsuccessful, without proceeding to the extremity of a deposition, which the military party would not have suffered, it was necessary to make up our minds to the anticipation of seeing all the gates of war thrown open. My impatience then augmented, and I laboured to accelerate the march of events. It was in vain that Davoust, in council, had reiterated to Napoleon that his presence at the army was indispensable; relying too little on the capital to leave it behind him for any length of time without mistrust, he did not resolve on his departure till everything was ready to strike an effectual blow on the frontiers of Belgium, in the hope of making his *début* by a triumph, and of re-conquering popularity by victory. He departed; he departed, I say, leaving the care of his *fédérés* to Réal; large sums of money to get them to cry "Napoleon, or Death!" and authority as to the publication of his military bulletins, with a plan of the campaign arranged for the offensive, and the secret of which was communicated to me by Davoust.

In this decisive condition of affairs, my position became very delicate as well as very difficult. I wished to have nothing further to do with Napoleon; yet, if he should be victorious, I should be compelled to submit to his yoke, as well as the whole of France, whose calamities he would prolong. On the other hand, I had engagements with Louis XVIII.; not that I was inclined to his restoration, but prudence required that I should procure for myself beforehand something in the shape of a guarantee. My agents, moreover, to M. Metternich and Lord Wellington had promised mountains and marvels. The generalissimo, at least, expected that I should provide him with the plan of the campaign, in the first instance. But the voice of my country, the glory of the French army, which appeared to me in any other light than that of the nation—in short, the dictates of honour, startled me at the thought that the word "traitor" might ever become an appendage to the name of the Duke of Otranto; and my resolution remained unsullied. Meantime, in such a conjecture, what part was to be taken by a statesman to whom it is never permitted to remain without resources? This is the resolution I took. I knew positively that the unexpected onset of Napoleon's force would occur on the 16th or 18th at latest. Napoleon, indeed, determined to give battle on the 17th to the English army, after detaching them from the Prussians and marching to the attack *sur le ventre* of the latter. He was so much the better justified in expecting success from his plan, since Wellington, deceived from false reports, imagined it possible to delay the opening of the campaign till the 1st of July. The success of Napoleon rested, therefore, on the success of a surprise. I took my measures accordingly. On the very day of Napoleon's departure I provided Madame D—— with notes, written in cipher, disclosing the plan of the campaign, and sent her off. At the same time I occasioned impediments on that part of the frontier which she was to pass in such a manner as to prevent her reaching the headquarters of Wellington till after the result. This is a true explanation of the inconceivable supineness of the generalissimo which occasioned so universal an astonishment and conjectures of so opposite a description.

If therefore Napoleon fell, it was owing to his own destiny; treason had nothing to do with his defeat. He himself did all that could be done in order to conquer; but he omitted to invest his fall with dignity. If I am asked what I think he ought to have done, I will reply, as old Horace did, " He should have died."

It was on condition of his coming out of the contest as a victor that the patriots had consented to give him their support. He was vanquished, and they considered the compact at an end. I learnt at the same moment the circumstance of his nocturnal arrival at the Elysée, and that at Laon, after his defeat, Maret, at his instigation, had broached the question of his quitting the army and proceeding without loss of time to Paris, in order to avert a sudden reaction. I was also informed in the morning that Lucien, keeping up his courage, endeavoured to derive resources from a desperate resolution; that he urged him to seize the dictatorship, to surround himself with nothing but military elements, and to dissolve the chamber.

It was then that I was impressed with the necessity of setting in motion all the resources of my position and my experience. The defeat of the Emperor, his presence at Paris, which occasioned a universal indignation, provided me with a favourable opportunity of extorting from him an abdication which he declined when it might have been of service. I set in motion all my friends, all my adherents, and all my agents, whom I provided with the watchword. As to myself, I communicated in full council with the *élite* of all the parties in the state. To the unquiet, mistrustful, and obnoxious members of the chamber, I said : "It is necessary to act, to say little, and resort to force; he is become perfectly insane ; he is decided upon dissolving the chamber and seizing the dictatorship. I trust we shall not suffer such a return to tyranny as this." I said to the partisans of Napoleon : "Are you not aware that the feeling against the Emperor has reached the highest pitch among the majority of the deputies. His fall is desired ; his abdication is demanded. If you are bent on serving him, you have but one certain path to follow, and that is to make head vigorously against them, to show them what power you still retain, and to affirm that his single word will be sufficient in order to dissolve the chamber." I also entered into their language and views. They then disclosed their secret inclinations, and I was enabled to say to the heads of the patriots who rallied round me : " You perceive that his best friends make no mystery of it; the danger is pressing; in a few hours the chambers will exist no longer ; and you will have much to answer for in neglecting to seize the only moment when you could prevent a dissolution."

The council being assembled, Napoleon caused Maret to read the bulletin of the battle of Waterloo; and concluded by declaring that, in order to save his country, it was indispensable that he should be invested with larger powers—in short, with a temporary dictatorship ; that it was in his power to seize it, but that he thought it more useful and more national to wait for its being conferred on him by the chambers. I left to such of my colleagues who thought and acted with me the task of contending against this proposition, which had already fallen into disrepute, and was incapable of making a stand.

It was then that M. de Lafayette, apprised of what was passing in the council and sure of the majority, made a motion for the permanency of the chambers, a motion which disconcerted the whole military party, and rallying the patriotic party, conferred upon it a considerable moral force.

Kept in check by the chambers, Napoleon did not dare to take any other step. He sounded Davoust as to the feasibility of effecting its dissolution by military means ; but Davoust declined.

The next day we all manœuvred to extort his abdication. There was a multitude of missions backwards and forwards, parleys, objections, replies—in a word, evolutions of every description ; ground was taken, abandoned, and again retaken. At length, after a warm battle, Napoleon surrendered in full council, under the conviction that longer resistance was useless ; then turning to me, he said, with a sardonic smile, " Write to your gentry to make themselves easy ; they shall be satisfied." Lucien took up the pen, and composed under Napoleon's dictation the act of abdication as it was given to the world.

Here then was a change of scene ! The power having passed away from the hands of Napoleon, who was to remain master of the field ? I soon detected the secret designs of the cabinet. I discovered that the Bonapartist party, now under the guidance of Lucien, intended, as a consequence of the abdication, to countenance the immediate proclamation of Napoleon II. and the establishment of a council of regency. This would have been to have suffered the hostile camp to triumph. In fact, that regency which had been for so long a time the drift of all my calculations and the object of all my desires, being now about to be organised under another influence than mine, excluded me from a share in the government. It was necessary, therefore, to recur to new combinations and to man counter-batteries, in order, with equal address, to defeat the system of the regency and the restoration of the Bourbons. I therefore conceived the creation of a provisional government established in conformity with my own suggestions, and which, in consequence, I should be able to direct according to my own views. I presented myself to the chamber with a view of inducing it to act with decision in consecrating the principles and the laws of the Revolution.

The chamber having accepted the abdication of Napoleon without noticing the condition it contained, Lucien exerted himself to procure the proclamation of Napoleon II. He had in his favour the *fédérés*, the soldiers, the populace, and a large part of the chamber of peers. I had on my side the majority of the lower chamber, a party also in the chamber of peers, the greater part of the generals, and the royalists, who courted and surrounded me in the hope that I should direct the throw of the die in favour of the Bourbons.

Lucien had already sent Réal to the Elysée in order to assemble the *fédérés* under the windows of Napoleon. It was with great difficulty that the assent of the ex-Emperor was obtained; it was only procured by remarking that my party intended to consider his abdication as a single and unqualified act; that if he did not at least preserve some shadow of his power, neither his security by flight nor the conveyance of his wealth could be answered for; that, moreover, the abdication in favour of his son might probably induce Austria to obtain more favourable conditions from the rest of the allies in his behalf. Réal immediately entered the field, and raked together all the *canaille* of Paris in the Champs Elysées; while Lucien on his side entered his carriage, and hurried to the chamber of peers, where he exclaimed in a harangue got up for the occasion: "The Emperor is dead: long live the Emperor! let us proclaim Napoleon II.!" The majority appeared to accede to this proposal. Lucien returned in triumph to the Champs Elysées, instructed the two or three thousand *brigands* whom Réal had assembled round the palace in their part, and got them to promise to proceed to the chamber of representatives, in order to determine the proclamation of Napoleon II. He re-entered the Elysée, and returned upon the terrace with his brother, whose countenance betrayed evident marks of depression. There Napoleon saluted the band of fanatics with some gesticulations of his hand, as they defiled before him with acclamations of "Long live our Emperor and his son! we will have no other!"

But these demonstrations of their zeal gave me little uneasiness. I had my eye upon the most inconsiderable movements, and the only staunch political string was in my hands. I had, moreover, secured to myself an initiative influence; and at the very moment of this ridiculous hubbub, the chamber named an executive provisional committee, the presidentship of which devolved upon me.

Meanwhile Réal had given the pass-word to the *fédérés*, ordering them to march in procession before the palace of the legislative body. They flocked thither in crowds; but it was too late; the terrified legislators had just abandoned the hall, after having appointed a committee. Night dispersed the mob, which, in passing through the streets of Paris, affrighted the citizens with the discharge of their muskets, and set up loud cries of "Death to all who refused to recognise Napoleon II."

The agitation of the day was terminated by nocturnal meetings, the preludes of one of the most animated of public sittings which was to occur on the following day. Next morning I and my colleagues, Caulaincourt, Carnot, Quinette, and General Grenier, entered on our new possession of the reins of government. We were proceeding in the task of our organisation, when I learnt that the deputy Bérenger, at the opening of the sitting, had just demanded that the members of the committee should be held collectively responsible. The obvious drift of this proposal was to engage each of them to separate themselves from my vote, and to supervise my proceedings, as a consequence of the mistrust which I occasioned the Bonapartist faction. As if he had not said enough, Bérenger added: "If these men be inviolable, you will, in case any of them should betray his duty, possess no means of punishing him."

I cared very little for these underhand attacks; as I have before said, my party was the strongest.

The councillor Boulay de la Meurthe, one of the most zealous partisans of Bonaparte, proceeded to deliver a philippic, in which he pointed out and denounced the Orleans faction. This was apprising the friends of the Bourbons and the Bonapartists that a third party was making its appearance in favour of the doctrine of *de facto* government, which three months before we had opposed to the doctrine of legitimacy.

It is certain that, finding myself embarked with a new party, more accordant with my principles than those which offered no other prospect than an absolute government or a counter-revolution, and feeling the impossibility of preserving the throne of Napoleon II., I was disposed to second the efforts of this new party, provided the cabinets did not exhibit too hostile a feeling towards it. The declamation of Boulay had for its principal object to cause the proclamation of Napoleon II. by the chamber. The party was strongly bound together, and it required some address to avert its attack. M. Manuel undertook the delicate task in a discourse which obtained universal concurrence, and in which it was fancied that the stamp of my policy was discernible. He concluded by opposing himself to the design of investing any member of the Bonaparte family with the regency; that was the decisive point, and that was abandoning the field of battle to me. The assent of the chamber was a new guarantee to the committee of government, and conferred upon me in my character of president an incontestable preponderance in public affairs.

Our first operation, after being installed on the 23rd of June, was to cause the war to be declared national, and to send five plenipotentiaries[1] to the headquarters of the allies, with powers to negotiate peace, and to signify assent to any species of government but that of the Bourbons. Their secret instructions went to the effect of conferring the crown, in default of Napoleon II., on the King of Saxony, or

---

[1] These plenipotentiaries were MM. de Lafayette, Laforêt, Pontécoulant, d'Argenson, and Sebastiani. M. Benjamin Constant accompanied them in quality of secretary to the embassy. —*Note by the French Editor.*

the Duke of Orleans, whose party had been reinforced by a great number of deputies and generals.

I confess that I, in this measure, made rather a large concession to the actual projectors, and that I secretly entertained strong doubts as to their attainment of the object they proposed. I had also so much the more reason to believe that the cause of the Bourbons was far from desperate, as one of my secret agents shortly arrived to inform me of Louis XVIII.'s entry into Cambray, and to bring me his royal declaration. Our plenipotentiaries, therefore, were at first amused with dilatory answers.

My position may be conceived. The party of Napoleon, always in activity, was recruited, if I may use the term, by eighty thousand soldiers, who arrived to make a stand under the walls of Paris; while the allied armies rapidly advanced on the capital, driving before them all the battalions and divisions which attempted to obstruct their passage. It was incumbent upon me, at one and the same time, to secure the generals, in order to control the army; to counteract the new plans of Bonaparte, which tended to nothing short of replacing him at the head of the troops; and to repress the impatience of the royalists, whose wish it was to open the gates of Paris to Louis XVIII.—and all this in the midst of the unloosing of so many contending passions, whence terrible convulsions were likely to be engendered.

I will not occupy myself with narrating in this place a multitude of minor intrigues, of accessory details, of collisions and chicaneries, which, during the tornado, inflicted upon me all the tribulations of power. Previous to the abdication, I was spied upon and continually kept on the *qui vive* by the zealous partisans of Napoleon, such as Maret, Thibaudeau, Boulay de la Meurthe, and even Regnault, who was sometimes in my favour, and sometimes opposed to me. Now, I had to defend myself from the requisitions of another party; I had to fortify myself against the mistrust of my own colleagues, of Carnot among the rest, who, from having been a republican, had become so attached to the Emperor that he had bewailed him with a flood of tears in my presence, after having stood alone, and that abortively, against the measure of his abdication.

It may be easily conceived that I did not succeed in muzzling this mob of high functionaries, marshals, and generals by any other means than pledging my head, if I may so express myself, for the safety of their persons and fortunes. It was in this manner that I obtained a *carte blanche* to negotiate.

I began with sending to Wellington's headquarters, my friend M. G——, a man of probity, and on whom I placed entire reliance. He was the bearer of two letters, sewed in the collar of his coat, one for the King and the other for the Duke of Orleans : for up to the latest moment, and while involved in protracted uncertainty as to the intention of the allies, no means could justifiably be neglected for returning into safe harbour. My emissary was introduced, accordingly, to Lord Wellington, and told him that he wished to be presented to the Duke of Orleans. " He is not here," the generalissimo replied ; " but you can address yourself to your King." And, in fact, he took the road to Cambray, and presented himself to his Majesty. Finding that he did not return, I dispatched General de T—— on the same errand; a man of feeling and intelligence, whom I expressly commissioned to sound the intention of Lord Wellington, to apprise him of my peculiar situation, to state how much the public mind was exasperated and public feeling inflamed; and that I could not answer for the preservation of France from the scourge of fire and sword if the design of re-seating the Bourbons on the throne was persevered in. I offered to treat directly with him on any other basis. The reply of the generalissimo was on this occasion peremptory and negative. He declared that he had orders not to treat on any other basis than the re-establishment of Louis XVIII. As to the Duke of Orleans, he could only be considered—so Lord Wellington expressed himself—in the light of a usurper of good family. This reply which I carefully concealed from my colleagues, rendered my position still more embarrassing.

On the other hand, our plenipotentiaries, having left Laon on the 26th of June, arrived on the 1st of July at the headquarters of the allied sovereigns at Haguenau. There the sovereigns, not considering it convenient to grant them an audience, appointed a commission to hear their proposals. The question which I had foreseen did not fail of being addressed to them: " By what right does the nation pretend to expel its king and choose another sovereign ? " They replied, " By an example derived from the history of England itself."

Apprised by this question of the inclinations of the commission, the national plenipotentiaries exerted themselves less to obtain Napoleon II. than to repel

Louis XVIII. They insinuated, in fact, that the nation might accept the Duke of Orleans or the King of Saxony, if it were not permitted to secure the throne to the son of Maria Louisa. After several unimportant parleys, they were dismissed with a note, implying that the allied court could not for the present enter into any negotiation; that they considered it as a *sine quâ non* that Napoleon should be placed for the future out of a condition to disturb the repose of France and Europe; and that, after the events which had occurred in March, the allied powers found it their duty to demand that he should be placed under their superintendence.

The committee of government then found itself frustrated in its hope of obtaining the Duke of Orleans or Napoleon II. Even before the return of the plenipotentiaries, I was directly informed of the real intentions of the allied powers.

I employed myself from that time in imparting such a direction to the course of events as should cause them to terminate in a result at once most favourable to my country and to myself. I had demanded an armistice, and with that view sent commissioners[1] to the allied generals, who had just commenced the siege of the capital. Blucher and Wellington eluded every proposal on the subject, raising more than objections against the government of Napoleon II., adverting to Louis XVIII. as the only sovereign who appeared to them to unite in his person all the conditions which would prevent Europe from exacting

----

[1] MM. Andréossy, Boissy-d'Anglas, Flaugergues, Valence and Labesnardière.—*Note by the French Editor.*

future pledges for its security, and vehemently complaining of the presence of Bonaparte at Paris, in
contempt of his abdication. That personage, as if a
fatality impelled him to plunge into the abyss which
yawned before him, had, in the first instance, persevered, instead of precipitately gaining one of our
seaports, in remaining at the palace of the Elysée;
subsequently at Malmaison, in the protracted hope of
repossessing himself of authority, if not as Emperor,
at least as general. Urged by fanatical friends, he
even went so far as to address to us a formal demand
of that description. It was then that I exclaimed to
a full meeting of the committee, " This man is mad
to a certainty; does he wish, then, to involve us in
his ruin ? " And here I am bound to say that the
whole committee, even Carnot himself, voted with
me for a definitive resolution to be taken with respect
to him. His actions were superintended, and Davoust
was determined to arrest him on the least attempt
which he might make to seduce the army from us.
It was so much the more incumbent upon us to take
a decisive step with reference to him, as the enemy's
cavalry, pushing their detachments even as far as the
environs of Malmaison, might capture him from one
moment to another ; and some share in such an event
would not have failed to be imputed to myself. It
was necessary to negotiate for his departure, and to
send a general officer to superintend it. The result
is known. This short explanation of facts will be
sufficient to rebut the accusations of blind and malicious detractors, who, perceiving some resemblance
between the captivity of Napoleon and that of the

king of Macedonia, Perseus, have attributed the former to treacherous combinations, which, computing days and hours, delivered him into the hands of the English through the operation of an underhanded and skilfully conducted intrigue.

We hoped, after the departure of Napoleon, to be able to obtain an armistice ; but it came to nothing. It was then that I wrote the two letters, which have been made public, to each of the generals-in-chief of the besieging armies. It may be remarked in those letters, wherein I feigned, in conformity with the necessity of the case, to plead the cause of Napoleon II., that I considered the question irrevocably decided in favour of the Bourbons ; but, in order to lull the vigilance of parties, it was indispensable for me to exhibit the appearance of alternately leaning towards the younger branch and the reigning branch. I hoped, moreover, that by aiding Louis XVIII. to remount the throne, I should induce that prince to detach some dangerous individuals from his presence, and to make new concessions to France, reserving to myself, if I could obtain nothing, the privilege of subsequently recurring to other combinations.

- I had at that time some nocturnal conferences with M. de Vitrolles, whose liberty I had just procured, and with several other eminent royalists, as well as two marshals, who inclined towards the Bourbons. I dispatched emissaries at the same time to the King, the Duke of Wellington, and M. de Talleyrand. I knew that M. de Talleyrand, after quitting Vienna, had proceeded to Frankfort, and subsequently to Wiesbaden, in order to be nearer at hand for the purpose of negotiating either with Ghent or Paris. Decided as he was against Napoleon, he, however, thought it proper, on his return to Paris, to come to an understanding with me, promising on his side to secure my interest with the Bourbons, whose re-establishment after the battle of Waterloo appeared to him infallible. I thought that he would at that time be near the person of the King, and I knew, beyond a doubt, that, in order to retain the control over affairs, he would require the dismissal of M. de Blacas. I arranged my measures accordingly. But it was almost impossible to avoid exciting the distrust of my colleagues. My proceedings were watched, and I was obliged to support reproaches and indignant declamations from some revolutionary and Bonapartist partisans, whose imputations I coldly repelled. Such was my position that I was obliged to have negotiations with all parties, and compromise with all the shades of opinion either attached to my interest or to that of the state. I did not disguise from myself that conduct such as this, which of necessity comprised something mysterious and underhand, was calculated to rouse all kinds of suspicions against me, as well as of resentment on the part of factions wounded in their dearest hopes. The formidable moment would naturally be that when light should dawn on this chaos of multitudinous and conflicting intrigues.

A more serious and dangerous consideration still was the ferment of the *fédérés*, and the violence of the fanatics in the chamber, who by turns excited against me the individuals of my own party, the soldiers, and the populace. I wrote to Lord Wellington that it was high time to put a stop to their ravings and excesses, or that they would shortly leave me without the capability of acting. But Wellington was thwarted by his intractable colleague, Blucher; that Prussian general, impelled by his native impatience and irritability, wished to penetrate into Paris, in order, as he said, to secure the better class of citizens from the pillage with which they were menaced by the mob; and he professed that it was only within the walls of the capital he would consent to the conclusion of an armistice. His letter exasperated us; but what could we do? It was necessary to sustain a siege, and give battle under the walls of Paris, or capitulate. Discouraged by the abdication, the soldiers appeared irresolute, and even the generals were intimidated by the uncertainty of the prospect. The minister of war and general-in-chief of the army, Davoust, wrote to me to the effect that he had conquered his prejudices, and was now persuaded that no other means of safety remained than that of instantly proclaiming Louis XVIII. I laid my answer before the committee. The members thought that I looked at the question of the recall of Louis XVIII. in too implicit a manner, and that I gave Davoust too great a degree of latitude. I got over this trivial difficulty, the marshal's determination having appeared to me so important that I had promised him safe conduct, on behalf of the King, through the intervention of M. de Vitrolles.

Compelled to deliberate upon our military position, the committee, in conformity with my advice, appealed to the intelligence, the counsel, and the responsibility of the most experienced individuals in the art of war. The principal generals were convoked in presence of

the presidents and official men of the two chambers.
A report of the situation of Paris was made through
the medium of Carnot, who had himself visited our
positions and those of the enemy. Carnot declared that
the left bank of the Seine was entirely uncovered, and
offered a wide field to the enterprise of the generals-
in-chief of the two combined armies, who had just
marched the major part of their forces in that
direction. I confess that I attached great national
importance to the circumstance of preventing a protracted defence of Paris. We were in a desperate
condition ; the treasury was empty, credit extinct, and
the government at the last extremity; in short, Paris,
in consequence of the existence and collision of so
many different opinions, was stationed over the mouth
of a volcano. On the other hand, its vicinity was
daily inundated by new arrivals of foreign troops. If,
under circumstances like these, the capital should be
carried by main force, we had nothing further to hope ;
neither capitulation, arrangement, nor concession. In
one single day, which would thus complete what
Leipsic and Waterloo left undone, all the interests
of the Revolution might be for ever engulfed in a
torrent of French blood. This nevertheless was what
the fanatics of a party, in its last death struggles,
desired.

In such a crisis, was it not deserving well of the
country to replace France without effusion of blood
under the authority of Louis XVIII.? Should we
have waited till foreign armies delivered us bound
hand and foot into the hands of our adversaries ?
I succeeded, by virtue of mingled insinuations and

promises, in persuading individuals who till that moment had been intractable.

It was decided that the military question should be submitted the night following to a council of war convoked by Marshal Davoust. The possibility of defending Paris was thus about to be determined. To capitulate would save Paris but compromise the national cause; to give battle would be attended by great and inevitable dangers to a capital distracted by all the excesses of popular fury, in case we should be vanquished. And, in fact, to what tremendous risks would those whose wish it was to give battle have exposed that immense city, and France itself, in the event of a defeat.

The discussions were solemn; and in consequence of the negative and unanimous resolution of the council of war, the committee decreed that Paris should not be defended, and that the city should be delivered into the hands of the allies, since they would not consent to suspend hostilities on any other condition. But Blucher required the additional surrender of the army. Such a clause could not be accepted; it was to require that everything should be delivered up to fire and sword. I hastily sent MM. Tromeling and Macirone, to the two hostile generals, to whom I consigned, without the knowledge of the committee, a confidential note conceived in these terms: " The army is dissatisfied because it is unfortunate; be easy on this point, it will become faithful and devoted. The chambers are intractable for the same cause. Tranquillise the mind of the public, and the public will be in your favour. Let the army be kept at a distance; the chambers will assent to this, if guarantees specified by the King be promised as *addenda* to the charter. In order to understand each other well, mutual explanation is necessary; do not therefore make your entrance into Paris till after three days. In that space of time everybody will have come to our agreement. The chambers will be gained over; they will conceive themselves to be independent, and sanction everything under that impression. It is not force which ought to be employed in their case, but persuasion."

Blucher soon became more manageable, and consent was given to negotiate the military surrender of Paris, which was concluded at St. Cloud on the 3rd of July. I objected to the name of capitulation being given to this treaty, and I caused that of convention to be substituted for it, which appeared to me less harsh, and therefore more unobjectionable.

Faction was still in too exasperated a state to allow of security from tumult and disorder. It was necessary to oppose the national guard to the *fédérés*, who were not restrained without difficulty by the mass of peaceable citizens. Réal, who had the direction of the *fédérés*, and who I knew was very easily frightened, yielded to my advice, affecting to be taken ill, and left his place of prefect of police to shift for itself. The faction gave the post to Courtin, a *protégé* of Queen Hortense, who, though exhibiting in her own person a wonderful intrepidity during the whole of the great crisis, vainly endeavoured to bolster up the relics of the expiring Bonapartist party. All these manœuvres concluded in their own defeat, by the greatest of all interests, the interests of the public. It was not long before imputations were made against the generals and the committee of having sacrificed Paris and betrayed the army. In order to justify the conduct of the government, I addressed an explanatory proclamation to the French people, in which I pointed out the vital necessity of a union of all ranks, without which there was no probability of reaching the term of our misfortunes.

After having capitulated to the foreigners, it was necessary to capitulate to the army, who, at the very moment of marching to the Loire, mutinied, in order to extort from us their arrears of pay. Thanks to some millions advanced by the banker Laffitte, the mutineers were disarmed and the needy satisfied. Meantime all the emissaries and agents of the King, and among the rest M. de Vitrolles, with whom Davoust and myself conferred, assured us that the King would shut his eyes upon all that had passed, and that a general reconciliation would be the earnest of his return. I had already conquered repugnancy in many quarters by the aid of promises when the royal proclamations, dated from Cambray and printed by order of the chambers, made their appearance.

This event created a new embarrassment in my position with regard to the chamber of representatives, who exhibited an increasing hostility against the Bourbons. We soon learnt, from the return of our agents and commissioners, that Wellington and Blucher declared, in an unqualified manner, that the authority of the chambers and the committees proceeded from an illegitimate source, and that consequently the best thing they could do was to dissolve themselves and proclaim Louis XVIII.

The committee then, at the instance of Carnot, deliberated, if it would not be proper to establish a rallying point, both for the chambers and the army, behind the Loire. I vehemently contended against this proposal, which would infallibly have rekindled the flames of foreign and domestic war. I maintained that so desperate a project would ruin France; that I was, moreover, satisfied that the greater part of the generals would not subscribe to it, and affirmed that I would be the last to quit Paris. Induced by my arguments, the committee took the more wise and prudent course of waiting the issue of events in Paris.

As soon as the convention of Paris was signed, the Duke of Wellington being informed of my wish to confer with him, expressed an inclination to come to an understanding with me respecting the execution of the convention. The committee of government did not object to an interview, which took place at the château de Neuilly. On that occasion I frankly opened my mind to the generalissimo of the allies. I knew well the efficacy of such words as moderation and clemency in seducing the higher order of minds; and, without seeking to diminish the culpability of those who had betrayed the Bourbons, I maintained that the re-established throne could only derive consolidation from an entire oblivion of the past. I represented how formidable and menacing the energy of the patriots still was, and referred to the management which would be necessary in order to calm their effervescence. I did not disguise the weakness of the royalists, their intractability and their prejudices; and I affirmed that there was no other means of restoring tranquillity than by opposing reactions and resentments, and by leaving no faction to indulge the hope of predominating in the state. I claimed the execution of the two authentic declarations of England and Austria, purporting that their intention was not to continue the war with a design of re-establishing the Bourbons, or imposing on France any government whatsoever. The generalissimo replied that that declaration had no other object than that of preventing war, and was resorted to in the hope that France would not take up arms in the cause of Napoleon, after he had been outlawed by the congress; but that, as we had risen in his favour, we had by that means liberated the allies from an engagement purely conditional. This sophistry did not leave a doubt upon my mind that we had been cajoled. Lord Wellington declared to me, without qualification, that the allied powers had formally decided in favour of Louis XVIII., and that that sovereign would make his entry into Paris on the 8th of July. General Pozzo di Borgo, who was present, repeated the same declaration on behalf of the Emperor of Russia; he communicated to me a letter from Prince Metternich and the Count de Nesselrode, expressive of a determination to recognise no one but Louis XVIII., and not to admit of any proposal at variance with the rights of that monarch.

I then insisted on a general amnesty, and required guarantees. On these conditions I consented to serve the King, and even to give him such pledges as might be consistent with my reputation and honour. The generalissimo answered me that it was determined to dismiss M. de Blacas, and that I should compose a part of the council, as well as M. de Talleyrand, the King having condescended to continue me in my office of general police; but he did not disguise from me that all kind of measures were taken in order that Napoleon might fall, as a hostage, into the power of the allies, and that it was required of me that I should do nothing to favour his escape. It was also required that the army should submit itself to the King, and that, for the sake of example, a few of its chiefs should be subjected to punishment. To this I objected; I protested that if Bonaparte had not made his appearance a crisis would have equally ensued. All my objections failed in shaking a thoroughly made up resolution. I regarded the evil to be without remedy, but at all events capable of being palliated by my presence in the council. The duke announced to me that the next day he would himself present me to his Majesty, or at least convey me in his carriage to the château d'Arnouville. I replied that it was my intention to address a letter to the King, which I had composed, and which I communicated to him. It was conceived in the following terms :

"SIRE,—The return of your Majesty leaves no other duty to be performed by the members of the government than that of divesting themselves of their functions. For the exoneration of my conscience, it is my request that I may be permitted faithfully to describe the state of public opinion and feeling in France.

"It is not your Majesty who is dreaded, since you have seen, during the space of eleven months, that a confidence in your Majesty's moderation and justice sustained the French people, in the midst of the terror which the proceedings of a portion of your court were calculated to inspire.

"It is universally known that neither intelligence nor experience are wanting to your Majesty. You understand France and your age; you understand the power of opinion; but your condescension has too often induced you to listen to the pretensions of those who followed you into adversity.

"From that time France was divided into two classes of people. It was, doubtless, a painful task for your Majesty to be continually obliged to repress the above pretensions by acts resulting from your own will. How many times must you have regretted that it was not in your power to oppose them by national laws.

"If the same system be reproduced, and, if deriving all your powers from hereditary title, your Majesty will not recognise any rights of the people but such as originate from concessions of the crown, France, as she was before, will be uncertain as to the nature of her duties; she will continue to waver between her love for her country and her love for her prince; between her inclination and her information. Her obedience will have no other basis than her personal confidence in your Majesty; and even if that confidence be sufficient to maintain respect, it is not by such means that dynasties acquire consolidation, and that dangers are averted. Sire, your Majesty is aware that those who urge the steps of power beyond its proper limits are very inadequate to sustain it when its unity is shaken; that authority impairs itself by a continual contest, which compels it to retrograde in all its proceedings; that the fewer rights there are left to the people, the more the well-founded distrust of that people will prompt them to preserve such as cannot be disputed; and that it is always by such means as these that loyalty becomes enfeebled and that revolutions are matured.

"We conjure you, Sire, deign for this once to consult nothing but your own sense of justice and your own enlightened judgment. Be persuaded that the French people attach in these days as much importance to their liberty as to their life. They will never consider themselves free, if there be not rights equally inviolable interposed between them and the claims of power. Have we not had, under your dynasty, states-general independent of the monarch?

"Sire, your wisdom cannot wait for events in order to make concessions. Under such circumstances, they will be prejudicial to your interests and, probably, increase in their extent. Concessions made at this time would soothe and pacify the public mind, and give force to royal authority; at a later period, concessions would only prove its weakness—such might be extorted by disorder—and the public mind would retain its state of exacerbation."

This letter was addressed on the day in question to his Majesty. On my return to Paris, I declared to the committee that the return of Louis XVIII. was inevitable, that such was the determined resolution of the allied powers, and that the time was even fixed to be the day after to-morrow. I concealed from them that I was retained in office: a circumstance which,

instead of being considered in the light of a guarantee
to the patriots, and a species of letting down, which
might enable a legitimate government, with less violence
of shock, to succeed a *de facto* government, would have
appeared to the fanatics in the light of wages for
my treachery, when, in fact, it was nothing but the
deserved reward of saving Paris. That very evening
the news got wind, and the same individuals loaded
me, in their harangues, with calumnies and maledic-
tions; the royalists alone addressed me in the language
of congratulation. Yes, I repeat, the royalists; and
among the most distinguished writers of that party
there are some who have since confessed that there
was a universal exclamation from all parts of the
country to the effect that without me there was
neither security for the King nor safety for France,
and that all parties had come to an understanding on
the necessity of continuing me in office. The next
day I proceeded towards St. Denis, and presented
myself at the château d'Arnouville, in order to have
my first audience of the King. I was introduced into
his closet by the president of the council, who leant
upon my arm. I entreated the King to tranquillise
the public mind by securing all individuals in the
enjoyment of their personal security; I represented
to him that clemency was, no doubt, accompanied by
disadvantages, but that the capitulation just concluded
appeared, as a matter of necessity, to reject every
other system; that a full and entire amnesty, and
without any conditions, appeared to me the only
method to impart stability to the state and durability
to the government; that, in this instance, pardon was

little more than another word for justice ; and that by an amnesty I understood, not only an oblivion of offences, but also a preservation of places, property, honours, and titles. My discourse appeared to have made an impression on the King, who listened to it with unbroken attention. That prince was fully aware of the need in which we stood of skilfulness and tranquillity, in order to re-assemble the elements which time and circumstances had dispersed. I thought I perceived that he comprehended the necessity of throwing a veil over past faults, and of gaining confidence, by exemplary moderation and good faith. I made a point of rendering this interview as public as possible, in order to give public opinion an opportunity of foreseeing a probable term to our discords and calamities.

I did not confine myself to entreaties ; I went so far as to represent to the King that Paris was in the most violent state of excitement; that there would be danger to his person in showing himself at the gates of the capital with the white cockade, and accompanied exclusively by the emigrants of Ghent. My plan consisted in maintaining the continuance of the chambers, in engaging the King to assume the tri-colour cockade, and to dismiss all his military household. In a word, it was my wish, as it always had been, to see Louis XVIII. heading the march of the Revolution, and so contributing to its consolidation.

These different views were submitted to deliberation in the council ; my proposals were only rejected by the majority of a single vote. The King, however, remained immovable. Sooner than consent to them he declared he would rather return to Hartwell. Accordingly his military household was not dissolved, and it was decided that the representatives should be expelled next day from the chamber. That chamber had just laid down, in a new Bill of Rights, the fundamental principles of the constitution which, according to the views it entertained, could alone satisfy the public desire. Although I had not expected much success from my proceedings, because my tact in public affairs had sufficiently apprised me of their tendency, it appeared to me that I ought to neglect nothing for the acquittal of my conscience.

The very evening of the 7th of July several Prussian battalions forced the gates of the Tuileries, and invaded the courts and the avenues of the palace. The committee of government, being no longer free, discontinued its functions, and announced the fact by a message. One particular circumstance rendered this separation of my colleagues remarkable. Carnot, one of the most decided in objecting to my retainment in office, and to his own subjection—if I may use the phrase—to my supervision, while waiting till a place of residence was appointed for him, wrote me the following note: "*Traitor!* where do you require me to go?" I answered him in the same laconic manner, "Simpleton! where you please." It must be confessed that I had in the council more than one altercation with Carnot, who never forgave me for having called him an old woman.

The next day, as early as eight o'clock in the morning, the deputies made their appearance, in order to enter the hall of their deliberations; but finding the doors closed, surrounded by guards and gendarmes, they withdrew. A few of them, repairing to the house of their president, there subscribed a protest.

The King made his public entry into Paris; nothing disturbed the excessive joy of the royalists, who hurried to meet their monarch, and exhibited themselves in very considerable numbers. I must confess that my presentiment was, in some degree, falsified, and that all my apprehensions did not receive confirmation. Thus finished the reign of a hundred days, and thus recommenced a reign interrupted during its first year. But what were the omens which accompanied this new accession? All the passions which inflame each other; all the resentments which thirst for satiation; all the interests which struggle and contend together; all the frenzy which lashes itself into outrage; in short, all the ulcerated feelings which burn for reaction! In so deplorable a conjuncture I did not withhold from my country the benefit of my labours and exertions.

The surrender of Bonaparte, the successive submission of all the towns and all the provinces in France, soon announced that the country was pacified in all such respects as could interest the allied sovereigns; but it could not be perfectly so as regarded the repose and welfare of the King unless everything was forgotten; unless there was an equal restraint upon all extreme opinions, from whatsoever source those opinions might be derived; and unless, in short, all the parties of the state enjoyed the protection of the laws with the same certainty and the same security.

Such were the counsels of moderation and clemency

which I gave to Louis XVIII. (as I had previously given them to Napoleon), at the same time that I proposed efficacious measures for averting the results of all such causes as tended to replunge France into the abyss of a new revolution. But all individuals, either in or out of the council, did not share my views. Examples and punishments were considered necessary. I had already, for a fortnight, constituted a part of the royal administration when the *ordonnance* of the 24th of July made its appearance. Fifty-seven individuals, divided into two categories, were therein proscribed without trial. It was asked how I could countersign such an act which affected individuals who had pursued the same line of politics as myself. Let it be understood, then, that ever since the day following the 8th of July the desire of proscribing had possessed all classes of the royalist party, from the *salons* of the Faubourg St. Germain to the antechambers of the palace of the Tuileries, and that thousands of names, obscure as well as notorious, were indicated to the police department for the purpose of being involved in a general measure of proscription. Heads were demanded of the minister of police as pledges of his sincere devotion to the royal cause. There only remained two paths for me to follow—that of making myself an accomplice in acts of vengeance, or that of renouncing office. To the first I could not subscribe; the second I was too deeply compromised to adopt. I discovered a third expedient, and that was to reduce the list to a small number of names, selected from persons who had performed the most conspicuous part during the late events; and here, I must confess, that I met, in the council, and more especially in the eminently French feelings of the monarch, with everything that was calculated to mitigate those measures of overstrained rigour, and to diminish the number of the victims.

But the torrent of reaction threatened to sweep away all the barriers opposed to it. I had conceived the design of acting the part of mediator between the King and the patriots. I soon perceived that the only intention was to make use of me as a necessary instrument for the re-establishment of a royal power without counterpoise and limit, and which would have supplied no guarantee to the men of the Revolution. The two *ordonnances* with regard to the electoral colleges and the elections which were about to furnish France with the chamber of 1815, left me no longer a shadow of doubt upon this point. It has been thought that I exhibited a culpable neglect in the formation of the electoral colleges; and it has been said that it was no longer excusable in a statesman like myself, grown old in experience and the exercise of important functions, to commit such a political error, nor to be mistaken as to the bias which the royalist faction, now repossessed of influence, exerted itself to impart to public opinion. My principles and my previous conduct ought to have secured me from similar imputations. This accusation of unprophetic levity and fatal indifference in grave conjunctures must be attributed to the amiable egotism and the *nonchalant* supineness of the president of the council, who indulged himself in sensual illusions, and did not wish to see anything else in the *fauteuil* of a minister but a bed of roses.

I was roused by this; it was now that my notes. addressed to the allied powers, and my reports, presented to the King in full council, appeared to the world. I had composed them in conformity with the wishes of the allied sovereigns, in order to supply them with materials for judging of the actual condition of France. The publication of those documents produced a profound sensation in enlightened minds; but their contents exasperated to the highest degree the ultra-royalist party,[1] who regarded its influence as lost if my disclosures led to a change of system. The King himself was displeased at the publicity given to reports of a confidential nature; but I had preconsidered my position. Deceived by M. de Vitrolles, whom I had introduced into the King's cabinet, deserted by the president of the council, whom the past did not oblige to sacrifice the present, I perceived that my fall was inevitable, unless I could succeed in giving preponderance to my designs.

Shall I confess it in this place? Yes. I have promised to disguise nothing. My notes and my reports were intended to impart unity and integrity to the dislocated and scattered members of the Revolution, and especially to give Europe cause to fear a national insurrection. By that means I hoped to intimidate her so much, on the score of an explosion, that she would consent to grant us, as the price of a definitive treaty of peace, that which I had never ceased soliciting since the congress of Prague—the

---

[1] It was Fouché who first made use of this expression, which has since become familiar, and which indeed has been quite worn out.—*Note by the French Editor.*

dynasty of Napoleon, which had become the single
object of our secret demands, of our desires, and of
our efforts. The interview of two powerful monarchs
contributed to disperse hopes which were not without
foundation. It belongs to history to collect and compare circumstances which it does not appertain to me
to elucidate. It appears as if I were summing up
my whole life when I declare that it was my wish
to conquer for the Revolution, and that the Revolution
has been conquered in me.

SHORT BIOGRAPHICAL SKETCHES

OF

NOTABLE PERSONS

MENTIONED IN THESE MEMOIRS

ALQUIER.

Charles-Jean-Marie, Baron Alquier, politician and diplomatist, was born at Talmont (Vendée) in 1752, died at Paris 4th of February, 1826. Sent to the States-general, then to the Convention, he voted for the death of the King with some reservations. Under the Directory and the Empire he fulfilled various diplomatic functions at Naples and Rome, and in Bavaria and Sweden. He was exiled in 1816 and recalled in 1818.

ARENA.

Barthélemy Arena, politician, was born at the Ile-Rousse (Corsica) towards 1775, died at Leghorn in 1829. He was deputy to the Legislative Assembly, then to the Council of the Five Hundred, in which he made a violent opposition to the 18th Brumaire. His brother Joseph died upon the scaffold at Paris in 1802 for conspiracy, the reality of which is doubtful.

COUNT D'ARTOIS.

Charles-Philippe, fourth son of the dauphin Louis (son of Louis XV.) and of Marie-Josephe de Saxe, was born at Versailles 9th of October, 1757, died at Goritz 6th of November, 1836. He passed his youth in great dissipation, his multiplied gallantries and prodigal follies costing the royal treasury fourteen million francs during the time of its greatest distress. This conduct, in conjunction with the course that he pursued in the Assembly, where he was one of the chiefs of the party which encouraged the court to make no concession, made him very unpopular. He emigrated shortly after the taking of the Bastille, and was joined by his elder brother, with whom quarrels soon ensued. The Vendean leader Charette wrote to the Comte de Provence concerning the Comte d'Artois: "Sire, the cowardice of your brother has spoilt all." He had been brought by an English fleet to the coast of France to assist Charette, but had not dared to disembark. He mounted the throne in 1824, but was obliged to abdicate in 1830.

AUGEREAU.

Pierre-François-Charles Augereau, Duc de Castiglione, Marshal of France, was born at Paris 21st of October, 1757, died 12th of June, 1816. Son of a servant, he enlisted, then lived in a very poor state at Naples, where he earned a living as fencing-master. Returning to France at the time of the Revolution, he enlisted again, and became captain of hussars in June, 1793. In the December of the same year he was made general of division in the army of the Pyrénées Orientales, and was very successful in his contests with the Spaniards. Sent to the Italian army under Bonaparte, he covered himself with glory in the very memorable campaign of 1796.

He rallied to Napoleon after the 18th Brumaire. He was sent to command the army in Holland, and was made marshal at his first promotion. In the campaigns of Austerlitz, Jena, and Eylau he covered himself with glory. In 1814, charged with the command of the army of Lyons, he, through weakness or treason, did not perform the *rôle* expected of him, and his inaction contributed to the capitulation of Paris. One of the first to acclaim the Restoration, he was made a peer. On the return from Elba he was proclaimed a traitor by Bonaparte and his offers of service refused. He was similarly treated by the Bourbons when they again returned, so, scorned by all parties, he retired to private life.

BABEUF.

François Noël Babeuf, journalist, born at Saint-Quentin in 1764, died upon the scaffold 27th of May, 1797. He founded at Amiens a journal, *The Picard Correspondent*, the violence of which caused him to be prosecuted. In July, 1794, he commenced to publish at Paris *The Tribune of the People, or The Defender of the Liberty of the Press*. He advocated the equal division of property. Unfortunately for him, he attempted to put his theories into practice, and organised a vast conspiracy against the Directory. Some days before the execution of the plot Babeuf was betrayed and arrested. He attempted to commit suicide, was unsuccessful, and was dragged bleeding to the scaffold.

BAILLEUL.

Jacques-Charles Bailleul, member of the Convention, was born at Bretteville (Seine-Inférieure) in 1762, died at Paris 16th of March, 1843. Advocate to the Parliament of Paris at the time of the Revolution, he was elected to the Convention, where he voted for detention at the trial of the King, and was one of the signatories of the protestation against the 31st of May. Proscribed and arrested, he obtained his liberty after the 9th Thermidor. He was one of the founders of the *Constitutionnel*, and published several articles on political economy.

BARAILON.

Jean-François Barailon, politician, doctor, and antiquary, was born at Viersat (Creuse) 12th of January, 1743, died at Chambon 14th of March, 1816. Elected member of the Convention, he voted for the exile of the King, and afterwards expressed his disapproval of Robespierre and his partisans.

BARÈRE.

Barère de Vieuzac (Bertrand), a celebrated member of the Convention, was born at Tarbes 10th of September, 1755, died 15th of January, 1841. Admitted as advocate to the Toulouse parliament, he was elected member of the Academy of the Floral Games for his brilliant eulogy on Louis XII. He was appointed counsellor of the seneschal's court of Bigorre, whence, in 1789, he was sent to the States-general. He founded a journal called the *Point du Jour*, in which he rendered an account of the sittings of the Assembly. On 19th of June he delivered a speech on the causes of the grain famine, in which he opposed the proposition that the goods of the clergy should be mortgaged for the loan required, and defended the liberty of the press. In 1790 he proposed a pension to the widow of Rousseau. In 1791 he supported all the measures proposed against the emigrants ; and he also caused it to be decreed that the "Serment du Jeu de Paume," by David, should be completed at the expense of the State. He put the first interrogatories to Louis XVI. at the trial, and voted for death without appeal or reprieve. Hesitating for some time between the different parties, he finally attached himself to the Mountain.

Appointed member of the Committee of Public Safety, Barère furnished more than two hundred reports upon all branches of administration. It was upon his reports that the arrest of Custine, the expulsion of the English sojourning in France, the confiscation of the goods of the condemned, the expulsion of the Bourbons, the judgment on the Queen, the destruction of the tombs of Saint-Denis, and the requisition of all men between the ages of eighteen and twenty-five were decreed. In October he caused the destruction of Lyons to be ordered. In spite of so many guarantees given to the Mountain, Barère was nevertheless denounced at the Jacobin Club, and Robespierre was obliged to undertake his defence. Barère's proposition that the English and Hanoverian prisoners should be executed was never carried out. Elected president of the Jacobin Society, he defended Robespierre until the eve of his fall ; but, seeing how the tide was running, he hastened to turn against Robespierre, and thus escaped the reaction of the 9th Thermidor. However, being accused in 1795, he was sentenced to transportation, but succeeded in escaping from the prison of Saintes. He was amnestied after the 18th Brumaire, and only reappeared on the scene during the Hundred Days. He was exiled in 1816, and returned to Paris after the 1830 revolution. His memoirs have been edited by MM. Carnot and David.

BARRAS.

Paul-François-Jean-Nicolas, Count de Barras, member of
the Directory, was born 30th of June, 1755, at Fos-Amphoux
(Var), died at Chaillot 29th of January, 1829. He served at
first in India, dissipated the greater part of his fortune, and,
returning to Paris in 1789, took part in the taking of the Bastille
and in the 10th of August. He voted for the death of the King
without appeal or respite. In October, 1799, he was sent to the
South on a mission with Fréron, distinguishing himself by his
severities ; and he followed all the operations of the Toulon
siege. Menaced by Robespierre, he was one of the most active
agents of the 9th Thermidor, and commanded the armed force of
the Convention which took possession of the Hôtel de Ville and
arrested Robespierre. Named director, he contributed materially
to the *coup d'état* of the 18th Fructidor. On the morrow of the
18th Brumaire he sent in his resignation and retired to Brussels,
where he lived in grand style, thanks to the immense fortune
made by his speculations. He returned to Paris during the
Restoration.

BARTHÉLEMY.

François Barthélemy, first count then marquis, statesman
and diplomatist, was born at Aubagne (Bouches-du-Rhône), 20th
of October, 1747, died at Paris 3rd of April, 1830. Brought
up by his uncle, he was, thanks to him, placed early in the office
of the Minister of Foreign Affairs. In December, 1791, he was
sent as minister of France to Switzerland, and it was he who
signed at Bâle, in April, 1795, the first treaty of peace of the
French Republic with a European power.

In June, 1796, the Royalists succeeded in getting him
elected member of the Directory. At the *coup d'état* of the 18th
Fructidor he was arrested and transported, first to Cayenne
and then to Sinnamary ; at the end of some months of captivity,
however, he escaped with Pichegru, Willot, and others in a
pirogue. After three days of perilous navigation, they reached
Holland, whence Barthélemy passed to England. Recalled to
France after the 18th Brumaire, he was elected a senator.

In April, 1814, he presided at the meeting of the Senate at

which was proclaimed the fall of Napoleon, and on 4th of June Barthélemy was made a peer of France. During the Hundred Days he was not employed. In July, 1815, he was recalled to the Chamber of Peers, and was soon appointed Minister of State and created marquis.

BAUDIN DES ARDENNES.

Pierre-Charles-Louis Baudin des Ardennes, a member of the Convention, was born at Sedan 18th of December, 1748, died 14th of October, 1799. Member of the Legislative Assembly in 1791, he was called to the Convention, where he voted for the detention of the King and his banishment until the peace.

EUGÈNE DE BEAUHARNAIS.

Eugène de Beauharnais, Duke of Leuchtenberg, Prince of Eichstadt, viceroy of Italy, known as Prince Eugène, was born at Paris 3rd of September, 1781, died in Bavaria 26th of February, 1824, in consequence of an attack of apoplexy. He was the son of Josephine and Viscount Beauharnais. Sub-lieutenant in 1797, he was charged by Bonaparte, who became the husband of Eugène's mother, with a mission to Corfu, and followed him into Egypt and Italy. At the creation of the Empire he was named prince, then Arch-chancellor of State and viceroy of Italy. In 1806 he married the princess Augusta-Amelia, daughter of the King of Bavaria. He distinguished himself in Austria, and especially at Wagram. When the divorce from Josephine was decided upon, it was his duty to announce that resolution to the Senate. Eugène took a glorious part in the Russian campaign, in which he commanded the 4th corps, executing a retreat in which were displayed the greatest military talents. He contributed to the victory of Lutzen, and set out again for Italy, where he was soon attacked by the Austrians, who were joined by Murat. Eugène gained another victory, but the fall of the Empire brought about changes in Italy. He then retired to Bavaria, and received from his father-in-law the title of Duke of Leuchtenberg and the rank of first peer of the realm.

BERLIER.

Théophile, Count Berlier, lawyer and statesman, was born at Dijon in 1741, died about 1840. Deputy from the Côte d'Or to the Convention, he voted for the death of the King without appeal or respite, and after the 9th Thermidor became member of the Committee of Public Safety. He was elected three times to the Council of the Five Hundred, and after the 18th Brumaire became Councillor of State, and finally count of the Empire. Exiled after the Hundred Days as a regicide, he retired to Belgium, and returned to France only after the Revolution of 1830.

BELLEGARDE.

Antoine Dubois de Bellegarde, member of the Convention, was born about 1740, died in 1825. He was admitted early to the body-guard, but was obliged to leave, entering then the service of Prussia, from which he deserted. He was elected deputy from Charente to the Legislative Assembly, then to the Convention, where he sat with the Mountain and voted for the death of the King.

BERNADOTTE.

Jean-Baptiste-Jules Bernadotte, King of Sweden and Norway under the name of Charles-John XIV., was born at Pau 26th of January, 1764, died 8th of May, 1844. Son of a lawyer, he enlisted when he was seventeen, and was only a non-commissioned officer in 1790 when an act of courage in an *émeute*, in which he saved his colonel's life, placed him *en évidence*, and thenceforth his advancement was rapid. He was general of division at Fleurus, and distinguished himself in the most brilliant manner in the campaigns of the Rhine and Germany. Sent (1798) on an embassy to Vienna, his mission met with little success, and on the renewal of hostilities was appointed general-in-chief of the army of observation of the Bas-Rhin, when he married the sister-in-law of Joseph Bonaparte. As Minister of War (1799) he displayed as much energy as ability, but was discharged by the influence of Sieyès. After the 18th Brumaire he offered a passive opposition to the Consular government, which did not prevent him being made marshal of the Empire in 1804 and Prince of Porte-Corvo after Austerlitz. Placed at the head of the corps of observation in the north of Germany, he knew so well how to obtain the sympathies of the populations that in 1810 the four states of Sweden chose him to replace the heir to the throne, who had just died. He obtained permission from the Emperor to accept the offer, arrived at Elsinore 19th of October, abjured Roman Catholicism, and, on 5th of November, was solemnly approved of by Charles XIII. He was hardly installed in this high position when grave disputes occurred between himself and Napoleon, the latter wishing to impose his policy upon the former; but Bernadotte was faithful to his adopted country, and after the battle of Lutzen joined the allies with 30,000 Swedes. His conduct proved fatal to the French, and contributed to a great extent to the reverses of 1813.

It was said that Bernadotte hoped that the allies would select him to succeed Bonaparte. Whether this be so or not, he received such a welcome from his late companions-in-arms when he visited Paris in 1814 that he was obliged to quit the capital promptly. He returned to Sweden, and succeeded to the throne 5th of July, 1818, under the title of Charles-John XIV. He administered his states with prudence and wisdom, and died in consequence of an attack of apoplexy. His son Oscar succeeded him.

BERTRAND MOLEVILLE.

Le Marquis Antoine-François de Bertrand Moleville, politician and historian, was born at Toulouse in 1744, died at Paris 19th of October, 1818. Minister of Marine, he was obliged to resign, and became minister of the secret police of the King. He was decreed to be accused after the 10th of August, but managed to reach England. He returned from England after the Revolution, but was entirely ignored by the Bourbons.

BESENVAL.

Pierre Victor, Baron de Besenval, a Swiss general in the service of France, was born at Soleure, in 1722, of a family of

Savoy origin, died at Paris 27th of June, 1794. At the time of the Revolution he was charged with an important command in the army collected round Paris. The public hate being raised against him, he fled, and was arrested and brought before the tribunal at Paris, but was discharged. Besenval remained hidden in Paris, and died there tranquilly.

BESSIÈRES.

Jean-Baptiste Bessières, Duc d'Istrie, marshal of France, was born in 1768, killed near Reppach (Saxony) 1st of May, 1813. He followed at first the business of a wig-maker, but enlisted in the Constitutional Guard of Louis XVI., and after the 10th of August he joined the legion of the Pyrenees. He distinguished himself in the army of Italy, and joined in the expedition to Egypt. Returning with Bonaparte, he contributed to the *coup d'état* of the 18th Brumaire. He distinguished himself at Marengo, and covered himself with glory in the campaign of Austerlitz, as well as at Jena, Friedland, and Eylau. After most stirring experiences in Spain and elsewhere, he was recalled for the campaign in Russia, in which he was in command of the cavalry of the Guard, and rendered eminent services. Remaining in Germany after the departure of the Emperor in order to reorganise the Guard, he commanded it on the eve of the battle of Lutzen, and was there killed by a cannon-ball. Bessières left behind him a reputation intact as regards honour and integrity.

BEURNONVILLE.

Pierre-Riel, Marquis de Beurnonville, marshal of France, was born 10th of May, 1752, at Champignolles, near Bar-sur-Aube, of a middle-class family, died at Paris 23rd of April, 1821. After having served some time in the Indies, he returned to France, and embraced the cause of the Revolution. He was attached as aide-de-camp to Marshal Luckner in 1792, and soon after was appointed marshal of the camp. He distinguished himself at Valmy, then at Jemmapes, and on this last battle-field was created general of the army of the Centre. At the head of this army he invaded Luxemburg. Sent with four commissioners to arrest Dumouriez, they were themselves arrested by the latter and given over to the Prince of Coburg. They remained imprisoned until given in exchange for the daughter of Louis XVI. Beurnonville manœuvred cleverly between the various parties, and was under Bonaparte successively ambassador, count, and senator. He afterwards assisted at the re-establishment of the Bourbons, and was created Minister of State and peer of France.

JOSEPH BONAPARTE.

Joseph Bonaparte, King of Naples, afterwards King of Spain, eldest brother of Napoleon, was born in Corsica 7th of January, 1768, died at Florence 28th of July, 1844. Chief of battalion at the siege of Toulon, he shortly afterwards married Mdlle. Clary, the daughter of a rich merchant of Marseilles. He followed his brother in the Italian campaign of 1796, and was appointed president at the court of Parma, and afterwards ambassador to Rome. Elected to the Council of the Five Hundred, he left it in 1799, and was involved in the intrigues which brought about the 18th Brumaire.

Although differences had occurred between the two brothers, when Napoleon became Emperor he sent Joseph with an army to invade the kingdom of Naples, and created him King by a decree of 30th of March, 1806. The situation was a difficult one, and in spite of Joseph's personal qualities and the improvements introduced by him, he had not gained the affection of his subjects when, by a decree of 6th of June, 1808, he was transferred from the throne of Naples to that of Spain. He therefore entered into a kingdom which had yet to be conquered. His only support was the French army, and he wished to be allowed to abdicate, but permission was never granted. The battle of Vittoria, where Joseph commanded in person (21st of June, 1813), finally decided the fate of the kingdom, and on 12th of July he definitely retired. In 1814 Napoleon made him commander of all the forces round Paris ; but Joseph, as previously, was not able to rise to the occasion. During the first Restoration he retired to Switzerland, but hurried to Paris on Napoleon's return. After the second abdication he crossed

to America, where he went under the name of Count Sur-
villiers.   After several voyages he obtained permission to
retire to Florence, where he ended his days.

LUCIEN BONAPARTE.

Lucien Bonaparte, Prince of Canino, second brother of
Napoleon, was born at Ajaccio 21st of March, 1775, died at
Viterbo 29th of June, 1840. He was brought up in France.
Imprisoned for six weeks as a Terrorist, he became afterwards
commissary to the army in Germany. Sent by the Council of
the Five Hundred, he played there a *rôle*, little by little, entirely opposed to the Directory. Elected member of the
Assembly some days after the return of his brother from
Egypt, he was one of the organisers of the *coup d'état* of 18th
Brumaire. Appointed Minister of the Interior in November,
1800, he was sent the same year as ambassador to Spain,
and signed the treaty of Badajos 20th of November, 1801.
He returned to France in 1802. His second marriage, in
1800, to the *divorcée* of an *agent de change* embroiled him to
such an extent with his brother that he left France and settled
at Rome. He repelled all offers of reconciliation, and was
made count by the Pope. He set out for America, but was
captured by an English privateer (1810), and being conducted
to England, remained there until 1814. In that year he became
reconciled to his brother, and during the Hundred Days served
him faithfully. After the second abdication he again returned
to Italy. His eldest son took a prominent part in the Roman
Revolution of 1848–1849.

PAULINE BORGHÈSE.

Marie-Pauline Bonaparte, Princesse de Borghèse, Duchesse
de Guastalla, third sister of Napoleon, was born at Ajaccio
30th of October, 1780, died at Florence 9th of June, 1825.
She married (1801) General Leclerc, whom she accompanied
to San Domingo and who died there. She married again
(1803) the Prince Camille Borghèse, who was not long in
separating from her. After 1806 she lived sometimes in Italy
and sometimes in France, but was banished from the Court

for having publicly insulted Maria Louisa. She with her mother visited Napoleon whilst he was at Elba. She was of rare beauty, and, as is known, was twice depicted by Canova, the first time in the character of *la Vénus victorieuse de Praxitèle*, the second in that of a *nymphe couchée*. These two sculptures are in England.

BOUILLÉ.

François-Claude-Amour, Marquis de Bouillé, general, was born 19th of November, 1739, at the château du Cluzel (Haute-Loire), died in 1800 in England. Governor of Guadeloupe, he served with great distinction in the American War. Appointed governor of Alsace and the Franche-Comté, it was his duty to repress the mutiny of the Swiss regiment at Nancy, which he did in a most rigorous manner. It was he who organised the flight of Louis XVI., and he emigrated when he heard that the latter had been arrested at Varennes.

BOULAY DE LA MEURTHE.

Antoine-Jacques-Claude, Comte Boulay de la Meurthe, politician, was born at Chaumousey (Vosges) 19th of February, 1761, died at Paris 4th of February, 1840. He served some time in the armies of the Republic, and after the 9th Thermidor discharged some judicial functions at Nancy. In October, 1798, he proposed that the nobility who had not yet emigrated should be expelled the Republic. He contributed to the 18th Brumaire, and under the Empire was made count, president of the section of legislation in the Council of State, and administrator of the disputed claims of the national property, and was awarded a seat at the Council of Regency. He was an exile from 1815 to 1819.

BOURDON DE L'OISE.

François-Louis Bourdon de l'Oise, member of the Convention, was born at Remy, near Compiègne, died at Sinnamari in 1797. Attorney to the Paris Parliament, he took part in the 10th of August business, and was elected deputy to the Convention by the department of l'Oise. He voted for the death of the King without appeal or respite, and took a prominent part in the

defeat of the Girondists.   In June, 1793, he was sent to La
Vendée, where he accused Westermann of pillage and suspended
Rossignol.   On his return he caused the Farmers-general to be
arrested (25th of November), fell out with the Terrorists, and
was excluded from the Cordeliers' Club as a traitor to the country.
He aided the fall of Robespierre, and from that time separated
himself more and more from the Revolutionary party, finally
attaching himself to the Clichien party (a Royalist club which
met from 1795 to 1797 in the garden of Clichy).   This was
dissolved at the 18th Fructidor, and Bourdon de l'Oise was
proscribed and transported to Sinnamari, where he died some
months after his arrival.

BOURGUIGNON.

Claude-Sébastien Bourguignon-Dumolard, lawyer, was born
at Vif (Isère) 21st of March, 1760, died at Paris 22nd of April,
1829.   He fulfilled divers administrative functions after the
9th Thermidor, and in 1799 was for a month Minister of Police.
After the trial of Moreau, where he was one of the judges, he
passed to the Court of Appeal.

BOURRIENNE.

Louis-Antoine Fauvelet de Bourrienne, diplomatist, was born
at Sens 9th of July, 1769, died near Caen in 1834.   He was
schoolfellow of Bonaparte at the Brienne school, and formed a
close intimacy with him.   Appointed secretary to the embassy
at Stuttgart, he was cashiered after the 10th of August, and
when he returned to France was imprisoned as an emigrant.
He was Bonaparte's private secretary during his consulship.
At the time of Bonaparte's fall, Bourrienne, who had been rudely
treated by the Emperor, was prefect of police, and followed
Louis XVIII. to Ghent, and on the return of the latter was
appointed Minister of State.

BRESSON.

Jean-Baptiste-Marie-François Bresson, member of the Convention, was born in 1760, died in 1832.   Sent to the Convention
by the department of the Vosges, he voted at the trial of the

King for detention and banishment. Proscribed on 31st of
May, he lived hidden in the Vosges until after the 9th
Thermidor, when he returned to the Assembly. After the
18th Brumaire he entered the Ministry of Foreign Affairs,
from which he became chief of division. He still occupied
this position in 1815, when in the month of December he
and his wife, at the hotel of the minister himself, where they
were lodging, gave shelter to Lavalette, who had been condemned to death and had escaped from the Conciergerie.

BRIOT.

Pierre-Joseph Briot, politician, was born 17th of April, 1771,
at Orchamps (Franche-Comté), died at Auteuil 16th of May,
1827. He followed, at intervals, a military career from 1792.
He was by turns imprisoned as reactionary under the Terror
and as Terrorist after the 9th Thermidor, was member of the
Council of the Five Hundred (1798), and opposed energetically
the *coup d'état* of the 18th Brumaire. He fulfilled later some
administrative functions in the isle of Elba, then at Naples
under Joseph and under Murat, whom he quitted when the
latter declared against France.

BROGLIE.

Victor François, Duc de Broglie, was born 19th of October,
1718, died 1804. He served with distinction in Italy, Bohemia,
and Germany. He was Minister of War in 1789, and he
emigrated and fought, in 1792, on the side of the Prussians.

BRUIX.

Eustache Bruix, admiral, was born at San Domingo 17th
of July, 1759, died at Paris 18th of March, 1805. Embarking
at the age of fifteen as a volunteer on board a merchant vessel,
he became a midshipman during the American war, obtained
the command of the *Pivert*, and during four years devoted
himself to the study of the coasts of San Domingo. His
career was a most creditable one. He had command of the
Boulogne flotilla, but his health gave way, and he was obliged
to go to Paris, where he soon afterwards died.

GENERAL BRUNE.

Guillaume-Marie-Anne Brune, marshal of France, was born 13th of May, 1763, at Brives-la-Gaillarde (Corrèze), assassinated at Avignon 2nd of August, 1815. Son of a lawyer, he was first destined for the bar, but became a printer. Attached to Danton, he was nominated (September, 1792) deputy to the adjutants-general of the interior, then (October) colonel adjutant-general, and in this position he followed Dumouriez in his Belgian campaign. He was sent (1793) against the Federalists of Calvados, and, returning afterwards to the army of the North, distinguished himself at the battle of Hondshoote, and held different commands in the interior. He gained the grade of general of division in the army of Italy (1796). From 1802 to 1804 he was ambassador in Turkey, and on his return was created marshal of the Empire. In 1805 he commanded the army near Boulogne, and in 1807 was named governor of the Hanseatic towns.

Having signed with the King of Sweden a convention in which was mentioned the *French army* instead of the army of his *Imperial and Royal Majesty*, he excited in the highest degree the anger of Napoleon, who caused Berthier to write to him that nothing so scandalous had occurred since the time of Pharamond. His command was taken from him, and he was not again employed on active service. In 1814 he rallied to the Bourbons, but during the Hundred Days he accepted a command. At the return of Louis XVIII. he submitted, and was on his way to Paris when he was assassinated and his body thrown in the Rhone. This murder remained unpunished, one man being prosecuted on the complaint of the widow and sentenced in default, but Madame Brune was mulcted in costs.

CABANIS.

Pierre-Jean-George Cabanis, a celebrated physiologist and philosopher, was born at Cosnac (Charente-Inférieure) 5th of June, 1757, died at Rueil (Seine-et-Oise), 5th of May, 1808. After having travelled in Poland, he gave himself up to the study of medicine. He was introduced by Turgot into the brilliant society of Madame Helvetius, and was also the friend of Mirabeau, whom he tended in his last illness.

CADOUDAL.

Georges Cadoudal, a celebrated Chouan leader, was born 1st of January, 1771, at Kerleano, near d'Auray, died upon the scaffold at Paris 25th of June, 1804. When the Vendean insurrection broke out, he joined the corps of Stofflet (June, 1793), under whose command he served as captain of cavalry. After the defeat of the Royalists at Savenay, he went to Morbihan, which he was endeavouring to organise when he was arrested and transferred to Brest, whence he escaped at the end of some months. He rejoined the insurgents, and became the most powerful and active chief of the Breton Chouans until the convention that he signed with Brune in 1800. Called to Paris, he had an interview with Bonaparte, but refused all offers made to him by the latter, and went to England, where Louis XVIII. made him lieutenant-general. He then set himself to organise a vast conspiracy against Bonaparte, but always denied being implicated in the infernal machine episode. Returning secretly to France, he conferred with Moreau and Pichegru ; but, seeing the futility of his efforts, he was about to return from Paris when he was arrested, after a fierce resistance. He did not belie his courage in the trial, which terminated by his condemnation.

CAMBACÉRÈS.

Jean-Jacques-Regis de Cambacérès, a celebrated statesman, was born at Montpellier 18th of October. 1753, died at Paris 8th of March, 1824. He was counsellor to the Montpellier court of accounts at the time of the Revolution, and was elected to the presidency of the criminal tribunal of the Hérault, being sent by this department to the Convention. He played an important *rôle* in the preliminaries of the trial of Louis XVI. : and after having contested the right of the court to try the monarch, he voted for provisional detention, with death in case of invasion. His conduct during the Terror was very discreet, seeing that, although he did not efface himself, he was able to get over those troublous times in safety. Nominated president of the Convention in 1794, he then passed to the Committee of Public Safety, of which he was elected president, and had charge of foreign affairs. An intercepted letter caused him to be charged with royalist tendencies, and prevented him becoming a member of the Directory. He was chosen second Consul by Bonaparte, then Arch-chancellor, perpetual president of the Senate, and Duke of Parma. In 1814 Cambacérès escorted Maria-Louisa to Blois, where he delivered her and her son to the Austrian commissioners. At the second Restoration he was exiled as a regicide, and was recalled in 1818.

CARNOT.

Joseph-François-Claude Carnot, politician and general, one of the most celebrated personages of the Revolution, was born at Molay (Côte d'Or), 13th of May, 1753, died at Magdeburg 2nd of August, 1823. Entering as second lieutenant of engineers at the École de Mézières, he left it (1777) first lieutenant, and was made captain in 1783, carrying off the same year the prize offered at the Academy of Dijon for an eulogy of Vauban.

At the time of the Revolution, the principles of which he embraced with enthusiasm, he addressed several pamphlets to the National Assembly—amongst others, one concerning the re-establishment of the finances, in which he proposed to pay the State's creditors by means of the property of the clergy. In 1791 he married the daughter of a rich merchant, and was sent to the Assembly by the Pas-de-Calais. Elected to the Convention, he was charged with the organisation of a *corps d'armée* upon the frontier of Spain ; then, after the trial of the King, at which he voted for death, he returned to the army of the North. In the month of August, 1793, he became a member of the Committee of Public Safety, in which was confided to him the administration of the war and the direction of military operations. It was to his great administrative capacity and his unceasing labours that the Republic owed that organisation and success of its armies which saved it from the foreigner. Denounced after the affair of the 1st Prairial, he was saved by Bourdon de l'Oise, who asked if they dared to order the accusation of the man who had " organised victory." At the dissolution of the Convention he was elected deputy by fourteen departments.

At the *coup d'état* of 18th Fructidor it was with difficulty that he escaped the soldiers charged to arrest him in the Luxembourg palace and was able to reach Switzerland, from where he retired to Augsburg. After the 18th Brumaire Carnot returned to France, and was appointed Minister of War. He soon resigned and retired to private life, which he left only in 1814, offering, by a letter which became celebrated, his services to Napoleon, who made him governor of Antwerp. Being only chief of battalion, it was necessary, in order that he could occupy the post, to confer upon him in one day the grades of lieutenant-colonel, colonel, general of brigade, and general of division. After having gloriously defended Antwerp, he returned to Paris, and soon published a *brochure* (" Mémoire adressé au Roi ") which caused an immense sensation. After Waterloo he tried in vain to organise a defence against the invasion. Proscribed in 1816, he retired first to Warsaw, then to Magdeburg, where he died.

CAZALÈS.

Jacques-Antoine-Marie de Cazalès, politician, was born at Grenade-sur-Garonne (Haute-Garonne) 1st of February, 1758, died at Engalin (Gers) 24th of November, 1805. He was captain of dragoons at the time of the convocation of the States-general, to which he was sent by the nobility of the bailiwick of Rivière-Verdun (Haute-Garonne). He was not long in showing himself to be one of the most remarkable orators, and was always the ardent defender of the rights of the King and clergy. The events of the 10th of August compelled him to quit France, and he was in the ranks of the emigrants when he wrote to the Convention requesting a safe-conduct to enable him to return and defend Louis XVI.

CHAMPAGNY.

Jean-Baptiste Nompère de Champagny, Duke of Cadore, statesman, was born in 1756, died in 1834. Nephew to the Abbé Terray on his mother's side, he was elected to the States-general, in 1789, by the nobility of the bailiwick of Montbrison, and joined the *tiers état*. After the 18th Brumaire he was

nominated to the Council of State, and became the spokesman
of the government in the Corps Législatif and at the Tribunat.
He adhered to the abdication, and was made a peer by Louis
XVIII. ; nevertheless he occupied office during the Hundred
Days, but retired into private life at the second Restoration.

CHAMPIONNET.

Jean-Etienne Championnet, general of the Republic, was born
at Valence (Drôme) in 1762, died at Antibes 10th of January,
1800. He first served in the Spanish army, but, returning to
France in 1791, was appointed commander of a battalion of
volunteers. Sent to the army of the Rhine, he soon gained
the grade of general of division, with which he passed to the
army of Sambre-et-Meuse, taking the most glorious part in the
victory of Fleurus. He was sent, in 1798, to the army which
occupied Rome. The weakness of the forces entrusted to him
compelled him to evacuate the city, seeing the superiority of
the enemy ; but, after having beaten General Mack, he did not
delay his re-entry into Rome, and took possession of Capua and
Naples. Having expelled an agent of the Directory on a charge
of extortion, he was cashiered, brought before a council of war,
and imprisoned at Grenoble ; the 30th Prairial, however, restored
him to liberty. Entrusted with the command of the army of
the Alps by the new Directory, he did not meet with complete
success, the defeat of Moreau and Jourdan leaving him exposed
to superior forces. His army was decimated by an epidemic,
to which he himself succumbed.

CHÉNIER.

André-Marie de Chénier, poet, was born at Constantinople
in 1762, died on the scaffold at Paris in 1794. In 1787 he was
appointed ambassador to England. On his return he adopted
the principles of the Revolution with fervour. Suspected by the
Jacobins, he finally provoked his arrest. After six months in
the prison of Saint-Lazare, where he might have been forgotten,
an imprudent act of his father recalled attention to him. He
was brought before the Revolutionary tribunal, condemned to
death, and conducted to the scaffold with the poet Roucher
two days before the 9th Thermidor.

CHEVALIER.

Chevalier, a mechanical engineer, died upon the scaffold at Paris in 1800. He was employed in the manufacture of powder under the Convention, and invented several firearms—amongst others, an explosive fuse. He was in prison for republican opinions at the time of the infernal machine explosion, and although quite innocent of it, he was sent before a military tribunal and condemned to death.

CHODERLOS DE LACLOS.

Pierre-Ambroise-François Choderlos de Laclos was born at Amiens in 1741, died at Tarente 2nd of November, 1803. He was captain of engineers when he published (1782) "Les Liaisons Dangereuses," a work cleverly written, but of a profound immorality. Its success was surprising. Attached afterwards to Philippe Egalité, he accompanied the latter to England. Returning in 1791, he drew up with Brissot the famous petition the result of which was the assemblage in the Champ de Mars. Implicated with his patron, he was arrested and detained until the 9th Thermidor.

CHOUDIEU.

Pierre Choudieu, member of the Convention, was born at Angers, died in 1840. Member of the Legislative Assembly, then of the Convention, he voted for the death of the King without appeal or respite. He was sent on a mission to La Vendée, and declared himself ardently against the Girondists. Compromised in the movement of the 12th Germinal, his arrest was ordered ; he was released after the 18th Brumaire. Pro scribed after the attempt of the 3rd Nivôse, he took refuge in Holland. He returned to France under the Empire and was banished in 1816.

CLARKE.

Henri-Jacques-Guillaume Clarke, Count of Hunebourg and Duke of Feltre, marshal of France, statesman, was born at Landrecies in 1765, died in 1818. Captain of hussars in 1784, he was afterwards attached to the embassy at London. Re-entering the army, he became general of brigade, but was discharged as a suspect; then, in 1795, he was nominated by Carnot chief of the topographical bureau of the Ministry of War. The next year he accepted a secret mission to watch Bonaparte in Italy; but he betrayed the Directory, and so was recalled and cashiered, only returning to service after the 18th Brumaire. He occupied several posts under Bonaparte, including that of private secretary; but he accepted a peerage from Louis XVIII., and followed that monarch to Ghent. His conduct towards his old companions-in-arms—amongst others, towards Marshal Ney, whose act of accusation he signed —raised against him bitter recriminations.

COLLOT-D'HERBOIS.

Jean-Marie Collot-d'Herbois, politician, was born at Paris in 1750, died in Guiana 8th of January, 1796. At first oratorian, he became afterwards an actor, and travelled in the provinces and abroad. He made his *début* in politics by a small treatise, "l'Almanach du P. Gerard" (1791), which had an immense success; was one of the promoters of the 10th of August, and, sent to the Convention, ranged himself with the most fiery members of the Mountain. Dispatched to Lyons, after the taking of that town, he made himself notorious by his cruelty, and escaped an attempted assassination. Though one of the most fervid opponents of Robespierre, he was nevertheless sentenced to transportation in April, 1795.

CONDORCET.

Jean-Antoine-Nicolas de Caritat, Marquis de Condorcet, the celebrated geometrician, philosopher, and politician, was born at Ribemont (Aisne) 17th of September, 1743, died at Bourg-la-Reine (Seine) 9th of April, 1794. After the defeat of the Girondists, he was, upon the denunciation of Chabot (9th of July, 1793), decreed for arrest and then for accusation. He remained for some time hidden in Paris, but not wishing longer to compromise his friend who had sheltered him, he left the city, and was arrested and imprisoned at Bourg-la-Reine. On the morrow he was found dead, having taken poison.

John Morley, in his "Critical Miscellanies," thus writes of Condorcet:—"This was the very day" (Danton's execution) "on which the virtuous and high-minded Condorcet quitted the friendly roof that for nine months had concealed him from the search of proscription. The same week he was found dead in his prison. While Danton was storming with impotent thunder before the tribunal, Condorcet was writing those closing words of his 'Sketch of Human Progress' which are so full of strength and edification."

BENJAMIN CONSTANT.

Henry Benjamin Constant de Rebecque, a celebrated publicist and *littérateur*, was born at Lausanne in 1767, died in 1830. After passing the early years of his life in England, Scotland, and Germany, he became chamberlain to the Duke of Brunswick, married, and settled down in France. There he joined the moderate Republican party, and was one of the most active of the constitutional party which supported Mme. de Staël, with whom he formed the closest intimacy. He entered the Tribunat after the 18th Brumaire, but was obliged to quit it in 1802. The following year he left France with Mme. de Staël, retiring to Weimar, and afterwards to Göttingen, where he married again. Returning to France in 1814, he attached himself to the Bourbons, but soon began to attack them. During the Hundred Days he accepted from the Emperor, whom he had at first opposed, the post of Councillor of State. After Waterloo he dwelt for some time in England, but on his return waged, either in *brochures* or in the *Minerva* journal, a bitter war against the government, and continued it when sent to the Chamber.

CORNET.

Matthieu-Augustin, Count Cornet, politician, was born at Nantes 19th of April, 1750, died at Paris May 4th, 1832. He assisted at the 18th Brumaire, and under the Empire became senator, secretary of the Senate, count, and grand officer of the Legion of Honour. He adhered to the act of forfeiture in 1814, and was created a peer by Louis XVIII.

COURTOIS.

Edme-Bonaventure Courtois, politician, was born at Arcis-sur-Aube in 1750, died at Brussels 6th of December, 1816. Sent from l'Aube to the Convention, he voted for the death of the King without appeal or respite, and took an active part in the 9th Thermidor. He was charged with the examination of the papers found at Robespierre's house, and published a report in two volumes on the subject. After 1802 he lived some time in retirement. In 1816 the Minister of Police caused his house to be searched and his papers, which were numerous and important, to be seized.

COUTHON.

Georges Couthon, a famous member of the Convention, was born at Orcet (Puy-de-Dôme) in 1756, died upon the scaffold in Paris 28th of July, 1794. Lawyer at Clermont, he pronounced himself with fervour in favour of the Revolution. Although almost completely paralysed, he was elected to the Legislative Assembly, where he was distinguished by his violence. Elected to the Convention, he voted for the death of the King without either respite or appeal. Hesitating for some time between the party of the Gironde and that of the Mountain, he at last delivered himself entirely to the latter, and contributed to the *coup d'état* of 31st of May. He became a member of the Committee of Public Safety, and, being sent to the army of Lyons, was remarked, after the taking of that town, by the vengeance which he executed upon the vanquished. At the 9th Thermidor, not wishing to be separated from Robespierre, he was included in the same decree of accusation and led at the same time to the scaffold.

DAUNOU.

Pierre-Claude-François Daunou, politician, scholar, and historian, was born 18th of August, 1761, at Boulogne sur-Mer, died at Paris 20th of June, 1840. He taught philosophy at the colleges of Troyes and Soissons, and brought himself into notice by his two pamphlets—the one, " The Influence of Boileau on French Literature " (1787), the other upon " The Origin and Extent of Parental Authority." He distinguished himself by the part he took in the Convention with regard to anything which concerned public instruction.

DAVOUST.

Louis Nicholas Davoust, Duke of Auerstaedt, Prince of Echmühl, marshal of France, was born in 1770, died in 1823. Pupil at the Brienne school, he became in 1791 chief of battalion in Dumouriez's army, afterwards serving as general of brigade in the armies of the Moselle and Rhine. He followed Bonaparte in Egypt. Commander of the third corps of the Grand Army, he took a most brilliant part in the campaign of 1805 and following years. On 14th of October, 1806, he gained over the Prussian army, with the King at its head, a victory at least as glorious as that gained at Jena the same day. He also showed rare ability at Wagram. Appointed governor of Poland, he exhibited that severity and inflexibility which were natural to him. After the Russian campaign he shut himself up in Hamburg, where he withstood a terrible siege, only consenting to evacuate when peace was signed and he received a formal order from Louis XVIII. He took service again during the Hundred Days. Commander-in-chief of the army collected around Paris after Waterloo, which clamoured to receive the signal for combat, he received orders from the provisional government to sign a convention with the enemy, which delivered again the town to the allies.

DECRÈS.

Denis Decrès was born in 1761, assassinated at Paris in 1820. Captain of a vessel in 1793, and vice-admiral in 1798, he distinguished himself at Aboukir. Whilst returning to Malta on the *William Tell* he was captured, after a glorious combat. He was afterwards appointed naval minister, which office he again held during the Hundred Days.

DELBREL.

Pierre Delbrel, member of the Convention, was born at Moissac (Tarn-et-Garonne) in 1764, died about 1832. He voted at the trial of the King for death with appeal. He combated energetically the 18th Brumaire, and was for some time proscribed. Member of the Chamber of Representatives during the Hundred Days, he was exiled in 1817 and recalled in 1818.

DESSOLES.

Jean-Joseph-Paul-Augustin, Marquis Dessoles, was born in 1767, died in 1828. At the time of the entry of the allies into Paris (1814) he was chosen to command the National Guard in the capital, and he decided the Emperor Alexander to set aside the regency and recall the Bourbons, when he was appointed Minister of State. He passed the Hundred Days in retirement. Ennobled at the second Restoration, he defended the liberty of the press.

DONNADIEU.

Gabriel Donnadieu, general, was born in 1777, died in 1849. General of brigade in 1811, he was implicated in a plot and arrested. During the Hundred Days he followed the King to Ghent, who on his return appointed him lieutenant-general. It was he who suppressed the Didier conspiracy.

DUBOIS DE CRANCÉ.

Edouard-Louis-Alexis Dubois de Crancé, politician, was born at Charleville (Ardennes) in 1747, died at Rethel 29th of June, 1814. Elected to the National Assembly, and then to the Convention, he voted for the death of the King and was violent in his denunciation of the Girondists. Sent against Lyons, which had rebelled, he assisted materially in the taking of the town. He was accused of moderate opinions, and suffered imprisonment for some time. Disgraced at the 18th Brumaire, he lived afterwards in retirement.

DUCOS.

Count Roger Ducos, politician, was born in 1754, died near Ulm, March, 1816. He was sent to the Convention by the department of the Landes, and voted for the death of the King. He was president of the Council of the Ancients, which position he held on the celebrated day of the 18th Fructidor. He conspired with Sieyès and Bonaparte against the Directory, and the 19th Brumaire he was elected president of the provisional consulate; and at the first sitting of the new government he and Sieyès shared the directorial chest, containing from 800,000 to 900,000 francs. He was made a peer during the Hundred Days, and was afterwards banished under the law against regicides.

DUPORT.

Adrian Duport, lawyer, was born at Paris in 1759, died at Appenzell (Switzerland), August, 1798. Arrested after the 10th of August, he was saved by Danton, and emigrated. He returned after the death of Robespierre, but emigrated again after the 18th Fructidor.

DUROC.

Géraud-Christophe-Michel Duroc, Duc de Frioul, was born in 1772, killed at Mackersdorf (Saxony) 23rd of May, 1813. Lieutenant of artillery, he soon became aide-de-camp to Bonaparte, to whom he remained attached until his death. He took part in the campaigns of Italy and Egypt.

DUVAL.

Jean-Pierre Duval, politician, died 1819. Sent from the Seine-Inférieure to the Convention, he voted for the detention at the trial of the King. He was proscribed after the 31st of May; was one of the Council of the Five Hundred; and became (1799) Minister of Police, then prefect under the Empire.

DUC D'ENGHIEN.

Louis-Antoine-Henri de Bourbon-Condé, Duc d'Enghien, was born at Chantilly 2nd of August, 1772, shot at Vincennes 21st of March, 1804. He was the son of Louis-Henry-Joseph, Duc de Bourbon, and of Louise-Marie-Thérèse d'Orleans. He followed his father when the latter emigrated, and he went through all the campaigns with the army of Condé. When this corps was disbanded he retired to Ettenheim, four leagues from Strasburg, on the right bank of the Rhine. It was in defiance of the law of nations that he was arrested by a troop of French soldiers, in obedience to the orders of Bonaparte. He was taken to Strasburg, and afterwards to Paris, where he arrived at twenty minutes to four in the afternoon. Transferred to Vincennes the same night, he was brought before a council of war. None of the usual formalities were observed, and no one was allowed to defend him. He was declared guilty of conspiracy, condemned to death, and shot between four and five in the morning in the ditch of the castle, where he was buried.

FLEURIEU.

Charles-Pierre-Claret, Comte Fleurieu, navigator, statesman, and member of the Institute, was born at Lyons 22nd of January, 1738, died at Paris 18th of August, 1810. Entering the marine at the age of thirteen, he made in 1763, with the clockmaker Berthoud, the first marine-glass ever seen in France, if an attempt of Julien Leroy be excepted. In 1776 he was appointed director-general of the ports and arsenals, and in this position rendered great services. It was he who drew up the plan of naval operations for the American War, and for the voyages of discovery of Lapérouse and Entrecasteaux. Imprisoned for fourteen months under the Terror, he occupied various posts under the Directory and Empire. The name of Fleurieu has been given to a bay in Van Diemen's Land, and to an island in its vicinity.

FRANÇAIS DE NANTES.

Count Antoine Français de Nantes, politician and *littérateur*, was born 17th of January, 1756, at Beaurepaire (Isère), died

at Paris 7th of March, 1836. Sent by the Loire-Inférieure
to the Legislative Assembly, he there proved himself an ardent
supporter of the Revolution. He became (1798) member of
the Council of the Five Hundred, prefect of the Charente-
Inférieure under the Consulate, and also Councillor of State
under the Empire.

LA FAYETTE.

Marie-Jean-Paul-Roch-Yves-Gilbert Motier, Marquis de la
Fayette, celebrated politician, was born 6th of September, 1757,
died at Paris 19th of May, 1834. His father was killed at
the battle of Minden (1759). At the time of the revolt of the
American colonies he equipped a vessel at his own expense
in spite of the remonstrances of the Court.

Appointed major-general of the American army, then general
of the army of the North, he was sent to Canada, where he
was unsuccessful. France having declared war against England,
he returned to his own country, where he was received with
enthusiasm, and arranged that a corps of 4,000 men should be
sent to assist the insurgents, himself to precede it.

He assisted considerably towards the capitulation of York-
town (1781), which decided the war. When France in its
turn had its Revolution, La Fayette was the first amongst
those who demanded reforms. At the Assembly of Notables
(1787), he demanded the convocation of the States-general.
On 15th of July, 1789, he was appointed commander of the
National Guard, and during the days of October 5th and 6th
did his best to prevent the populace going from Paris to
Versailles, but was obliged to succumb to the torrent which
drew him and the guards to Versailles. On 16th of June,
1792, La Fayette addressed a letter to the Assembly against
the Jacobins, which was supported by seventy-five departments,
and a few days after he quitted the army to defend himself
at the bar, but was unsuccessful in his efforts to organise
the constitutional party. Returning to the head of his troops,
he was cashiered, and upon the point of being accused, when
he quitted France.

He was captured and imprisoned by the Austrians at

Olmutz, and was treated with unheard-of rigour. When released he lived in retirement until the Hundred Days. He was then elected a deputy, and was a prominent member of that opposition which paralysed in part the national defence. In 1824 he visited America, and received a handsome recompense from the government and an enthusiastic reception from the people. The last days of his life were ended sadly in consequence of the attacks from the members of the extreme parties. George Washington stood sponsor to his son.

GARAT.

Dominique-Joseph Garat, politician and *littérateur*, was born at Ustaritz (Basses-Pyrénées) 8th of September, 1749, died 9th of December, 1833, at Urdains, near Usteritz. Sent to the States-general with his eldest brother, he was during the session one of the principal editors of the *Journal of Paris*. Nominated Minister of Justice (1792) in place of Danton, he passed afterwards to the Ministry of the Interior, and remained there until the month of August, 1793. He rallied to Bonaparte after the 18th Brumaire, and became under the Empire count and senator : and he made return for these favours in the same manner as for those he had received from the Mountain under the Convention—by the most unworthy and base flatteries. He changed the object of his adulations in 1814, and made the most pompous eulogy of Wellington and the Czar.

GAUDIN.

Martin-Michel-Charles Gaudin, Duc de Gaëte, statesman and financier, was born at Saint-Denis (Seine) 19th of January, 1756, died at Paris 26th of November, 1844. He occupied a superior position in the general direction of public contributions at the time of the first ministry of Necker, and was one of the six commissioners of the public treasury. On the morrow of the 18th Brumaire he received the portfolio of finance, and retained it until April, 1814, receiving it again during the Hundred Days. He remained faithful to the Emperor, who had treated him well. During the second Restoration he was sent to the Chamber by the department of l'Aisne, and was governor of the bank from 1820 to 1834.

MADAME DE GENLIS.

Félicité Ducrest, Comtesse de Genlis, a celebrated woman of letters, was born 25th of January, 1746, died at Paris 31st of January, 1830. Admitted at the age of six years a canoness in the noble chapter of Alix, near Lyons, she bore the name of Countess of Lancy. Married for love (1746) to the Comte de Genlis, from whom she separated after some years and who was guillotined during the Revolution, she succeeded in obtaining the appointment of lady-in-waiting to the Duchess of Chartres, and was charged with the education of the twin daughters of the princess. She was able to exert such an influence over Philip Egalité that she was named by him *governor* to his children, one of whom was Louis Philippe, a nomination which excited great scandal. She then showed herself a most prolific writer, and received a pension from Napoleon, but in spite of this she rallied to the Bourbons.

GOHIER.

Louis-Jérôme Gohier, member of the Directory, was born at Semblançay in 1746, died at Paris 29th of May, 1830. Lawyer at Rennes, he took an active part in the liberal movement which signalled in Brittany the approach of the Revolution. He was sent, in 1791, to the Legislative Assembly by the department of Ille-et-Vilaine, and was appointed secretary-general of the Ministry of Justice in October, 1792. On his return from Egypt Bonaparte sought in vain to attach Gohier to him.

GROUCHY.

Emmanuel Grouchy, marshal of France, was born in 1766, died in 1847. General of brigade in 1792, he went through the Vendean campaign, but was excluded from the army on account of being a noble. He was recalled and reinstated in 1795, serving under Hoche in the expedition to Ireland. He served under Moreau, and under the Empire distinguished himself in the campaigns of the Grand Army and the campaign in France. At the return from Elba he forced the Duke of Berry to capitulate, and was created marshal, being charged with the chief command of the cavalry in reserve of the army. On 16th of June he took possession of Fleurus and forced Blucher to retreat. At the battle of Waterloo Grouchy received such contradictory orders from Napoleon that he was not able to act with the necessary decision. At the return of the Bourbons he went to America, but was recalled in 1821. He was ennobled in 1832.

GUIDAL.

Maximilien-Joseph Guidal, general, was born in 1765, shot in 1812. He was detained at La Force when the Malet conspiracy broke out, and was delivered by the latter. He arrested the prefect of police, but was soon himself again arrested with his accomplices, and with them condemned to death.

HAREL.

F. A. Harel, *littérateur*, was born in Normandy in 1790, died at Paris August, 1846. Prefect during the Hundred Days, he was exiled on the return of the Bourbons, but afterwards became director of the Odéon and of the Porte-Saint-Martin. His best work is " L'Eloge de Voltaire," crowned by the Academy in 1844.

HÉDOUVILLE.

Gabriel-Théodore-Joseph Hédouville, general, was born at Laon 27th of July, 1755, died near Arpagon 31st of March, 1825. He was chief of the army near Brest, and captured Stofflet and Charette. Later he assisted in the pacification of La Vendée.

HENRIOT.

François Henriot was born at Nanterre in 1761, died upon the scaffold 28th of July, 1794. After having spent a disgraceful youth and having been sentenced for theft, he took an active part on the day of the 10th of August, then in the massacres of September. Commander-in-chief of the National Guard, he marched against the Convention on the 9th Thermidor. Outlawed with Robespierre and his adherents, he was for a time imprisoned, but, being delivered by Coffinhal, he put himself again at the head of his troops, who abandoned him. He retired to the Hôtel de Ville, but was thrown from the window by Coffinhal. Picked up half-dead, he was conveyed to prison, and was executed on the morrow.

HOCHE.

Lazare Hoche, one of the most celebrated generals of the Republic, was born at Montreuil, near Versailles, 25th of June, 1768, died at the camp of Wetzlar (Rhenish Prussia) 28th of September, 1797. Son of one of the guards of the kennel to Louis XV., he was, at the outbreak of the Revolution, sergeant in the *Gardes Françaises.* Entering, in 1789, the National Guards, and afterwards, with the epaulet of lieutenant, joining the regiment of Rouergue, he distinguished himself at the siege of Thionville and at the battle of Neerwinde, when he was aide-de-camp to General Le Veneur. Upon the proposition of Carnot he was created general of brigade, and, having defended Dunkirk against the English, was appointed commander of the army of the Moselle. He chased the Austrians from the lines of Wissembourg, raised the siege of Landau, and caused Alsace to be evacuated. It was owing to his intelligence and strategy that, in 1796, the Directory was able to announce the pacification of the provinces of the West.

Hoche organised and commanded an expedition against Ireland, which was destroyed by tempests. After the 18th Fructidor the army of Germany was confided to him, but it was not long before he felt again the pains of a disease of the chest, which soon carried him off. The funeral ceremony, celebrated at Paris, was very magnificent.

HULLIN.

Pierre-Augustin, Count Hullin, was born in 1758, died in 1841. He was general of brigade and commander of the foot grenadiers of the Consular Guard when he was called upon to preside over the military commission which judged and condemned to death the Duc d'Enghien. He commanded the armed force in Paris at the time of Malet's conspiracy, and was seriously wounded by that individual. Hullin published a pamphlet concerning the trial of the Duc d'Enghien.

ISNARD.

Maximin Isnard, politician, was born 16th of February, 1751, at Grasse (Var), where he died in 1830. Sent to the Legislative Assembly, he at once declared against the monarchical government. Re-elected to the Convention, he voted for the death of the King without appeal or respite. When he was proscribed, he caused the rumour of his death to be published, and so escaped the fate of the other Girondists. He retired entirely after the 18th Brumaire.

JOUBERT.

Barthélemy-Catherine Joubert, a celebrated general, was born at Pont-de-Vaux (Ain) 14th of April, 1769, killed at the battle of Novi 15th of August, 1799. Engaging himself, in 1789, as a volunteer, he was made chief of brigade in 1796, and general of division in the same year. He distinguished himself in a striking manner at the battle of Rivoli, and the result of his campaign in the Tyrol was to compel Austria to sign the preliminaries of peace at Léoben.

Joubert was sent successively (1798) as commander-in-chief in Holland, of the army of Mayence, and of the army of Italy – where in three days he took possession of Piedmont. Resigning during some months in 1799, he was sent back to the army of Italy some days after his marriage with Mdlle. de Montholon. Attacked at Novi by Souwarow at the head of superior forces, he was mortally wounded at the commencement of the action.

JOURDAN.

Jean-Baptiste Jourdan, count and marshal of France, was born at Limoges 29th of April, 1762, died 23rd of November, 1833. After having been for six years (1778-1784) a private soldier, and having also served in America, he established himself as a mercer at Limoges. When the Revolution commenced, he was appointed commander of a battalion of volunteers (1792), and distinguished himself under Dumouriez, Dampierre, and Custine. Appointed general of division in 1793, he replaced Houchard in the command of the armies of the North and the Ardennes, and beat the Austrians at Wittignies; but, being forced into inactivity the following winter, he returned to his business. Recalled for a few months, he was most successful in his engagements with the enemy, rendering himself master of Cologne, Bonn, Coblentz, and Maestricht. The campaign of 1795, however, was not so fortunate.

Next year his defeat forced Moreau, who had penetrated the heart of Bavaria, to execute his celebrated retreat. Jourdan was now replaced by Beurnonville, and played in future only a secondary part in history. He was ennobled in 1819, and during some days (after the July Revolution) was Minister of War.

JUNOT.

Andoche Junot, Duke of Abrantès, was born in 1771, died 1813. Engaging himself as a volunteer, at the siege of Toulon he made himself known to Bonaparte, to whom from that time he devoted himself, being his aide-de-camp in the first Italian campaign, and in the Egyptian campaign. He was taken by an English cruiser whilst returning to France, and recovered his liberty only some days before the battle of Marengo. He distinguished himself at Austerlitz. Charged with the invasion of Portugal, he was able, in spite of unheard-of difficulties, to take possession of Lisbon and other important places, which performances obtained him his title. The rising in Spain and Portugal and the landing of Wellington compelled Junot to agree to a convention, by which it was arranged that the French should evacuate Portugal. In 1813 his mind became affected, and after a violent attack he threw himself from a window, breaking his thigh. He died from the effects of the amputation.

KELLERMAN.

François-Christophe Kellerman, Duke of Valmy, marshal of France, was born at Strasburg in 1735, died in 1820. He had filled various missions abroad, and was marshal of camp at the time of the Revolution, the principles of which he embraced. Joining Dumouriez in 1792, he obtained a victory over the Prussians at Valmy, which had an immense effect. He served in Italy in 1795, and became under the Empire senator, marshal, and Duke of Valmy.

François-Étienne, marquis, son of the above, was born in 1770, died in 1825. He served with distinction under the Republic and Empire, and covered himself with glory at Marengo, where he commanded a brigade of heavy cavalry, whose charge decided the victory. He assisted at Waterloo, and did not take service under the Bourbons.

LABORDE.

Alexandre-Louis-Joseph, Comte de Laborde, member of the Academy of Inscriptions, was born in 1774, died in 1842. After having served in the Austrian army during the Revolution, he returned to France in 1797 after the treaty of Campo Formio, and was attached to the embassy of Lucien Bonaparte in Spain. Deputy from 1822 to 1824 and from 1827 till his death, he sat on the Left until the July Revolution, when he was for some days prefect of the Seine.

LAHORIE.

Victor-Alexandre Fauneau de Lahorie was born in 1766, shot 12th of October, 1812. Chief of Moreau's staff, he was compromised in the Pichegru conspiracy, but succeeded in escaping. On returning to France he was imprisoned in La Force. He took part, from his prison, in the Malet conspiracy, and was arrested and condemned to death.

LAIGNELOT.

Joseph-François Laignelot, a member of the Convention, dramatic author, was born at Versailles in 1752, died at Paris 23rd of July, 1829. He voted at the trial of the King for death without reprieve or appeal. He was exiled in 1805, after his tragedy " Rienzi," originally played in 1792, had been revived at the Théâtre Français.

PRINCESS LAMBALLE.

Marie-Thérèse-Louise de Savoie-Carignan, Princesse de Lamballe, was born at Turin 8th of September, 1748, murdered

3rd of September, 1792. She lost her husband a year after their marriage. Later she became superintendent of the house of Marie-Antoinette, who showed her the greatest kindness, which was repaid by a devotion that knew not any bounds. Imprisoned at the Temple with the royal family after the 10th of August, she was taken from there to the prison of La Force and cruelly murdered.

LAMETH.

Théodore, Comte de Lameth, politician, was born at Paris 24th of June, 1756, died 19th of October, 1854. Colonel of cavalry at the time of the Revolution, he was elected by the department of Jura to the Legislature, where he sat on the right and courageously defended the monarchy. He emigrated at the last moment, and returned only after the 18th Brumaire.

LANNES.

Jean Lannes, Duke of Montebello, marshal of France, was born at Lectoure (Gers) 11th of April, 1769, died at Vienna in 1809. He was a dyer when he enrolled himself. He left the service, but returned when Bonaparte set out for Italy, and soon became general of brigade. In the second Italian campaign he distinguished himself in a glorious manner at Montebello, and afterwards at Marengo. With the army of Germany he signalised himself at Essling, but on the morrow was mortally wounded.

LAPLACE.

Pierre-Simon, Count then Marquis de Laplace, a celebrated geometrician and physician, was born 23rd of March, 1749, at Beaumont-en-Auge (Calvados), died in 1827. His parents were poor cultivators. At first professor at the military school at Beaumont, he became, thanks to D'Alembert, professor of mathematics at the military school of Paris. He is accused of having shown an extraordinary servility as regards political affairs—he subordinated everything, doubtless, to his scientific studies. As geometrician Laplace has the honour of being credited with the discovery of the laws which govern our planetary system, and also of being the most clever continuator of

Newton's work. From his youth he had formed, says Fourier, the project of consecrating his efforts to theoretical astronomy; and he passed his entire life in the accomplishment of this aim with a perseverance to which the history of the sciences does not offer any parallel example. He accepted honours from the Empire and Royalty.

LAVALETTE.

Antoine-Marie Chamans, Comte de Lavalette, was born at Paris in 1769, died there in 1830. He was aide-de-camp to Bonaparte in Egypt. One of the most active agents of the 18th Brumaire, he became director-general of the postal department and Councillor of State. At 7 a.m. on 20th of March, 1815, he presented himself at the Hôtel des Postes, and took possession in the name of the Emperor, for which he was made a peer. At the return of the Bourbons he was excepted from the amnesty, and on being brought before the court was condemned to death. All efforts for his pardon proving ineffectual, on the eve of the execution his wife assisted him to escape, she taking his place. With the aid of English officers, and in the uniform of an English colonel, he reached Bavaria. His wife, unable to sustain such an amount of trouble, lost her reason.

LEBRUN.

Charles-François Lebrun, Duc de Plaisance, statesman and *littérateur*, was born 19th of March, 1739, died 16th of June, 1824, at the château de Saint-Mesme (Seine-et-Oise). Thanks to Maupeou, he was appointed Royal Censor, then general inspector of the Crown domains. He quarrelled with his patron, however, and lived in retirement until the time of the Revolution. He was sent to the National Assembly by the bailiwick of Dourdan, and gave his attention solely to the state of the finances. A member of the Council of the Ancients, he was after the 18th Brumaire named third Consul, and was charged with the reorganisation of the finances and the administration of the Interior. After the abdication of King Louis of Holland, Lebrun was charged with the administration of that country, with the title of lieutenant-general, a position which he occupied until the evacuation of Holland by the French troops. In 1814 he rallied to the Bourbons, by whom he was ennobled. Accepting office during the Hundred Days, he was excluded at the second Restoration, and was recalled in 1819.

LECLERC.

Charles-Emmanuel Leclerc, general, was born at Pontoise 17th of March, 1772, died 2nd of December, 1802. Engaging himself as volunteer, he was adjutant at the siege of Toulon. General of brigade in 1797, he married at Milan Pauline Bonaparte, and took an active part in the 18th Brumaire, which brought him the grade of general of division. In December, 1801, he set out at the head of a great expedition directed against San Domingo, but, after some success, he saw his army decimated by illness, to which he himself soon succumbed.

GENERAL LEFÈVRE.

François-Joseph Lefèvre, Duke of Dantzic, marshal of France, was born at Ruffach (Haut-Rhin) 25th of October, 1755, died at Paris 14th of September, 1820. Sergeant in the *Gardes Françaises* at the time of the Revolution, he became general of brigade in 1793, and general of division in 1794. He assisted in the *coup d'état* of 18th Brumaire. He was appointed senator in 1800, marshal of the Empire in 1804, and Duke of Dantzig after the taking of that town in 1807. In Spain he won the battle of Durango. Nominated to the Chamber of Peers in 1814, he sat there during the Hundred Days, and was recalled only in 1819.

LEGENDRE.

Louis Legendre, a member of the Convention, was born at Paris in 1755, died there 13th of December, 1797. He was a butcher in Paris when the Revolution broke out, in which he was one of the principal actors on the days of 14th of July and 5th and 6th of October, 1789, and 20th of June and 10th of August, 1792. Deputy from Paris to the Convention, he voted there for the death of the King without appeal or respite, became member of the Committee of Public Safety, and contributed to the fall of the Girondists.

LEMERCIER.

Louis-Jean-Népomucène Lemercier, a celebrated writer, member of the Institute (1810), was born at Paris 21st of April, 1771, died in 1840. He belonged to a rich family. After writing "Méléagre," a tragedy, he wrote for the theatre a comedy, "Clarisse Harlowe," and finally "Agamemnon," which proved to be a brilliant success, and was crowned on the Champ de Mars by order of the Directory. He undertook to strike out a new line in the theatre by his drama "Pinto," in which he proposed "to despoil a grand action of all poetical ornament and disguise, to present persons speaking as they do in everyday life, and to reject the prestige—sometimes unfaithful—of tragedy and of appropriate verses." Faithful to his republican principles, he broke with Bonaparte at the creation of the Empire, and never ceased to attack his government. On every occasion he showed the disinterestedness of a noble character.

LINDET.

Robert-Thomas Lindet, politician, was born at Bernay (Eure) in 1743, died there in August, 1823. Priest at the time of the Revolution, he was sent by the clergy of Evreux to the States-general. In March, 1791, he was elected constitutional bishop of l'Eure, and was sent to the Convention, where he voted for the death of the King. He married, and became a member of the Council of the Ancients, being exiled in 1816.

Jean-Baptiste-Robert Lindet, brother to the above, was a member of the Convention. He voted for the death of the King, and pursued the Girondists with much ferocity. He was charged with implication in the Babeuf conspiracy, but was acquitted, and soon after retired into private life.

MACDONALD.

Étienne-Jacques-Joseph-Alexandre Macdonald, Duke of Tarento, marshal of France, was born at Sancerre (Cher) 17th of November, 1765, died 24th of September, 1840. Second lieutenant in the regiment of Dillon at the time of the Revolution, he served under Dumouriez, and distinguished himself, becoming colonel, general of brigade, and, after having served under Pichegru in Holland, general of division. Governor of Rome, he beat General Mack. Replacing Championnet, he was forced, in consequence of the defeat of Scherer, to evacuate the kingdom of Naples, but soon effected a union with Moreau. He received from the First Consul the command of the army of the Reserve, with which he made a memorable campaign in the Tyrol. Showing an attachment to Moreau when the latter was on his trial, he was disgraced, and recalled only in 1809. His conduct at Wagram brought him the degree of marshal and title of duke; but he was at last beaten by Blucher (1813). He left Bonaparte only at the last moment, and supported the Bourbons, escorting Louis XVIII. to the frontier. At the return he was made Grand Chancellor of the Legion of Honour.

MALET.

Claude-François de Malet, a celebrated conspirator, was born in 1754, shot at Paris 29th of October, 1812. General of brigade in 1799, he served in the army of Italy in 1804. On attempting to promulgate a republican propaganda he was sent back to France and shut up in the prison of La Force, where he remained ten months. Being again arrested, from his prison he planned another conspiracy, which, however, was revealed by a fellow prisoner. In 1812 he obtained permission to be sent to a *maison de santé* in the Rue Faubourg Saint-Antoine, and there, with a small band of confederates, he organised a new plot. During the night of the 22nd of October he escaped from the house, accompanied by Rateau, corporal of the guard, and a student named Boutreux, and visited various posts, announcing the death of the Emperor and the nomination of a provisional government. Generals Lahorie and Guidal were placed in La Force, General Hullin was wounded by a pistol shot, but Malet himself was arrested by two officers, Laborde and Doucet. This terminated the *émeute*, though Lahorie and Guidal had conducted the Minister and the Prefect of Police to La Force. Malet and twenty-four others were brought before a military commission, and fifteen were condemned and shot the same day.

MARET.

Hugues-Bernard Maret, Duke of Bassano, statesman, was born at Dijon 1st of March, 1763, died at Paris 13th of May, 1839. Editor of the *Moniteur* for the National Assembly bulletin, he was after the 10th of August sent as envoy extraordinary to England. Ambassador to Naples in 1793, he was captured by the Austrians, and, after a detention of thirty months, was one of the prisoners exchanged for the daughter of Louis XVI. He became the confidential friend of Bonaparte, and followed him in almost all his campaigns, being in return loaded with benefits.

MARMONT.

Auguste-Frédéric-Louis-Viesse de Marmont, Duke of Ragusa, marshal of France, was born at Châtillon-sur-Seine (Côte d'Or) 20th of July, 1774, died at Venice 22nd of July, 1852. Son of a captain in the Hainault regiment, he entered as pupil at the school of artillery at Chalons, and was lieutenant of artillery at the siege of Toulon. He went with Bonaparte to Italy and Egypt. After the 18th Brumaire he was appointed Councillor of State, and received the command of the artillery. He was then commander of the army in Holland.

In 1806 Marmont received the command of Dalmatia, beat the Russians and Montenegrins at Castelnuovo, and administered with intelligence the country confided to him, which caused him to be created Duke of Raguse. He beat the Austrians, and was created marshal of the Empire on the battlefield. Sent to Spain, he beat and was in turn severely beaten by Wellington. In the campaign in France he was finally crushed by superior forces at Fère-Champenoise, and had to retire under the walls of Paris; but, in spite of an heroic defence, Marmont was obliged to conclude an armistice which gave up the capital to the allies. At the Restoration he was created a peer, and went with the King to Ghent. In 1817 he was sent to Lyons to restore order, a terrible Royalist reaction having taken place in the town. On his return he was created Minister of State, but in 1818 was disgraced and exiled from court for some months. At the time of the 1830 Revolution he was in command of the troops who had to take action against Paris. At St. Cloud, on 30th of July, he had a violent scene with the Dauphin, who caused him to be arrested. He accompanied the King (Charles X.) to England, and never again saw France.

MASSÉNA.

André Masséna, Duke of Rivoli, Prince of Essling, marshal of France, one of the most illustrious generals of the Republic, was born at Nice 6th of May, 1758, died at Paris 4th of April, 1817. After having made, as midshipman, two voyages to distant lands, he enlisted in the Royal Italian regiment in the service of France, and left it after having remained fourteen years non-commissioned officer. He was at Antibes when the Revolution burst, and he returned to the army as chief of the battalion of volunteers of Var in 1792. Appointed general of brigade in 1793, and four months after general of division, he took an active part in the campaign of Italy, and was the principal actor in the victory of Loano. When Bonaparte took command of the army Masséna was put at the head of the vanguard, and covered himself with glory. In this memorable campaign his division in forty-eight hours fought two battles, Rivoli and La Favorite, distant twelve leagues from one another, and his exploits were worthy of the name " Beloved child of victory " bestowed upon him by the general in command. He was sent to Rome to replace Berthier : but the extortions of the commissariat had raised such an amount of discontent among the troops that the officers refused to recognise him, and he was compelled to retire. His next command was that of the three armies of Switzerland, Danube, and the Rhine, which in all only amounted to 30,000 men ; but, ably seconded by his lieutenants, he executed that famous campaign, which remains a *chef d'œuvre* in the art of war, and which terminated in the victory of Zurich, thus breaking up the coalition and saving France from a formidable invasion.

After the 18th Brumaire he was sent to the army of Italy ; and although repulsed at Gênes, he sustained a siege which showed most conspicuously the heroism of the soldiers and the ability and indomitable energy of their chief. Bonaparte, not caring to have a rival in glory, replaced him. Member of the Corps Législatif in 1803, he made some opposition to the government concerning the trial of Moreau. Created marshal, he gained over the Archduke Charles the decisive battle of Caldiero. The following year he conquered the kingdom of Naples for King Joseph. After the campaign of 1807 he was created Duke of Rivoli. He performed wonders in Austria, and after the battle of Wagram was made Prince of Essling. Sent to Portugal, he did himself credit, but the scarcity of provisions in a hostile country, added to the fact that Wellington was in front of him with a superior army, compelled him to retreat to Spain. He was soon after recalled by Bonaparte, and was not again actively employed. He did not accept service during the Hundred Days : and he refused to form part of the council of war before which Marshal Ney was brought.

MAUPEOU.

René-Nicolas-Charles-Auguste de Maupeou, the last Chancellor of the ancient monarchy, was born in 1714, died in 1792. His name has been associated with a *coup d'état* which raised against him the hatred and anger of all France, but which, however, to a certain extent brought about some reforms of which the Revolution was one of the consequences. The fight sustained against the King by the parliament of Paris, with which the other parliaments joined cause, became more and more bitter. The parliament of Brittany continued the prosecution of the Duke of Aiguillon, in spite of the opposition of Maupeou. A bed of justice was held by the King (Louis XV.), when the action of the parliament was annulled. Five days afterwards the parliament, ignoring the action of the King, condemned the duke. The result of this dispute was that the members of the parliament who opposed the King were exiled.

[NOTE.—For full particulars of this struggle, with details of the private life of the Duke of Aiguillon and all other personages of importance in the reign of Louis XV., see the "Memoirs of Madame du Barri," 4 vols., H. S. Nichols' Historic Memoir Series.]

MENOU.

Jacques-François, Baron de Menou, was born in 1750, died in 1810. He was sent by the nobility of Touraine to the States-general, but soon rallied to the *tiers état*. Sent to La Vendée in 1793, he was unsuccessful; and on being brought before the Convention, he was defended by Barère. General of division after the 9th Thermidor, he repressed the insurrection of the 2nd Prairial at Paris. He was superseded in his command by Bonaparte; and, on his accusation being ordered, he was saved by his successor. He took part in the expedition to Egypt, and after the death of Kléber took chief command; but here as elsewhere he showed a total incapacity, and was forced to capitulate (1801). He afterwards became administrator of Piedmont and governor of Venice.

MERCIER.

Louis-Sébastien Mercier, a prolific writer and member of the Institute, was born 6th of June, 1740, at Paris, where he died 25th of April, 1840. Member of the Convention, he voted for the detention of the King. He was proscribed on 31st of May, and afterwards passed to the Council of the Five Hundred. He commenced with some *héroïdes*, but soon renounced poetry for prose, saying that the *writers of prose are the true poets*.

MERLIN DE DOUAI.

Philippe-Antoine, Comte Merlin de Douai, a celebrated lawyer and politician, was born at Arleux (Nord) 30th of October, 1754, died at Paris 26th of December, 1838. Sent to the States-general by the bailiwick of Douai, he rendered the most eminent services in all questions of jurisprudence raised by the changes brought about by the destruction of the old legislatures and the creation of the new. President of the criminal tribunal of Douai, he was sent to the Convention by his fellow-citizens, where he voted for the death of the King. After the 9th Thermidor he was President of the Convention, and entered the Committee of Public Safety. Called to the Council of the Ancients, he was immediately (30th of October)

named Minister of Justice, becoming in the following January
Minister of the General Police, which office he quitted to retake
his former functions. He did not take any part in the 18th
Brumaire. He became, in 1801, Procureur-general to the Cour
de Cassation (Court of Appeal), and in this high position displayed his profound knowledge of jurisprudence. He was
created successively Councillor of State for life, count and officer
of the Legion of Honour.

Dismissed at the first Restoration, he retook his place during
the Hundred Days, and was appointed Minister of State. Exiled
in July, 1815, he returned to Paris in 1830.

MIOLLIS.

Sextius-Alexandre-François, Comte Miollis, was born in 1759,
died in 1828. Captain at the time of the Revolution, he was
in 1794 appointed general of brigade, and covered himself
with glory at the siege of Mantua (1796–1797), of which he
was made governor. Having voted against the Consulate for
life, he was for some time condemned to inactivity : but in 1805
he was again governor of Mantua, and afterwards (1808) of Rome
and the States of the Church. Commanding the division of
Marseilles at the time of the return from Elba, he sought in
vain to oppose the progress of Bonaparte.

MIRABEAU.

Honoré-Gabriel-Riquetti, Count de Mirabeau, the greatest
orator of the Revolution, was born at Bignon (Seine-et-Marne)
9th of March, 1749, died at Paris 2nd of April, 1791. His
youth was a stormy one, and in 1774 he was, in consequence
of his debts and other disorders, confined in the Château d'If.
Transferred to the Fort de Joux, he made the intimate acquaint-
ance of the Marquise de Monier, with whom he fled. They
were soon arrested, and he was sent to Vincennes. He was set
at liberty in 1781, was obliged to defend himself in actions
brought against him, and did so with an eloquence that established his reputation. When the States-general were assembled
he, being rejected by his own class, the nobility, made himself
a tradesman in order to be included in the *tiers état*.

From the first days of the meeting of the Assembly he manifested an energy and an eloquence which placed him in the first rank. The address that he made to M. de Brézé, when the latter ordered the Assembly to dissolve by order of the King, is well known. His death, which occurred after a few days' illness, caused great grief. The funeral ceremony was remarkable for its extraordinary solemnity.

MONCEY.

Bon-Adrien-Jeannot de Moncey, Duke of Conegliano, marshal of France, was born at Besançon in 1754, died at Paris in 1842. Officer at the time of the Revolution, he soon became general of brigade. His success in Spain decided that country to sign the treaty of Bâle. Major-general of the National Guard in 1814, he made himself illustrious by his defence of Paris. The letter which he sent refusing to be a member of the council of war to try Marshal Ney caused him to be cashiered, and even imprisoned for a time. He commanded a *corps d'armée* in the Spanish war (1823), and in 1834 was commander of the Invalides.

ABBÉ DE MONTESQUIOU.

François - Xavier - Marc - Antoine, abbé de Montesquiou-Fezensac, politician, was born in 1757 at the château of Marsan (Gers), died in 1832. Agent-general of the clergy, he was sent by them to the States-general in 1789, and refused to unite with the *tiers état* until he received the order from the King. He took an active part in all discussions in the chambers regarding ecclesiastical matters, but fought in vain against the majority. Emigrating to England in 1792, he returned after the 9th Thermidor, and was until the Consulate one of the agents of Louis XVIII., on the part of whom he presented a letter to Bonaparte. [This incident is referred to on page 128 of this volume.] He took part in the provisional government of 1814, and again at the second Restoration.

MATTHIEU DE MONTMORENCY.

Matthieu-Jean-Félicité de Montmorency-Laval, politician, was born in 1766, died in 1826. He went with La Fayette to fight for the independence of America, and was nominated by the bailiwick of Montfort-l'Amoury as deputy from the nobility to the States-general. One of the first to unite with the *tiers état*, he voted constantly with the majority of the Assembly. After the 10th of August he retired to Switzerland, near Mme. de Staël. He returned to France in 1795, and was detained for some time. living then in retreat until the end of the Empire. At the Restoration he became aide-de-camp to Monsieur, marshal of camp (1814), and chevalier of honour to the Duchess of Angoulême. He followed Louis XVIII. to Ghent, and at the return was raised to the peerage. Although no *littérateur*, he became a member of the French Academy. His *liaison* with Madame Récamier is well known.

MOREAU.

Jean-Victor Moreau, one of the illustrious generals of the Revolution, was born at Morlaix 11th of August, 1763, died at Laun in Bohemia 27th of September, 1813. Son of a lawyer, he first engaged himself as a soldier, but was bought out, and consented to resume his studies of the law at Rennes, where he played an important part in the fight of the parliament against the court (1788), and then in that of the people against the parliament. Chosen chief of the battalion of volunteers of Ille-et-Vilaine in September, 1791, he went to serve under Dumouriez, and succeeded rapidly to the grade of general of division, which was obtained for him, in 1794, by Pichegru, to whom he succeeded (1795) in the command of the army of the North. Placed, in 1796, at the head of the army of Rhine-et-Moselle, which was to act in concert with Jourdan (then chief of the army of Sambre-et-Meuse), he passed the Rhine, and, after eight victories over Wurmser, etc., penetrated to the Danube, and advanced into Bavaria; in consequence of Jourdan's defeat, however [*see* JOURDAN], he was obliged to retire. His army accomplished one hundred leagues of the enemy's country in forty days, and gained a signal victory at Biberbach.

Moreau afterwards served under Scherer, who, after reverse upon reverse, decided to abandon to him the command of an

army demoralised by several defeats and having in front of it
forces numerically four times as strong. Defeated by Souwarow
at Cassano, he executed with marvellous ability a movement
of retreat, with the object of rejoining Macdonald, who advanced
towards him from Naples. This manœuvre, however, was unsuccessful, and the command of the two armies was ultimately
given to Joubert, who was killed at the battle of Novi, and
Moreau was replaced by Championnet.

Now arrived the 18th Brumaire, in which Moreau assisted
Bonaparte, which brought to the former the command of the
Rhine and Swiss armies. The campaign which followed was
a series of brilliant victories for Moreau.

Being of a feeble character and dominated by his wife, a
Creole, Moreau allowed himself to be connected with Pichegru
in a treasonable intrigue : and although the evidence at the trial
was favourable to him, he was, thanks to the efforts of the
public prosecutor, condemned to two years' detention and the
cost of the trial. His punishment was commuted into exile,
and soon after his name was erased from the army list. He
then went to the United States until 1813, when, tired of
inaction, he allowed himself to be influenced by the Royalist
party, and joined Bonaparte's enemies. Disembarking at Gotten-
burg (Sweden), he went to Prague, and was received with *éclat*
by the allied sovereigns. On 27th of August, in the midst
of the battle fought under the walls of Dresden, his right knee
was shattered and his left calf blown away. He died some days
after. His widow received from Louis XVIII. a pension of
12,000 francs, and from the Emperor Alexander a gift of
500,000 roubles and a pension of 30,000 roubles.

MURAT.

Joachim Murat, King of Naples, was born 25th of March,
1771, at the Bastide-Fortunière (Lot), shot at Pizzo in 1815.
His father was an innkeeper. He was at first destined for
the Church, but, quickly disgusted, he enrolled himself in the
cavalry. Discharged for insubordination, he was enabled by
influence to enter the Constitutional Guard of Louis XVI.
He showed so much enthusiasm for the Revolution that it is

said that when the "Friend of the People" was assassinated by Charlotte Corday, he demanded to be allowed to change his name to Marat. This caused him to be denounced after the 9th Thermidor, but he was saved by Cavaignac and sent to the army of the Pyrénées-Orientales, where he advanced rapidly.

Following Napoleon into Egypt, he signalised himself by the most brilliant feats of arms, especially at the battle of Aboukir. Some months after the 18th Brumaire, at which he assisted, he married Bonaparte's youngest sister, and received the command of the Consular Guard. In the Italian campaign he was placed at the head of the vanguard, and, after several fortunate engagements, entered Milan 2nd of June, 1800, and commanded the cavalry at Marengo. He was fully employed for the next five years, always giving a good account of himself, and contributing to the victory of Austerlitz. It was to him that Blucher surrendered himself at Lubeck. He covered himself with glory at Eylau.

Sent to Spain in 1808, he took possession of Madrid, and had to quell a terrible insurrection. When Joseph Bonaparte exchanged the throne of Naples for that of Spain, Murat succeeded to the first-named, and was proclaimed King of the Two Sicilies under the name of Joachim-Napoleon. He introduced the most sagaciously-planned reforms into the administration of his kingdom. The two brothers in-law disagreed the next year, but Murat took part in the Russian campaign. He gained several victories, but was unsuccessful when left in charge after Napoleon's departure. Murat then left for Italy, and although he appeared at the battle of Dresden, he entered into negotiations with Austria and England, promising to join the allies with 30,000 men. This defection paralysed the army of Prince Eugene.

Remaining upon the throne after Bonaparte's first abdication, he declared for the Imperial cause : he was, however, unsuccessful, and had to fly. He sought refuge at Cannes, offering to support Bonaparte ; but the latter refused to see him, and prohibited his sojourn in Paris. After Waterloo Murat decided to accept the hospitality of Austria. Being led to attempt a descent upon his former kingdom, he collected 250 men and set out in boats. A tempest dispersed this expedition, and Murat, finding himself alone, disembarked at Pizzo. He had hardly advanced into the interior when he was arrested, brought before a military commission, condemned, and shot the same day.

NECKER.

Jacques Necker, the celebrated financier, was born at Geneva 30th September, 1732, died at Coppet (Canton of Vaud) 9th of April, 1804. He founded in 1762, at Paris, a bank which soon became the first in France, and which in difficult circumstances came more than once to the assistance of the government.

He was appointed Controller-General of the Finances 29th of June, 1777, but, being a Protestant, was not allowed to enter the Council. In 1781 he published a statement of the financial situation, which was well received by the public. Thinking himself now strong enough, he requested admittance to the Council, was refused, and resigned 19th of May, 1781, The government were obliged to recall him, but he was not able to control the situation of affairs, and was ordered to quit France. This caused a riot, resulting in the taking of the Bastille. Once more he returned, but finally retired in September, 1790, and reached Switzerland with difficulty. He lived there rich and tranquil. His complete works were published (1820-21) in 15 vols. 8vo.

FRANÇOIS DE NEUFCHÂTEAU.

Le Comte Nicolas-Louis-François de Neufchâteau, statesman, man of letters and agriculturist, member of the French Academy (1816), was born at Saffoy (Meurthe), 17th of April, 1750, died at Paris 10th of January, 1828. He was successively member of the Legislative Assembly, minister of the Interior (1797), and under the Empire senator and count.

NEY.

Michel Ney, Duc d'Elchingen, Prince de la Moskowa, marshal of France, was born 10th of January, 1769, shot at Paris 7th of December, 1815. Son of a cooper, in 1788 he enlisted in a regiment of hussars, and became lieutenant in 1792. His indomitable bravery and his intelligence soon caused him to advance. He served under Hoche in the army of Sambre-et-Meuse in 1797, and was taken near Steinberg, but was soon exchanged. In 1799 he served in the army of the Danube under Jourdan. Temporary general-in-chief of the army of the Rhine, he knew how, by his clever manœuvres, to contribute to assuring the results of the victory of Zurich. The *coup d'état* of the 18th Brumaire caused him some dissatisfaction, but on returning from the campaign in Germany in 1800 he allowed himself to be gained over by the First Consul, who made him marry Mdlle. de Lascano, the friend of Hortense de Beauharnais. For the next few years Ney gave a very good account of himself, and contributed considerably to the victories of Eylau and Friedland. From 1808 to 1811 he served in Spain and Portugal, and signalised himself above all in the retreat from Portugal, where, in spite of the inferiority of his forces, he held his own with Wellington. Placed under the orders of Masséna, he showed such an amount of insubordination that his command was taken from him, and he was sent back to France. The disastrous Russian campaign was the most glorious epoch in the life of the marshal. His conduct at the terrible battle of the 7th of September gained him the title of Prince of Moskowa; and when the army commenced its retreat it was he who commanded the rear-guard. Then it was that by his prodigies of valour and ability he succeeded, at the head of a *corps d'armée* reduced to 3,000 men, in rejoining the body of the army, from which he had been separated. After the abdication of Bonaparte he rallied to the Bourbons, who appointed him member of the Council of War, commander-in-chief of the cuirassiers, dragoons, light infantry, and lancers of France, governor of the sixth military division (Besançon), and peer of France. At the return from Elba he made at Paris the most solemn protestations of devotion to the King, and set off to oppose his former master; but, led away by his own soldiers, he joined Napoleon. His manœuvres before and during the battle of Waterloo have been differently appreciated. Returning to Paris, he was one of the first to declare it necessary to recall the Bourbons. Although the twelfth article of the Capitulation of Paris should have sheltered him from any penalty, by a royal decree of 24th of July he, with nineteen other generals, was sent before a council of war. He was badly advised in questioning the competency of this tribunal, seeing that it was favourably disposed towards him. The Chamber of Peers tried him and condemned him to death on 6th of December. The sentence was carried out at nine o'clock the next morning, at the place where now stands his statue in bronze.

ALEXIS DE NOAILLES.

Louis-Joseph-Alexis, Comte de Noailles, politician, was born in 1783, died in 1835. Arrested for some months under the Empire, he quitted France, and served in the army of the allies during the campaigns of 1813 and 1814.

D'ORLÉANS.

Louis-Philippe-Joseph, Duc d'Orléans, called " Égalité," was born at Saint-Cloud 13th of April, 1747, died upon the scaffold 6th of November, 1793. His title at first was Duc de Montpensier, then (1752) that of Duc de Chartres. Opposed to the *coup d'état* of the Chancellor Maupeou, he was exiled, and only returned to the court at the accession of Louis XVI. His conduct during the war with England (1788) gave rise to much dissatisfaction. He was unpopular at court, especially with Marie Antoinette. Member of the second Assembly of Notables, he violently attacked the ministry, but was compelled to retire to England, whence he returned in 1790. After the flight to Varennes, " Égalité " was credited with arranging the meeting in the Champ-de-Mars held to promote the signature of a petition for the deposition of the King. When it was decreed by the Assembly that the princes could not be elected by the people, he renounced both his privileges and rank. Elected deputy of Paris to the Convention, he received from the Commune of Paris the title of " Égalité." The vote that he gave in

favour of the King's death excited against him universal indignation. Arrested April, 1793, he was condemned to death,
and, demanding to be led at once to the scaffold, died with
courage. He married, in 1769, Louise-Marie-Adelaide de Bourbon, daughter of the Duke of Penthièvre.

OUVRARD.

Gabriel-Julien Ouvrard, financier, was born 1770, died
at London, 1846. The enormous fortune which he made as
army contractor forced upon him such disputes with the Emperor that he tendered a statement of accounts. He was afterwards arrested and lodged in Saint-Pélagie. In 1823 he was
again arrested, in consequence of his action with regard to
the furnishing of the army for Spain.

PASQUIER.

Etienne-Denis Pasquier, statesman, member of the French
Academy, was born in 1767, died in 1862. He saw his father
perish on the scaffold 21st of August, 1794, and was himself
arrested some days before the 9th Thermidor. When Malet's
conspiracy broke out he was arrested by the conspirators and
detained for some hours at La Force.

PERIGNON.

Dominique-Catherine, Count Perignon, marshal of France,
was born in 1754, died in 1818. He was commander of legion
in the army of the Pyrénées-Orientales. General of division
in 1793, he commanded the centre at the battle of Montagne-
Noire, where Dugommier was killed, whom he replaced. He
rallied to the Bourbons, who raised him to the peerage.

PICHEGRU.

Charles Pichegru, a celebrated general, was born 16th of
February, 1761, at Arbois (Jura), died 5th of April, 1804, at
Paris. Enrolled (1783) in a regiment of artillery, where he
became adjutant, he embraced with enthusiasm the principles
of the Revolution. He was elected at Besançon (1792) chief

of a battalion of volunteers of the Guard, with whom he joined
the army of the Rhine, distinguishing himself to such an extent that he was appointed general of division and, some days
after, general-in-chief of this army. He made a junction with
Hoche, who commanded the army of the Moselle, and contri
buted to a great extent to the success of the latter against the
Austro-Prussians. After the arrest of Hoche he, thanks to
Saint-Just, obtained the command of the two armies. He
also had a most brilliant campaign in Holland. He was in
Paris at the time of the rising of the Faubourgs against the
Convention, and, being placed at the head of the troops, he
soon got the better of the *émeute*. Soon afterwards he commenced to be involved in Royalist intrigues, and compromised
Jourdan by his false manœuvres : and, being deprived of his
command, he declined an ambassadorship in Prussia. Elected
to the Council of the Five Hundred, he continued his intrigues,
and was arrested the 18th Fructidor and transported to Sinnamari, whence he succeeded in escaping in June, 1798. Some
time after he organised the conspiracy of Georges Cadoudal.
Arriving secretly at Paris, he was able to escape all search for
him, but he was sold to the police by an intimate friend, named
Leblanc, and arrested 28th of February, 1804. He was imprisoned in the Temple, and was found there strangled. At
the second Restoration statues were erected to him in the
cemetery Saint-Catherine and in his native town.

POULAIN DE GRANDPRÉ.

Joseph-Clément Poulain de Grandpré, politician, was born
at Ligneville (Vosges) 23rd of December, 1744, died at Graux
(Vosges) 6th of February, 1826. Sent from the Vosges to
the Convention, he voted there for the death of the King
without appeal or respite. He was a member of the Council
of the Ancients, and afterwards of the Council of the Five
Hundred, from which he was excluded by the 18th Brumaire.
Later he became president of the Imperial Court of Trèves, and
member of the Chamber of Deputies during the Hundred
Days. He was exiled in 1816.

PRADT.

Dominique Dufour de Pradt, publicist and diplomatist, was born in 1759, died in 1837. Sent by the clergy of Rouen to the States-general, he emigrated, in 1791, with his protector the Cardinal de la Rochefoucauld, and published several pamphlets which created some sensation. Presented by Duroc to the First Consul, he became, as he said himself, *aumonier du Dieu Mars.* In 1805 he was named Bishop of Poitiers, and followed the Emperor, whom he aided in his action against the Bourbons of Spain, to Bayonne. The same year he was raised to the archbishopric of Malines and created baron. He was disgraced in consequence of his negotiations with the Pope relative to the National Ecclesiastical Council in 1811. He then became ambassador to Warsaw, but was afterwards again disgraced. Next time he entered France it was with the allies. He opposed the government of 1824 with such vehemence that he was brought up for trial, but was acquitted. He never ceased writing pamphlets until his death.

QUINETTE.

Nicolas-Marie Quinette, Baron de Rochemont, politician, was born at Soissons September, 1762, died in exile at Brussels in 1821. Sent from l'Aisne to the Legislative Assembly, he was re-elected to the Convention, where he voted for the death of the King. He was one of the four commissioners sent to arrest Dumouriez, who, however, were themselves arrested by him and given over to the enemy 1st of April, 1793. Released in 1795, he occupied various posts under the government.

RÉAL.

Pierre-François, Count Réal, politician and administrator, was born at Chatou (Seine-et-Oise) 28th of March, 1757, died 7th of May, 1834, at Paris. He was a friend of Danton, and contributed to the fall of the Girondists. When his patron fell he was imprisoned until the 9th Thermidor. He filled several offices under the Directory, was one of the agents of

Bonaparte at the 18th Brumaire, and was one of the four Councillors of State charged with the police of the Empire. He was exiled in 1816, but obtained permission to return to France in 1818.

MADAME RÉCAMIER.

Jeanne-Françoise-Julie-Adelaide Bernard Récamier was born at Lyons 4th of December, 1777, died at Paris 11th of May, 1849. She married, at fifteen years of age, a rich banker, who was never her husband, and who died in 1830. She was celebrated for her beauty, for the illustrious friendships which she knew how to gain, and, above all, for the brilliant society which until the last day she gathered round her in her *salon* of l'Abbaye-aux-Bois.

RÉGNIER.

Claude-Ambroise Régnier, Duc de Massa, statesman, was born at Blamont (Meurthe) 6th of April, 1736, died at Paris 24th of June, 1814. Lawyer at Nancy at the time of the Revolution, he was deputed to the States-general, where he sat on the Left. From 1795 to 1799 he was member of the Council of the Ancients, and was one of the most active agents of Napoleon at the 18th Brumaire.

LA REVELLIÈRE DE LÉPEAUX.

Louis-Marie de la Revellière de Lépeaux was born at Montaigu (Vendée) 25th of August, 1753, died at Paris 27th of March, 1824. Member of the Constituent Assembly, then of the Convention, where he voted for the death of the King without appeal or respite, he was proscribed after the 31st of May. Returning to the Assembly after the 9th Thermidor, he became a member of the Committee of Public Safety. He was president of the Directory at the 18th Fructidor, and was expelled from power 18th of June. Refusing to take the oath to the Empire, he was deprived of the place that he held at the Academy of Sciences.

REWBEL.

Jean-François Rewbel, politician, was born 8th of October, 1747, at Colmar, where he died 23rd of November, 1807. Lawyer to the Sovereign Council of Alsace, he was elected by the bailiwicks of Colmar and Schlestadt to the States-general. Deputy from the Haut-Rhin to the Convention, he was sent to the army at Mayence : and although absent at the time of the trial of Louis XVI., he agreed by letter to his condemnation. Member of the Council of the Five Hundred (September, 1795), he was named member of the Directory, and remained there until 16th of May, 1799, when he was replaced by Sieyès. Elected then to the Council of the Ancients, he returned to private life after the 18th Brumaire.

ROBESPIERRE.

Maximilien-Marie-Isidore de Robespierre, a celebrated member of the Convention, was born at Arras 6th of May, 1758, died upon the scaffold at Paris the 10th Thermidor, year II. (28th of July, 1794). Son of a lawyer of Artois, he was brought up as foundation scholar at Louis-le-Grand College, and returned to Arras to exercise the profession of lawyer there, where he acquired enough reputation to be sent as one of the deputies from Artois to the States-general. It was not until the second year there that he brought himself into notice, giving utterance on 30th May, 1791, to a very eloquent speech in favour of the *abolition of capital punishment*.

The austerity of his manners, his integrity, and his impassioned declamation at the Jacobins' Club made him popular with the mob. He became a violent opponent of the Girondist party and the leader of the Mountain. After the death of the King the conflict between the two parties became very violent, ending in the victory of Robespierre.

Thanks to the terror with which he inspired the Assembly and to the Revolutionary tribunal, which was no more than the instrument of his will, or of that of the committee that he ruled, he sent to the scaffold first the Hebertistes (13th of March, 1794), then Danton, Camille Desmoulins, Fabre d'Eglantine and others (5th of April), and Chaumette (12th of April).

He caused it to be decreed that the Convention recognised the existence of a Supreme Being and the immortality of the soul, and would celebrate (8th of June) a solemn fête. Two days later a law was proposed in the Assembly by which accused were taken at once to the Revolutionary tribunal without being referred to the Convention. This law, which allowed 1,285 persons to perish in forty-five days, was voted by the terrified Assembly, but it raised in its midst and in the committees such a reprobation that a vast conspiracy was at once organised against its authors. The parties until now divided and inimical came to an understanding, and on the 8th Thermidor (26th of July) the struggle commenced in the Convention. On the morrow it recommenced with more violence, and ended in a decree of arrest against Robespierre, against his brother, Couthon, Saint-Just, and Labas. Released the same evening by Coffinhal and led to the Hôtel de Ville, Robespierre and his defenders were outlawed, and, the Convention having collected some thousands of National Guards, the Hôtel de Ville was invaded at 2 a.m. Robespierre, whose jaw was smashed by a pistol-shot, was arrested, with forty others. The same evening, at six o'clock, he was guillotined on the Place de la Concorde.

In Carlyle's "French Revolution" Robespierre's wounding is thus described: "Robespierre was sitting on a chair, with pistol-shot blown through not his head, but his under jaw: the suicidal hand had failed."

John Morley, in the essay on Robespierre included in his "Critical Miscellanies," thus describes the end: "It was half-past two. Robespierre had just signed the first two letters of his name to a document before him, when he was startled by cries and uproar below. In a few instants he lay stretched on the ground, his jaw shattered by a pistol-shot. His brother had either fallen or leaped out of the window. Couthon was hurled over a staircase, and lay for dead. Saint-Just was a prisoner.

"Whether Robespierre was shot by an officer of the Conventional force, or attempted to blow out his own brains, we shall never know, any more than we shall ever be quite assured how Rousseau, his spiritual master, came to an end. The wounded man was carried, a ghastly sight, first to the Committee of Public Safety, and then to the Conciergerie, where he lay in silent stupefaction through the heat of the summer day. As he was an outlaw, the only legal preliminary before execution was to identify him. At five in the afternoon he was raised into the cart. Couthon and the younger Robespierre lay, confused wrecks of men, at the bottom of it. Henriot and Saint-Just, bruised, begrimed, and foul, completed the band. One who walks from the Palace of Justice, over the bridge, along the Rue Saint-Honoré, into the Rue Royale, and so to the Luxor column, retraces the *via dolorosa* of the Revolution on the afternoon of the 10th Thermidor."

RŒDERER.

Pierre-Louis, Count Rœderer, statesman, publicist, and *littérateur*, was born at Metz 15th of February, 1754, died at Bois-Roussel (Orne) 17th of December, 1835. Counsellor to the Parliament of Metz, he was elected by his native town to the National Assembly in 1789, several months after its opening. It was he who persuaded the King to go to the Legislative Assembly. One of the most active promoters of the *coup d'état* of the 18th Brumaire, he was afterwards created Councillor of State, senator, Minister of Finance to King Joseph, and peer during the Hundred Days.

ROSSIGNOL.

Jean-Antoine Rossignol, politician and general, was born at Paris in 1759, died at Anjouan (an island near Madagascar) in April, 1802. The part he took in the days of the 20th of June and 10th of August made him very popular, and he was given the command-in-chief of the army of la Rochelle. Arrested in 1795 as being implicated in the Babeuf conspiracy, he was acquitted ; but, in consequence of his opposition to the Consular government, he was suspected of implication in the affair of the infernal machine, and was transported to the coast of Madagascar.

LA ROCHEFOUCAULD.

Louis-Alexandre, Duc de la Roche-Guyon et de la Rochefoucauld d'Enville, politician. was born 11th of July 1743. killed at Gisors 14th of September, 1792. Elected to the Assembly of Notables, and afterwards to the States-general, he was one of the first to join the *tiers état*. He was named president of the department of Paris. Obliged to resign and to quit Paris, he was massacred at Gisors.

SAINT-JUST.

Louis-Antoine de Saint-Just, a celebrated member of the Convention, was born 25th of August, 1767, at Decise (Nièvre), died upon the scaffold 28th of July, 1794, at Paris. His father had been captain in the cavalry. Coming to Paris at the end of 1797 in order to publish a poem, he manifested for the Revolution an enthusiasm which caused him to be nominated deputy for the Aisne to the Convention. He spoke there for the first time on the trial of the King, and voted for death without appeal or respite. His clear, incisive speaking had great effect. It was in consequence of his report that those of the Girondists who had left Paris were outlawed and those who remained put upon trial. At the 9th Thermidor he was accused, arrested at the Hôtel de Ville, and executed.

SALICETTI.

Christopher Salicetti, politician, was born at Basti in 1757, died at Naples 23rd of December, 1809. He was a member of the National Assembly in 1789, then of the Convention, voting there for the death of the King. Member of the Council of the Five Hundred, he opposed the 18th Brumaire. He was General Minister of Police at Naples under Joseph (1807), then Minister of War, of which office Murat relieved him in 1809.

SANTERRE.

Antoine-Joseph Santerre, republican general, was born 16th of March, 1752, at Paris, where he died 6th of February, 1809. Son of a brewer, and a brewer himself in the Faubourg Saint-Antoine, he took an active part in the *émeute* of the Champ de Mars and in the days of 20th of June and 10th of August. As commander of the national guard, he was in charge at the execution of Louis XVI. He was sent to La Vendée, but only experienced reverses. Recalled and arrested, he recovered his liberty after the 9th Thermidor, but did not again take any active part in public affairs.

SAVARY.

Anne-Jean-Marie-René Savary, Duc de Rovigo, general and politician, was born at Marcq (Ardennes) 26th of April, 1774, died at Paris 2nd of June, 1833. He was chief of squadron when he followed Desaix in Egypt, and after the death of the latter was aide-de-camp to Bonaparte. He presided at the execution of the Duc d'Enghien. In the campaigns of Austerlitz and Jena he distinguished himself, and beat the Russians at Ostrolenka. In 1810 he replaced Fouché as Minister of Police, but, in spite of his vigilance, he allowed himself to be surprised by the Malet conspiracy. After the capitulation of Paris in 1814, he followed Marie-Louise to Blois, and was made a peer during the Hundred Days. He wished to accompany Bonaparte to St. Helena, but was taken to Malta. He escaped, however, and went to Smyrna, where he lost his fortune in commercial speculations. Going to Trieste, he was arrested and brought back to Paris to purge the judgment which had been passed upon him in contumacy. He was acquitted, and lived in retirement until 1830. He was in command of the army in Africa from 1831 till 1833.

SCHERER.

Barthélemi-Louis-Joseph Scherer, general, was born 18th of December, 1747, at Delle (Haut-Rhin), died 19th of August, 1804, at Chauny (Aisne). Officer at the time of the Revolution, he was named general of division 28th of January, 1794, and some months after was appointed general-in-chief of the army of the Alps, being transferred the year following to the army of the Pyrénées-Orientales. Sent to Italy in 1795, he beat the Austrians at Loano, but did not know how to profit by his victory, and was obliged to resign. On retaking command, he was disastrously defeated by the Austrians. He was then recalled, and appeared no more on the scene of war.

SEBASTIANI.

François-Horace-Bastien Sebastiani, marshal of France, was born in Corsica 10th of November, 1772, died at Paris in 1851. Colonel of dragoons at the 18th Brumaire, in which he actively assisted, he acquitted himself well in various missions in the East, and became general of division after Austerlitz. He was ambassador at Constantinople when the English fleet forced the entry to the Dardanelles ; and it was largely owing to his efforts that Constantinople was put into such a state of defence that the enemy's fleet was obliged to retire. His last days were embittered by the fact that his daughter (Duchess de Praslin) had been assassinated by her husband.

SEMONVILLE.

Charles-Louis Huguet, Count then Marquis of Semonville, politician, was born 9th of March, 1759, at Paris, where he died 11th of August, 1839. He was sent as ambassador to Turkey, but was arrested on neutral ground by order of Austria, and recovered his liberty only when the daughter of Louis XVI. was given up. He was created marquis by Louis XVIII. in 1819.

SERURIER.

Jean-Matthieu-Philibert, Comte de Serurier, marshal of France, was born at Laon 8th of September, 1742, died at Paris 21st of December, 1819. He served as officer in the Seven Years' War, in Portugal, and in Corsica. He became colonel and then, on being sent to the army of the Var, general of division. He acted a brilliant part in the victory of Loano and in the campaigns of 1796 and 1797.

SIEYÈS.

Emmanuel Joseph, Count Sieyès, publicist, politician, and member of the Institute, was born at Fréjus (Var) 3rd of May, 1748, died at Paris 20th of June, 1836. He was vicar-general, canon, and chancellor of the church at Chartres, then (1787) councillor, commissioner to the superior chamber of the clergy, and member of the Provincial Assembly of Orleans. He published, in the first instance, an " Essay on the Privileges " (1788) in 8vo, and finally his celebrated pamphlet, " What is the Tiers État ? " which had an immense success, and caused him to be nominated deputy from Paris to the States-general. He exercised a preponderating influence there during the first period. Elected to the Convention by several departments, he there voted for the death of the King, but under the Terror completely effaced himself. Member of the Committee of Public Safety (5th of March, 1795), he was sent to La Hague, where he signed the treaty of peace with the Batavian Republic. He conspired with Bonaparte at the 18th Brumaire. Appointed one of the provisional consuls, he was soon replaced, and became successively senator (1799), president of the Senate, and count (1808). Peer during the Hundred Days, he was exiled at the second Restoration, and returned to France after the Revolution of 1830.

SONTHONAX.

Léger-Félicité Sonthonax, politician, was born in 1763, died 1823. Sent in June, 1792, to San Domingo, he took Port-au-Prince from the blacks and abolished slavery. This led to a rising of the whites, who sought the aid of the English, to whom he was obliged to surrender Port-au-Prince. Sent again to San Domingo, Toussaint-Louverture soon forced him to quit the island. His opposition to the 18th Brumaire caused him to be imprisoned for some time.

SOULT.

Nicolas-Jean-de-Dieu Soult, Duke of Dalmatia, marshal of France, was born 29th of March, 1769, at Saint-Amans la Bastide (Tarn), died 26th of November, 1851. Son of a notary, he enlisted in 1785, becoming sub-lieutenant in 1791, and mounting rapidly from grade to grade. He took a most glorious part in the operations which preceded the battle of Zurich, and also at the defence of Gênes under Masséna. There he had a leg smashed, and was taken prisoner. He contributed to the success of the campaigns of Austerlitz and Jena. From 1808 till 1811 he had a busy time in Spain and

Portugal, but after several differences with King Joseph he was recalled to Paris. In 1813 he was sent to oppose the progress of the English in Spain, and, in spite of the inferiority of his forces, he showed rare ability in this struggle, which terminated in the indecisive battle of Toulouse. Under the first Restoration he became a zealous Royalist. He was cashiered 11th of March, 1815, and in spite of a proclamation in which he treated Bonaparte as an adventurer, he was ennobled by the latter and appointed major-general of the army. His conduct at Waterloo was faulty. At the second Restoration he issued a memorandum of justification, but was nevertheless banished. Soult was recalled in 1819, and his baton of marshal was returned to him. He was sent as ambassador-extraordinary to attend the coronation of Queen Victoria, and was enthusiastically received by the populace in England.

MADAME DE STAËL.

Anne-Louise-Germaine Necker, Baroness de Staël-Holstein, a woman as celebrated for her wit as for her writings, was born 22nd of April, 1766, at Paris, where she died 14th of July, 1817. Daughter of Necker, she married, in 1786, the Baron of Staël-Holstein, Swedish ambassador to France. This union was a failure, and separation was agreed upon. At first she embraced with ardour the cause of the royal family. Rallying afterwards to the Directory, her *salon* became after the 18th Brumaire the rendezvous of the adversaries of Bonaparte. Persecuted by Bonaparte, she was obliged to remain in exile. She married secretly, in 1812, a young officer, M. de Rocca, this union being only made known by her will. Her complete works were published by her son in 1820-21.

TALLEYRAND.

Charles-Maurice de Talleyrand-Périgord, a statesman celebrated for his wit and his diplomatic talents, was born 13th of February, 1754, at Paris, where he died 17th of May, 1838. Destined for the Church against his will, he became, in spite of the notorious irregularity of his manners, agent-general of the clergy of France in 1780, and Bishop of Autun in 1788. Member of the Assembly of Notables in 1788, he was sent by his diocese to the States-general, where from the first he showed himself a decided partisan of the Revolution, and proposed the first appropriation of the property of the clergy. He celebrated the mass at the Champ de Mars at the time of the Fête of the Federation, took the oath to the civil constitution of the clergy, and resigned his bishopric. He consecrated the constitutional clergy of the Aisne and Finisterre in 1791, which brought him an excommunication from the Pope. Sent as ambassador twice to London, he was finally expelled, whereupon he went to the United States, thence to Hamburg and Amsterdam, at which latter place a decree from the Convention reached him permitting him to return to France.

Foreseeing the high destiny of Bonaparte, he gave to him all his support. He rendered services which brought the Concordat to such a successful termination that the Pope not only withdrew the excommunication, but gave to him a brief of secularisation, which enabled him to marry Mme. Grand, an Englishwoman, with whom he lived seven years. He rose to the very highest pinnacle of favour, but, disagreeing with the declaration of war against Spain, fell into disgrace and severed himself from Bonaparte.

Talleyrand contributed to the return of the Bourbons, and was a member of Louis XVIII.'s first cabinet. He was sent to the Vienna Congress, and was there when the news of the return from Elba arrived. He refused office during the Hundred Days, but was recalled to power at the second Restoration. Until the end of this reign he played a very unimportant part in public affairs ; but after the Revolution of 1830 he was sent as ambassador to London, and succeeded in realising the dream of his earlier days—an Anglo-French alliance. Recalled at his own desire, he ceased to occupy himself with political affairs.

TALLIEN.

Jean-Lambert Tallien, politician, was born in 1769 at Paris, where he died 16th of November, 1820. He was a solicitor's clerk at the time of the Revolution, the cause of which he embraced with fervour. He took an active part in the 10th of August, and was one of the organisers of the September massacres. Deputy from Seine-et-Oise to the Convention, he seated himself with the Mountain, and voted for the death of the King. On 21st of January, 1793, he entered the Committee of Public Safety, and contributed to the fall of the Girondists. Being sent on a mission to Bordeaux (September, 1793), he distinguished himself by his cruelties and extortions. He conceived an affection for the daughter of Cabarus (a celebrated financier), Mme. de Fontenay, whom, having saved from the scaffold, he married 26th of December, 1794. Considering himself menaced, he put himself at the head of the party which was being organised against Robespierre. Becoming a member of the Five Hundred, he followed Bonaparte to Egypt; and, sent back by Menou, he was captured by an English vessel and conveyed to London. He was allowed to live in peace at Paris after the Restoration, in spite of the law against regicides.

TOPINO-LEBRUN.

François J. B. Topino-Lebrun, painter and politician, was born at Marseilles in 1769, executed at Paris 30th of January, 1801. Pupil to David, he adopted republican principles. He was named juryman to the Revolutionary tribunal, but was so moderate that he was arrested as a suspect. He was also implicated in the Babeuf conspiracy and acquitted. Compromised in the plot of Arena and Ceracchi against Bonaparte—a plot organised by the police—he was, in spite of the little evidence brought against him, condemned to death 9th of January, 1801.

VERGNIAUD.

Pierre-Victurnien Vergniaud, the most illustrious orator of the Girondist party, was born at Limoges 31st of May, 1753, died upon the scaffold at Paris 31st of October, 1793. He was the son of an army contractor. After being destined for the Church and having studied theology, he decided for the bar, and was already a celebrated lawyer at the epoch of the Revolution. In the Assembly he allied himself with the Girondists. At the trial of Louis XVI. it was he who, as president of the court, had to pronounce the result of the vote. Some time after he was brought before the Revolutionary tribunal, and, in spite of an eloquent defence, was condemned to death.

VILLENEUVE.

Pierre Ch. J. B. Sylvestre de Villeneuve was born in 1763, died in 1806. He distinguished himself in the American war, and was captain of a vessel in 1793. Vice-admiral in 1796, he took part in the expedition to Ireland, and afterwards in the expedition to Egypt. It is said that the battle of Aboukir was lost to the French by the indecision and inability of Villeneuve. Owing to the protection of his friend Decrès, he did not lose favour with Bonaparte, who confided to him the execution of a plan to attract the English fleet a distance away, so as to allow the concentration of that of the French. Incapacity and indecision, however, made him commit fault upon fault, the result being the loss of the battle of Trafalgar. Taken prisoner, he returned to France to be exchanged, but committed suicide at the hotel where he alighted.

VITROLLES.

Eugène-François-Auguste d'Arnaud, Baron de Vitrolles, politician, was born in 1774, died in 1854. He emigrated, and served in the army of Condé. After the 18th Brumaire he rallied to the government of Bonaparte, and was appointed inspector of the imperial pastures. In 1814 he was the secret agent of Talleyrand at the congress of Châtillon, and contributed to the acceptance of the Bourbons by the allied powers. At the return from Elba he was sent to Toulouse to organise the defence, but was imprisoned until after the abdication of Bonaparte. He then recommenced his intrigues, and formed in the South, under the Duc d'Angoulême, a partly independent government, which Louis XVIII. put an end to by recalling the prince near him.

THE END

H. S. NICHOLS, PRINTER, 3 SOHO SQUARE, LONDON, W.